Dracula's Guests

A Vampire Anthology

Compiled by Dr. Chris McAuley

A HellBound Books LLC Publication

Printed in the United States of America

Contents:

Introduction to Dracula's Guests

I'm truly honored to be asked by my great friend and co-writer, Dr. Chris McAuley to write the introduction for the terrifying anthology *Dracula's Guests*, which celebrates the 125th anniversary of this classic work of gothic horror.

I was introduced to Dracula at the age of six thanks to an elder brother who decided to dress up as the blood-thirsty count for Halloween. I became his unwilling victim to immortalize the event. I still remember him leaning over me with fake blood oozing out of his mouth, white plastic fangs closing on my innocent flesh as I screamed and my mother took a photo. Who could have known that one moment would have such a drastic effect on my life? Bram Stoker has a lot to answer for!

From there, I was exposed to Bela Lugosi, Christopher Lee... I still remember watching the classic Universal Horror and Hammer Horror films half under blankets on a Saturday morning in New York on WOR, channel 9. As I got older, my literary interests continued in the horror and gothic vein with H. P. Lovecraft, R. Chetwynd Hayes, M. R. James and others. But still those sharp fangs coming closer and closer haunted me and if there was a book or a movie that had Dracula or any form of vampire in it, I would be there like a shot.

I even married a horror writer, Scott Ciencin, who was writing a Vampire trilogy when we first met and I just happened to look exactly like his heroine – Dani Walthers. Could there be anything more romantic or fated for a vampire fan?

Scott and I shared an interest in vampires and all things horrific. In fact, we were even given the opportunity to write a couple of Buffy: The Vampire Slayer books as well as an Angel book.

For me, Dracula has always meant so much more than a tale of gothic horror or movies I watched half under the blankets as a child. I have always been called to that darkness and there I found kindred spirits as well as soulmates.

I suppose that's why Dracula is still so popular today and why it's still finding new audiences as well as new formats to terrify its victims. There's something in all of us which calls out to the darkness of the void and if we listen closely, it will answer us… and invite us to know its depths… to face our shadow selves and come out stronger on the other side.

I want to thank Bram Stoker for creating the most famous vampire of the past 125 years and may he continue to terrify readers and viewers for the next 125 years. I also want to thank Dr. Chris McAuley for inviting me to write a short story with him for this collection. The character of Quincey Morris is truly a fascinating one and is often removed from the Dracula adaptations to concentrate on the "core" characters of Dracula, Jonathan and Mina. As an American, I truly enjoyed writing the first American vampire hunter.

In closing, I want to extend my gratitude and appreciation to all the fans of vampires, in whatever form they take, the world over. You keep Dracula "alive" so to speak and you allow us poor horror writers to earn our moldy crust of bread.

Denise Ciencin
July 17, 2022

Dracula in Recovery
Michael Zimecki

I awoke to the sound of chalk squeaking on a board. It made me think of fingernails scratching at the inside of a coffin lid, of a body trying to arise and escape the grave. I was stuck here.

I'm a night-shift guy and these daylight sessions are tough on me. I looked around to see if anybody noticed I'd nodded off. Fortunately, our T-group leader had his back to me.

Chalk clicked on the board as our leader, Arthur Holmwood, a sensitivity coach from Godalming Diversity Builder, Inc., listed behaviors we should avoid: "crude jokes and sexual innuendoes" . . . "sexually oriented gestures" . . . "looking a colleague up and down (elevator eyes)" . . .

None of this applied to me, which perhaps explains why I zoned out. Louche conduct's not my thing. I'm an old-world gentleman who ardently believes in the art of seduction, aided in my case by hypnosis and mind control.

Holmwood flipped the chalkboard over and started

writing on the other side. "Touching an employee's hair, clothing, or body" . . . "pinching, patting, or grabbing a colleague's body parts" . . . "brushing against another worker" . . . "sinking one's fangs into her neck."

The last one wasn't on the board, of course. The last one was mine, the reason I was here. I'd like to say it was Lucy's fault, but the terrible truth of the matter is I have only myself to blame. Our T-group leader made that very clear.

"You don't get a pass," Arthur Holmwood said, looking straight at me, "if the unwelcome behavior occurs after work hours or off-the-premises."

I was thinking of the couch in Lucy's apartment as he said this, of the freckles on her bare shoulder, of a throat as white as the chalk in Holmwood's hand, of skin so translucent you could see blood coursing through the veins. I remember staring at the nape of Lucy's neck and tracing her jugular with my eyes. I was lingering longingly over the spot where the carotid meets the subclavian, poised to bite, when Lucy unexpectedly stirred.

Later, she accused me of slipping her a roofie, something I would never deign to do or need to, thanks to my telekinetic powers. It didn't matter. After Lucy filed her complaint, everyone in the office started comparing me to Cosby.

My manager, Abraham Van Helsing, called me to account. I was asked to meet with him and a Human Resources officer named Quincey Morris.

They wanted to know what I was doing in Lucy's room.

"She invited me in."

Morris looked nonplussed. Frankly, I didn't understand his reaction. From my perspective, the invitation was everything: I wouldn't –- I *couldn't* – have done anything if Lucy hadn't asked me to cross her threshold. Any student of vampireology knows that.

"After our date, she asked me back to her apartment," I said by way of further explanation. I raised a finger and pointed at the employee handbook on Quincey's shelf. "Dating a co-worker isn't prohibited in that manual of yours," I stammered.

"No, but date rape is."

"Stop right there," my lawyer, Jonathan Harker, interjected. "I've read Lucy's statement and she isn't clear about what happened, if indeed anything did. She doesn't allege that Vlad here even kissed her let alone had sex with her."

Van Helsing wasn't mollified. After Morris and Harker left, he backed me into a corner and insisted on some candor.

"I like women," I shrugged, although, to be honest, the sex and gender of my victims doesn't make a whit of difference.

Van Helsing frowned.

"It's an addiction," I confessed.

His eyebrows arched high. "A sex addiction?" van Helsing asked.

"No," I replied. "It's more like a hunger. Or a thirst."

Van Helsing crossed his arms. "You're an alcoholic," he declared.

Not exactly, but how might I explain it? Like an alcoholic, it isn't the taste that excites me; it's the buzz.

If you've ever pricked your finger and sucked it to staunch the flow, you know it's nothing like fine wine, no comparison at all to vintage Port or top-rated Cabernet, one of those ones Robert Parker likes. It even loses the taste-test to Barefoot Pinot Noir or Bota Box Merlot—take your pick of supermarket wines.

Blood's metallic, like licking a copper pot or swallowing a handful of multivitamins rich in zinc and iron and chromium. It's slightly alkaline; it has a salty mouthfeel and a bitter aftertaste.

If I had to drink something red and gluggy in the throat, I'd rather have a V8.

Not that choice has anything to do with it.

Not for me.

Van Helsing ordered me to attend sensitivity training and addiction treatment at Hazelden Bettie Page, a detox facility named for the Queen of Pinups, a late-life convert to evangelical Christianity.

"Clean up your act," he demanded. "Or you won't be coming back."

Blood's memory, the biochemical equivalent of language, or, to put it more precisely, it's what words don't need to teach us, the stuff that's imprinted on our brains at birth, the innate knowledge that fire burns and love is eternal, the impulse that draws the infant's mouth to his mother's breast or the instinct that makes us fear heights and edges. Knowing how to breathe, how to respond to pleasure and retract from pain, how to smile, to laugh, to cry and to grieve are all in the blood.

Like the Bible says, life's in there.

Which is to say, I didn't think I could do without it.

At Hazelden Bettie Page, I was asked to take a blood test. It was negative for drugs or alcohol – 0.00% -- but the phlebotomist noticed needle marks on my arm. She suspected I was mainlining drugs, which, in a way, was true -- since the incident with Lucy, I had been giving myself periodic blood transfusions to keep my need to bite and feed under control.

Fortunately for me, Dr. Seward understood. Jack— Dr. Seward's nickname, which is what he wanted me to call him—said he had seen symptoms like mine in patients with porphyria, a rare blood disorder. "Your photosensitivity," he said, pointing at some sunspots on my skin. "People with porphyria often benefit from blood transfusions," he added. "But I don't think you have porphyria. People with the disease don't need or want to drink blood, and those fangs of yours are less indicative of porphyria than a condition called hypohidrotic ectodermal dysplasia, a genetic condition affecting tooth development. Perhaps you have some other kind of rare disease. Or maybe this blood addiction of yours is psychosomatic."

Okay, he didn't really get me. Dr. Seward didn't understand what made me tick, but he knew I needed treatment. He decided to take a "warm turkey" approach to my addiction, transfusing me occasionally while tapering down the volume of plasma I received. After a trial period of moderation, Jack put me on the vampire equivalent of methadone, an experimental blood substitute and natural oxygen carrier derived from the aquatic species *Arenicola marina*--in common parlance, lugworm blood. It's super-rich in hemoglobin and I can testify it works.

But perhaps the best thing Jack did for me was to hook me up with a recovering bloodoholic named Renfield, a courtesy for which I am eternally grateful. It was Renfield who taught me about The Big Book (a.k.a. The Anti-Vampire Codex) and The Twelve Steps, starting with the first one, "I admit that I was powerless over blood." Renfield and I hit it off immediately, and he became my V.A. sponsor. (That's V.A. as in Vampires Anonymous, not the Veterans Administration). Renfield accompanied me to a V.A. meeting, where I stood up and for the first time said, "Hello, my name is Dracula – you can call me Vlad—and I'm a vampire."

Since then, I've told my story at V.A. meetings

several times. How I became a vampire after my wife, Elisabeta, died. Why I couldn't accept that she had been taken from me, and how I sought in vain – v-**e**-i-n—for an answer. (Polite, if insincere, laughter from the group.) How I came to believe in a Power greater than myself and found Him amongst the Carpathian Mountains near Hermannstadt at a place called Scholomance. "His name was Satan," I told rapt audiences, "and he introduced me to the black arts."

In my V.A. confessionals, I related how I came under the Devil's spell, and started drinking blood to express my undying love for my long-lost bride. A quirky way of showing grief, I know.

The rest is history, one familiar to every vampire. The blood took over. I mistook it for life and allowed death to define me. In fact, everyone who had been close to me was dead. I couldn't have pets. There were so many days when all I could do was look out my window to see if it was dark yet.

I finally hit bottom. (Violins, please.) Like other bloodsuckers – by which I mean, not just creatures that suck blood, but people who prey on others (fill in the blank with the name of your favorite asshole) – I overstepped the bounds of decency. I thought I was above and beyond the laws of God and Nature, not to mention the manmade ones that define consent and the capacity to give it. I assaulted Lucy Westerna and came face-to-face with #MeToo, or #VeeToo (whatever you want to call it), the mirror in which I could not see myself, but where my true image was revealed.

That's my story. I've told it and I own it.

After spending 90 days at Hazelden Bettie Page and nearly a year in recovery, I got my life back. I was even reinstated to my job. Under the terms of my re-employment, I couldn't work anywhere near Lucy, so I was transferred to an office out-of-state where I would be supervised by one of the organization's rising stars, a talented young woman named Mina Murray.

I couldn't believe it when I saw her. She had the same sweet countenance as my Elisabeta, the same dear face, framed by long, dark hair that swooped over her cheeks, bobbing and curling under her chin, and partially concealing a graceful swan-like neck. The likeness was so striking, in fact, that I couldn't take my eyes off her.

Holmwood's voice echoed in my head, cautioning me to stop, but I couldn't keep from looking her up and down. I studied Mina as an anatomist might, visually inspecting the sinuous curves of her neck for an artery, the smalls of her wrist for an ulnar, the hollows behind her dimpled knees for a femoral vein.

As I stared at her, my pulse quickened with desire. From the moment I met her, I knew. I could hear it in the rustling of my blood. Mina was my soul mate, or would be, if I actually had a soul.

"Don't go there, Drac," I told myself. "Relapse isn't a part of recovery." Wasn't that what Dr. Seward said?

I didn't know what to do.

I couldn't ignore my feelings for Mina, but I also couldn't ask her out. The company's new non-fraternization policy, put into effect in no small part due to me, absolutely forbade it. Besides, we were much too March-December, way too daughter-father, and I wasn't sure if she knew about my parlous past.

I tried to suppress my desire for her, I really did, but every evening I awoke with thirst for Mina and the goodness I didn't have.

I found myself making excuses to be in her presence, hanging around her office every chance I got, sitting next to her at meetings, and acting like her Boy Friday--fetching coffee for her, running errands, constantly displaying my willingness to perform any menial task she wanted done, all the while waiting for some small token display of gratitude in return.

One day, a few weeks into the job, I asked her to join me after work for a drink.

She refused.

Disappointment washed over me in wave after wave of tears.

I fretted like Troy's Hector before his final battle. I sulked like Achilles in his tent. Life sucks, I thought, appreciating the irony.

I was in crisis mode.

I stopped going to V.A. meetings. I wouldn't take Renfield's calls. Ignoring the Twelve Steps and every other rule Dr. Seward taught me, I plotted and schemed to get Mina alone.

Finally, the opportunity arose.

Mina asked me to accompany her to a business conference in Las Vegas.

Vegas is my kind of place. It has an artificial environment that appeals to me: you can sit in air-conditioned comfort without caring whether the sun still shines or even knowing what time of day or night it is. Vegas is unreal.

The Strip is the city's beating heart. We were staying at one of the hotels there, The Mirage, which has a large volcano sculpture outside its entrance; the volcano erupts every night with fireworks and a percussion soundtrack from The Grateful Dead's legendary drummer Mickey Hart.

The conference organizers had purchased some casino chips for our use and, of course, there were free drinks and snacks. After our meetings were over, we left the Grand Ballroom to spend the evening at the casino.

Mina had slipped into a cocktail dress. I was

sporting a shirt with a spearpoint collar, the kind Joe Pesci used to wear. I watched from the shadows while Mina played the slots. She hit the booze heavy and ran through her tokens pretty quick.

Gallant that I was, I offered her mine, but Mina demurred. She was a little wobbly on her feet and said she needed to get some sleep.

I followed her back to the hotel. She took an elevator to her floor. I took another one, and stepped out into a hallway that looked like it stretched for miles. I spied Mina at the end of it, swaying like a buoy in the tide. She had a keycard in her hand but was either too drunk to know how to use it or simply couldn't get it to work.

I sprinted down the hall and offered to assist her. I took the keycard from her hand and opened the door to her room.

Mina staggered inside, got as far as the bed, and kicked off her shoes.

I watched her remove her jewelry and take off her dress. She was about to slip out of her underwear when it dawned on her that I was still standing in the doorway. Instead of scolding me for gawking or just shooshing me away, she pointed to a desk by the window and told me to put her keycard there.

Bells and whistles went off in my head. She was inviting me into her room.

Mina was staying in one of the hotel's volcano view rooms with a king-size bed. She was roosted on the runner at its foot, her tiny feet dangling over the edge. The volcano was erupting outside the window and I felt myself getting into the vibe.

I crossed the room, bringing myself almost close enough to taste her.

As I set the keycard down, Mina patted the bed with

a hand, beckoning me to sit beside her.

I turned toward the bed and caught a whiff of her perfume. It smelled of meadow flowers with softly musky, woody notes that reminded me of the dark forested hills of my native Transylvania.

Light flooded through the window from the neon ocean of The Strip, the lambent colors of its glittering facades, ad displays, and LED's filling the room. I closed my eyes to the light.

When I opened them again, I was touching elbows with Mina on the bed.

Clearly, something magical was happening.

Outside the window, a full moon loomed over The Mirage.

Inside the room, a transformation was taking place.

Mina brushed her hair back with a paw, exposing a pointy ear. Her eyes shone with an amber light as she fixed her gaze on me, like an animal locking on its prey.

Mina narrowed her eyes to slits when I returned her look. She emitted a low growl. Take-away message No.1: it was a stare-down contest I couldn't win. No. 2: Mina definitely needed to have her eyebrows plucked and it wouldn't hurt to get acquainted with some depilatory cream. I was about to ask her if she had ever heard of Nair when she curled her lips up in a snarl, revealing a pair of long, sharp canines.

"My what big teeth you have," I said in a falsetto, playfully quoting Little Red Riding Hood's words to the wolf disguised in Granny's bedclothes.

Mina replied with a snap of the jaws that drained all the blood from my face. "The better to eat you with, my dear," she said.

A Final Supper
Trev Hill

The smell hits me as I approach the campsite. It is the stench of death. It is nothing new to me, nor is it anything I fear, although it does put me on my guard.

The wagons are burning and overturned, the tents are torn to shreds and their inhabitants, or what is left of them, are scattered around the site. When I say scattered, I don't just mean individual people, I mean parts of people as well. It is all too familiar... and all too quiet. They have been here, that's obvious. But are they still here? That is the question I ask myself. Quite a pointless question as it is obvious they still are. They wouldn't leave all this fresh meat just for one ranger, even me. No, the question is, *where are they?*

The blur of movement to my right gives me my answer. I spin to my left, swinging my sword in a wide arc as a large male one charges me. My movement has confused him and he finds himself running into the space I once stood, as my blade cleaves into his spine, snapping through it and cutting him almost in half. Not breaking the motion, the sword completes its arc and I pull back and lunge forward, skewering the hell-bitch who is running towards me shrieking in fury because her decoy tactic didn't work. The shock on her face as my sword's point enters her belly is almost comical. However, the force of her dash makes her run almost the length of the blade. Even dying, her bite could prove hazardous, so my chain-mailed forearm smashes into her face, stopping her suddenly and allowing me to wrench my sword from her rancid guts. She writhes around in circles on the ground until I get a decent aim and lop her head off. Best take no chances.

That was a wise move. Dropping to one knee I avoid the axe of the third one as it circles where my head was a second before. Rising quickly, I jam his arm with my body, preventing his reverse swing, and drive the sword upwards, under his ribs and into his upper-body. I slam his face to the side to direct his bloody vomit away from my face. I pull the sword out and let his putrid corpse drop.

I spin around at the ready, ready for the next one wherever it may be. But nothing. No sound, except the first one twitching and drowning on his own blood. No movement. The third one must have been the last of them. I relax slightly and proceed to detach the heads from the two males before dumping them into the fire. Then, sheathing my sword, after wiping their foul fluids from it, I drag their carcasses over to the fire and toss them on to burn.

Now it happens.

As I drag the third corpse to the fire, I have to bend down to pick it up so that I can put it on top of the other two. As I begin to lift, I see the flash of movement from the corner of my right eye. I manage to turn and hold the headless carcass between us as the female slams into me.

Dropping the body, I stagger and trip backwards into the fire. Immediately I begin rolling, trying to extinguish the flames but the bitch-fiend is at my throat, trying to extinguish me.

Her fangs snap at my throat as her filthy claws swipe at my face, drawing blood. Jamming my forearm across her throat, I continue to roll, taking her with me. My weight on her squeezes some of her stinking breath out (unfortunately, into my face… damn, I almost puke!). I pull her over until I am below her. Thinking I am at a disadvantage, she moves in for a throat bite only to meet my mailed fist, and again as I reach behind her head and pull it onto the metal knuckles. Forcing my knee up, I kick upwards and send her flying backwards. Now we are both standing, both ready. She snarls and edges towards me, flexing her taloned fingers. She draws back her lips to expose her filthy, saliva coated fangs and hisses. Then her head explodes.

This surprises me. But I don't have time to be surprised. As her knees fold and her body flops to the ground, I see the boy standing behind her, the slingshot in his hand. He stands still staring at her corpse then slowly raises his face to look into mine.

"She's the last one," he says, his voice quivering.

"Are you sure?" I ask.

"Yes, there were four… I saw them…" his voice begins to speed up as the emotion comes flooding out, "… I saw it all, I saw them attack. The men tried to fight them off but they were too quick, too strong. I hid, I couldn't help… I…"

His voice trails off.

"You did right. You'd have been taken had you tried," I say brusquely. Perhaps I should try to comfort him but I no longer have those skills, those feelings. "And maybe, if not for you, I would have been that hell-bitch's dinner. So I thank you!"

He still stands. Lost, uncertain. I break the silence. "We should go. We can't help the dead and the fire may draw more. If you have things, get them."

We leave.

***

We ride along mainly in silence. Little by little he either volunteers pieces of information or answers my direct questions. His name is Ethan. He is an orphan (well, if he wasn't already, he is now!) and joined the wagon-train somewhere in the west, he forgets the name of the town. The vampires attacked the camp not long after sunset, while the people were still eating. They were fast, picking off the guards and then the so-called "safe wagon" where the women and children sheltered. They had just shredded all before my coming was noted and they laid an ambush for me. Ethan had watched them feed and knew my approach might be his only chance to escape alive.

The boy is lucky to have survived. In some cases, the lucky ones are the dead. The fiends are known to have taken children and…*initiated* them. In other cases they keep them around for sadistic amusement, or to simply feed on them, alive, when they get bored. These aren't the old-style blood suckers of children's stories, these feed on human flesh, the innards especially. A man, even a child, can live for some time as his organs are plucked one by one.

Yes, Ethan has been lucky, as have I. If he wishes to ride with me, his experiences will make him a useful apprentice, not least because children have an ability to smell out the creatures.

***

Arriving at the next settlement, I leave the horses with the boy and go to the local guard commander to report the massacre and pick up any new assignments. The reaction is a mixture of tired despair and resignation. Perhaps someday we'll all end up this way, they mumble. Perhaps, but not today. I leave the guard room. I've done my work, the matter of the retrieval and burial is theirs, if they even bother to do it. I return to the horses and find Ethan sitting watching a cat tormenting a mouse before eating it.

"It does that to make the meat taste better," I explain, "It looks like it's playing for fun, but it makes the humours in the body spread and softens the flesh." The boy speaks without taking his eyes from the scene.

"But do you think the cat enjoys the game as well?" he asks. The cat, if it had been enjoying the game, must have become bored, as it finishes it abruptly by biting the mouse's head off and devouring the rest.

"Who knows? But at least when the game is over, the end is swift. I've seen times when it wasn't. That's what marks men out from the animals, from the hell-spawn. We don't play before the end."

The boy favours me with a long gaze before standing and picking up his bag. We stable the horses, as I need to eat and sleep for a few hours before we go to the market area of the settlement to buy supplies before continuing.

***

The market stinks, they all do. Cheap meat burning on spits, unwashed souls trying to beg scraps while the sweating stall holders try to sell their shoddy wares for an outrageous price. Having done what we need to do we once more saddle up and move towards the settlement gates. On the edge of the market we see a makeshift gallows with several furry bodies hanging from them and a number of blood-spattered men carving up carcasses below. Ethan gazes at the swinging bodies, one or two of which are still twitching and kicking.

"Were they men-wolves?" he asks quietly. I shake my head.

"No, just ordinary dogs, wolf people would have been beheaded, staked and burned, like vampires."

"But why hang a dog? What has it done?" he queries. I snort in amusement.

"Have you never seen dog meat before, boy? It's the poorer people eat it but it is still common."

Ethan favours me again with one of his long looks. "I know people eat dogs, but why hang them? You don't hang pigs or cows." This comment makes me laugh out loud.

"Have you ever tried to pull something the weight of a pig or a cow, boy? Perhaps that's why they don't hang 'em. But as for dogs, I suppose it is like the cat and the mouse, hanging it makes the meat better, or so they say."

The boy looks forward and rides for a while in silence. When he speaks, it was a strange kind of distant voice, strange for one so young.

"I had a dog once, it was my friend. I wouldn't have eaten it, but then I would eat pigs. I suppose some people might make a friend of a pig. Strange how people eat animals, even ones which would be their friends, and yet when the vampires eat people, they are evil." He pauses, looking me in the face. "Could you be a friend to a vampire?"

I snort once again, "Never! They don't want to be

friends anyway. Man was put on earth to rule it and we kill them to defend ourselves. Now if you have no sensible questions, hold your tongue, boy!" We ride on in silence.

The sun will soon be setting and we need to make camp but the area is too open. There are no defensive areas. We'll be easy to see and prone to attack during the night. This is an area I don't know well but I have been told they are here and are known to attack travelers. We must be wary. Ethan has learned well and suggests several places which might be better than others. Eventually he suggests riding to the brow of a hill and taking stock of the landscape to see if there is anywhere suitable… of course, I would have done this myself but it is good to know his mind is working like that of a ranger.

The land below the hillcrest reveals a small outcrop a few miles below. There seem to be a few wisps of smoke coming from behind it. This creates a problem. It might be that there are wagoners there, or perhaps a camp or settlement. While that might suggest safety, it also makes a potential target. Still, perhaps it is better to check it out, if the company is good, then we can sleep safely. If not, then they'll need our help.

The truth becomes obvious as we skirt around the base of the outcrop. To my surprise, there is a stone building, a little like a small monastery, although it looks long deserted. In front of this building, a small train of three has been hit and the smoke is from the burning remains of one of the wagons. Scattered around are the familiar shapes of their victims. This time it looks like nobody escaped. This presents us with a serious problem, do we make camp here in the hope that they will not return or do we move on in the hope of finding somewhere? Also, what do we do with the corpses?

Burning them might attract attention to ourselves yet leaving them might allow some to rise, if they were attacked by a specific sort. A quick look tells me that this won't be a problem. The attackers have fed and apparently dragged some bodies away, presumably for the rest of the nest, wherever that may be. They will probably stay away tonight. A few beheadings will ensure none of the victims rise.

We decide to look through one of the remaining wagons to see if there is anything of use before searching the monastery to see if it is possible to defend it if need be. It is in the second wagon that we make our discovery. As I am about to climb in, I spot a movement from a bundle of cloth by a sleeping mat. I motion to Ethan to stay back and I draw my short sword.

"It would be better if you come out slowly. You might not like me dragging you out!" I call. The mound stays still. "You have one more chance. If you are human, you have nothing to fear from us!" The mound shuffles slightly and from within its folds appears a small, tousled haired head, with two staring blue eyes.

"Is Mama with you?" it asks.

The little girl climbs down the ladder looking straight ahead, as I told her to.. I don't want her seeing what is left of her family. As she walks towards the building Ethan emerges. The two children stop and stiffen slightly as they see each other, then cautiously relax. Ethan introduces himself and the girl announces her name as Caitlin.

We sit around the fire in the building eating a meal. I have erected some makeshift defences and traps to let us know if we have unwanted visitors. Caitlin is happily chatting away, apparently oblivious to what has happened outside. Ethan told her Mama and Papa have gone to town and asked us to look after her and to my astonishment, it has worked. As soon as the sun rises, we will turn around and take her back to the town. The boy is at least old enough to be of use in my work but I cannot take care of an eight-year-old little girl.

She tells us that her family travelled out from town two days ago and were heading out to the new lands to try and make their fortune. I smile at her innocence, although there is nothing pleasant about either her present situation or those which make poor families risk all in the hope of some ill-conceived dreams. I ask her how long they had been camped here.

She thinks a little before replying, "Oh just a few hours, I think. We were just going to make dinner and then mama told me to go into the wagon and hide under the blankets and stay there until she came for me." She smiles and begins to draw in the sand.

"Oh, and why do you think she did that?" I ask.

She shrugs and giggles, "I don't know! Sometimes we played hide and seek. I liked it very much," she replies. I nod and suddenly remember that we need some water for the horses. Without a sound, Caitlin smiles and walks over to the corner of the room and points to a pump hidden by some old wooden planks.

"You can get some from the well, here," she declares. I tell Ethan to fill one of the old buckets and to water the horses. I sit across the fire, smiling at the girl.

"So how long have you lived here, Caitlin?" I ask. She goes still and quiet for a moment. "I mean, you know your way around this building very well, especially for someone who has only been here a few hours." She stares at me a second before looking at the ground.

"Well Mama showed me where it was!" she mumbled. I nodded.

"Of course, she did. Was that when you were washing the dishes after dinner?" I ask. She nods enthusiastically. My hand is moving inside my cloak.

"But I thought you said that you had just started to make dinner when your mama told you to hide, and you don't seem very hungry. You haven't touched the meal." I see her jaw tighten and her little hands ball into fists.

"No, I forgot, we had dinner," she snaps.

"Of course you did, Caitlin, then you set fire to the wagon to attract any passers-by. Isn't that what you usually do? In fact, is your name really Caitlin?" I demand. I roll to my right as she pounces across the fire towards me. Standing straight up from the roll, I plant my boot in her little backside and send her flying into the wall. She slams into it and turns, snarling, her face bloodied from the impact. At last she is showing her fangs.

"Not such a sweet little thing now, are we?" I taunt.

She runs towards the other wall and jumps at it, bouncing off and flying towards me. I dodge to the side and bring my sword swinging round, catching her across her back with the flat of it. She sprawls across the floor and I move in for the kill. But she is faster than I expected. Swiveling around onto her back, she catches my sword between her hands and stops my swing. Now I feel the first indication of her true strength. I wrench the sword back and aim it towards her head. Once again her speed takes me by surprise and she dodges the blow and catches my sword arm, using my own force to send me flying across the room.

My back slams against the wall, winding me. I barely manage to keep hold of my weapon. Before I can react, she has charged across the room and is driving her head into my stomach, making me double up. Now she is on my shoulders, snapping at my neck with her little fangs, although they are no less dangerous for their size. I snap my mail glove across her face and force it into her mouth, trapping her head with my other hand. Spinning around I slam her little body against the stone wall, again and again, using my own body weight to sandwich her against the wall. At last I feel her body slacken and I throw her limp form to the floor before picking up my sword to finish her off. Her little head swivels around to face me.

Two large, teary blue eyes stare up at me pitifully and she whimpers, "Please don't hurt me!"

I pause for a second, almost fooled by her innocence, but that is her weapon. I raise my sword to bring it down on her neck but as my arm reaches its full height, I hear a crunching squelch and am aware of all the feeling in my body draining away. My legs buckle and I realize my bowels are emptying. My face thuds into the floor and I lie there motionless, save for the involuntary twitching of my limbs.

Ethan walks around me, licking the blood from his hand. Caitlin is picking herself up, spitting her own blood on the floor. She approaches the boy.

"You took your time!" she snarls. Ethan smiles at her before turning to look me in the face. He smiles at me whilst talking to her.

"Well, it was a good fight and for a moment you didn't seem to need any help," he shrugs. Apart from that, I needed him where I could get him properly, like this."

I stare at him, trying to speak, but my muscles refuse to work. I can barely manage a grunt. Caitlin walks over and stands next to him. She picks up my fallen sword.

"Why not just kill him?" she asks. Ethan chuckles and lays his hand on her sword hand. He looks me in the eyes with a smile of increasing malevolence.

"Are you really as young as you look, Caitlin?" he chuckles. "I was initiated a few years ago by the nest who he found me with. I won't say I liked them, in fact, I was glad to see him dispose of them. I even took the opportunity to finish the bitch who sired me. Still, what I did learn was a few gastronomic tips." He keeps his smile fixed on me as he takes his little knife from his belt.

"Are you going to kill him now?" she asks.

He shakes his head, "No, no," he chuckles, "As I said, I know a few little things. One of the reasons I let you slam him around was that it tenderized the meat a little. Do you remember, like the cat and the mouse?" he asks me. "But there are other ways to improve the taste of fresh meat," he explains, slowly walking towards me. "It took me a while to learn to puncture a man's spine this way but it is worth it. The paralysis creates all kinds of movement of the humours, for one."

He kneels down beside me and turns me over onto my back. I follow his movements with my eyes, unable to move anything else. Slowly he pierces my stomach with the point of his knife and begins sawing a cut across my body. Although I feel only the pulling sensation, I cannot help but moan. Ethan looks across at the slavering girl.

"You see? It's starting to work already. Keep them alive and the fear increases. The humours enter each part of the body making each morsel sweeter. Sliding his hand inside my torso, he plucks something from within before extracting it and taking a bloody bite. As my life juices trickle down his chin, he hands the organ to the girl. "Try and see," he invites her.

She takes a bite and smiles a bloody smile of delight. "And the best thing is," he grins, "if we take each morsel separately and slowly, we can keep him alive at least until his heart," at which, as I watch helplessly, he begins sliding his hand back inside me for his next portion.

An Interview in the Garden of Earthly Delights
Albert N. Katz

The wait is unbearable. The pain afterwards is even worse. The thrill of sexual excitation and release is a cruel joke now. I wait for Carmen, with dread, not joy. I want to shout out loudly, "Damn you, Charles Reyno, Damn you to hell", but know that would only give him extra pleasure.

It had started so innocently, with such expectations that the downward spiral of my life was about to turn around and that, once again, I would take my rightful place among the elite. I had an "in" to interview the richest, most reclusive man in the world, and would parlay that into regaining my job and position.

I had known Reyno since we were both in our teens as fellow students in secondary school. Unlike the rest of us, he was a 'charity case', coming to the Academy from a foster family. We used to make fun of him. But that was then. When I contacted his New York agent asking for an interview I fully expected to be rebuffed but instead received a very nice, personal hand written note inviting me to stay with him and his wife at his foreign "hideaway shack", up in the mountains.

I was met at the airport by one of his employees, a muscular cruel looking man, who said not one word for the nearly four hours it took him to drive me to the estate. On arrival, he took my bags and motioned me to a guesthouse, adjacent to the main house. There was a note inside: "Dinner starts at 9:00 sharp. Do not be late. Come to the front door of the main house where you will be met and taken to the dining room. Dress is Casual suit."

A flash of anger came over me as I read the impersonal dictatorial tone of the message. I used to order people and now found myself being ordered, like a servant. I was no servant.

***

I, like everyone else, knew only the bare bones of Charles' story. His little mining company had struck it rich in some god-forsaken corner of the world. He seemed to possess an uncanny ability to buy stock when the price was low, watched it rise, sold them before the market dropped. Except that his wealth and power was unimaginable, his life was cloaked in secrecy otherwise.

I made it to the front door just before 9:00. Waiting for me was an incredibly beautiful woman. Tall, with curves like a river valley, her auburn hair snaked down and across her breasts. "Please come this way, Mr. O'Seau." I followed, mesmerized by the seductive sway of her hips. Charles was waiting at the entrance. Not the Charles I knew once, but a trim tanned man looking decades younger than me, although our birthdays were only months apart. He clapped me on the shoulder as if we were old buddies. "I see you met Juliana's niece, Carmen. And here, let me introduce you to my wife Juliana." Carmen was stunning but Charles' wife was, if anything, even more beautiful.

Dinner started brilliantly: the food, witty conversation, perfume from the two beautiful women. I was seduced by the opulence. This was a life I had dreamed of in my youth; the life that rightfully should have been mine, not handed to someone like a Charles Reyno.

I asked a few questions, journalist that I am, but Charles disapproved, interrupted me in mid-question. "Not tonight and not over dinner. We can talk shop if you wish in the morning but not now. I am a stickler about such things, David." I reacted to the dismissal with a flash of irritation, quickly repressed. I knew, and suspected he did as well, how much I needed the exclusive interview. Pissed off, I ended up drinking too much, talking too loudly. My flirting with Carmen got more blatant with each drink. She seemed to find my futile efforts quite funny. Finally, Charles raised his voice a bit. He was slightly cold and commanding. "David, we are not at St. Thomas Academy anymore. In my house we act civilized, not as animals. You will apologize to Carmen immediately or I will have Vuk drive you to the village and you can make your own way back to whatever hole you came from."

I recognized immediately this was no longer the kid we once bullied, but a powerful dangerous man. Although it galled me, and the words almost stuck in my throat, I needed the interview badly. I apologized, blaming my actions on my failure to control the amount of wine I had imbibed. All during that humiliation, I was thinking 'what a smug, urbane bastard you've become

Charles; I remember you when'. He looked at me as if he could read my mind, his smile thin and snake-like.

As a sign of her acceptance of my mea culpa, Carmen took my arm after dinner and walked me back to the guesthouse. Once, women like her would have almost begged me to take them back to my place but she just walked away, not looking back once. The scent of her perfume and sight of the curve of her barely clad breasts clung to me as I tried to sleep.

After breakfast the next morning, Charles and I had our first interview session. I asked if I could tape our conversations.

"No you cannot. You are free to take notes. I have no intention that my speech patterns be available for whoever wishes to analyze them, use them. There are good reasons I keep my private life hidden. This is my Garden of Earthly Delights, my oasis," he said, looking at me expectantly. When I said nothing, he continued.

"You should know that while you are here we are basically cut off from the world. We are quite self-sufficient here. We need nothing from the outside world. No one comes here except those I permit. You won't see them, but this place is under 24-hour surveillance by my personal cadre of very skilled and dangerous people. So even if you— or anyone else— did make it up here without invitation you would be stopped. You've probably noticed already your cell phone is inoperative. Let me be blunt. If I wanted I could have any intruder disappear from the face of the earth. Including you, old friend. Am I clear?"

A chill of fear embraced me. "Was that a threat Charles?"

He smiled, seemingly delighted at my reaction. "Nonsense. You are a journalist, my guest, personally invited to interview me, so let us begin." He raised his hand, and Vuk arrived with a single glass of gin and tonic. The symbolism was clear: he was the master and I was mere staff. I so hated him at that moment.

"I am curious why after refusing interviews in the past, you have agreed to have me talk to you."

"Well, for starters, I have over the years followed your career and others from our school days. I've enjoyed reading your books and am sorry that you haven't written any for quite a few years now. But more importantly because I wanted to see how you were progressing since the tragic death of your wife and two daughters."

I was somewhat taken aback, not expecting that he, of all people, had been following my career and life. "I handle my loss, unfortunately, with too much drink and attempts at work. So please let us just do the interview. Start where you wish and we'll take it from there."

Just then Vuk entered and whispered in Charles' ear. "I am so sorry but some matter has come up. It shouldn't take long, just hang in."

He kept me waiting almost two hours, returning without an apology for leaving me so long. I was livid but said nothing. I needed him and he knew it. Charles took up the conversation as if gone only a minute.

"Do you remember our days at St. Thomas Academy; me the poor waif and you the golden boy?"

I nodded uncomfortably.

"You and your buddies made my life a living hell in those days."

"Charles…."

"Please let me continue. Those were difficult days for me. I was filled with all the diseases of the soul: self-loathing, hatred, anger. I didn't know it at the time but I was at a crossroads."

"Look Charles, I truly am sorry for what I did in

those days. But I did it, and though I now wish otherwise I can't take that back, I'm afraid."

"Don't apologize. You wanted to know where I wanted to start, and I want to start at St. Thomas because it was there that I realized that I had a choice to either feed the diseases of the soul, or not. Recognizing that freed me from being a victim, a prey to the hurts meted by the likes of you and your clique."

Ever the journalist, I thought this was a good place to start my questioning. "So if you are no longer prey, do you then consider yourself a predator?"

He smiled, a thin sinister smile. "Some might think so. I think it better stated that I am leading a crusade for good. I invited you to meet with me because I see you as someone to help me meet that aim."

I was taken aback. "You want to hire me?"

At that Charles just smiled again. "Something like that. We'll talk of my plans later."

He stood up abruptly. "But that is enough for now. I have other duties to attend. It is a beautiful day, so enjoy the grounds, perhaps take a swim. Anything you want can be found somewhere on these grounds. Anything. I will see you again at lunch."

Frustrated, I could have screamed at the brevity of our interview, and the suddenness of it's end, especially with promises left hanging. He knew that he controlled the situation and had no qualms in showing me that he was master, and me an insignificant supplicant.

***

Charles' hideaway "shack" did seem to offer a host of earthly pleasures. However, wherever I went either Vuk or Carmen was nearby, oozing a threat to my physical or mental well-being. Though I knew Vuk could snap my neck without raising a sweat, it was strangely Carmen that seemed to me the more threatening. I knew instinctively she could erase the memory of the death of my wife and children from my consciousness but that there would be a cost to pay for that relief.

At breakfast, and then again at lunch it was clear that Carmen was flirting with me, seeing I suppose how far she could string me. I can feel my penis hardening and was relieved that my excitement was hidden under the dining cloth. She approached me in the garden after lunch, she the huntress and I, poor sad I, her victim.

"So David. I can call you David, no? Last night you talked too much and now you talk too little. I liked it when you said I was beautiful. You think me beautiful?"

I decided the safest response was honesty. "Yes. You are incredibly beautiful. But I need this interview with your uncle if I have any hope of recovering my career, so I will appreciate your beauty as I do a fine painting hanging in the Prado."

She pouted when I continued, "with appreciation from a distance. I will not jeopardize my opportunity here by a fling with you Carmen, beautiful as you are."

"We shall see, n'est-ce pas?" And at that she twirled away. I floated in the perfect balance between relief, desire and disappointment.

I met with Charles again later that evening in his library before dinner. Like everything in the estate, it was extensive. Books lined the room to the ceiling, a sliding ladder to get to the uppermost shelves. Charles showed me some of his prize possessions, priceless ancient texts, a copy of Shakespeare's first folio, an original Gutenberg bible. And I just stood there as the bastard shoved his wealth, his success in my face.

"This is my special place, David. Here I am surrounded by the beauty of the human spirit."

"I see an original of 'The Prince', and a first edition of 'Mein Kampf'."

"Yes, signed by Hitler himself."

'You think those beautiful?"

"Of course. The human spirit is beautiful in all its expressions. The greatest works of art, scientific insights, and acts of altruism come from, at their roots, that dark part, the most hidden and evil parts of the human spirit where absolute pain resides. True creativity comes from transforming the energy generated by psychic pain to psychic ecstasy."

"That's not my experience, Charles."

He gave a dismissive shrug. "Here is a tidbit for your notes. Before I studied mineralogy, I received a graduate degree in cognitive neuroscience. I did research on consciousness, trying to find the material source of the soul, the human spirit. I tried to find the neural sites of our darkest wishes and a means to transform them into something good and beautiful."

"Seems somewhat esoteric to me Charles."

"Not practical enough? Well I was hoping that if successful I could monetize the project. Alas, a research dead-end."

"Since you mentioned your degree in mineralogy, why that field?"

"Ah, because I thought I could get rich. I thought with wealth I would have the ability to change the world."

"Perhaps also to rectify the lack of wealth in your youth?"

Reyno looked long at me with a thin, snake-like smile on his lips. "Maybe. But in truth I found a place of much greater richness, you know."

"Where you found the diamond field that got you started!"

"No, that was only material. Something far greater."

"And that place is?"

Charles smiled, "I could tell you where that place is, but then I'd have to call Vuk to kill you." I must have looked frightened because he just laughed loudly, enjoying my unease.

"Let me just say that it was in one of those infrequently visited places in which I went looking for minerals to mine. Let us call this place, Shangri-La for its literary connotations. Are you familiar with the allusion David?"

I nodded. "It was a book by Hilton about utopia. I saw a copy in your library."

'Yes. First edition, signed."

At that moment, Vuk knocked on the door, entered and handed Charles a note. He glanced at it. "I am sorry, David. Even when I wish otherwise, business intervenes sometimes. Let us take this up again later, perhaps after we all meet for dinner. Vuk, please ask Carmen to come." Turning to me, "She'll show you around the property while I take care of matters."

Frustrated at the abrupt end to our talk once again, I was made aware once again how unimportant I was to Charles and his enterprises. He seemed to relish in showing me that I was a nobody. And it was clear to me that he recognized that Carmen was the last person I wished to see, and so ensured she would be the person I would have to be around. I did not know how to extricate myself gracefully.

Carmen made a dramatic entrance, in a dress more revealing than hiding. "So David, how do you like my perfume? It is made from certain pheromones guaranteed to bewitch men, I am told. Are you bewitched?"

And indeed it was intoxicating. And I was excited

and so much wanted her and longed for the world in which she was living with Charles and Juliana, a world that had been promised to me by my birth, and then cruelly never realized.

"Carmen, why are you teasing me like this?"

"Teasing? Like this?" She reached forward, cupped my scrotum and as I started an erection, withdrew her hand and slapped me across the face. "Why tease? Because I can, David. Because I find your reactions are quite humorous. Because I wish to."

And then, as if I were a mere piece of meat, Carmen dropped playing the seductress and took on the role of estate guide. She showed me around the mansion, the guest rooms, a film theatre, a game room, some meeting rooms, family quarters, including at one point a room she announced coquettishly as "This is my bedroom. Would you like to enter it?" Oh God yes, I thought but course I demurred. She giggled. "Oh, it is almost too easy to play with you."

She showed me room after room, walking for miles, each room filled with the finest that the wealth of mankind had produced. In the lowest levels, beyond the wine cellars I noticed a closed door and asked what they store there. Carmen shrugged. "It is a workshop. Charles likes to putter, doing things."

Walking through the endless gardens, I thought I saw Vuk, or someone just like him, stabbing a man in the distance. When I mentioned that to Carmen, she just laughed. "The sun must be playing tricks with your eyes." Finding a shaded spot with benches we sat. Carmen called out. "Please bring me some tea, from Assam. Is there anything you want, David?" I asked for a glass of good single malt whiskey.

From seemingly nowhere, Vuk arrived with our drinks. I was sure I saw blood splatter on his clothes. He smiled at me broadly, with teeth capped in gold. Carmen laughed, the sound of wind chimes, as I picked up the glass, my hand shaking. "You are shaking. Do I excite you that much? I hope you are not going to lose control and do something unfortunate. Try to ravish me?" I put the glass down. She laughed. "Don't be foolish David. Enjoy your drink."

I remember little of our conversation because my barely controlled lust for Carmen clouded everything. I only remember later her telling me that there were untold thousands of guests at the estate, but it was so large we were unlikely to bump into any accidentally. I remembered at that moment Charles' description of this vast estate as his "garden of earthly delights", with inchoate unease.

I limited myself to one glass of wine at dinner. The food was magnificent, the conversation clever. Juliana sat next to me, asked if I had family. I talked about my life, especially about the house fire and the loss of my family. "And your friends?" I told the truth. "Long gone. Tired I guess of my mood swings, the pathetic spectacle I exhibited after the deaths of my family, my drinking." She touched my arm gently, "So you are all alone in the world? So sad." Carmen added. "Then let him stay with us." There was warmth around me, and I felt at home.

After dinner, I asked to continue the interview. Charles promised me an hour, no more. Before starting, and, after some hesitation, I mentioned Carmen's advances towards me, looking for his reactions. He just laughed. "You are both adults."

When I mentioned that I thought I saw Vuk assault someone, he dismissed it. "Impossible. He is capable of it of course but would do something like that only if I ordered him. Which I did not. Not today at least." He gave me his thin smile. "Do you not have an interview to do?"

Trying to be professional, I worked to ignore the veiled menace of his words. "Let us pick up where we left off. Please tell me of this place you called Shangri-La."

"It was during a low period in my life. I had started my own company but was quickly going bankrupt. I staggered into this little village. The people were ragged, and looked at me as an outsider more appropriately robbed than helped. I found out later, during my sojourn in that place, there were villagers that sheltered rebels who were fighting government abuses, and were wary of potential spies. I hadn't eaten for days and begged for food at a local cantina, but was rebuffed. I thought I was going to die in that godforsaken outpost. I must have fainted. When I awoke I was in a hut being tended to by an old man and his wife. They slowly had me eat some rice and drink some milk. I stayed with them for three years."

"This was Shangri-La?"

"Yes, for me that hut was more wondrous than is the estate we are in now. Those two gentle souls became the father and mother that I had never known. They papered over diseases of my soul. Under their guidance and love, I freed my repressed inner goodness, and was instructed in their abilities."

"I'm afraid I don't understand. "

"There is good in all of us. If we just let our innate love, trust, and empathy grow it will flower. They had the ability to unleash that part of the human spirit and the powers that came with its unleashing."

"You've mentioned abilities, and now powers."

"David, the bright soul is a part of cosmic unity. If you could unleash it you would have the power to create gold out of tin. Light out of dark. They could do all that and more but did so only for purposes of discipline, never for personal gain as that would be a perversion of the 'unity' as they called it."

"Are you fucking with me Charles? Creating gold out of other materials?"

Sounding irritated, he asked "Do you want my story or not?"

Again recognizing how easily I could be evicted without a complete interview, I merely nodded.

"Good. These, my new parents, were humble folk deeply knowledgeable and immersed in ancient philosophies. They understood that one cannot create out of nothing, but one can transform. Knowing this, and seeing how everything is related, one can learn ways to turn one thing into another. We do it all the time. Water into steam into power. Mass into energy and vice-versa. Why not base metals into gold? The alchemists knew it was possible they just never figured out how to do it."

"Did they teach you these tricks?"

"More than tricks, David. I was the child they had not had, and they instructed me. Showed me the face of God. Incantations. Deep, deep magic. Their only rule was that I only use these skills they taught me for self growth, and only for the sustenance of the bright soul."

"Charles, I'm sorry, but I don't believe any of this."

He just gave me a pitying smile. "Of course you don't". Then he continued. "I asked my parents why we could not use our abilities to unleash the diseases of the soul and transform it into something bright and beautiful. I tried to tell them about my studies into the material nature of the human spirit, that the diseased soul possessed its own sources of power. They just laughed at the thought that the mind could be material. To them it was, as they put it, "so American" of me. And they completely rejected the notion that the human spirit had a dark side. They claimed the dark is merely an absence of the bright and not something separate with its own powers to transform. Alas, I didn't heed them and experimented with the powers of the diseases of the soul. The magic here was deep. So deep David. It needed blood sacrifices to make it work, but I got the chants to work."

"You killed people?"

"It was necessary. I only took the old and the infirm. When my parents found out I violated their one rule, what I had done, they banished me from Shangri-La."

"Was it worth it?"

"No! I was happy for the first time in my life and I threw that away. And my abilities have come with a cost. All magic requires a balance. I used blood magic to make forays in time. In the unity there is a balance, you can't add or subtract. So the short times that I've spent in some other times is subtracted in some ways from this timeline. I already know that the time spent in the future erases some of my memories of my past, so I transform time sparingly. I used it enough to access news from the future to learn where mineral finds will occur, which companies will succeed, when governments or other events will impact my investments. That is the source of my material wealth. I give you permission to tell this story on how I became so wealthy."

"Why are you doing this to me Charles? I came here to interview you and you end up feeding me this rubbish. Do you imagine I could get any of this published, without tapes of this conversation? Nobody will believe me. I'll be a laughing stock. Ruined even more than I am now. Is that your plan, to ruin me completely?"

"I have told you the truth whether or not you wish to believe me. As for whether others believe what you write, well that's not my concern."

"I see." And then like a child I dared him. "So can you see my future?"

He smiled. "I've done so already. That is how I know you will help me in my crusade to bring brightness to the world."

"Fuck you!"

He seemed to enjoy my anger, "I've also peeked at your past."

At that my blood turned cold. I thought of my wife and children, and then, inexplicably, about Carmen.

Charles abruptly stood up. "Enough. Your hour is up. Enjoy the evening air. Go for a walk. Refresh yourself."

My anger and unease was not abetted in the fresh air. I encountered Carmen, waiting for me like a spider for the fly. She invited me back to her room and we made love. I experienced an ecstasy, greater than any ever I had known, my wife and children forgotten.

When we met for our interview the next day, after breakfast, I had decided on how I would headline the write up of the interview: "The wealthiest man in the world belongs in a lunatic asylum."

Whatever Charles Reyno was, he was not stupid. "So I gather you did not believe what I told you yesterday and yet here you are, back again for more. Did your time with Carmen change your mind?"

I ignored his jab. "I came for an interview, and I intend to leave having completed one. My interactions with Carmen have nothing to do with my work." At this Charles just smiled. "When we talked last, you mentioned that through your ability to peek into the future you became unimaginably wealthy."

"More than you can imagine. But it was insufficient. I tired of killing people. I thought of my parents, and how my selfishness, my greed for material goods, my inhumane activities was indeed a perversion of the unity. I went back to the village planning to beg for their forgiveness, but soldiers had come and burned it. My parents were butchered. The village women raped. In my sorrow I had an epiphany. I decided to celebrate their lives by becoming a spiritual Johnny Appleseed, manufacturing and sprinkling good around the world from evil mined from dark souls."

"Sounds like a major engineering job." My sarcasm must have been obvious, because Charles gave me a crooked smile.

"Oh it was David. It is no easy task transforming the base darkness of the human soul into its most sublime positive characteristics: Hate to love, Selfishness to altruism, Fear to Confidence. I had to figure out how to extract the negative soul, transform it, store it and then spread it where it is most needed. Yes, it posed huge technical problems."

"And you think those problems are solvable?"

"Of course. I solved it! Not through neurosurgery, but as it turned out something more traditional. I just extract it, much like milking a cow."

"Pray tell."

"Still sarcastic are you? Believe me I conducted experiments. Sadly the early ones were failures and our early subjects died in agony. A pity really, but needed. Fortunately we have many here in my little hideaway on whom to experiment. To sacrifice for the magic required."

"Charles, do you recognize at all that you are a fucking nutcase?"

He just ignored me, continued talking as if giving a lecture.

"You need to start with the right type of person. I

found the best donors possess a sense of lost entitlement in which their needs, angers, insecurities, fears, excesses, and jealousies lie close to the surface."

I grew quiet. Charles smiled. "Yes. Exactly. People like you David. Once you herd these people, you have to keep the diseases of their soul replenished. I find that what works best is by encouraging people to express their most base natures and experience their most abject shortcomings. In short, fatten them up, and keep them fattened, so their diseases never run dry. Much like we do with our cows. I have created such an environment here. I thought you were a lover of art David. But even at that you are superficial and I was not really surprised when you did not react when earlier I called this hideaway my 'garden of earthly delights'. Look up the art of Bosch when you have a moment; you'll understand better."

"I don't understand."

"Now, now, David. You are not a fool and I am sure you know the answer to that question. I could not believe my luck when you contacted me. I must admit I have my petty side and the thought of milking the person who made my life a hell on earth when I was young was one I could not pass up."

"So why the charade of an interview?"

"You of all people must appreciate the joy in extending one's pleasure. The last few days have given me much joy watching your jealousy, greed, and lust express itself, and knowing that I could put it to good use. Watching you as I contrived to leave the interview just as you were getting hooked, feeding your frustration. Putting you into Carmen's path to exercise your lust. Just talking them over with my wife added to our lovemaking."

"I don't deserve whatever you plan for me Charles."

"Of course you do, you sniveling coward. I looked into your past and saw your family burn. I saw how you could have saved them, but being a coward you did not even try. I could actually smell your fear, and then your self-loathing."

"For God sake, what do you want from me?"

"I want something good to come from the rot that is your soul."

Vuk dragged me downstairs, stopping in front of the room Carmen had called Charles' workshop. Juliana and Carmen were waiting. Juliana smiled, "So you are joining us, after all." Carmen kissed me gently on the lips. Vuk went forward and opened the door. Inside, there were cubicles, hundreds of them, about a quarter of which were closed. We went inside. Charles pointed to one of the open cubicles.

"This will be your collection room. Over there is the machine where we hook people up and extract negative soul, and over there is the storage container. My personal touch is needed to change that sewer of dark soul into something bright, beautiful and sublime. I think of myself as a vintner of souls."

"You'll never get away with it, you madman, People know I am here."

"David, David. I have gotten away with it already with hundreds of thousands of other people, around the world, and will with you too, you little insignificant worm."

"Please, Charles."

"I believe I may have said that to you more than once at St. Thomas. An ironic twist is it not? So let me tell you your future. You will stay here until I have no more use for you and then you will be fodder for another of my donors. Perhaps one will murder you for the sheer joy of it. But I think when the time comes, I will murder you myself for the dark magic needed to transform the dark to the light. Until then, for three out of four weeks a month, you will have the run of the place. The best of food, wine, and whatever pleasures you wish. Drink to your heart's content. Rape someone. Murder someone who is no longer useful. There are herds of humans in my grounds for those purposes. As for sex, Carmen will feed that lust. You will find it an ecstasy only for a while. I can assure you, however, that you will wish for death long before she tires of you. Vuk will be around to hurt you, do very unpleasant things to you, but that too is needed to bring out the fear and anger and hopelessness and wish for revenge that fattens the dark part of your soul."

"And in the fourth week?" I asked, but I knew the answer.

"In the fourth week you will be hooked up to that very nice looking machine, and we will milk you of your hatred and lusts and envies. It will be painful. You see the unity works by equilibrium. The euphoria we manufacture from your extractions will be paid for in your agony. I hope you will feel some perverse satisfaction in knowing that every pain, every jealousy, every self-loathing we milk from you is being used to make the outside world turn slightly more sunny."

***

I used to count the times I was hooked up, but have stopped doing so. I no longer feed well in my three weeks grazing and there is increasingly less being milked from me. Soon I will be put out for pasture to be used and abused and finally murdered by Charles for his cursed blood incantation. I hear Carmen coming for me. She will see if she can still get me sexually excited.

When I am completely incapable I will be put out to pasture. She is coming, carrying the tubes to hook me up. She is singing.

All the Missing
Paul Wilson

One

Joel Kincaid slept in a tangle of sweat and sheets as the muggy July air molested him. Thunder muttered over his home. The remains of his dinner rolled in his stomach. Strained, scared, and in pain, he was a man ripe for nightmare.

"Daddy."

Joel woke. He came awake all at once. He sat up, the sheet pulling taught at his shoulder. His hair was a wild helmet, his eyes wide in the dark. The skin at the base of his neck crawled. He called his lost daughter's name in the dark, his voice a dry croak.

"Molly?"

"Help me, Daddy."

He jumped from the bed, looked around the room, eyes bugging from their sockets. He called her name again. The wind talked to the eaves. Then silence. Joel went to the window and watched the pines bend in the strengthening gale. His throat was dry, yet he found the courage to call out. Her name puffed a blue circle against the window.

"Molly?"

Nothing. He walked backwards to bed, falling in, watching the window until he slept again. In the morning, he told himself the night-voice was only a product of a hopeful heart, penance for putting off the confrontation he should have finished already.

Two

Joel started his day as always: he thought about his lost daughter.

Molly had the usual childhood troubles: talking back, throwing tantrums, and snitching whiskey from Joel's stash. It wasn't until her teenage years that she found real trouble. She fell in love with a boy named Christoph.

Joel hated the name. It was an incomplete *Christopher*, or even better here in the country, *Chris*. The punk was tall, lean, and always smiling. He looked like he knew too much and was laughing about it.

Jenny fell hard. It started with drawings on her notebook covers. Joel didn't interfere, only hoped they would have a falling out as kids do. But Annie immediately began threatening and forbidding Molly from seeing ". . . that no-account boy." So naturally their daughter began sneaking out, meeting Christoph in the corn—until Annie caught them one night.

Joel came out to find mother and daughter screaming at each other. Christoph stood with arms crossed and his painted-on smirk. Joel marched past the arguing women and told Christoph to leave. Joel told him up close. The boy-man never lost his infuriating smile. He simply looked at Molly with lazy good humor and faded towards the road while she cried for him to come back.

Tears, curses, and pain made a thick cloud in the house as the sun rose. The arguing didn't cease all day. That night, Annie snapped.

Molly told her mother that she could not be stopped from following her heart. In the sliver of exasperated silence that followed, Annie struck hard enough to send Molly to the faded linoleum in a spray of blood. Unbelieving, daughter looked at mother, then scurried to her room, holding her bleeding nose. Annie was white.

"I didn't mean to do it that way, Joel."

Joel said he knew and took Annie to bed—but he did so gingerly, as if she were a gun that might still be loaded. When they woke the next morning, Molly was gone. By nightfall, the only sign they found of their daughter was her bloody coat crumpled by the side of the road.

Three

Joel stopped thinking about the past. It was a truly shitty way to distract himself.

All morning he found odd jobs to keep himself supposedly busy. A leaky sink was repaired, the front porch swing was oiled, and laundry just had to be finished. Finally, around one in the afternoon, he was out of excuses. For a last-ditch effort, he walked the porch to check the weather. The sun had been growing weaker all day. As he studied the sky, the black clouds quit fooling around and made rain.

You should do the same. Stop avoiding the confrontation and get behind the typewriter.

Ivy had asked him to write about his experience as

the father of a missing child. He had written some, but the effort stirred up emotions Joel thought were buried. He promised he would finish before Ivy got back from the city, but he was afraid. He had opened a grave in himself. It was ghoulish self-harm. Ivy said it would help him heal, but Joel didn't understand how. He didn't feel exorcised. He felt violated.

Just get it done. Then maybe you can put it all behind you. You have to at some point. You can't live like this forever.

Joel was torn. Putting it behind him meant accepting Molly was gone forever. What kind of father would do that? With Annie dead, it was his duty to carry Molly's torch.

But at what cost? Your sanity? Your soul?

Joel leaned against the kitchen doorway and watched the soaked wind blow the curtains. Lightning lit the house in a purple x-ray. He didn't see the red eyes watching him from the corn now that the sun was safely covered.

"You have work to do, old man."

He made himself a deal. If he finished, he would reward himself with a shower.

"And if Ivy makes it back to town tonight, I'll go out there and stay. Her house doesn't talk in the middle of the night."

Joel pushed off the kitchen wall. He balled his fists, swallowed the lump in his throat, and marched to his daughter's room. The ugly green typewriter smiled at him with ancient key teeth. He sat at her desk and pulled it closer. Tall and thin, his knees bumped the underside of her child's furniture.

"Okay. Let's get it done."

His thick, blunt fingers picked out the letters. He punished the keys as he typed:

The rain comes down the panes and I wonder where they were formed, these little drops. Are they lost to their cloud parents? They smash themselves on my window, never to go home again. Is that the fate of my daughter? Smashed somewhere, never to return home?

Joel paused. Was Molly dead? Two years now and he realized that was likely the truth. But she was his daughter, his flesh and blood, his little girl with the flying ponytail who always wanted to play in the corn. He could not give up on her just because the statistics said she wasn't coming back. Joel stopped to cry. Because he was alone, he sobbed. Then he screamed. When his storm passed, he went on, hammering the keys. He had to finish this now. He would never summon the courage to return here. Something was rising from the internal coffin he had dug up; a purple-blue hand gripped its edge. He didn't want to see any more of it.

I may never know. And that is the worst part. Is she gone to a new life and too happy to let me know? Did I anger her or fail her in some way and she's punishing me? I just want to know. Where is my child? How have I misplaced her? May God forgive me for letting her leave my sight. Please God forgive me for failing her.

Joel tore the page out of the machine and laid it atop the pile beside the desk. His words weren't many, but they were true.

"There. It's finished. Ivy can have it. I'm done."

Joel was surprised by a new wave of tears. He thought it a squall, but his breath hitched, his eyes screwed themselves shut, and he wailed. The sound that came from him was long, loud, and scared him with its power. The fact that he was alone, and there was no one to help him, intensified the fear. He fell from Molly's chair and curled himself smaller until he fit under her desk, falling into the coffin he had exhumed from himself.

In the corn, those red eyes continued to watch the house. Agitated claws shredded the sword-like leaves.

Four

Joel decided on the old L & M for supper. The low and wide brown building was a landmark place to the old families. Depending on the day, you could get a home-cooked meal or a fat, greasy burger. Today was the latter.

"Slap some cheese and A1 on it," Joel requested. He took his usual table near the jukebox and read the paper. The waitress, a young thing all of seventeen, brought him his food. As he ate, he thought about the long afternoon ahead of him.

Ivy had complained about the leaking of her shed roof for weeks now. It was a small thing and just needed a few new sheets of tin. Joel checked his watch. He had time. With luck, he would finish just as she pulled into the driveway.

Five

Joel was able to buy most of the materials at the hardware store, but they were out of the nails he needed. He didn't want to go to Wal-Mart but there was no way around it. At least he could buy dinner to cook for him and Ivy tonight.

He fought his way through the crowds and the check-out, leaving with three bags. Their weight turned him into a metronome as he exited.

"Hey there, Joel."

The Greeter was a friend he knew from the library, Margo. She was standing by the buggy corral. As she approached, a kid pushed between them, followed by his mother whose buggy set off the squalling siren. Everyone turned, knowing it was a false alarm, but Margo had to check anyway. While she worked, Joel studied the wall, the one he knew as well as any in his home, the one that caused him to avoid this store.

Posters filled the glass case. Many were yellowed and curling. Some were faded to shadows of type. A few were printed on colored paper, as if by choosing a pink or blue the grieving families could win extra attention for their child. Have you seen *my* baby? Don't look at the others, they're surely dead, but not *my* child. Joel knew how they felt.

He found his poster, his girl, his Molly. She had become folded against a picture of a beautiful Mexican boy last seen over a year ago.

"Shame," Margo said. Joel nodded without turning.

"I clean it every morning and afternoon and see their faces through Windex. I wonder about them. I'm so sorry, Joel. Truly I am."

He nodded again and tried a smile for her sake.

Margo wanted to say more, but a harried mother asked about returning a vacuum and Joel made his escape. Despite Margo's sympathies, he had a job to do. Despite his pain, the world moved on. Children were going to sit down at dinners tonight—so were wives for that matter. It wasn't fair, but the world moved on. So should he.

Six

Ivy's place backed against the woods, a squat square lovingly stuffed with junk. She had a reputation as a kind of wise hippie, a charming oddity. She was that writer-woman up the hill who wore all the bracelets and rings and feathers. She moonlighted as a Fortune Teller. Every February and Prom Season lovesick girls flocked to her place for potions and crystals and advice.

Her shed housed a riding mower and boxes of God-only-knew-what. A motorcycle was covered by a dusty tarp. There was a story there, but Joel had never pushed. Ivy was a private woman. An extension ladder was an easy find and Joel set to work on the roof. He enjoyed the distraction. Unlike the writing, he understood how to do this.

As he worked, Joel thought of Ivy, his beautiful woman from Greek heritage. She was a great cook (his own miserable attempts in the kitchen were applauded but laughed at) and a better conversationalist. She was the perfect complement to the post-family Joel. Life with her was easy, unlike life with Annie. Annie, the woman he had shared twenty-three years with—until she decided to check out.

Joel thought of his dead wife.

Seven

Annie was the power player in the house. She was the heavy, the disciplinarian. Joel always wondered how much she enjoyed it; how much was extracting a little balance for the abuse Annie's mother had heaped on her?

Molly had her share of fuck-upery as a kid, most memorably the time she climbed aboard the tractor while Joel was clearing some old pines and got the machine going, but as Molly grew older, as her breasts began to develop and boys started sniffing around, Annie changed. She grew meaner. Joel called her on it one exasperated night.

"Do you have to be so hard on her? She's going to date. She's going to be curious. You start putting a choke on her and she'll pull further away."

"We got to watch out for her, Joel. It's our job." Annie used her hard look, the one that turned her baby-blues to ice.

Then came Christoph and the fight and the slap and then the sheriff found Jenny's bloodstained jacket. Then came the waiting, the worry, the drifting apart, and Annie's final gruesome decision.

***

Joel always woke before Annie. That morning he came fully awake, fully aware in the first blink of his eyes. He knew, he said later. He just knew.

He got out of bed. It was quiet, with none of the smells that had populated their long marriage—no breakfast, no coffee, no sounds of a shower running, only the southern spring heat baking the house. Joel walked every room. The back door opened onto the carport. He walked through and saw his wife swinging by her neck. A bedroom slipper had fallen off. Her housecoat was open around pale legs. Her hair was a mask covering her face. Joel swallowed once, feeling everything in him and around him settle.

"Okay then."

He went back inside and called the police.

***

The sheriff asked again if Joel was all right.

"This must be a hell of a shock, coming after Molly's disappearance."

Joel nodded. He knew the answer before he asked, but hope is a damnable weed.

"Anything new on my daughter?"

The sheriff shook his head.

"If I didn't know you better Joel, I'd consider that question suspicious with your wife's body bag not even out of the driveway."

"Annie hadn't been here for a while. She was distant. Lost." A new idea came to Joel. It was horrible, but—

"Is there any chance Annie could have done something to Molly? If she was damaged enough to hang herself—"

"Don't think about those things," the sheriff said.

"I have to. What the hell else can I do?"

Eight

Joel first met Ivy when the library was being rebuilt. Talbot Woods finally decided the old mill building needed replacing. Some of the town guys got together and pitched in to move the books and periodicals. One of Joel's neighbors suggested him for duty and Joel found he liked the work. It occupied his mind instead of Molly or Annie.

Ivy was one of the volunteers. They spoke between scratch lunches and dusty cardboard boxes, and before long Joel marveled that he had made a friend. Ivy was a warm woman who seemed to realize he couldn't talk easily on his own. She did all the work. In his pain, Joel let her. Somewhere between the library and getting together for dinner they discovered they were in a mellow sort of relationship.

"I was thinking of writing a new book," she said the first night they spent together. The wind was playing the eaves like an instrument. Her head was on his chest. "A book about missing children."

"Okay."

"I want to talk about it. I think it will help you . . . and help us."

"Us?"

"I don't have any other interests, you know." She looked up at him and smiled. "You're my only boyfriend."

The idea of him being anyone's boyfriend made him laugh. His laughter greased the wheels. He agreed to help Ivy with her book. Unspoken but no less true, Ivy agreed to help him start living again.

Nine

"Who is that handsome man on my roof?"

He came down the ladder to hug her. "How was the trip?"

"Terrible." She looked at the replaced tin roof. "But it's getting better."

"I aim to please."

"Can you make my night better, too?"

Joel took her inside to try.

***

After dinner Ivy made love in her usual eager way. She liked being on top, bending over where they joined. It was good and when they finished, they fell asleep together, her hair over his chest, both smiling in satisfaction.

While they snored, eyes appeared at the window, red eyes full of pain and misery. Claws scratched at the glass. When the voice called for him, Joel woke. He leapt from the bed and hurried across the room.

"Did you hear that?"

Ivy rose, naked, and joined him. They went to the

window together and looked out. Joel saw a figure by the end of the house. His mouth dried at the sight.

"Oh. My God. Is that?"

Ivy put a hand on his back.

"Joel, wait!"

He ignored her. He moved, walked, and finally ran. He didn't feel his toes connect with the bed nor his elbow with the wall. Joel flung open Ivy's front door, calling his daughter's name. He found Molly at the foot of the porch, glowing in the moonlight. Life's great clock stopped. She was there, she was *right there*! His little girl. Her skin was pale, her eyes dark. He held out his hands, reached for Molly, and Ivy grabbed his nuts.

Joel crumpled as Ivy twisted. Shock fought with pain and pain fought with anger for supremacy. He fell back, mouth open.

"Trust me," she said, then turned her attention to Molly.

"Are you happy to see your father? Then why don't you embrace him? Why don't you help him?"

Molly's eyes flared as she looked between the two. She growled.

"Help me, Daddy," she said in her musical little-girl voice. Despite the pain, Joel struggled to get to his feet.

"Wait," Ivy said. "Let her come to you."

Joel looked at his daughter, at his dream realized, then at the woman he might love, and wondered if his grief hadn't finally driven him mad. Maybe he had fallen off the shed roof and this was all a dream as he lay dying.

"She can't come to you because I haven't invited her up."

"What?" Joel gasped.

"Prove me wrong if you can, Molly." Ivy wore a peculiar smile that looked two sizes too small.

"Daddy, invite me in."

Ivy said: "It's my house."

Joel croaked: "That's my little girl."

"No, she's not." Ivy spoke with finality and Joel broke. He struggled up, meaning to step out and touch his lost daughter, but a silky voice called from the side of the house.

"Oh, for God's sake! Can't you people move it along!"

Joel sensed more than saw movement. He couldn't take his eyes from the daughter he was sure he'd never see again. He watched hands wrap around Molly's throat, pulling her away again. Then Joel found his voice.

"No you don't!"

He charged, not hearing Ivy call him, only knowing the night had Molly again, but this time he would not lose her.

*****

The moonlight showed Christoph choking Molly. Joel moved with no thought, only fury. The bastard's smiling face was beside her terror-filled one. Joel hit him hard. The punk's head snapped back, his hand slipped from Molly's throat, and he laughed. He opened his mouth to say something, but Molly whipped her head with the speed of a snake and fastened her teeth into his arm. Christoph roared in pain, unbalanced enough for her to skip away. Joel wasted no time in hitting him again, relishing the feel of lips squashing under his knuckles—but the boy's teeth felt so strange! So big! Christoph wobbled, but even as he fell, he reached for Joel. The kid's hand closed around Joel's throat and the reaction was simple and clear:

He's not human!

Molly was a blur, a shadow bending. The moonlight flashed on what she had in her hand and Joel pushed himself back. His feet tangled and he fell as the ax split the air. The blade opened Christoph's neck. Blood exploded. His head flopped backward, eyes wide, his pupils reduced to pinpricks. But Molly wasn't finished. She swung the weapon again. The connection was solid. Christoph's head flew, finally landing against Joel's truck. Molly swayed. She leaned on the ax like an old woman.

"Molly?"

When she turned her eyes on her father, they were glowing red.

Ten

They sat in the living room. Molly huddled to herself in a leather recliner. Joel sat on the couch. He wanted to hold her, but Molly gave him no sign he could.

"Is that . . ." Ivy asked, creeping close to Molly.

"What?" Then Joel saw. Molly's hair was a wig. It sat low and crooked, giving her a skewed visage and a touch of unreality. She eyed Ivy with barely concealed hostility. She turned to her father.

"Daddy, I came home." Finally, the weird ice-lock broke, and Joel was able to touch her. He caressed her cheek, and the same thought went through his mind: *She's not human.*

But she was still his daughter.

"Honey, what do you need?"

"Water, please. It helps. My throat is always dry."

Ivy went to get it.

"I came home because I was scared. I came home because you deserved to know what happened to me. But mostly because I was scared."

"My baby . . ."

"Tell us," Ivy said, handing Molly the water. "Tell us everything."

Eleven

"It was Christoph who took me. He turned me by the road. He bit my neck. I bled on my coat, and he threw it on the ground. He said I didn't need it anymore."

"He bit you?"

"Let her talk, Joel."

***

"He shuffled us from place to place but always headed south. The second night we picked up three more runaways, two girls and a guy. I was more upset that I didn't have Christoph's undivided attention. I was still a stupid girl in love, and he used that. I guess it's no more than I deserved. He told me later—I don't know how long or even where we were—that I was his favorite and I cried with relief. Then, one night, we were all shoved in a barn. He took me to a corner. It smelled of cow. He told me his bite started the transformation, but if we made love, it would finish. He said if we made love, we would be closer and so we did. We made love. I made love. He fucked me and I became a vampire.

"We moved on a steady course and finally wound up in Shy Town. Georgia. We came to this plantation house about four in the morning. It was beautiful. The women lounging on the porch were beautiful. A fat man in white spread his arms to us. We had picked up six more on the trip. I wasn't special anymore, just one of the herd.

"The fat man's name was Arlington. He hugged Christoph and told him he had done well. I found out that Christoph was a recruiter. He traveled around finding stupid boys and girls to bring to houses like Arlington's throughout the world.

"Each of us newbies had to sit with Arlington to be judged as worthy stock. Not everyone made it. I did. He told me he was trying to rebuild his species. He said that many runaways were brought to his home and became his children—if he judged them worthy. He said this while running his hand up and down my neck.

"I didn't have the courage to resist. I only realized that if his mansion was my new home then I was going to have to run away from home again. I began to think of my escape.

"The mansion was surrounded by hills. Inside the hills were chambers carved out of the earth. All the new recruits remained there until they had finished *becoming*.

"Arlington gave us a final pep talk before he sealed us down there. 'It can be a scary process my children, but those who survive will become family. Those who don't . . . deserve their fate.'"

"What's the change?" Ivy asked in a breathless little whisper. "What's it like to become a vampire? Does it hurt?"

Molly regarded her with eyes that glittered red like the dying embers of a fire.

"The change happened in stages. Arlington said that some of us would evolve faster than others. He said that we would start out as low vampires—ghouls—and we would have to learn to control our base urges. Way down deep in the tunnels was a huge room with people for us to practice on. To . . . to feed on. Our goal was to become useful members of our new society, what Arlington called elegant, sophisticated. He said the most important attribute was to be able to pass for human so we could go into the world and help recruit more family members.

"But first we had to learn to eat. It's hard to pass as human when you can't stop eating people.

"The process hurts. You puke a lot. For weeks Christoph didn't come to see me. He changed me, gave me this thing, and then left me. There were nurses, but they had to deal with so many. They were cold. Sometimes they hit if someone wouldn't stop crying. And there was a lot of crying.

"I began losing my hair. My fingernails grew thick and long. I bit them off, but they grew back. It's the same with our fangs. They come back if something happens to them. My teeth and gums hurt all the time. My stomach shriveled. I learned to cry quietly."

Joel sat forward. His eyes were wet. "How did you get away?"

"They were taking some of us in for a feeding. Only three at a time, because when a vampire is taken with bloodlust, they can overpower almost anyone. The nurses were careful. What they weren't counting on was that the humans had made a plan. They knew that when we came to feed, they had their best chance for escape. Only then did they outnumber us. The cage door opened that morning and the humans rushed at once. The nurses were knocked down. It was chaos. The humans headed up, towards the light. I chased, I ran, because I knew this was my own best chance for escape. I pretended I was trying to catch the humans, but I wasn't. I was trying to get away.

"Thank God they tried this when it was dark. If it had been during the day, the sun would have killed me as soon as I got up top."

"So, it's true," Ivy asked. "About sunlight?"

"Yeah. Sunlight. Garlic. Mirrors. I can't stand the sight of roses or silver or running water now. I don't understand it, but . . ." Molly shrugged, drank water, and continued.

"I got topside and into the swamp. I kept going. I got away. I came home."

Molly finished. She was tired and curled into herself. But she wouldn't close her eyes. Those nests of rubies glittered.

"I came home because I was scared, Daddy. I guess I messed up good. You were right about Christoph."

Joel knelt in front of her and brushed the wig hair out of her eyes. He felt Ivy behind him. Her breath was cold as she spoke.

"Why don't we put her in the back bedroom for now? No direct sunlight comes in that room."

Joel nodded, unable to speak. Ivy told him she would take care of it. The two females exchanged looks over Joel's head.

"Daddy, we should move Christoph's body. Would you?"

"Okay."

***

Joel used a tarp to wrap the boy's remains and drag them into the shed. The act took twenty minutes. He wondered why Christoph hadn't turned to dust like in the old legends. But the answer was obvious. Because he wasn't a vampire. Vampires were fiction.

Joel returned inside, eager to say goodnight to his daughter, to see her again, but Ivy had shut the bedroom door and greeted him with coffee. She said nothing, but her huge teal eyes studied him.

"We have to keep vigil tonight. Let Molly rest. She

came a long way to find us."

Joel sat. His emotions were an avalanche crashing down on him. He waited to see if he would be crushed.

"We'll have to call the sheriff," Joel said.

"Soon," Ivy said. "Not yet."

Twelve

Molly slept all day. As the orange light leaked out of the sky and darkness took over, Ivy pulled herself close to Joel.

"You have to be strong when you open the door."

"What are you talking about?" He sounded weak and hated himself for it.

"Molly told me a lot last night while you were dealing with the vampire's body. She told me she loved you and that she was sorry."

"Why didn't she tell me any of this? What's going on, Ivy?"

"She was tired, and she knew she owed you an explanation first. She didn't know how long she had left before—"

"Before what? Do you really think that punk took her to some kind of vampire commune? She's been through something horrible, something I have to help her with, but what you're saying is crazy. You're crazy."

Joel stood, meaning to get his daughter and go home. That thought was clear and well formed, everything else would have to wait. Joel walked down the hall to Molly's room. He stopped when he saw the ax leaning beside her door. Ivy had followed him.

"She told me she felt her humanity draining."

Inside the room, something was thrown against the wall.

"Ivy . . . She just came home to me."

"You have to accept that she didn't."

"I don't know if I can."

"Don't leave her like that."

"Ivy . . ."

"Do your duty as her father. You have to."

How long did he hesitate? Time didn't seem to pass at all. Joel picked up the ax and opened the door.

Molly had lost her wig. She was bald. Her eyes had grown to large black saucers and Joel's breaking mind told him it was so she could hunt better. Her hands were five-bladed claws. Her mouth hung open. Drool splattered the floor.

"She didn't survive the change, Joel. You can't leave her like this."

Molly swung her head around. Her nose flared. She was scenting them.

"She'll kill us both and you know it. She came home, but she's changed."

Molly lowered her head and hissed. She rushed them. Ivy screamed.

Joel swung the axe.

Thirteen

Joel stopped at Wal-Mart and looked at Molly's poster a final time. No one was around. He had a copy of the case key, given so he could change out Molly's information. Joel reached in and took down the paper. It crackled between his fingers. He looked at his daughter and remembered who she used to be. He folded the flyer, put it in his pocket, and left before the tears could blind him.

Fourteen

The sheriff laced his hands behind his head and stood. His back cracked in complaint. To quiet the rumblings of his stomach, he finished off coffee that had been fresh six hours ago.

He walked away from the desk, a tall man with clothes-hanger shoulders. He walked away from the cracked and peeling notebooks. He walked away from the pictures. Someone had put a beige piece of tape on the top notebook and written in magic marker: THE MISSING.

Alec had seen movies where detectives taped pictures to a wall and then paced, posed, and look oh so cool. Those guys never had sweat stains under their Wal-Mart shirts and they always found the missing kids.

So many children. Where did they all go? The air? Join the circus? Start an underground society?

He gazed from the window to the desk again. On top of all the other pictures was Joel's daughter, Molly. How old was that picture now? Alec had been a cop long enough to know that Molly's fresh-milk face and honey hair were surely more dead than missing. She had the kind of looks that hurt to appreciate. She was perfect fodder for a monster's eye.

It started to rain, making a lonely sound. Alec stood by the window, but he still saw Molly's face. When it stopped raining, he would go out and begin looking again, for all the good it would do.

A Visit From Lady Lydia
Ken Goldman

"In a world of diminishing mystery, the unknown
persists."
— Jhumpa Lahiri, The
Lowland

"Known is boring; unknown is tempting!"
— Mehmet Murat ildan

"There is no such thing as the supernatural. There is
only the natural that we
don't understand."
--- Lady Lydia Zephyr,
online vampirette

The scene played like a bad horror movie, the two
characters standard Hollywood issue. The vampire, her
victim. Check and check.

But the scene was real...

From the shadows she appeared like an apparition, a full-bodied beautiful woman whose appearance did not suggest the strength of which she was capable. The young man hardly resisted as she pulled him backwards into the darkness of a nearby alleyway. Maybe he expected an anonymous blow job from this dark female seemingly emboldened by alcohol. He'd had enough beers himself to let that happen, even under this bizarre circumstance.

"Do you know what I am?" she asked.

"I have no idea who you are..."

She tugged him closer. "Not **who** I am, you fool. I asked you **what** I am!"

The man managed to stare at her, but said nothing. In the pale wash of moonlight she appeared heavily made up yet still alluring, although her skin was white as porcelain. She loosened her grip, allowing him to speak freely.

"**What** you are? I'd say you're a bit presumptuous, if this is a mugging. I'm carrying little cash, and you don't seem to have a weapon. I could break you in half, you know, so you're fucked all around." He struggled, but again she held him fast."Look, if this is some drunken attempt at a seduction, or if you have some irrational hatred of men--"

The woman crooked her arm around the man's throat "You are a fool. I need no weapon, and this is no seduction. This is my survival. And yours!"

"And you, lady, are a bad cliché. So get your fucking hands off me."

The man laughed, unaware he had proven the woman's statement accurate.

He **was** a fool...

***

One of Len Haskin's dutiful students turned on the lights as the young teacher slipped the DVD back into its case. Facing his class, he grinned and slipped into hip mode. "Okay, gang. Movie Review time. Questions? Comments? Thumbs up or down for this morning's creatures of the night?"

Adele Somers, always bucking for an 'A', took the shot. "A good movie, Mr. Haskin. But vampires aren't real, are they?" Her pearly toothed smile followed. "I mean, no one lives forever, right?"

Ronny Corbin, his testosterone bubbling at full boil, whispered, "Not as real as those tits, Adele! They'll always live forever right here." The kid pointed towards his crotch. Haskin ignored him, although he agreed the kid was right about Adele's attributes. If he were ten years younger and not her teacher -- Christ, the girl could pass for a full grown woman *now*.

The girl's question wasn't unexpected. High school kids were always curious when it came to the darker realms. Haskin's senior class responded on cue, having just viewed that teenage angst '80's classic, "The Lost Boys." *("Worms, Michael! You're eating worms!")* The vampire flick was part of his film class's horror unit, so of course some student had to ask if the movie depicted real vampirism.

"No, Adele. I highly doubt it. Not if you're talking about someone transforming into a bat and flapping around the room. However..." Len paused for dramatic effect. "I imagine there are those who practice vampire-like customs. Cults exist for all kinds of aberrant behavior, including the urge to administer some serious hickies. But I'd guess those folks are mostly wack jobs, outcasts whose lives would otherwise be empty, or, more likely, who are just pissed off at the world."

Craig Rabin, a heavy-set tattooed and body pierced Goth wannabe, looked up from his smart phone. "You mean guys like me, don't you, Mr. Haskin?" Len had never seen the boy attempt to smile or to pay attention, which of course came with the ever-present black attire. But in the age following Columbine, ticking time bombs like Rabin had to be taken seriously.

"For some that lifestyle is a sort of religion, Craig, like those who pay endless homage to their smart phones. And finding like-minded peers often serves as a bonding experience for other ersatz vampires. It may not be the Scouts, but cults do serve a purpose, a kind of emotional meth for those needy enough." Haskin felt like adding ... *And you would know something about that, wouldn't you, you unemployable prick?* Preferring to keep his job, Len kept that judgment to himself. Even the best teacher had to remain safely open-minded and essentially spineless, not an easy thing when asked about premarital fucking or the existence of vampires.

Rabin's attention returned to his phone. Another student offered commentary.

"But vampire bats are real, isn't that right?" The question came from Bart Guffman, a good looking and likable enough student, whose I.Q. probably was similar to his shoe size. "I mean, they suck blood just like those kids in the movie, right?"

Seeing his opportunity for some cleverness, Haskin went into full Bela Lugosi mode. "Geeve me a bite of yourrr neck, yesss?" The joke fell flat. What would millennial kids know of a movie made more than fifty years before their parents were born? "Okay, yes, vampire bats are real. There are several species of the little suckers, and they all drink blood, Bart. It's their primary food source and readily available. Mammals, birds, but rarely humans. They do hunt at night, though. And they're ugly as hell, little fanged flying rats. But they're mostly harmless."

Craig Rabin spoke again, an event about as common as Halley's Comet. "I found something on my phone that may interest you, Mr. Haskin." The kid got to his feet, held up his phone. "There's this site online -- It's filled with people who say they're vampires. *Real* vampires! They have chat rooms, web pages, all kinds of shit. There's this woman online now. She's no kid, either, if you look at her photo, which means she's not jerking around. She's local, too. Interested?"

"Bring up your phone, Craig. I'll put it on the screen, make some use of this high technology the school has graciously supplied." He hooked the phone into the large HDTV unit. The image onscreen caused some girls to gasp.

Rabin was right. These weren't kids' photos online; these were adults, and their photos showed bleeding fanged creatures whose faces probably were enhanced by photoshop to look like the real deal. Many of them had active text addresses; that meant they were willing to talk, and remaining anonymous seemed of no concern. The young woman Craig had selected could have come from central casting. Erotic and raven haired but with milky white skin, she seemed some gothic Cleopatra. Her name flashed beneath her photo.

"Lydia Zephyr?" Haskin asked. "That can't possibly be her real name."

"I think she prefers Lady Lydia. Women vampires like that sort of royalty shit."

The bell rang, signaling Haskin's Film Class period was over, but Craig and his classmates didn't budge. They seemed to expect their Goth pal Craig to make his point.

"Text her, Mr. Haskin. See for yourself. Maybe this Lydia lady will want to visit our class. That'd be cool, rustling up a real vampire, don't you think? None of those sparkling '*Twilight* 'Hollywood pansies, but the real deal? And a female yet!" Haskin's students nodded in agreement.

"Text her, Mr. Haskin! Will you. Please?" from Adele.

Len shrugged. "Yeah, Craig, That'd be cool. It might cost me my job, but what the hell. Now scram, all of you..."

***

Well, what the hell...

His class gone, Len hit the computer's FaceTime button and waited before the large monitor. Incredibly, within seconds Lydia Zephyr appeared onscreen, live, or seemingly so. Her dark eyes appeared almost cat-like. Or maybe bat-like.

"Your chubby Goth student told me you'd make contact. Am I his homework assignment?" The woman's voice was breathy, sexy enough to seem well rehearsed.

"Lady Lydia, huh? Your real name?"

The woman managed a shit eating grin. "Well, Lady Lydia sounds a bit affected, but 'Linda Smith '-- that's an unimaginative moniker for a creature of the night, don't you think, Mister...?"

"...Haskin. Leonard. Film Studies teacher over at Washington High on the South Side. And it's my real Judeo-Christian name. Well, Jewish, actually. So you won't have to worry about crucifixes from me." The woman's expression seemed a blank slate, so he dropped the clever repartee. "Okay, so, Lydia, you're on the level, then? See, my senior class seems to think there may be such things as--."

"...as vampires? Real bloodsuckers? I know you're skeptical, but we all harbor our own nasty little secrets, don't you think? I'm not ashamed of mine."

Len grinned. The woman's flirtation was obvious but effective. "Fine. You want to put your money where your fangs are?"

"This isn't Tinder, Mr. Haskin. I don't show my goods so easily."

"So, you've got nothing?"

"Well, I won't do the bat-transformation right now -- that's so amateurish. But here's something for you..." Lydia's onscreen image sank out of sight for a moment, then reappeared. Smiling now, she displayed elongated fangs. "Convinced, Leonard?"

Haskin had to laugh. "Very clever, but nuh huh. You slipped some false teeth into your mouth while you weren't onscreen. Big whoop, but no cigar, Lady Lydia."

"Well, I would morph into a bat, but I don't think you're ready for that." The woman managed a Playmate-of-the-month pout. "Don't tell me the teeth aren't a turn-on, Leonard. You want a little bite, maybe? I'd be happy to oblige."

Her flirtation came full throttle now, but this was no hormonal teenaged girl. Lydia Zephyr *(no, Linda Smith!)* was a woman in full bloom, but also maybe a bit warped.

Len knew it was game-on now. "No bites, Lydia, not unless we get to know each other better. However, you *can* do something for me."

Lydia leaned forward. Her lips puckered as if she were about to leave a lipstick smear on the screen. Seething with innuendo, she whispered, "And what would that be, Mr. Haskin?"

"Len, okay?"

"Fine."

Their verbal sparring felt tacky, but the woman's breathy utterance coupled with her image on the monitor had the desired effect on Haskin's libido.

"You know where Washington High is?"

"I can find it."

"My Film Class students asked about vampires. You know kids. The supernatural fascinates them. And a vampiress such as yourself must be a wealth of infor-"

"--Vampirette, okay? That's the correct term. And there is no such thing as the supernatural. There is only the natural that we don't understand. Capeesh?"

"Got it. So, care to stop in around 10:30 for a little Q and A? I'm in Room 215. Tomorrow's a double period. Plenty of time to strut your stuff."

Lydia laughed loud. "Why, Leonard, you know what they say about vampires appearing during daylight. You wouldn't want me to dissolve in a pool of goo on your floor, would you?"

"So it's thanks, but no thanks?"

She spoke low, as if sharing a secret. "Well, you also know what they say about having to invite a vampire in, right? You've invited me. So I'll be there, Leonard. Tomorrow. Although I have some plans tonight. Midnight plans."

"A rendezvous with another creature of the night, I'm thinking."

Lydia giggled, but the response fell short of girlish. "Not quite. A feeding. Probably from some young stud like yourself. Don't misunderstand, Mr. Haskin --- *Len*. It's harmless stuff, really. A pricked finger, at best. Most guys are usually grateful for the experience that follows." She licked her lips and smiled, faux fangs still in place, and the screen went dark.

Len Haskin grinned at the young woman's moxie, the same dopey grin he'd worn as a horny adolescent on the prowl. He had good reason. He was nursing one enormous erection. Well, then...

He had a few minutes before his next class to take care of business.

***

At the bar the young woman sat, her legs on full display from the high stool. She waited for the inevitable. Near midnight, it wouldn't take long.

"Mind if I sit here?" The well-dressed collegiate-type didn't wait for her answer. "What're you drinking, hey? Wine?"

"It's red, isn't it?" Smiling, the woman applied a brief Blush touch-up, then gave the guy the once-over. The man appeared younger than her usual selections. Probably a pre-law or pre-med student. Looking him over, she laughed to herself. "Isn't it a little late for you to be out?"

The guy didn't appreciate the joke coming from a woman clearly older than himself, but nonetheless she was beautiful. He ignored the comment. "A cabernet, then?"

The woman finished the last of her drink. She nodded.

He called the bartender over, pointed to her glass. Extending his hand, he leaned towards his new companion. "I'm Cliff."

Squeezing the young man's hand lightly, the woman spoke close to his ear. "I'm whoever you want me to be."

Within the half hour the two walked together beneath the boulevard's dim street lamps. Being late and a weeknight, traffic was light. The woman waited for the right moment. She stopped cold, kissing her escort near the entrance of an alleyway. He seemed surprised but quickly responded. She slipped her tongue into his mouth, crushing her body against his. The young man followed her into the alcove's darkness. She knew he would. Easy.

"*I don't even know your--*"

"*Shhh...*"

Moments later the woman exited the alleyway alone. In thick rivulets, blood dripped down her chin.

***

"It's sunny out, Mr. Haskin. Not promising weather for a vampire's visit." Adele Somers had a point. Ten minutes into 3rd period already had passed.

Len shrugged. "When we spoke yesterday, our Lady Lydia didn't seem concerned about daylight. I'd say that sunlight thing is probably a myth anyway. Miss Zephyr is probably a bored woman playing 'Let's Pretend.'"

"A bored woman with huge ta-ta's," Craig Rabin mumbled.

As if on cue the door opened and there she stood, displaying a toothy grin -- but showing no fangs. The woman wore a black skirt that stopped at her knee with a plain white shirt, a surprisingly conservative ensemble. "Okay, then, kids. Let's pretend, shall we?" She winked at Haskin, an action noticed by Len's students. Two girls giggled when the woman, crossing long legs, parked her ass on Haskin's desk. Someone wolf whistled.

Len extended his hand. "Thanks for coming. I'm glad you didn't enter through the window, Miss Zephyr. Our principal would frown on that."

"No one sees me except those I choose to see me."

Haskin's brow raised, but he kept his thoughts to himself. "Class, our guest speaker is your basic practicing vampire, Miss--"

"They know what I am, Mr. Haskin." She turned to the class, pointed to the window. "It's a bit bright out today. Would someone mind pulling the shades?"

Several students looked at each other. Quick on her feet, Adele Somers darkened the room. Lydia mouthed a quick 'Thank you.' She straightened her posture, still perched on Len's desk.

"Okay, then. Your teacher mentioned you had some questions for me. I'm all ears, kids. Except for the part that's teeth." Practically every hand went up. "Not necessary to follow school rules today, guys. Just ask. Okay?"

Suzette Davis took her shot. "Are vampires really dead? Or undead? Are you--?" Suzette never spoke up in class before. As far as Haskin knew, she never spoke at all.

"I'll let your teacher decide that. He pressed my hand, my flesh, a moment ago. So, Mr. Haskin, tell your students -- What did you feel when we...touched?"

Len went flush before he realized where Lydia's question was going. "It felt cold, Suzette. Miss Lydia's touch felt very cold."

"Want to feel, Suzette?" Lydia asked.

Falling silent again, the girl shook her head. She clearly didn't want to know.

From the back of the room came a male voice. "Do vampires live forever?"

"I live in the moment. Forever consists only of moments. So, yes, in that sense vampires live forever. As do I."

Behind her, Haskin leaned close to the woman so that only she heard. "Nice save. I'm writing that one down."

Another student, a girl, spoke up. "Will you show us your fangs?"

"No."

An uncomfortable silence followed before the next question came.

"Do you drink blood?" asked Bernie Huffman, a boy who never failed to spit whenever he talked.

Lydia didn't miss a beat. "Tell me -- If you cut your finger, do *you* drink blood? Or, perhaps when you were younger, your mother kissed the boo-boo?" She turned to Len, saw him smile at her answer. She smiled too. "A question most ask of me, knowing so little of what I really am, Mr. Haskin. Next question?"

"Do you kill?" from the Indian kid, whose name Len never could pronounce.

"We all kill."

"No, I mean do you kill people? Bite them?"

"Only if they appear tasty."

Craig Rabin shouted, "*Answer the damn question!*"

"Very well. In nature, it's the female who kills. Almost always. As for myself -- well, I *am* female, as you can see." A laugh from Lydia, and that was all.

Haskin leaned forward and spoke low. "And the Oscar goes to..."

Rabin interrupted. "About sunlight..."

"A lie based on superstition," Lydia answered.

"But you wanted the shades pulled!"

"The sun was in my eyes."

"Crucifixes? Stakes in the heart? Morphing into a bat?"

"Those beliefs make for good fiction."

Rabin sneered, mumbling something to himself.

Honor Roll Student Adele spoke up with one hell of a question. "Who made you?"

"The same who made you. Your maker. My maker."

"Do you mean God?"

"No. Do you?"

Adele's attempted smile didn't work. The woman's answer would have to do.

Craig Rabin wasn't buying any of it. "Tacky, Lady Z. Very tacky." Stepping forward, he raised his phone and snapped the woman's photo. Holding the screen for all to see, he added. "See? *She's visible!* Lady Z., that raises serious questions about your authenticity, don't you think? For a vampire, you're more like Donald Trump!"

Without losing her grin, the woman motioned for Craig to come forward. She cupped her hand and whispered to him.

"Don't fuck with me."

***

At the bell, Lydia got to her feet. Heading to the door Len's students thanked her, while a few kept their distance. Adele Somers bravely shook the woman's hand, then whispered to her, "Yeah, your skin, it's cold. Like death." Craig Rabin smirked and moved on. With the classroom emptied, Len closed the door, turned to his dark guest.

"That was heavy stuff. Not entirely informative, though. You fudged a bit."

"Much better to keep them guessing, Leonard. Adolescents, they're such curious souls. Like that Goth kid with all the ink and piercings, the headbanger that found me online."

"Craig Rabin is a curious kid, all right. But I think he's in training to be a full-out ass hole. The nose ring is a dead giveaway. You want to bite someone, he'd be a good start."

"Taking a chunk of Mr. Rabin's favorite arteries can be arranged."

"For all that, you really didn't admit to much, you know. Rabin had a point. Your answers were mostly cryptic bullshit, textbook vampire lore -- *Lady Lydia*."

The woman managed a warm smile unlike those she previously offered. Her eyes locked with Len's.

"You can call me Linda."

Haskin smiled too. "So much for the vampire act, then?"

'We're mysterious beings, we creatures of the night, Leonard. But I'll share one secret." She extended her hand. "Your cell phone, please."

Haskin appeared puzzled. "A selfie to show you really don't appear onscreen after all?"

The woman tossed her thick black hair provocatively and took the phone. "No, Leonard, that's vampire Hollywood hype. What I want is --- I want to give you my number. Okay, there, I said it. No bullshit." She punched the keys and handed the cell back. "However, if you'd like, I *can* let you in on something else." Reaching into her small purse, she added, "Have a look?"

She inserted the false fanged teeth. Haskin leaned close, took the woman's face into his hands pretending to examine it.

"I knew it! The lovely Lydia emerges from the dark to reveal herself as mortal!"

She tapped her palm across her chest. "Very mortal. Be still, my heart."

"No stake required?"

Her smile appeared again, now faux fanged.

"None at all."

***

Craig Rabin put away enough beers to drown a moose. He topped those off with one potent bomber of a joint. Leaving his pals at the school ball field, he found himself on Main Street near midnight, passing the local watering hole called Moxie's. Soon he would be old enough to enter, not that he hadn't tried. But his eighteenth year wasn't far off, and before long he'd be bumping uglies with the local sluts he'd seen entering the place. The crowd inside was shouting whatever lyrics they could figure out from "*Louie Louie.*"

Taking in the bump-and-grind music that drifted to the sidewalk, he noticed the woman in the black mini emerge. She was alone, and stopped to stare at him. He stared back.

"Craig! It's you! Out this late, and on a school night!"

It took a moment for the voice to register, a longer moment for him to recognize the woman's face.

"Adele? Jesus, I never would have recognized you in a million years. You look so --- so *old!"*

"Older, you mean, right? I wouldn't want to look *old*, Craig."

Rabin burped a taste of his beer. "Jesus, Adele, I didn't mean--" He paused, trying not to slur his words. "I mean, look at you! You're so made up, you could pass for thirty!"

"It's a rare talent, Craig. Gets me into these local bars every time. You think they'd let in a high schooler?"

Craig laughed. "I guess girls can pull off that kind of shit. Me, not so much, not even with a phony I.D. But I'd never figure someone like you would want to be in this place. I mean -- **you, *here?"***

"A girl can get thirsty."

"Yeah, but, I mean -- *You're Adele Somers! You're on the fucking Honor Roll!*"

"Only during school hours. That 'A 'student is off duty now. And my parents -- well, since the divorce, my dad doesn't give two shits where I go."

"I guess we have that in common."

"And maybe more," she added.

The two started along the boulevard, although it was more like Adele walked and Rabin followed.

"You sure don't talk like a Washington High senior, 'Del. I mean, tonight you don't look like one, either. Not even close!"

"I'm actually a little older than most kids think. And much smarter. The Honor Roll, that's kid stuff."

Front Street appeared vacant, a side artery that saw no traffic at this hour. The girl made the turn, and the two walked in silence. Adele Somers could be damned intimidating, but she was also one major piece of ass. That ass looked fine in the pale light.

"Do you think of me as a kid, Adele? I'm not, you know. I've been around."

"I'm sure you have, Craig. I've watched you in class. You really put that phony Lady Lydia in her place today. I detest phonies too."

"Especially wannabe phony vampires," Rabin added. He paused, looked at Adele. "Are you really older than everyone thinks?"

"Oh, yes, Craig, much older. Want proof?" She smiled beneath a dim street lamp. Pushing him against a beat up Chevy, she wrapped her arms around him and pulled him close. The boy's wide grin spread. This was more than Craig Rabin could have ever asked for. His erection nearly shot through his pants.

"Right here?" he asked. "I mean you want to do it right --?"

"I'm old enough, Craig. Are you?"

"Fuck yes!"

Smiling, the girl showed teeth. "That's good. Me, I'm pushing three hundred!"

Grabbing Rabin by the throat, Adele Somers sank her fangs deep into his neck.

All the Way
Eamonn Murphy

A girl screamed.

'What the…?' Sean stopped rummaging through the ruined chest of drawers looking for jewelry and jumped to his feet. I had been examining an old clock on the mantelpiece that had long stopped but might be fixed and might be valuable.

'Come on, Will!' Sean ran.

I replaced the clock and went after him. The only girl downstairs was Karen, my sister, and a chap had a duty of care for his little sister, even if she was sixteen going on thirty. Sean may have been in love because he sprinted across the landing and bounded recklessly down the stairs, which bounced under his heavy tread. Sean was six foot four and built like the proverbial outhouse. He was in the second row of the local amateur rugby team.

I followed more cautiously, using my torch to scan the floor ahead of me. It was Saturday 17 October, a dark night, a new moon only the day before. The house was an impressive ruin: a massive solid block of red brick with doors and windows framed in bath stone and a neoclassical portico at the front door. A mansion in its heyday - but still a ruin with missing floorboards, loose bannisters and several other traps for the unwary. I would be no use to Karen if I broke my neck, and no use to Niamh O'Kelly, either.

For a moment, I regretted coming here. When I had my brainwave for a Halloween party venue, it seemed perfect. The Barker place was a local legend. Old rumour, the kind that no one can substantiate but everybody knows, had it that the Barker family were involved in witchcraft, or seances, or devil worship, or something. The Barker place was our town's 'haunted house', sitting on this lonely hill for as long as anyone could remember. It was derelict, the grounds overgrown with weeds and saplings that would soon grow to blend in with the surrounding woods. With property values so crazy, it was a wonder no one had grabbed the land and built an estate of detached houses. No one had, but British land laws were full of anomalies, and there were plenty of old buildings lying idle in both urban and rural settings. I guess no one could.

As I made my way down the stairs, Sean called out. 'Will! Come quick!'

I jumped the last few steps and landed on the bare floorboards with a hollow thump. Like many old houses, this one had a cellar below. We hadn't got around to exploring it yet, and it looked like we wouldn't now. I dashed into the front room. The windows were all shuttered. The light of our torches revealed a large lounge, what the estate agents call a surprisingly spacious reception room. It was mostly empty of furniture except two large armchairs leaking their stuffing and a tatty old chaise lounge of the type you see on those old Agatha Christie dramas repeated endlessly on ITV3.

Sean was clutching the arm of a slender girl with blonde hair, finely drawn cheekbones, large blue eyes and all the equipment needed to be a star of stage or screen. My sister, Karen. The arm was bleeding heavily.

'What did you do?'

She nodded at some broken glass on the floor. 'I picked up that dirty old whisky bottle and dropped it. When I went to catch it… Oh, just help, Will!'

I scanned the room, but everything was old and dirty. The cleanest cloth available was on me. I shrugged out of my fleece and felt cold immediately in the chill October air, but that was a small matter. I ripped the sleeve off my shirt.

Sean stared. 'What?'

'Put that over the wound,' I said. 'Press tight. And raise her arm to slow the flow of blood.'

While he did that, I ripped my other sleeve off and twisted it into a makeshift rope. 'A tourniquet,' I said in answer to his raised eyebrow. Just then, Lenny wandered in. Dressed all in blue denim with shoulder-length, lank dark hair, he looked like a sixties dropout, as usual. Lenny had been out in the overgrown garden, looking for marijuana perhaps.

'What's happening?'

'Karen's cut herself,' explained Sean while I tightened the tourniquet around her bicep. Blood had dripped from her arm onto the bare floor and I saw it slip between the boards, headed for the cellar, no doubt. Well, the house was a complete mess anyway. A few bloodstains wouldn't make much difference.

'We need to get her to A and E,' I said.

'Yeah, right.' Lenny didn't seem all that interested. He wandered over to the chaise lounge and examined it.

Lenny was always broke and may have been looking for something he could sell.

'Come on.' I took Karen's unwounded arm and hustled her out towards the front door, Sean following. My old Ford Escort was parked on the weed-covered gravel out the front. The nearest Accident and Emergency Department was in Bristol, maybe ten miles away.

The front door was closed. As I approached, it creaked open. A tall, lean figure was just about visible. My torch had been pointing at the floor, looking for hazards. Now I raised it level. The man in the doorway put an arm up to cover his eyes.

'Who the Hell are you?' said Sean.

He dropped his arm. I saw a man in his thirties, maybe forties, with a long, pale face, sort of washed-out looking as if he was ill. He had a narrow nose and a wide mouth. He was still blinking from being torch blinded which gave him an air of confusion. I didn't really notice his clothes until later, but he was smartly dressed in a suit and tie of old-fashioned cut, all buttoned up and formal. He looked like a young fogey on his way to the Conservative club.

'I'm terribly sorry to bother you,' he stammered apologetically, 'but I'm a bit confused.'

He sounded it. Then he noticed Karen and his eyes widened. His whole expression changed, took on an eager look, almost hungry.

Well, my sister is a good-looking girl. I had seen that look before. I noticed there was blood on his lip and pointed at it.

'What happened?'

He wiped his mouth. 'I was asleep in the basement. I woke to something dripping on me.'

'Blood,' said Karen. 'Mine.' She had calmed down

considerably since her initial panic.

'You were asleep in the basement?' I said. He didn't look like a tramp though his clothes were old and somewhat dusty.

'Get out of the way!' shouted Sean. 'We have to get this girl to the hospital!'

Sean was right. Whoever this oddball might be, we had more important things to do than chat. I waved my torch at him to move aside.

'Sorry.' The newcomer stepped aside and we rushed down the broad stone steps to the car.

I helped my sister into the back seat and Sean sat beside her. I jumped in and started the engine. 'Lenny!'

'Leave him,' said Sean. 'He can walk back.'

I didn't like it, but he was right. If Lenny was still mooching about doing *Bargain Hunt* when my sister needed a doctor...well, that was his lookout. I gunned the accelerator and sped off down the long drive. Just before I got to the bend that would take the house out of view, I saw Lenny running out the front door. Too late.

'We left Lenny behind,' said Karen. She always had a soft spot for the little man, as did I. For many years, he was my best mate.

'Fuck him,' said Sean. 'We'll see him soon enough. Too soon.'

As it turned out, Sean was wrong. We never saw Lenny again.

***

The Accident and Emergency Department wasn't busy (one of the benefits of Covid-19). Karen was seen almost at once. Her arm needed stitches. The nurse asked a few questions about how it happened, mostly to rule out domestic abuse I suspect, and let us go. I dropped Sean home. Karen gave him a warm kiss goodnight. No tongues because I was there. I didn't like him, but brothers don't get a veto over their sister's boyfriends, and I knew he wasn't going to get what he wanted. Karen had told me more than once that she never went 'all the way' with any boy. She was saving herself for Mister Right.

I had already phoned ahead to tell our parents about the accident, so mum came rushing to the front door to greet us with dad following close behind. I prepared to get it in the neck. Clearly, as the big brother, the responsible one, I was to blame. Well, it had been stupid messing about in the old Barker place, but my scheme was a good one. Nightclubs were still closed; pubs might close again at any time. Even when they were open, it took ages to get served. In this time of national emergency, it was the duty of irresponsible young people to organise illegal parties and what better place to have one on Halloween than in a so-called haunted house.

Halloween fell perfectly party-wise this year of our lord 2020 on Saturday 31 October, two weeks away, and I planned to go ahead. It would surely impress Goody Two-Shoes, and there was still plenty of time.

That Wednesday, we were having a quiet night in. Karen was catching up on her schoolwork while I read about old clocks. I loved old clocks and was fascinated by horology generally: the phases of the moon, eclipses, all the ways that we and the cosmos marked the passing of time. Grandad had been a watch repairer and amateur astronomer, and I learned it all from him when I was a kid. When his time ran out two years ago, I kept the tradition going.

Mum and dad had gone down the pub for a pint and

a chat to the locals about the appalling state the country was in, how bad the youth of today were (no respect) and how in their day you could have a good night out and still have change from a tenner. I guess I will be doing the same in thirty years.

The doorbell rang and when I opened it there stood the fogey from the Barker house. You could have knocked me down with a bow tie.

I blinked in surprise. He was dressed in the same clothes - white shirt, brown tweed suit, bow tie - but looked as if he had dusted himself down. Also, he looked sharp, alert, wide awake. The first time we met, he had been dishevelled and confused. Now he was composed and confident.

'Will Jenkins?'

I nodded, for I was me. 'How did you…?'

'Your friend Lenny told me where to find you, Mister Jenkins.'

'Right.' I didn't know what else to say to a complete stranger who came to the house unannounced. I suppose the British thing to do was invite him in for a cup of tea, but it wasn't very British of him to just turn up. While I pondered how to get rid of him without being rude, he spoke again.

'I came to enquire about the young lady who was hurt. Is she all right?'

Just then, probably glad of any excuse to interrupt her maths homework, Karen came to the door. She stared at the middle-aged man and pointed, undermining all my attempts at politeness. 'Oh! You're the bloke from the Barker place.'

'Yes, ma'am.' He bowed to her. 'Henry Barker, at your service.'

Karen smiled, charmed perhaps by the olde worlde courtesy or maybe just by attention from an older man.

Infamously, young girls like that. Older men have better cars than the callow youths usually fawning over them; and money, too. Modern kids often grunted their greetings, so this formal flattery was a new experience. Karen seemed to like it.

She opened the door wide. 'Come in. Come in.'

Henry Barker hesitated. 'I only came around to make sure you were well. I wouldn't want to intrude.'

I didn't believe him. She did.

'You're not intruding. We're only doing homework. Come in.'

I wanted to object but had no grounds. It was Karen's home as much as mine. I moved back out of the way. Henry Barker stepped over the threshold and smiled a smile that didn't reach his eyes. They were cold. He looked at me, and there was something triumphant about it as if he had just won something.

He needed the invitation, of course, but we didn't know that then.

'I'll put the kettle on.' Karen bustled away to the kitchen, leaving me to make conversation with my unwanted guest. Fortunately, his name gave me an ice-breaker.

'Henry Barker? Does that mean you're related to the family who owned the old house on the hill?'

'Own,' he corrected absently. As if to demonstrate his complete lack of interest in me, he had pulled out an antique pocket watch from his waistcoat and began to fiddle with it. 'My family owns the Barker place, young man.' The way he said 'young man' was contemptuous, and again I caught that coldness about him. 'In fact, I own it. It has never been sold.'

'Oh.' Well, that explained why it had never been developed. I wasn't sure what to say next. He seemed distracted by his watch. To be honest, he made me nervous. After a few moments wondering what to do with a man who came into your house and wouldn't talk to you, I picked up *The Price Guide to Collectable Clocks 1840 - 1940* by Alan and Rita Shenton. My examination of the mantle clock at the Barker place had been interrupted. Still, it looked familiar, so I was checking the book for it. Of course, nearly all information is available online now, but I still like a real book. Henry and I sat there and politely ignored each other.

Karen re-entered with a tray bearing a teapot, a milk jug, a sugar bowl and some beautiful teacups. With saucers! We usually drank from mugs. She was out to impress.

I told her that Henry owned the old house.

'You own it?' she said, understandably surprised. 'But it's been deserted for decades. Maybe a century. Nobody knew who owned it. We just assumed...' She finished the sentence with a shrug.

'It's been neglected.' He frowned at the pocket watch and held it out to me. 'Set this on the right time for me, Will.' No 'please'. No 'thank you'. Just an order, as if I was his lackey. When I took it, he turned to face Karen and accepted his tea. 'It's been neglected,' he said again.

'You weren't living in the basement, were you?' It seemed unlikely, but I thought I should ask.

He shook his head. 'I have been...away. On Saturday, I came to look over the ancestral home with a view to starting the renovation. I was in the basement when fatigue got the better of me, and I took a nap on a settee down there.'

'It really is your house.' I didn't quite believe it. 'You're not very old.'

'Obviously, I have never lived there. As you say, it's been derelict for a century. My family moved away. Now

I am back to claim my inheritance.'

'Oh.' Karen frowned and looked at me. 'I guess that scuppers our party plans, dear brother.'

'Party plans?'

Reluctantly, I explained to Henry that we had intended to host a noisy Halloween party for a lot of rowdy teenagers in his ancestral home. 'Obviously out of the question now. We thought it didn't belong to anyone.' I shrugged away my disappointment and focused on his watch. It just needed a little winding and the time adjusted. I glanced at the clock on the wall and set the watch to nine thirty-five. 'Done.' I handed it back.

He looked at the timepiece thoughtfully. Then his lips curved in a salesman's fake smile. 'A party, you say? Why, you must go ahead with it.'

I saw Karen's eyebrows go up and I suppose mine did too. 'Really?'

He threw back his head and laughed. Not a full-bodied roar with mouth open - he was too refined for that - but real amusement nonetheless. 'Why not? The place is a wreck anyway. A few teenage hi-jinks aren't going to cause any real damage, and the place is being tidied up and renovated after, so what harm. Now is the right time for a party. I will be your host.'

'Well, that's brilliant!' I was delighted. 'It won't even be illegal if the owner is hosting it. An Englishman's home is his castle.'

'Indeed.' Henry rose to his feet. 'I have things to do and must leave you, alas.' He made another slight bow to Karen. 'I'm glad you are well, miss.'

She jumped up. 'I'll see you out.' One would never guess, watching her, that she already had a boyfriend.

I stood up politely. 'Better get back to my homework.'

'We shall meet again.' Henry had no interest in me

and followed Karen to the door without a backward glance.

I picked up my antique guide and resumed looking for the mantle clock. Not that I could take it now - I'm not a thief - but just out of curiosity. Henry Barker, I decided, went well with the house. There was something antique about him, and a hint of menace too. I shrugged it off. Quickly engrossed with my beloved horology, it was a while before I noticed that the goodbyes seemed to be taking a long time. When Karen finally came back in, she looked dazed and a little confused.

'All done? Said farewell to Little Lord Fauntleroy?'

She grunted and sat down on the chair opposite. I resumed reading and thought no more of it.

***

Next day was Thursday. Karen said she felt a bit poorly and stayed home. I went to school, where I continued with my mission to corrupt Goody Two-Shoes.

That wasn't her real name, of course. She was Niamh O'Kelly (obviously of Irish descent), and Goody was her nickname because Niamh didn't sin. Chipping Oldbury Academy was an average small-town English school in the twenty-first century with the usual teenage temptations: fags behind the bike shed, a little hash and maybe something stronger for the bad boys on Friday nights too. Booze was known. Sixth formers went to the local pub, and no one cared. Sex? Well, it happened, and most of the girls were not one hundred percent pure. I knew my sister still hadn't gone 'all the way', but there were rumours she had done other things with her favourites.

Goody - Niamh O'Kelly - hadn't done anything with

anybody. She had been on dates with some nice boys, but hands that slid up her slender thighs were quickly slapped. She was a charming, pleasant girl, even funny at times. Her blue eyes and long dark curls were set atop the figure of a film star, and I don't mean Lassie. But she had Victorian morals, and no sex was allowed. It was the Catholic upbringing, of course. She went to Mass every Sunday with the old man from County Cork and the rest of the family - five brothers! She even wore a crucifix for Christ's sake. Literally.

She seemed to like boys, but the lads with roving hands were promptly excluded, which left room for more subtle players. Me. I shared a few classes with her and had managed to make her acquaintance. We went on a couple of dates during which I was a perfect gentleman. The last one had been the previous Saturday, and when I dropped her home, I had the feeling that she wanted a goodnight kiss, but I didn't try. I would make a move in my own time. The other thing was, to be honest, I liked her and didn't want to fuck it up. What started as a game, a bet with the lads, was turning into something more serious.

If the Halloween party went well, she might let her hair down a bit. I lingered after the History lesson and caught up with her on the way to lunch.

'Off to the canteen?'

'No, I'm going to get my rifle and kill something fresh.' She smiled to take the sting away. 'Yes, Will, I'm off to the canteen.'

'Mind if I join you?'

'Not at all.'

I fell in step beside her as we ambled past the rows of lockers. A couple of lads were watching me. Ron Difford smiled ruefully and shook his head. He had besieged the citadel of Niamh's virtue and been repelled.

'What are you doing for Halloween?'

She bit her lip. 'Probably nothing. It's not my sort of thing, all those ghouls and ghosts and the real meaning is darker than...Ah, but you wouldn't care about that. Anyway, it's all a bit American, isn't it?'

'Better than Guy Fawkes Night,' I said, 'when we celebrate burning Catholics.'

'Not really. All these things are just an excuse for a party.'

'Well, I'm having a party.'

'At your house?'

'No, that would be boring. I'm organising a bit of a do at the old Barker place up on Quarry Hill.'

She shook her head. 'Never heard of it.' She had only lived in town for a few years and didn't know all the local legends and folklore.

'It's an old ruin south of here. I was going to use it anyway, but now I have the owner's permission.' I explained what had happened.

Niamh looked pensive. 'It's weird that the owner should turn up just like that.'

I shrugged. 'Coincidences happen.' I was tempted to say it was all part of God's plan and decided that sort of remark wouldn't go down well.

'They do,' she agreed.

'So, are you coming?'

She wrinkled her nose in distaste.

I stepped in front of her, blocking her path. Careful plotting forgotten, I gave her a piece of my mind. It was a reckless move, but I am not by nature a manipulative little shit, and I really did like her.

'Look here, Niamh, I know you're a good Catholic girl and all that, and I respect you for it and I like you but, you know, this is the world you live in. You have to take part in it. You can't live in an ivory tower like some mediaeval princess waiting for a knight in shining armour to come along. Just because you're not a slut, it doesn't mean you have to be a bloody nun.'

I felt like kicking myself, pretty sure I'd just ruined my chances but, damn it, this wasn't about sex or winning a bet with Josh. She really would be better off adapting to her environment.

For a second, she looked stunned. Then she smiled, leaned forward and kissed me on the lips. Only a peck but it was enough to raise a cheer from the boys and girls at the lockers.

'I'll come to your party, Will.'

She stepped around me and strode off down the corridor, hips swaying like a real live sexy woman.

I put a finger to my lips. 'Well, I'll be damned.'

Little did I know.

***

On Friday morning, Karen skipped school again. The previous day she had surfaced late and stayed up late, which annoyed mum but she didn't say anything. Karen was seldom ill. Dad was heading out the door to work while I munched my cornflakes and called out to me.

'Will! A letter for you.'

A letter? They were as rare as rocking horse shit in the modern era, except for bills and I didn't get any of those yet. It was odd, too, because the postman didn't come until eleven nowadays. I answered pater's summons. He handed me a good quality white envelope with my name written on the front in a beautiful copperplate script. It was the sort of writing you only see on restaurant menus and at the start of old Hammer horror films.

'A letter,' I agreed, opening it clumsily. Inside was a single sheet of watermarked cream paper and in the same classic handwriting these words.

Dear William,
There are a few arrangements still to make for your Halloween party. If it is convenient would you call on me this Saturday 25 October at around 7 pm?
Please bring your sister and her friend Sean as they may have some ideas to contribute.
Yours Sincerely
Henry Barker, Esq.

By the time I read it, dad had hurried off to work. Karen was in the kitchen with mum, so I took it there for consultation.

She read it, yawning sleepily, still in her dressing gown. 'You happy to come along?' I asked.

'Certainly.'

I elbowed her gently. 'Are you happy to bring Sean or is three a crowd with him and Henry Barker?'

'What do you mean?'

'Well, you took a long time saying goodbye to him the other day, and he seems to like you. Maybe it's mutual.' I nudged her again. 'He's got money. Good catch.'

She twisted away from me impatiently. 'Oh, leave off. Of course, I'll bring Sean. Are you bringing Lenny?'

'No.' In fact, I hadn't seen Lenny since last Saturday, which wasn't that unusual. He finished school after doing his GCSEs - obtaining none - while I had gone on to the sixth form. Lenny worked now in a small convenience store. I had meant to pop in and apologise for leaving him stranded at the Barker house but hadn't got around to it yet. In any case, I didn't want to bring him. Lenny had been a good mate, but since he left school, our paths had diverged, and we were growing further apart.

No. I wanted to bring Niamh O'Kelly to reccy the Barker house for the party but would she come?

***

She came.

The sun was down when we pulled up outside. My clapped-out old motor had struggled on the narrow road up the hill and I had to go into second gear, but we made it. The woods were spooky at night, which was all the better for our party. I parked the car on the weed-covered gravel area in front of the house. Sean had ridden in the back with Karen, who seemed in better health for the weekend. Niamh sat up front with me. We exited the car and stared up at the neoclassical portico on the front, northern face of the old mansion.

After a few seconds, Henry Barker approached along the left side of the house to greet us. He must have heard my noisy engine climbing the hill.

'Come in. Come in.' He led us back the way he had come. I had supposed we would go in the front door, but he was in charge. The ground sloped downwards to the rear of the place. Around the back was an overgrown garden and almost concealed by the greenery a small door. Sean looked up and pointed. 'That's the ground floor.'

'I haven't cleaned it up yet,' apologised Barker. 'The cellar is half tidy. We'll have a look at the rest shortly. Come in.' He stood aside to usher us into the cellar.

It was getting darker rapidly. I helped Niamh over a crumbling stone threshold. We stepped down into a dank room with a low ceiling of joists and floorboards. A couple of oil lamps provided dim illumination.

Once we were all in, Barker closed the door behind us. He locked it with a long metal key which he then slipped into his jacket pocket.

I didn't like that.

'No electricity, I'm afraid,' he said, 'nor water either. But I have sherry.' He went to a sideboard against the nearest wall, opened a drop-down door and revealed a few old bottles. There were glasses on the shelves above it and he poured golden liquid into four of them, put them on a tray and brought them over, still smiling. He offered it to Karen first and when she took one, winked, quite obviously. She favoured him with a little smile. When Sean took his glass, he scowled. Barker didn't seem to notice.

Niamh stood very close to me, and I felt her tremble. She watched Barker the way a mouse watches a cat. I think she had noticed him locking the door as well. She slipped her arm through mine and whispered, 'I don't like this place, Will.'

Before I could answer, Henry was in front of me with the tray. 'Drink up, old chap; young lady.'

We both took a glass. Our generation, and a few before, like to pretend we are free spirits who have broken with convention but put us in an awkward social situation and we'll do the polite thing, especially we of the well brought up lower middle class. I don't like sherry, and I like it least of all in a dusty cellar but...well, you can't be *rude*, can you?

Karen and Sean were sipping theirs and looking around at rickety brown furniture that must have been at least a century old. I gave it a quick survey and lost interest at once. We watched a lot of *Bargain Hunt* at home. Mum loved the knick-knacks, I was interested in antique clocks. I knew there was currently no market for brown furniture, and these elegant objects weren't worth a damn.

Niamh nudged me. I focused and saw Barker holding out his watch. 'It looks to have lost a bit again,' he said accusingly. 'Put it right for me, could you? I do like to know the time.' Phrased as a request, it was uttered more like a command. I wanted to tell him to stuff his elegant chronometer up where the sun don't shine. Instead, I took it politely.

'Yeah, sure.' I glanced at my own modern watch. When adjusting Barker's, I remembered what day it was and put the time accordingly, almost without thinking about it. It's a horologist thing.

'Sit, friends. Please.' He waved to a long settee, and we all sat down together, four in a row, squeezed in tight, while he sat on a chair opposite.

'I'm so glad I met you young people,' he said. 'Of course, I have Karen to thank for that.' He nodded at my sister.

'Bit of a rude awakening,' said Niamh. 'Blood.'

Barker chuckled. 'Nothing else would have worked.'

Sean looked confused. 'How do you mean?'

I wondered what he meant too. Why blood? My head was swimming and I felt as if I could go to sleep right there. But it was barely eight o'clock.

'How long were you asleep?' slurred Karen. Her head dropped onto Sean's shoulder.

'Oh, a century or so.'

I laughed, trying to keep my eyes open. 'Rip Van Winkle.' I felt like I might sleep for a century myself.

Niamh fell against me. Her hand clawed at my chest. 'Will! It's drugged. The sherry is drugged. We have to....'

Oblivion claimed her, and me too.

***

When I woke, my head was pounding. I lay belly down on the floor with one arm tucked under me. Awkwardly, I pulled it out. I opened my eyes to semidarkness. There was a candle or something over to my left providing faint illumination. Too much, as it turned out.

Inches from my face was Sean's. His eyes were wide open but not seeing. His mouth was open and his tongue lolled out. His clothing had been pulled away from his neck. His neck was covered in blood.

Sean was dead.

I had never seen a corpse before. Almost vomiting but still too fuzzy to get up, I rolled over on my side. This brought the sofa into view. Niamh and Karen were still on it, collapsed together in an ungainly heap. No blood and they seemed to be breathing. I was gasping, hyperventilating. Fighting nausea, I rolled onto my back.

A few feet away, Henry Barker sat in a chair. He looked like a gentleman at his club, one leg crossed elegantly over the other and a glass of something red in his hand. He favoured me with that cold smile.

'Who are you?'

'I am Henry Barker. That is no lie.'

I stared at Sean's corpse. He hadn't been my favourite bloke in the world, but he was just an ordinary man. He didn't deserve this. I struggled to get to my feet and made it to my knees.

'Bullshit. You...you're a fucking psychopath!'

That had to be it. The man calling himself Barker had escaped from somewhere and hidden out in this derelict house. We stumbled across him, and he decided to kill us. Lured us here by pretending to go along with the party. A cold chill ran through me. I looked left and right for something I could use as a weapon.

He seemed entirely at ease. 'No. I really am Henry Barker. I've been resting in this cellar for a hundred years; too weak to move but too immortal to die. Your virgin sister's blood revived me just enough. Your friend Lenny restored me to full vigour.'

I wondered briefly how he knew Karen was a virgin. 'Lenny? Where's Lenny?' My oldest friend and I had forgotten all about him. I felt even sicker.

'Well, he's dead. An unfortunate side effect of my hunger.'

Hunger? I looked at Sean again and realised that his throat was bitten, not cut. Oh, Christ. He wasn't just a psychopath. He was a psychopath who thought he was a vampire.

I was beginning to feel better. I looked at Niamh and Karen on the sofa then back at the murderer. 'Why aren't we all dead?'

He laughed. 'I like fresh meat, dear boy. You three are my larder to keep me going while I get established here. You can be both slaves and food supply. I don't need to kill you to feed unless I'm starving.'

I wondered how crazy he was. If so-called Henry Barker believed he was a vampire, it might give us a chance. 'You have to sleep in the day.' I looked at my watch. Whatever he put in the sherry had knocked us out for most of the night. 'Not long now.'

Barker chuckled. 'Dawn is at 7 am. As I told you, I do keep track of time. And I don't need to sleep all day, as long as I'm not in sunlight, I'm safe. And once I take a small piece of you, Will, you will lose your own will, Will. You will be my slave.' He laughed at his own wordplay and stood up.

I jumped to his feet. The room seemed to spin around. Damn drug!

Barker took a step closer. 'It won't hurt. Much.'

I stared at him, then over his shoulder. 'Behind you.'

He shook his head to let me know that old trick wouldn't work.

Niamh clouted him with a vase.

Barker staggered, not severely hurt. He grabbed my coat lapels and snarled as he lowered his head towards my neck. The crazy bastard really did think he was a vampire!

I reached into his pocket and took out the door key. With it clenched in my fist, I gave him a solid left-hand uppercut. I'm no brawler but desperation lent it force. His head snapped back. He just grinned.

Niamh had something in her hand. She stabbed it into his neck.

He screamed and backed away, clutching at whatever it was. With a cry of rage, he yanked it out and flung it across the room. It chanced to land near the candle, and I saw what it was.

Her crucifix!

'Papist bitch! You will die for that!'

He was gasping for breath, trying to recover. It had hurt him. He raised his right hand to wipe his brow, palm facing me.

There was a crucifix shaped burn mark on his hand. Mind over matter? Or....?

But that was impossible. Wasn't it?

Maybe his belief in his own vampirism was that strong. In any case, it gave us a few seconds.

'Niam! The door!' I threw her the key. She caught it cleanly, thank God and turned to put it in the lock, scrabbling desperately. I grabbed Karen from the sofa and picked her up in my arms.

Barker staggered toward me.

Niamh flung the door open and ran outside. Ignoring

me, Barker ran after her. He was infuriated by the crucifix attack. I put Karen down on the ground so I could run after them.

I looked at the sky. Dawn at seven, he had said.

Mind over matter?

I closed the cellar door, locked it and put the key in my pocket. Then I chased Niamh and Barker as if her life depended on it because it did.

He had caught her. She was on her back with him on top of her. She was fighting like a wildcat.

I launched myself in a rugby tackle and knocked him off. As we tumbled over in the gravel, I wrapped my arms around him like Stan Laurel in that old black and white film where he fights the bloke with a horseshoe in his glove. It wasn't a brave tactic but it kind of worked. If nothing else, it confused him.

He was too strong for me. Wriggling free, he pinned my arms to my side. I was as helpless as a child. He picked me off the ground and glared at me. I stared into his cold, mad eyes and prepared to meet my maker. There was one chance.

'Now you die, mortal.'

I shook my head. 'Look east.'

'What?'

Something in my voice, something in his own senses must have alerted him that I wasn't joking. He hesitated.

'Look east,' I repeated. 'Dawn.'

He dropped me and turned in the direction of the sunrise. A red glow was forming on the distant hills.

'No! No! It's impossible.' Barker pulled out his watch and stared at the dial. 'It's only six. Dawn isn't until seven.'

Standing up, I told him the facts of life and horology. 'I did you a favour last night. I put your watch back an hour, ready for today.'

'What are you talking about?' He stared towards the east dumbfounded. It was as if nature herself had betrayed him. 'Sunrise does not change!'

'Clocks do. Daylight saving time. It was introduced this century. The clocks go back an hour to give the farmers extra daylight in winter. Seven o'clock yesterday is six o'clock today.' Surely even a lunatic knew this? It happened every year. I was counting on him having forgotten and on his belief in his vampirism.

He stared at me, eyes wide and frightened. 'Madness!'

He stared eastward again and realised he was exposed. Like a terrified child, almost falling over his feet in his haste, he ran back to the house.

I had locked the cellar door. Barker pulled desperately at the handle.

'No! No!'

Mad. Completely mad. Niamh was staring at him wide-eyed. I grabbed her arm. 'Get in the car. I'll get Karen. We have to get out of here before he realises the sun can't hurt him.'

She pointed. 'Look!'

The sun was higher in the sky now. A beam of light fell on him. He sank to the ground to avoid it, cowering, trying to protect himself with his arms. 'No!'

Karen was finally awake. She cast a frightened glance at Barker and staggered over to stand beside Niamh and me. 'What's happening?'

'He thinks he's a vampire,' I said. 'Come on, let's get out of here.'

Niamh wouldn't budge. She stood there, watching Barker. He could cower no lower, and the sun fell full on him now.

He screamed.

Then he exploded.

It was like a firework. A big one. I took three steps backwards. Karen screamed. Niamh gasped. There was a flash, a bang and then...nothing.

I walked to the cellar door, the girls behind me. A few burnt tweedy rags were all that remained of Henry Barker.

Niamh said it.

'He was a vampire.'

That was impossible. 'No. No, he couldn't. There's no such thing. It was...psychosomatic. That's why the crucifix hurt him because he really…'

'You can't psychosomatically explode, Will.'

'Damn. I killed him. But... the trick with the daylight was just to make him believe it. When I set his watch last night, I *did* think I was doing him a favour.' I remembered something else. Karen had been unconscious when I carried her out of the cellar. 'Niamh. Wait in the car, please.'

She wandered around to the front of the house, out of sight.

I told Karen about Sean.

'He's dead, Karen.' I put my arms around her.

I held my sister, eyes closed, and I wondered what we were going to tell the police. As far as they knew, Henry Barker didn't exist. The only proof I had was some burnt tweed. Sean was dead, and they might think we killed him. How could I prove the existence of a vampire who no longer existed?

I opened my eyes. My sister's neck was right in front of me.

There were two holes in it.

I pulled back and stared at her. 'But Barker drugged you, same as he drugged the rest of us. You can't…'

She opened her mouth to reveal pointed fangs and

smiled.

'He had to drug me too. I was still undercover. Fooled you, didn't we?'

I pulled away, but she kept her arms wrapped around me. I remembered the long goodbye at the front door on Wednesday, three nights earlier. Three nights! I struggled, but she held me tight.

'The daylight doesn't affect you!'

'Oh, it stings. Fortunately, I'm only a bit of a vampire for now.' she sighed. 'As I often told you, Will, I never go all the way.'

Of course, I thought. It's Karen. She never goes all the way.

'But I'm still hungry.'

She lowered her head to my neck.

Almost-dry January
Judith Newlin

"It was a bad break-up," Laney said as the drinks arrived. "It's why Christopher messed up on the contracts."

"That's no excuse," I said, playing with the glass. She didn't know that I was the one who had broken up with Christopher. He was loud and opinionated and a bad boyfriend, and now he was just another bad coworker.

"Can you imagine if a woman pulled that?" She asked.

We sighed, and I took a sip of my drink. It was a Diet Coke; it was dry January and I had committed. "Remind me to drink more water."

"Why are you doing this to yourself?"

I rolled my eyes. "It's my New Year's resolution." Mid-December, I had gathered up ten wine bottles from around the apartment for recycling; when I ran into a neighbor in the stairwell I had to pretend that I had a party.

"Going well?" She gestured at the glass.

"Well, if Christopher keeps this up, dry January is

going to end real quick."

"Seriously." Laney took a sip, then frowned at her rancid glass. "You're not missing much."

"Speaking of resolutions," I deflected, "how's your yoga thing going?"

Laney started talking about crow pose and balances and I looked up at the clock above the bar. There was a lot of night left to endure. Happy hour with a colleague at the closest bar to the office was better than being alone at home, hiding my phone under pillows to keep me from calling Christopher.

The Cart and Horse was a true dive - heavy chipped wood stained from a thousand sticky beer spills, stinking of mothballs, run by a gruff pale man who we all believed lived in the basement during the daylight hours. As I turned back to the table, my eye caught the gaze of someone at the bar, leaning one arm against the rail, holding a glass of scotch, neat. Tall, dressed in all black, a swimmer's body with arms so wide they could engulf you, drown you with them.

"Anyway," Laney was saying, "I'm gonna try to take that new class tomorrow."

I hadn't thought about tomorrow. I realized I had a whole weekend to try to avoid calling my ex.

If I was hungover tomorrow, I wouldn't be in the mood to call Christopher.

I caught the eye of the man at the bar again. He was as hot as sin; he would make a great distraction. Laney was poking around in her purse, jumping when he slid into the booth next to me. "Hello there."

It was unfair how his voice was like silk, how it made my ears tingle and buzz. I tried to look sweet but was painfully aware of my dry lips stuck on my teeth. "Hi there."

"I'm Desmond."

"That's a fancy name." He stood out from the finance types in the bar; nothing about him said casual Friday. His eyes were so dark they were black; I was mesmerized.

He turned, a thin smile across the table at Laney. "I promise, I'm not too fancy."

I felt my heartbeat stutter at the thought he might flirt with Laney. He was my distraction.

As if sensing my discomfort, he turned back, his hand on my arm. "What are you ladies drinking?"

"Chardonnay," I managed to say.

Laney gave me a look as he moved over to the bar to get two more glasses. "What are you doing?"

"I changed my mind."

Laney mimed waving a fan. "Well, he's hot."

When he returned to the table, he slid his arm around behind me as he handed me my glass. "Is it any good?"

I took a sip, my first in two weeks. It could have tasted like battery acid, I would have relished it like. I took another sip, a gulp. "It's good."

"I could make it better." He said.

Laney's eyes widened. "How?"

Desmond pulled something from the pocket of his leather jacket, a small glass vial no larger than a chapstick. He was a stranger and we had barely exchanged pleasantries. No matter how much I wanted to lick him, this was, objectively, a terrible proposition.

"No," Laney was saying. "No drugs."

"This isn't drugs," he said, and his voice floated through my ear and down my spine, hypnotic. Like a current jolting through me, I felt a new certainty that I wanted to have fun with him.

"What is it then?" She asked.

"A flavor enhancer," he said.

My better sense made a weak effort, half-heartedly

trying to derail this. "Tomorrow is my long run."

Desmond put his hand on my thigh with a little squeeze of reassurance. When I looked up into his eyes, I had the feeling as though I could lose myself in him searching for stars. "You won't feel it tomorrow." He said, "Trust me. Way better than the house chardonnay."

It was a cheap bar; vagrant piss would be better than the house chardonnay. Laney was looking at me; concerned. It had been a long week; a Friday night of drinking and bad decisions was a long tradition of beleaguered assistants.

It would keep me from calling Christopher.

"We could use more fun," I said.

The liquid in the tube was dark, reddish, almost like a cabernet; our new friend poured a teaspoonful into our glasses. "Drink it slowly." he instructed.

"Aren't you going to have some?" I asked.

He leaned in close, the musky scent of him overwhelming. "I already did."

My heart was racing. Before I could open my mouth again, Laney smiled at me, not willing to be left out, following my lead, "L'chaim!"

It was thicker than wine, almost gloopy, and sweet, the sip lingering on my tongue, soaking into the muscle, into my gums. I was reminded of biting the inside of my cheek, bleeding into my mouth. Rusty, but gently sweet like a French macaron. I closed my eyes, wanting to savor it.

The effect was immediate.

I opened my eyes to a dim room lit in neon. Handprints shone in front of me, glow-in-the-dark. My legs were moving, back and forth in some sort of dance, arms aloft. My back teeth shook in their sockets. My shirt — black, tight — pasted to my chest with beer and sweat. I felt a muscular arm slip around my shoulder, a muscular body close.

"Join me," his voice whispered at my ear, crisp amid the pounding noise. My head turned; his gleaming black eyes the only thing I could see. I felt a little bolt of clarity at my temple; he wanted me.

I sank into his fingers at my hip — somebody else's hip, I realized now, far more bony than my own — and I gazed dizzily around the room through somebody else's eyes. I swayed with him, feeling all of this life pulsing around me in the club.

"May I?" he asked, his lips at my neck, each word drizzling like syrup.

I breathed in to respond, feeling as though the air was closing in around me. Now I was in a booth at the bar, looking into my empty glass, a stray drop rolling down the side.

"Wow," Laney was saying.

"Good, right?"

As the hallucination receded, I realized that the post work crowd had begun clearing out. The clock above the bar read 10:05. Usually, we peaced out once the Goldman Sachs types started loosening their ties, to move on to White Claws and gossip in our tiny apartments. Desmond was still next to me, so close I could smell him, the same as the man in my vision.

"It's late!" Laney was saying.

I heard myself tell her. "Don't worry about it. You know what? I'll get the bill, you can Venmo me on Monday."

"You sure?" She asked, but already she was pulling on her coat.

"Text me when you get home." She instructed.

I'd just dosed myself with an unknown drug given to me by a stranger, whose fingers still rested gently on the edge of my hip as they had in the dream of the club, who I was already planning on going home with tonight.

"I'll call you tomorrow," I promised.

***

I found myself on the platform of the W train, the cold air of the night bristled against my skin, and sweat dripping down beneath my bra. I swiped my hand at the sweat on my neck, feeling some grit, a little blood forming a scab. It must be a bug bite. That bar was getting worse. It was one of those slushy winter Fridays, where the snow had piled up on the street corners, and your feet would slip right out from under you. I had worn cute boots, and cautiously stepped my way along the platform, high knees like a baby giraffe.

The approaching train was too loud, the screech of the brakes filling my head like smoke. I wrapped my coat tighter around me, too focused on the gap between car and the platform, my senses now wildly alert, too keen for midnight. I felt giddy, like I could dance till sunrise; I may have lost a sense of time, but the drug had replaced it with all the others. Each color, each sound seemed so precisely in front of me, like I could grab it. I stared like a creep at the thousands of shining colored threads of my neighbor's scarf. My lips were still dry: I had forgotten to drink any water.

***

On Monday, Laney and I crossed paths in the pantry as I refilled my coffee. Her boss was there, head in the fridge searching for leftover snacks, so we exchanged inane comments about the state of the kitchen, how no one washed their mugs. I was grateful she didn't ask about the gorgeous guy from Friday night; it was embarrassing to admit that I must have drunk too much; I had blacked out until I got to the train.

The day was so busy fixing Christopher's screw-up with the files for production that I was on the train home before I had time to scroll through the headlines on my phone:

D.A. Files Charges Against Mobster
Rare Fish Spotted in Hudson
Nightclub Disappearance Raises Questions

The sense of a half-memory pricked at me, and my scabbed neck began to itch as I clicked through on the last headline, ready to indulge in some healthy fear of spiked drinks and strangers in crowded rooms.

Her name had been Julie Emerson, and she had last been seen dancing at Eclipse in the Meatpacking District. There was a photo of the club: a dark room, neon lighting—it looked familiar. Julie Emerson had been with her girlfriends when she came in, but her body had been found a mile away by the river, completely exsanguinated. As we rumbled through midtown, I imagined a wash of oily red in a halo around her as she lay beatific against the rocks. I shuddered as I put my phone away — what a disgusting mental image.

I should be more careful, drink a little less. I had given up on dry January, and was enjoying a celebratory glass of wine every night with dinner. Just one, I bargained with myself. One was fine.

It was rainy now, a biting rain that was neither hail nor snow, each sting loaded with misery. I ducked into a pizza shop, letting the heat soak into my hands. My vision focused on the guy behind the counter, the quickness with which he cut the pizza, sliding the tray down to a customer, speedy like a machine. The buzz of the restaurant filled my head; there was so much life pulsing through the room while Julie Emerson was dead.

My lips were dry again, and I recalled the picture of the club. So much like the one I kept seeing in my dreams. I felt a tingle at my hip, where his hand had been. What was his name again? It struck me then that I couldn't remember his face, just the feeling of his lips at my neck.

I stepped back out into the rain, worrying my own dry lips between my teeth. I needed to drink more water.

***

When Friday came and Christopher hadn't cleaned up his act, I confessed to Laney that I was the source of the break-up. She alternated between rage at him and worry for me. I was refilling my thirty-two ounce Nalgene for the third time that day; it seemed like I was endlessly parched these days.

"Happy hour tonight. You in?"

I tried not to grimace. I had been meaning to talk to her about the previous week, about drinking less, but the work week had been mayhem. Precisely the reason we kept going to Friday night happy hour; we needed a break. I promised myself I would leave when she left; no strangers with mystery substances this time.

Except as we took up our spot in our usual booth, I found myself looking up at the clock, hoping to see him again, leaning against the bar.

"You in a rush?" She asked, after I looked for a third time.

"No," I shook my head, coming back to the conversation. "Sorry."

"You're just disappointed," Laney laughed. "About the hot guy. Desmond, right? You never told me how that went."

I shrugged.

"Not good?" She asked.

I shook my head. "I think I drank too much. I don't know how you got home. I don't remember anything till I got on the subway."

Laney moved around to sit on the bench next to me, putting her arm around my shoulder. "Oh, honey."

I shook my head. "I was fine. I was fully dressed. Just tired. Don't worry."

Laney gave me a squeeze. "I'm glad you were safe."

"Better to avoid that stuff in the future?" I suggested.

Laney sighed, "It was so good."

"And he was such a good kisser," I said, feeling dazed, at the edge of a memory. "Really focused on my neck."

And sitting in that same seat, looking down at the awful house wine, I had a flashback to the nightclub, the man's lips at my neck, "*May I?*"

"Shame," I murmured, stealing another glance at the clock.

He was leaning casually against the bar, his eyes fixed on our conversation. I felt the sweat on the back of my neck, the cold of the night air passing over it, though it was pleasingly warm and dry in the bar. I scratched at the itchy spot from my bug bite.

"Hey there," he said, sliding in across from us.

"Hey there," I said, this time taking a cautious sip of water, trying to memorize his face. I would remember it. His smile, wide but tight, showing no teeth. His hair, dark, falling about his eyes.

His eyes, black like the night sky, with galaxies in them.

***

I was walking through the classical statues at the Met, meandering between the pedestals, feeling a chill from the marble, from the long cold fingers he had wrapped around mine. He pulled me to a bench in the corner, held me close under his arm, to observe. There weren't many visitors this late. We sat in the chill, his right hand kneading my shoulder as I leaned into him, whispering made-up details about each ancient Greek into my ear. I heard myself laugh, too bright, an airy giggle unlike my own. His voice was like ice cream on the tongue, rich as he laughed, "this one is just a head. He must have lost his mind."

He kissed me, down, down to my shoulder, back up to my neck, sweet like drips of honey.

"*May I?*"

***

I found myself on the subway home, everything too bright against the dark tunnel. I had a cheap plastic water bottle in one hand; my phone in the other. It was late, and I had no idea how I had gotten to the train.

My stop was too loud; the world spun faster with each step. I paused against a wall to orient myself. I hadn't been at the Met, had I? I had been in a bar with Laney. I had been looking up at the clock and there had been black eyes.

I must have taken his drug again. His — what was his name? — it was too bright out here. I wished for the quiet dark of his eyes.

The Met was another trip; those sugary kisses weren't for me. It had felt so real, like I was living someone else's life. I shivered again, the sweat on my neck crystalizing in the frigid air, like a fever.

I picked up a gyro from a cart on the way home, but the slick fat felt too heavy on my tongue. I dropped it in a trash can down the block, unable to stomach it.

***

"I need to drink more water," I said at lunch the following Wednesday with my desk-neighbor Ashley. "My lips are always dry."

"Wasn't that your New Year's resolution?" Ashley asked.

"I was doing dry January," I explained. "*Was.* Clearly, it's going great."

I kept talking about my efforts at drinking more water, but Ashley became distracted, looking anywhere but her salad. Eventually, she blurted out, "Have you seen Laney?"

"I heard she was out sick." I shrugged.

"No one's heard from her since Friday," Ashley said. "You guys went to happy hour, right?"

"Yeah," I nodded. "She seemed fine on Friday. She's probably sick."

"I guess you're right," Ashley said, looking across the cafeteria. "It's just not like her not to call in."

"She's fine," I insisted, but there was a lump forming in my throat. I didn't remember much of Friday at all until I had found myself on the subway. I couldn't remember Laney after I had seen those black eyes.

I needed to drink less.

***

Laney's body washed up on the bank of the East River two days later. When the call came from HR asking me to stop by the office, I dropped my water bottle, drenching my keyboard. I spoke to the police about my memories of the bar, but I couldn't tell them about the man or the drugs. Would they believe I was his accomplice? I told the half-truth, that I didn't remember much, that I must have had too much to drink. The officer taking my statement didn't seem to care what I said; it was looking like a suicide, he told me.

On Friday night all of the assistants went out to the bar, a last happy hour in honor of our fallen coworker. I felt unmoored. Nothing fundamental had changed about the place, but we were returning to the scene of the crime. Not that the police were treating it as a crime scene; video showed Laney leaving the bar alone. There was no sign of the tall man on any of the cameras. Maybe my hallucinations were just getting out of hand.

We drank quietly, a round of cheap wine in honor of our friend, a few murmured reminiscences about the way she welcomed newcomers, the warm arm around your shoulder on a bad day, wild tales of Friday nights in the city turning into Saturday brunches in Brooklyn. When we ordered, I asked for a glass of water, and Christopher chuckled, brightening up the table with a joke that I was always thirsty these days.

I made it through two thirds of a rapidly warming glass before I escaped to the bathroom.

"I just don't get it," I snuffled to myself, grabbing at toilet paper to dab at my eyes and blow my nose. "How did it happen?" I leaned against the wall. "I didn't do anything wrong."

Except I still felt those black eyes settling on my neck.

"She lived a good life." Desmond said from my right. I hadn't heard the door open.

I sniffled again. "She was too young."

He nodded. I stepped over to the sink to wash my

hands and straighten myself up. "I'm fine. I can do this."

"Do you want to take the edge off?"

I startled, jumping around. His voice had been close in my ear, but I hadn't seen him come up behind me in the mirror. "That's probably not a good idea right now."

His dark eyes captured mine, cold now.

"I didn't hurt Laney." I said, even as a certainty pooled in my gut. I felt cold, like my heart had stilled; I needed to get out of the bathroom. "I need to stop drinking. I need water."

"No you don't," he said.

The door opened, and Desmond hid behind it. Ashley stepped in. "Talking to yourself?" She giggled, tipsy.

I put my hand against the sink to steady myself. Ashley pulled me in, a sideways squeeze of reassurance. I buried my head in her neck, my hand gripping at her forearm, holding on tightly. She was so alive, and Laney wasn't. I pushed her hair over her shoulder, away from where it was tickling my nose.

"May I?" I asked.

I remember nothing else, until I woke up with a dreadful thirst.

Be Like You
Jack Nash

For the sixth time in an hour, Louis Lioncoeur, Prince of the Vampires, extended his fangs and pulled the woman with flowing blond curls to him. She moaned as his lips brushed her skin, then leaned sideways to expose the delicate blue veins of her neck. His nostrils filled with the warm scent of her taffeta lace dress, mingled with the spice of her perfume.

"And cut!" A voice rang out. "That's a wrap."

Louis vanished, subsumed back into the body and mind of Mark Bronstein, leading man of *Prince of Blood*. His co-star, Tania, stepped out of his embrace and adjusted the folds of her costume. A phone appeared from her bodice, and she snapped her fingers for the Starbucks coffee held in the wings by a stagehand.

"Nice work," Mark said. "Really liked that last take. Great energy."

Tania glanced up.

"Heard you didn't get the part in the biopic," she said, then shrugged and turned back to scrolling through photos. Mark was grateful his heavy white makeup hid the flush growing on his cheeks.

"Great job, but listen up, everybody." The director, a thin man in a sweater and baseball cap, waved his hands in the array of lights, microphones, and technical equipment that surrounded the stage like a metallic forest. When the hubbub of the actors, makeup artists, and onlookers quieted, he continued.

"I was planning to save this for later, but what the hell. The producers just texted me this morning, we're renewed for a tenth season. Congrats everyone!"

A whoop erupted from the sound booth, staff writers hugged, and the camera operators high-fived everyone around them. At a signal from the director, a woman at the catering table produced buckets of ice, a champagne bottle in each.

Mark's stomach turned to concrete. Another season? Again? He eyed the stage exit. It's red letters beckoned like a lighthouse, offering harbor and safe passage. He managed one step toward it before the director leaped up and pulled him into a lopsided embrace.

"You must be so happy," the director said as he released Mark.

"Happy," Mark repeated. "Of course."

"We wouldn't have made it here without you. Just think, another season as television's most famous vampire." He grinned with porcelain veneers so white they reflected the blue of the special effects screens behind them. Over the catering table, a cork popped to applause. "C'mon, let's celebrate!"

As the director wrapped his arm around Tania's waist and steered her toward the waiting drinks, Mark slunk outside, exchanging the cheers of the crew for the distant and ever-present hum of L.A. traffic. Despite the sun having set an hour ago, the asphalt and concrete of the studio lot still radiated with its warmth. Mark hurried down a side alley to the stars' trailers.

He let his trailer's aluminum door slam shut with a bored clang. In the darkness, he flexed his fists, willing his heart to slow, to relax.

Ten seasons. Ten years. A decade as Louis Lioncoeur. This was supposed to be over by now. He was supposed to be doing something else.

He sucked in a breath and then grimaced at the odor assaulting his nose. Like meat left too long in the back of the refrigerator. Had catering left a lunch for him in here he'd forgotten?

Mark pulled down a window and waved a hand to force an exchange of air. Flipping on the light, he scanned the living area for the stink's source. Nothing. Maybe a trailer nearby had an overfilled toilet.

Breathing through his mouth, Mark flopped down on the couch and stared at the ceiling. The beige and sepia paint job pulled him in, slowing his breath with its monotony and familiarity.

"I am grateful," he muttered, then repeated it with more conviction. "I am grateful."

It was true. Mostly. Another season would mean the continued flow of paychecks, each fattening the already obese sum in his bank account. And what had he been before *Prince of Blood*? Just another actor in a long audition queue. It was a miracle he got the part, really. And the success, the unprecedented popularity of the show had been shocking. At first it had been everything he wanted – Emmy nods, wild parties, "Sexiest Man Alive." What fun it had been, too, with the producers insisting that the actors remain in character and costume whenever they were in public.

He sat up, resting his head in his hands. Now it felt like it was going to last forever. The echo of this morning's conversation with his agent still reverberated in his head.

"Mark, I'm sure you would do great, but they're not looking for the sexy kind of leading man for this film. They need a more nuanced portrayal, with someone who's had more experience. A better track record with Oscar-worthy roles. Maybe next time, right?"

His agent had hung up before Mark could insist that he did have the range, that he did have the ability, if only someone would give him a chance to prove it. He'd done Shakespeare before and had done it well. Didn't that count?

Mark stood, circling the confines of his trailer like a caged dog. Couldn't anyone see past the vampire shtick?

He caught his reflection in the window above the couch. A dribble of corn syrup blood still clung to the corner of his mouth. Under it, makeup was slathered over his forehead and cheeks, each season requiring more to maintain an illusion of immortality. Never mind the never ending injections of Botox around his eyes and forehead. He sighed. Maybe this is all one saw. Mark Bronstein—another cautionary typecasting tale.

"Louis Lioncoeur?" a pale voice asked from the darkness of a doorway.

Mark spun as a girl stepped from the bedroom into the halogen lights of the living area. Bulging black eyes, peeping between limp strands of brown hair, stared at him.

"Shit," Mark said, stumbling backwards. She jumped at his sudden movement, almost dislodging the notebook she clutched to her chest. A promotional photo from the show's first season was taped to its cover, with "Louis Lioncoeur – Vampire Prince" scrawled in sharpie.

Mark's chest relaxed. Just a fan. Early twenties perhaps. Probably looking for an autograph.

"Who let you in here?" he asked. "My manager?" He took in her formless sweater, the too large jeans, the poorly applied makeup. One of her breasts seemed to be larger than the other. He promised himself to speak to security. If they were going to let fans in, at least they could be more…selective. He chided himself for the thought. What had this job done to his humanity? Another reason to get out.

"You're the Prince of the Vampires," she said, her voice hushed as if reciting a prayer. "You're him."

Mark pulled the chair from his kitchen table and sat, rubbing a hand over his forehead.

"News to me," he said.

"Louis Lioncoeur…"

Mark rolled his eyes and leaned back. A fan, and a starstruck one. So often they just stood there repeating his name, but she didn't look like the typical ones who made it to his trailer. They almost always had on some vampire gear. Wigs, makeup, even fake fangs. Something to emulate the show and demonstrate just how devoted they were. But this girl looked like she came straight from a homeless shelter.

Her eyes fixed on him, she took a step closer.

"I want to be like you."

Mark sighed. "Like what? An actor? I don't do lessons, but I can recommend some people downtown. Workshops and stuff."

She shook her head; tendrils of hair swirled before resettling like vines around a tree.

"I want to be a vampire like you." Her eyes widened until they were almost perfect circles. "Be my Master."

"Oh," Mark said. "Like that."

Vampire fetishist. So that's how she talked her way in. There were always fans a little too into role play. Girls who wanted to be bit with his stage fangs—never really to draw blood or anything, just to pretend to be the victim in distress with the real Prince of Blood. Not that he minded. It was fun, or at least had been fun. Mark had never really been into the role play and using his character for sex. And when he did, it was a means to an end. Fans who acted out their fantasies always told the press about sleeping with the vampire. Those tabloid stories would drive more people to watch the show, where they would imagine themselves in his arms, his teeth on their necks.

But that wasn't why he agreed to keep acting in the series year after year. He wanted to do Shakespeare and perform the dramatic, award-winning stuff. Besides, after the third or fourth season, sex in his costume had become trite.

Mark scrutinized her. She stared back with obsidian eyes. She wasn't even his type. He doubted she was anyone's type.

"Sorry, not interested," Mark said. He gestured a thumb at the door. "Stop by catering on your way out. They have champagne."

The girl sat on the edge of the couch, sliding close until she was inches from him. Mark swallowed a gag. So, the smell had been her this whole time. How long had she been in in his trailer? Did she ever bathe?

She extended her arm and pulled back her sleeve, revealing a thin sinewy wrist.

"Bite," she said. "Make me a vampire like you. Beautiful, like you."

Mark placed a finger on her arm and guided it back to her lap. "Look, I'm flattered, but I'm really not interested. This used to be fun and all, but that was a long time ago." He reached into his mouth and popped the stage fangs off his teeth. He managed a half-smile and a shrug at the unexpected sensation of nudity.

The girl recoiled, her hands leaping to her mouth, stifling a gasp.

"What? Don't tell me you believe that story that I had the fangs implanted permanently?" He chuckled. "That was a rumor started by *People,* you know."

Mark stood and went to the dresser where he placed his fangs in their case like dentures. Tugging a tissue from a box, he began to wipe away the makeup from his eyes and nose. He caught the girl's reflection in the mirror. Hands still over her mouth, her breathing rapid.

Mark turned. "You okay?"

She didn't answer or move, save for her eyes which flicked at his semi-makeup-less face.

"Look, I know you may have gotten all excited for some vampire pillow talk or whatever, but I'm beat. It's been a day. If it makes you feel better, find the stage manager, tell him I told you that you can get some signed posters at the studio gift shop, okay?"

The girl said nothing, only stared. Mark swallowed. Maybe he had gotten this wrong. She might not be one of the fans looking for role play…

"Everything alright?" he asked.

The girl opened the book on her lap. "On April twelfth, you went to the Emmy awards under the cover of black tents so you wouldn't be in the sun, and you showed your fangs to the cameras. You didn't drink any of the food and were filmed all night only drinking from bags of blood."

Mark barked a laugh. "Oh, yeah. That was for the show. 'Make it real' and all. Method acting. The blood was wine by the way. Got super drunk."

The girl shuddered as if he had punched her in the gut.

"May tenth, on *The Tonight Show*, you leapt into the audience and bit into a woman's neck to feed. The audience saw her collapse and die before you continued your interview."

Mark glanced at the door. This was getting weird.

"It was a stunt. She was an actress we hired. And she didn't die, she lives in Seattle. I think she has two kids now."

The girl stood, her voice rising in pitch as she read, "Audience members were spattered with blood and swear they saw holes in her neck." A page tore as she turned it, her hand shaking. "You were known to avoid the sun while shooting in Florida and didn't go to the beach with your co-stars." More paper ripped. "People go missing in cities that you visit, because vampires hunt for people and need blood to survive. Animal control has found an unusual number of bats in Ventura, where you keep a home."

A page fluttered to the ground as she read on. Mark snatched it up. Plastered to it was a collection of printed out comments from a Twitter thread, a clipping of a magazine article, even half a page of what looked like a novel, all taped and glued together like a child's collage. Everywhere were handwritten notes scribbled in tiny, indecipherable writing.

Sweat tickled to life on his forehead. She was no fetishist. She was crazy. One of those people who couldn't separate reality from the fiction of the show. Mark inched toward the door.

The girl darted forward, blocking him.

"You can do this," she said. "You can. Make me a beautiful vampire like you."

"Vampires aren't—"

"I can be like you. I already live all the rules. I stay in the dark, I avoid the sun. I'll even sleep in your coffin. I don't mind the killing, because there are people who need to be killed, who deserve it. Just make me beautiful, and strong, like you. I don't want to be like this anymore, but you can show me how. You have the power. You can be my Master."

She put her wrist to his face. Mark recoiled at the odor wafting from under her sweater.

"Security!" He hoped not everyone was busy getting drunk.

The girl reached into her pocket and produced a pocketknife. She flicked it open, its tip dull and tainted with rust. Mark stumbled back against his chair and half fell against the wall.

"Help!" His voice broke as he cried out. Stories of celebrities gunned down and murdered by their most devoted fans flew through his head. Would Mark Bronstein be added to that list of unfortunates?

"I'll even help," she said. The girl turned the knife and jabbed it into her extended wrist. Blood welled up in a ruby pool, running along the blade, then over its handle, and to the floor.

"Drink, Master," she said. Tears cut rivulets down her cheap makeup. She waved her arm at Mark. Thick globs of blood splat against linoleum and stainless-steel appliances. "Please, drink."

"Shit. Shit!" Mark pushed himself up, fumbling for the hand towel draped under the microwave. He grabbed the girl, gagged again, and held the cloth against her wound. Crimson bloomed through the fibers.

"It's deep." Mark retched, keeping down the rising gorge. "You need a hospital," Mark said. He pressed his face against the screen of the open window. "Help! Somebody!"

"Please," she sobbed.

"Mark?" A voice called, followed by a knock on the trailer door. "You okay?"

"Call an ambulance," Mark shouted.

The door opened. A security guard and a boom mic operator, holding champagne flutes stopped and stared, unmoving. Their eyes darted from Mark, to the girl, to the blood drenched cloth, and finally to the pocketknife lying on the floor.

The security guard moved first. He tossed his drink aside, leapt up to grab the girl, and dragged her down the trailer steps. The mic operator dug for her phone, her fingers fumbling with the screen.

"No," the girl said, struggling against the guard. "Master!"

But she was pulled away, her pleas melting into wails, sobs, and screams.

***

The police came. They asked questions, and Mark answered. No, he hadn't seen her before. Did she threaten him? Not exactly. Did she give him her name?

Mark blinked. "Didn't she tell you? When you arrested her?"

To this, a short officer with bags under her eyes, shrugged.

"She slipped out when the security guard went to grab a first aid kit. We're checking hospitals, but…" Another shrug.

Mark handed them the notebook the girl had dropped. The officers rifled through it, raised their eyebrows at some risqué photos of his character glued to the back cover, then thanked him and put it in a Ziploc bag. Then they left Mark to deal with the aftermath.

Studio lawyers argued about who, if anyone, was at fault. Co-stars demanded to know 'What it was like?' and a few journalists with large mugs of coffee tried to get quotes from anyone who was within arm's reach.

In a few hours, interest had waned. In a few weeks, it was forgotten. Mark pushed the memory of the girl, her notebook, and the knife to the back of his mind. An incident to tell at parties, or to be pulled up at some future interview. Nothing more. But even as life resumed its normal pace of cast readings, shootings, and long hours in the makeup chair, he doubted he would ever forget that smell.

Two months later, Mark once again held Tania in his arms, this time at the edge of a swamp somewhere east of Baton Rouge. The director hovered around them, muttering character motivations and scene goals, all while fussing over the placement of the extras in the background. Bored, Mark let his gaze wander. Portable lights fixed to cypress trees attracted a tornado of insects. A smattering of rubberneckers and onlookers watched beyond a cordon at the edge of the mobile studio. Most held up phones, some waved, attempting to get his attention.

The breeze changed, and its odor transported Mark's mind back to his trailer. Meat gone wrong. Mark nearly dropped Tania, ignoring the director's reprimand, and scanned the crowd. A father holding up his daughter, pointing at the cameras and actors. Two teenagers, giggling as Marks' gaze rested on them. An elderly man struggling to keep his dog from sniffing the leg of a passing extra covered in fake blood.

Mark's breath caught in his throat. There she was, half hiding behind the teenagers. She stared at him, her eyes as black and glimmering as the swamp water around them. She raised a hand, pulling down her sleeve to expose her wrist and a twisted purple scar.

Mark yelled for a security guard and pointed to the girl.

"Yeah?" the guard asked, jogging up to him.

"She's—" Mark's finger indicated nothing. The girl was gone.

It happened again three weeks later. Back in L.A., Mark let a makeup artist apply powder to his nose and cheeks. His own skin tone this time, in preparation for an interview promoting the upcoming season of *Prince of Blood*. The interviewer, a striking man with a helmet of auburn hair, smiled and chittered about a recent interview with a well-known producer, now accused of impropriety.

"I mean, during the whole thing he was sweating like a pig. I mean just buckets of it, and I…" his voice trailed off as he sniffed. His smile waned, then inverted on itself into a grimace.

"Do you smell that?" He sniffed again. "Dana, did someone not take the trash out or something?"

Mark's skin prickled. He spun, jerking his head side to side to scan the studio. Posters, computer monitors, technicians behind computers. Nothing, except for a side door easing itself shut under the phosphorous green glow of an Exit sign.

Mark didn't sleep much the next month.

Anytime they shot a scene outside the studio, he could smell her. Faint at first but then growing stronger until he couldn't detect Tania's perfume or the earthy notes of the makeup covering his skin. Security found nothing and no one. How could she get past them? Impossible. But at his insistence they added more guards and changed all the studio locks.

After a long day under the camera, he returned to find his trailer rank with the smell. He burned candles and incense until he set off a fire alarm. At home, it seemed to be in his clothes. He showered, scrubbed, applied lotions and colognes. Still, when he went to bed, the odor was there, vaporous and seeping into his dreams.

He added security cameras until every inch of his house was watched with robotic eyes. It made his home feel like the studio – cameras always watching, he always on edge. But still, nothing. The police came, looked around, and after he described the persistent smell, referred him to a plumber.

Mark bolted awake one night. It was stronger than ever, nauseating and viscous. She couldn't be here. This was all in his head. Mark flung the covers aside and grabbed his phone from the nightstand. In five minutes, he had bought a one-way ticket to New York. He had a condo near the Finger Lakes. No one knew about it. Or almost no one. But not her, surely. He just needed some time to relax, get away.

In three hours, Mark was airborne. He composed a text to the director, fabricating a family emergency and expressing apologies for the abrupt schedule change. He then turned off the phone. The plane landed, he rented a car, and drove, enjoying the way New York City withered into suburbs, and the suburbs into trees.

It was dark when he got to his condo. His mind was clearer, his nose happier, and his body looking forward to a deep, dreamless sleep. He parked, exited the car, and took in a deep breath of clear, forest air.

It was rank. Like a deer had been gutted and left to the sun. He coughed, spun and twisted, probing the darkness for her.

"Leave me alone," he shouted.

She stepped from the shadow of a tree into the silver moonlight. She wore the same sweater and loose jeans. Only her hair was different. Tangled, knotted, and falling over her face in ropes.

"Louis." Her voice was ice in his ears.

"I'm not Louis, dammit. Why won't you leave me

alone?" Mark said, fumbling for his keys. They slipped from his grasp and clattered to the ground. Mark swore and knelt to grope for them.

"Make me like you. I want to be a beautiful vampire like you." She glided to him, knelt and then put her hand on his.

The awfulness wormed into his mouth, down his esophagus and through his sinuses. He could taste her. A wave of vertigo crashed over him.

"Beautiful?" Mark said. "You want to be beautiful?"

She nodded and guided him to his feet. Her midnight eyes glimmered with stars of hope.

"Yes, please." She pulled up her sleeve. The scar sat on her skin like a violet worm.

"You can't be beautiful," Mark said, grabbing her wrist.

Her face flickered as she squirmed in his grasp. He held tight, squeezing.

"I don't know what could make you beautiful. Not me, that's for sure."

She grabbed at his hand. He yanked her sideways. A part of his brain told him to stop, to let go. Months of exhaustion, resentment, and rage slapped his conscience aside.

"You've been following me, hounding me. Vampires aren't real. I'm not Louis. I'm Mark. I work on a television show. Don't you get that? Fiction. I'm not a vampire."

She whimpered, digging at his fingers to free her wrist.

"And you, what are you? You're nothing. Got it? Nothing. You're skinny, you're wearing rags, your hair is a mess, your boobs are weird, and you stink. Do you know how bad that smell is? Do you ever bathe? Even if I was a vampire, what on earth makes you think someone like me would ever want to help someone like you?"

Mark pushed her to the ground. She looked up at him, cradling her wrist. Knowing he was yelling but unable to stop himself. He leaned down, stopping inches from her face.

"You're a pathetic, deluded, nobody fan girl. Only a blind, deaf person with no sense of smell could ever think you are beautiful, got it? Do you?"

Her lip trembled. Then she covered her face and stifled a sob. Mark stood. His breath slowed as his stomach twisted and knotted in on itself like a pile of eels.

"I—I'm...Shit. You okay?" Mark stooped to offer her a hand, but she scuttled back, hiding her face. Tears dripped from her chin and her chest heaved.

"Look, I didn't mean it," Mark said. He reached for her again. She shoved his arm away. Then, with catlike swiftness, she leapt up and darted into the forest. Branches swayed for a moment, then fell still to the retreating sounds of her feet on dead leaves.

In the moonlight, Mark stood alone with his growing shame.

***

Months passed. Sourness filled the back of Mark's throat at the thought of that night in New York. He should have offered her some help. Pointed her to a shelter or something.

He would catch himself scanning faces in crowds, hunting for her black eyes or lumpy sweater. She was never there. The studio smelled of makeup, rubber props, and corn syrup blood. His trailer of pine scented candles and fresh linen. All familiar, all pleasant.

Perhaps it had been for the best, he concluded.

Tough love. There was no point coddling her delusions. She would be fine.

He found comfort in routine. The new season was different. The writers were stretching Louis beyond his sex appeal. It felt good to act out his newfound emotional depth. Early reviews raved.

The best happened when his agent called.

"There's a role. Not Hollywood, the UK. Great film, war epic. The real Oscar-baiting stuff critics love. Your name's been floated for the lead, and they want to talk to you. Could you be on the next flight to London?"

Mark tried to sound nonchalant as he muttered, "Oh, it's tight, but I'm sure I can make it work."

He hung up and pumped his fist in the air. Mark told the director they would just need to do without him until Monday, perhaps even Tuesday, as he dashed for his trailer. What clothes he didn't have he would buy. He had the money.

As he threw a blue sports coat against his gray denim jeans, the trailer door opened.

"Minute, okay?" he said.

Nothing. Then it hit him, pushing its way into his lungs, clawing at his tongue, and sliding down his throat like slime.

The stench.

Still holding his potential outfit to his chest, Mark turned. He only recognized her by the eyes—irises of black glass set in creamy white, glinting under the fluorescent lighting. The sweater and jeans were gone, as well as all her other clothes and adornments. Not even makeup. She, this thing, stood before him naked, tendons and veins wriggling under gray skin that glistened with dampness.

Mark's tongue glued itself to his mouth. He understood now why the sweater was formless, her jeans so loose. There was nothing on her. Ribs hung over her stomach like the maw of a cave, and her breasts dangled on her chest as desiccated sacs.

"Mark," she said. She reached into her mouth and extracted dentures.

He recoiled and dropped his clothes. Rows of long, thin, and translucent fangs curving into wicked points remained in her mouth. Mark's mind flashed to childhood trips to the aquarium and the deep-sea exhibit, the displays of monstrous fish with mouths wider than their bodies. They too had rows upon rows of glass-like teeth. All of them predators.

Mark moved his jaws, but no words came.

She stepped toward him, her bones flaring under her paper skin as she moved.

"I wanted to tell you, you were right." Her teeth flashed as she spoke. "You couldn't make me beautiful." She ran a hand along her thighs, her stomach, her hair that dangled like discarded twine about her cheeks. "I'm already beautiful. Don't you think?"

Mark glanced at his phone on the dresser. She followed his gaze and then snatched it up. She examined it a moment, and then bit into it. Shards of glass fell to the floor, winking like black stars. She spat its metal frame to the ground, licking the tips of her glossy teeth, still intact.

"I wanted to be like you because I thought you had power. A vampire who is loved, who is desired." She closed her eyes and purred. "I wanted that. I wanted to be a vampire like you. No more hiding under the city, no more eating strays. People flock to you, so willing to be taken."

Her eyes snapped to him. Mark stepped back and bumped against the closet.

"But you are a liar. Just a pretender with fake teeth."

"I—I—I'm sorry," Mark said. He looked around the trailer. She blocked the door; the windows were closed. With the new locks, even if he could yell for help, no one could get in.

"Do you know how long I was in the dark? Huddling beneath the sewers? Alone, starving because I was too ashamed to let even my victims see my face? But then I found your show."

She grinned.

Mark spun and scrambled for the bedroom. She darted forward, slamming him into the bed frame. He fell with a groan. She was on him, crouching on his back like a cat. She pressed a foot on his neck and put her mouth to his ear.

"The way you spoke, the way you fed. How beautiful. I watched every episode ten, a hundred times. On lost phones, in homes of addle-brained junkies— wherever I could find you."

"Please." Mark whimpered.

She pressed him down until he coughed because he couldn't breathe.

"And then I found out it wasn't just for the show. Newspapers said you hid from the sun. I saw you bite people, even in the open. I believed you were one of us, but different. You could go above; you could be with them. More than that, you were loved and admired. I wanted to be a vampire like you, but I'm a vampire like me. I have power. I am power. And what are you?"

Mark swallowed, tried to rise, but she jumped down, squashing him into the floor. Carpet fibers dug into his eyes, and his teeth cut into his lips, and he struggled to speak. Then she eased just a touch.

Gasping for breath he cried out, "What do you want?"

She leaned in and whispered, "For you to be like me."

Beer in a Bar
Jerry Purdon

D ean savored each bite from his meal as though it
were his last. He sunk the final morsel of bread
into the au jus and let the taste melt away in his
mouth. The tanginess brought a smile to his face.

He loved food and as a road warrior, he managed to
sample some of the best cuisine around the world. For
the most part, pub entrees surprised him. He didn't
always desire fancy eats, those three course gems
covered by a daily per diem, but sometimes found
delight in something as simple as a French dip. This
particular sustenance definitely fixed his exhausted
mood.

He checked his phone and regretted it. Not enough
time had passed for him to stop looking for her texts.
Every time he did, too many painful memories crashed
his consciousness.

"You're married?" A woman asked while grabbing
his ring finger, lifting his whole hand as if to obtain a

closer inspection of his wedding band. His inner thoughts dissipated. Her upbeat mood intruded on his personal space.

"Yes," he said.

"Why are you here?"

"Food and Beer."

He pointed to his unfinished pint and barren plate. Her brows creased as if she didn't believe him or she had another question.

"Is she here?"

"No."

"So empty seat?"

"Yes."

She slipped onto the red vinyl covered stool. Her hair bounced as she settled. She waved the bartender over. With a toothy grin, she turned back to him with an extended hand.

"Anna."

"Dean."

They performed a quick shake. She pointed at his hand.

"Manicure?"

"Yes."

The mixologist walked up. Anna maintained her cheerfulness while turning to order "gin and tonic," while holding out her credit card to open a tab. She then turned her attention back to Dean and said "Interesting."

"What?"

She gave the slightest shake to her head as if it helped her contemplate an answer. The pause allowed for the appearance of a more pensive response.

"People with money tend to be well groomed."

He chuckled, "I assure you, I have to go to work every morning like everyone else."

"Sure you do."

He didn't respond and ignored her by checking out his empty plate. The way things sounded, she appeared to be having a conversation with someone else. Not only did she have an in-your-face kind of happy personality but brought a lot of volume with every word. He thought she was nervous being around strangers in a bar and obviously unaware of his somber only wanting to be left alone persona. At least he thought he gave off that particular vibe.

He reached for his almost depleted pint and took the last swallow. Before he sat the empty down, the bartender pointed and Dean nodded. He figured one more would not be a big deal. Besides, he did not want to sit in a hotel room all night.

No longer than a minute passed for a refreshed glass. In the meantime, he struggled not to check his phone. For years, he and his wife kept in touch through texts. A life changing event had to occur for him to realize they maintained contact more when he was away than when they were together. Instead, he studied the worn wooden bar top. The dark stain almost gave the place a true English pub ambience, but he pondered if this were by design or sheer luck.

"Done with the plate?" The barman asked.

"Yes."

The artwork on the man's hand stood out to Dean. A detailed eye on the back of the hand alone with very ornate vines entwining around the wrist. He wanted to see more but the long black sleeve of the shirt covered what he thought would have been at least a grand's worth of investment.

The bartender took off with the dinnerware before Dean could comment about the ink. Exceptional artistry fascinated him and quite a few people wore some of the best. For his one and only, it hadn't turned out well.

Being inebriated tended to lead him into making poor decisions and picking out a tattoo artist named Shaky Bob had been one of those. Plus, his wife hated any sort of tat, so he hadn't tried to repurpose or cover it. After a couple of beach summers, the trembling sketch faded and lacked the same standout quality when he had first obtained the thing well before meeting his bride. Funny thing how life meanders on its own course; now, an opportunity existed for something new.

He peeked at his phone. Damn. A twinge gripped the empty pit in his chest. One he related to sorrow and depression since he moped after such a thing happened. Dean continued to stare at the screen, lost in thought. Maybe one of his kids texted. Then again, maybe not.

The lack of any relationships with them was on him, and he owned it. He stayed on the road or worked long hours and didn't make the usual list of events overachieving children tend to have while growing up. They were tremendous girls. He loved the family vacations but the love of his life was who did all the parenting, thus bonding with all three of their daughters. He had no idea how to gain a relationship with them, other than be patient and keep trying.

"You still married?" Anne asked.

"Yes," he said with rapidly successive nods.

Her eyes had a waver to them. He hadn't paid attention to how much she drank, and apparently, she had a lot in a short period of time. He concluded she probably had taken a little something extra.

"Well, that's too bad, but please let me know if anything changes."

She laughed and turned back to who he assumed were friends. To Dean, younger Anna offered none of the charm his wife exhibited. Plus, he actually loved his longtime bride. Though he spent most of his career away from home, he made sure they traveled together. He flew her first class on each vacation and for every location he already experienced the lay of the land. He maintained acquaintances at the right places to obtain the maximum enjoyment for their adventures. As far as he believed, she always appreciated those. He wanted everything to be special for her and in his view do his best by her. Including never cheating. He hadn't ever before when she was alive, and he wasn't ready now.

Someone else sat on the other side of him taking him away from his self-reflection. He glanced at his cell again and deemed stopping such a habit as impossible. He wished way too often for her to pull off what Houdini did not and make the connection from the great beyond. He sighed, turned the device face down and gazed at his empty glass. He chuckled and thought about how fast that one went down.

"Another?" The bartender asked.

"Yes," Dean responded then added, "any meaning about the eye?"

The barman stared blankly at Dean then smiled, "Not really. My aunt is an artist and we kind of came up with this sleeve concept together. She's awesome, and because of being family, it's the only way I could afford this."

The man unbuttoned the cuff and rolled it up to show a bit more. The vines that ended into the eye on the back of the hand went up the arm but wove into many patterns. One was a face, another a flower, and another a wolf. It was all Dean had the chance to make out before the man slid the fabric down.

"It's the full length. It took a couple of months over five four-hour sessions."

"Amazing," Dean said, "I guess you can't get away with showing biceps here?"

"Only on manager-less days. The uniform here is black shirts, long sleeves," he said, then gave a nod toward the windows behind Dean, "that's something to make a crappy drive home."

The bartender went off to pull another pour. Dean turned to see the front door. The patio he had walked through after coming down the stairs from the sidewalk was completely covered in a cloud. He had seen Seattle smothered in the murky soup before but never quite this heavy.

"Fascinating," a feminine voice stated. The word came from the non-Anna side.

"What's that?" He asked still staring at the fog. He hoped this guest was nothing like Anna.

"The permanency of ink," she said.

He caught the slightest hint of an accent. Very unsure of where from but kind of reminded him of an old Romanian friend.

He faced her and became captivated by her allure. The dark hair and eyes were accentuated by sallowness. He thought she might be ill. With high cheeks, a crisp jawline, thin nose, and almost completely translucent skin. Though terribly pale, she had a familiarity about her. He focused on her in an attempt to place her.

"I'm Esther," she said.

He didn't know how to respond. The words to introduce himself did not come to mind. He felt like she controlled his thoughts.

"Spellbound?" she asked.

Her question broke the enchantment. He caught himself.

"Oh, sorry," he said, "I'm Dean." He didn't turn away. At this moment he was only aware of her. He tried to think of something else to say. "Can I get you a drink?"

Her eyes pierced him. "I don't think anyone is working."

He glanced around the bar which had been manned by three people the whole time he sat there. The place had been almost packed, yet now sounded like things had quieted down some. He found the current emptiness odd and himself a bit ignored with no one was around to take an order.

"Wow," Anna said from his other side, "check out the fog."

A number of people did glance toward the door as did Dean again. The dense vapor made the glass doors and windows appear as though they had been coated with spray paint.

"I didn't think it ever got that thick here?" he asked aloud.

"Mist forms in many ways," Esther responded.

Her reply elicited a look from his overly cheerful neighbor who leaned across him.

"He's married," Anna said.

"Monogamous?" Esther questioned.

Anna shrugged and he nodded.

"How castigating," Esther added.

"If he decides not to be married, I had him first." Anna stated right to Esther. The pallid woman didn't change her facial demeanor. Dean's wide-eyed expression appeared to be missed by the young woman, who sat back with her own jovial face then turned to her conversation with her friends.

"Possessive," Esther commented as she stared at him.

"I've agreed to nothing of the sort," he said, and her smile never faltered. "Besides, I have kids older than her. I think."

"Sounds like an occasion for aberration." She said,

reaching over and patting his arm, "I believe you." Her steady expression unnerved him. In the back of his mind, danger existed behind her reassurance. He didn't fathom how and the thought evaporated the more he concentrated on her.

Her hand slid onto the bar near his. The comparison of his color next to hers made her own skin unnatural in every way. It was as if someone washed away her pigmentation.

"I'm unusually pale," Esther said as she examined her own hand pressed against the side of his. He noted not only her pallidness but also how long her fingernails extended. They were almost sharp to a point and due to the thickness made him think of claws.

With a sudden urge to confess, Dean leaned closer to Esther. "Actually, my wife passed…four months ago," he paused and took a breath, "so yes, technically I am not married but I still act as such."

"Hmm, still act as such?" He took her question as rhetorical. "And, now she's dead?" He had no doubt he could lose himself in her eyes. They were dark to the point her irises were opaque, there was a subtle color difference with the pupil. Yet the small smirk had a definite shit-eating quality to it. "Not til' death do us part?"

Dean was unsure on how to respond. He wished he had never blurted out his true status. His stomach acid started tracking up through his esophagus. The subtle burning rising inside. "Not for me."

"Hmm," she nodded, "not for me." Her eyes focused on his. "You miss her?"

"Every minute of every day."

"What do you miss about her?"

"Every part of her, from her beauty to her wonderful wit." He paused through a deep breath, "she was way smarter than me."

"Hmm, smarter. This is what you miss?"

"Actually, yes." He glanced at his beer and peered around for bartenders. "One of many things about her that I miss. Well, not the thing she did that was as obnoxious as all get out. She'd always give three possible explanations and start with saying, 'would you believe'. Something she picked up from an old TV show."

"You miss such obnoxiousness now?"

"I do, though at the time her little routine caused me to become completely unhinged." He wiped his eyes a bit. A tear hadn't formed but water was building on his bottom eyelashes. "She was an amazing person and I miss her."

"Was she a doctor or a scientist? Or a professor?"

"No," he thought it sort of funny Esther asked. "She wanted to go to med school and even got accepted to several close to home, but in the end she decided not to go."

"Hmm, she decided." Esther peered back to the kitchen, "I wonder why she would go to the trouble then decide against going."

"Economics. She was almost fifty, but by the time she'd finish any residency she'd have been near sixty. There's simply no way to get a return on the investment."

"Hmm, return on investment," she nodded, "so brain power, this is why you don't like her," Esther said pointing at Anna.

"It's not a matter of like," he creased his brows and glanced the younger woman's direction. "I'm just not interested."

"Hmm, not interested."

A new mixologist walked up. Her short hair emphasized a long neck along with sharp facial features.

She wore a sleeveless, black leather blouse. It wasn't shaped like a corset nor did it accentuate any body parts, but fit blocky almost as if it were styled like surgical scrubs. With a hand decorated with the identical style of fingernails as the woman sitting next to him, she placed a filled wine glass in front of Esther.

"A recent vintage," she said.

Esther lifted the drink by the stem. She held it up to the ceiling lights and then swirled the liquid. After, she brought it under her nose. Dean heard her inhale. He regarded, with interest, as Esther showed considerable patience in her tasting as well as pure gratification. She sampled the dark crimson contents, and he thought of his last bite of his own meal in how he savored the moment. She must have been doing the same.

Her eyes closed. The small grin she had maintained for as long as he had seen her finally widened. Dean thought he saw a tinge of rouge appear on her cheeks.

"That good?" He asked.

"You have no idea," Esther said while opening her eyes focusing on him. She took another sip.

"Would you like some?" The new mixologist asked Dean.

"Oh, no, thank you, I tend not to mix when drinking." He pointed at his beer.

The bartender left while he observed Esther relish her drink. He wished he appreciated anything as much as she did this. The whole display of her partaking and the enjoyment brought out a glamor he had to have ignored before. She was gorgeous in an exotic way but this was like viewing a supermodel perform in front of a camera. He became aware he held his breath.

"Am I making a show?"

Her question prompted him out of his observation, and obviously he had been caught doing more than watching. He hoped he hadn't been leering.

"I haven't quite seen anyone be this grateful for wine."

"Hmm, grateful indeed."

He chuckled, "indeed."

Her dark eyes consumed him. The thought of holding her flashed across his mind. With tremendous effort, he stared at his beer and not her. It had only been four months. He shouldn't think like that. He may not have been the most attentive husband in the world but still loved his wife. His heart ached, damnit.

Something within her long almond eyes. They were so dark and soothing. He had a deep desire to disappear in them. His faint inner voice told him things weren't right, he needed to observe anything other than her face. He fixated on her bare arms, somehow her skin was less translucent than before. Possibly her drink restored her like his meal had done for him. Except he wasn't ever deathly pallid. She raised her eyebrows as if to question him.

"Oh, nothing," he shifted in his chair then used his finger to circle the air around his face, "It appears the wine refreshed you a bit." He simpered in an attempt to feign happiness to cover his nervousness and instead focused right into her line of sight. Yes, he wanted to be enamored by her and never to glance away again.

He liked the confidence behind her relaxed expression and with her chin held up, it gave her more of a regal manner. From way back in the crevice of his mind, those thoughts yelled at him, but he lacked the understanding as to why. He sure as shit didn't need another beer, but he needed a reason to continue to sit next to her. He thought about ordering a water.

She nodded. Her countenance remained, relaxed and predominant. She stared into him as if grabbing hold of his soul. The draw to her came from deep within. All he wanted was to dive back into her and grasp any part of her, never to let go. This wasn't physical but emotional as if his heart already belonged to her. Nothing about what he desired was sexual, he yearned for something more. He blinked a few times as if coming out of a stupor.

"My thoughts," he said, "I may have had a beer too many since my mind seems to be cloudy."

"Must have come with the murk outside."

"Yeah."

"Would you like to have a stroll?"

"Yeah, stroll." He nodded, riveted on her. Esther began to get up as did he.

The leather clad bartender came up as if waiting for an instruction.

"Rochelle," Esther said, "his is my charge."

"As you wish," Rochelle responded.

"When did you get her name?" Dean asked.

"I frequent here."

"Reg-u-lar." His speech was slow with a solid effort on all three syllables. He chuckled. Wow, he thought, and only after a few beers. Somewhere along the way he had become a real lightweight.

"Sir," Rochelle said, "don't forget your phone."

He blindly picked up the device. His mind heavy as if in a dream.

Anna pushed through between Dean and the bar. "Hey," she said pointing at Dean. Her legs faltered once she faced Esther. "Where are you guys going?"

"We are retiring for the evening," Esther answered.

Anna dropped her hand and abruptly raised her finger again, directed right back at Dean. "But he's married."

"And what does piernik have to do with a

windmill?"

Dean didn't quite understand all the words but caught onto probably comparing one unrelated thing to another. He stared at Anna waiting for her to respond. She wavered a bit in her stance as she attempted to say something.

"What?" Her question came out as almost as unsteady as she appeared.

He hadn't seen Rochelle leave the bar, but she walked up behind Anna placing her arm around the woman's shoulders.

"Are you okay?" Rochelle asked.

Anna motioned to nod but as she glanced up at Rochelle, the young woman changed her reply.

"I'll take her," another server in a white short sleeved blouse said. This one was pale as well but nowhere near as colorless as Esther. Dean ascertained there was another person out of the bar's uniform. She escorted Anna in the direction of the restrooms.

"When do you start your next shift?" Esther asked Rochelle.

"A few minutes ago but need to clean up here."

"In this weather, it's safer to walk with us." Esther nodded toward the bar, "ask Amara if she approves."

Rochelle went to another bartender. Dean tried to say something but the words never surfaced. He thought if he possibly didn't watch all the commotion around him, he might be able to focus. He forced his head down in order to stare at his shoes. His frontal lobe already berated him for not keeping in Esther's sight. After a couple of seconds of being attentive to his feet, the self-chastising stopped and it became easier to keep his head downward.

But the urge to study Esther still remained. He missed her. He searched for something else. The memory of his wife. Something safe. Something real. The familiar pang in his chest rang true, but somehow not as strong as the impulse to admire Esther. Those dark pools of timeless curiosity. He desired to be there. They were peaceful. Here in his mind with his eyes cast down, he yearned for the woman he just met.

"Where is her next shift?" He asked without ever looking up.

"At the hotel, where I reside," Esther's voice lured him to face her. How he loved to gaze at her. "Dean, shall we?" He nodded. "No one should ever walk in this gloom alone." She added.

"Yeah, alone." His eyes never left her.

She went beyond her smug expression to show the whiteness of her teeth. "Thank you for the escort."

He gave a simple nod as if he'd been a formally trained gentlemen and held out the crook of his arm. She slid hers around his at the elbow as they headed toward the doors. Rochelle followed. Dean glanced once more around the restaurant. The amount of patrons had decreased. He noticed it had become more quiet, but the thing that bothered him was none of the servers wore long black sleeve shirts. The manager had to be out and Dean pondered if this was the only change.

Navigating the outdoor patio proved to be a challenge for him due to the impossibility of seeing the next table even as they stood next to one. No customers sat outdoors. The classic 80's rock playing inside was louder outside. He turned back to the glass doors they had exited only a few feet behind him but didn't see them. The fog encompassed everything around their group and for some reason his initial worry about going forward dissipated. He found a sense of security within the dense air blanket.

Dean kept steady and allowed Esther to lead the

way. He assumed she had been to this pub many times before since she knew the patio so well. He never saw when they hit another rise of the veranda but took the step up when Esther did. Before he realized it, they were on street level.

The music became distant as they stepped away from the restaurant. They took a left on the pavement.

"Where are we headed?" He asked.

"To the Mayflower," Esther said.

"Yes, the Mayflower," another arm wrapped around his elbow on his free side. "I reside there." His smirk was more of an attempt to please Esther instead of showing joy. Though he didn't turn away from her to acknowledge Rochelle on his other side.

It wasn't long before they reached the intersection. Dean was unsure since the traffic lights were hidden underneath the dense urban nebula but the echo of street lamps in the fog created enough glare for him to see as he moved along the sidewalk where they crossed the road and turned left heading down Pike.

He did pry Esther from his view to check ahead a few times, but each time his head drifted back to where he peeked at her. Though she never glanced his way, her profile inveigled him. He only wanted her.

They turned right, and Dean recalled the hotel wasn't far. He remembered there should be a park but they wouldn't be able to see it in the opaque vapor anyway. On his way for a meal, he wondered how the area seemed at night. It was a small city plaza but appeared to be a great place to hang out. Well, not for his age bracket, there had been plenty of younger people there all day. Some with longboards, others talking in groups. They were there when he went to work and still there when he came back at the end of the day. Except an hour later, when he left to find something to eat, all were gone.

Now, his observations did not matter, only Esther did. He never met anyone as enticing as her. That he had not checked his phone popped in his mind and for a second, a flash of an internal debate began about whether the mourning for his wife was over. Even if it had been only four months. The familiar pang erupted once again but faded.

Though he walked between their grasps, it was more like he followed. What would happen next Dean did not know. He hoped to only be their escort back to the hotel but he knew he was being led. More like pulled no matter how essential it was to stick his feet to the ground and not budge. He was going. On top of it all, once he pushed back those deep thoughts, he was delighted.

Seeing the buildings snapped him into the moment. He missed the park in the fog, and the mist lightened up since he saw various entrances all with closed signs as they passed.

On entering the hotel, the cloud dissipated. Once inside, there was no one else in the lobby. They had entered through the side doors close to the elevator bank. Everything, though old fashioned, appeared clean and well kept, including the lift buttons and door. Dean took a glimpse of the front desk and saw nobody It was only the three of them.

He turned to Rochelle who had no expression on her face of any sort. Her stare reflected back to him as blank as he felt. He switched back to Esther, she maintained her slight smile, that continuous coprophagous grin. It is possible he had too much to drink.

In no time, they were opening the door to Esther's room. When they entered the space, he realized it was bigger than any other room he had ever stayed in at the hotel. He had no idea the old building packed a room this size. They must be on one of the higher floors. Come to think of it, he never did ask what Esther did for a living nor did she ask him.

The ornate curtains and extra tapestry around the window was the same in his room, but he didn't have a table with chairs, or love seats, along with a coffee table and sofa. This was a definite suite. It rocked all the hotel neutral colors but held its own level if individuality that seemed to fit this place and nowhere else.

She came close to him. He didn't hear her breathing or feel it, but she was near enough he should have sensed it. Her lips almost touched his. He wanted them to touch, but then again he didn't. He stood there with his eyes closed. The pang in his chest became larger. He could not do this. He was not ready.

"Still married?" Esther asked.

He silently indicated yes. So, this was why he conjured up the unusually foul halitosis. It reminded him of the dead rat he had to pull out from underneath his shed. It was the identical smell. Rotted animal flesh. Death. Decay. This was the stench from her mouth.

What he sensed was impossible. She had only wine at the bar and nothing to eat. So the scent came from his head. Something subconsciously made up to throw him off from liking her, and he thanked his internal self.

She backed away from him, raised her eyebrows up and with a playful grin asked, "Did I offend?"

He shook his head, and though he desired those mystifying eyes, he closed his own to keep from them. The eagerness to stare at her faded moment by moment.

"Why don't you relax on the sofa?" She said.

Rochelle took him by the arm as an escort. He was thankful he was able to sit without seeing where to put his backside. He imagined Esther spied his every move. It must have been Rochelle who sat next to him. Well, almost on him. Her leg squeezed right next to his and her hand landed on his lap. He wanted to brush it away but thought it was best not to interfere. He wasn't sure what they were after but it was apparent they desired something.

Dean heard some movement followed by the slight scuff of something being lifted from the floor then moved to be in front of him. Most likely a chair, then he knew when someone settled on it. He assumed it was Esther.

"Let's break the ice," Esther said.

"Let's not," he responded, "just let me go back to my room."

"Can't do that now. You realize that."

"No, I only had a tad too much to drink." He hoped this would work.

"Two things you should know," she paused with a sigh, "one is I hate lies. Lying to me," she hesitated, "what's today's slang for it?…Yes, about as useful as nuts on a priest because I know, without a doubt, when a lie is presented. Just as I know what you said is a non-truth."

Dean didn't know what to say much less what to do, he only wanted to go back to his room and sleep this off. He had been pleasant to her this evening and even walked her back to the hotel. Why couldn't she just leave him alone?

"By the way," her words were smooth, controlling, and comforting, "your closed eyes don't work. I'm already in your head."

He still wasn't going to open his eyes or move Rochelle's hand. It laid still. She wasn't moving it or caressing so it was only an extra weight. He thought it was kind of nice so he knew exactly where she was and by sound he had an idea where Esther sat.

"For example, I can flash an image in your head. One that will cause an instant reaction."

More than a picture flashed across his mind. A movie took over his brain. Something like a hologram he could not shut off or turn away from. One of Esther and Rochelle standing in front of him, clad in lingerie, and making out. The smacks of the lips caressed his nerves, a citrus scent filled his nostrils followed by lavender. The last odor was one his wife burned from a candle whenever he returned home from trips. He felt his arousal.

"That was fast," Rochelle said moving her hand.

He ignored the comment and thought he heard movement. Possibly others entered the suite or were there already.

"Now open your eyes," Esther commanded.

He did as instructed. Esther stood in front of him but behind the chair where another woman sat. He recognized her immediately but what he saw was impossible. He blinked a few times.

"Barbara?" he asked.

"Hi dear," the woman said, "is that for me, or Rochelle, or Esther?" She pointed at his crotch.

"What have you done to me," he said, "this isn't funny."

"Oh, I concur, it's not humorous, especially to make an agreement then to not honor it," Esther nodded in the direction of the woman who sat in front of her and resembled his deceased wife.

"What did I not honor?"

Rochelle leaned into him and whispered in his ear, "med school."

"I didn't say not to go," he stared at the woman he still didn't believe was his wife.

"Correct, you didn't, but you did make it seem like

if I went, then it would have been the most selfish and stupid thing I could ever had done," Barbara said. Except this phrase did sound like her. He didn't know how they pulled this off but she was an exact duplicate of his bride as was her voice and her sayings. Her mannerisms, but the type of clothes she wore at the moment was not her style.

"I saw you dead. I was there when the doctor said it."

"I know and then you went against my last wishes for me to be buried and signed me right up for cremation."

"When did you say you wanted to be buried?"

"Anytime we talked about it." She placed her hands on her hips, "thanks for listening. Plus, you ignored the file in the safe where I had bought the plots for us both along with the tombstone. Luckily Esther intercepted my body, otherwise, I'd have been really pissed to wake up in hell."

She took the chair and scooted it against him. The edge pressed against his knees and his feet were under the seat. Barbara sat right in front of him and spread her legs to where her knees were on the outside of his. Her short dress revealed her thighs and Dean glanced at where a mole on the inside of both legs matched the other. She lifted her skirt up and stretched out.

"Is this what you are looking for?" she asked, pointing at the beauty marks.

He saw them. They were the same and in the exact spot he had caressed many times during the course of their marriage. He stared into her eyes. The irises were the same color of amber they had always been. This was impossible, he had seen her dead.

"I don't know how you are doing this…"

"Dean, honey, look at me," she smiled a big toothy

smile exposing sharp canines.

"This doesn't scare me. I know fake teeth when I see them," he paused attempting to think of an answer and nothing came to mind. "What do you want? Who are you?"

Esther's grin widened. "I think you know what we are," this time she expanded her lips.

Dean glanced over to Rochelle who showed her teeth as well. Her canines were as pointed as the others. He sighed, "stop messing around."

Esther never wavered, "it's amazing how humanity can ignore the supernatural even when standing right in front them." She shook her head as if she disapproved of him. Then her smile disappeared, "And it really pisses me off." Her words were cold. Her once charming eyes steeled and now penetrated right through him. The anger shot into him causing his hardened condition to die down.

Dean sat up as much as he could. It was an attempt to defy her and all of them. He made sure his back was straight and his shoulders squared. He stared at Esther. If he was going to be killed then, he might as well face it all head on.

Esther resumed a relaxed position and her smirk returned as she no longer focused on Dean. "Thank you for coming tonight," Esther said to a group of women he just now paid attention to as they stood on either side of Esther. All in front of him. Many he recognized from the restaurant.

He knew they were all against him. The realization from the experience with his recent condition, through the fog, the bar, the walk home, and to how quick he became fascinated with Esther, his racing thoughts of vampires and his dead wife, it was possible this could be real.

He started to shake, tears flowed, and he took shallow gasps of air. He glanced up at Barbara, "This can't be you. You'd never be mean or hurt anyone."

"Let's just say betrayal changes one's nature."

"I never betrayed you. I have never been with another woman."

"I know. I'm still talking about med school. When we got married, we shared our dreams together. Mine was to have kids first then go on to become a doctor. I even received a Masters to get prepped to go. I was accepted to every med school I applied to and you said to wait until our youngest is in high school. Remember?"

"You agreed."

"Yes, only until our last daughter reached high school, but did I have a choice?"

For some reason, he peered over at Rochelle, her blank look with the same slight smile she had painted on her face as all the others and without a doubt he was the only one on his side. No matter how cozied up to him she happened to be at the moment.

"And then our youngest started high school," she said, "and I got accepted again to every school in the area. And you said, it didn't make financial sense to pursue such a thing. I was shattered."

Dean could see the burrowed brows and scathing squinted eyes. He recognized she was pissed. He had seen her angry, but not to the point of clenched fists held at her side by straight arms. Then she raised her hand and pointed right at him.

"I should rip your throat out, just on principle."

He shook his head. "This isn't you. I was good to you. I gave you everything."

"Except what I wanted and agreed to do when we first started out."

"That's not true. You agreed with me."

"No," her voice softened, "I never did. However, I did agree with Esther."

Dean considered the woman he first met in the evening. He could not believe he even thought about being with her. He hated her and blamed her for everything.

"Blame yourself," Esther said, "Besides, it's a small matter, we all are born crying, live complaining, and die disappointed."

Dean started to sob and blubber more than he ever had in his life. No way this was all his fault. Barbara had agreed, and she was there. Somehow he received a death sentence with her becoming undead.

Esther stepped toward him, reached down and patted his knee, "compose yourself, mon chéri."

"Listen," Barbara said, "I thought for sure you were not only redoing the definitions of our marriage but also cheating on me. For that, I was going to tear your heart out, but because you're only a selfish ass, I'm going easy on you." She laughed, stood and walked away.

"What now?" He asked viewing his former wife's back.

"Rochelle knows what to do," she said without turning around.

Within a few seconds everyone in the room disappeared and the lights dimmed. Rochelle moved and extended her hand to him. She escorted hm out of the suite and to the elevator. They took the ride down to his floor where he opened the door and Rochelle led the way inside.

"What now?" He asked again.

"I'll carry out the sentence."

"But I don't want to die. I didn't do anything wrong."

"You killed a dream. Or you were, at least, a party

to it dying. So yes, you did something wrong."

A tear formed and trickled down his cheek. Rochelle kissed the wetness and smiled at him. His tears stopped.

"It's way too late for tears," she said, "don't worry, you'll die like a man. I know how important that is to you fellows."

She took him over to the bed where she turned to kiss him, and they both sat.

"Why are you being nice to me?"

"Because, well, you remind me of my old boyfriend."

"What happened to him?"

"He was killed in the Battle of the Bulge."

She sighed, "I met Esther one night after I found out he'd died. She said if I joined her we could put an end to the war. So I did, and we went." Her eyes searched around the room. "It's a pain in the ass for us to travel, especially over bodies of water, but we went taking our coffins full of our native soil, finding great places to operate from and proceeded to create a ton of havoc."

Dean repositioned himself with his back on two pillows leaning against the headboard.

"Sounds like you are the good guys, but you just killed those people in the bar and even poor Anna."

Rochelle laughed aloud. "No, we didn't. We take a bit of blood while implanting memories of them having sex with one another. Real top notch recollections of their sexual encounter based on their own fantasies." she paused for a second, "they awake nude or partially clothed, these thoughts flood in very much like it is for when someone wakes up with a hangover from a night of binge drinking. Things trickle in and people feel ashamed as they recollect. Most people are so embarrassed by how much they enjoyed it. They get dressed and go home feeling a bit weak."

"Why sexual encounters?"

"Because, still to this day, people will not talk about sex, especially their wildest fantasies, so we get our dinner without creating a trail of bodies and the general population gets their jollies without the slightest transference of a STD. We hit different areas of the world and keep on the move."

Dean struggled with how the implanted remembrances worked.

"For example," Rochelle said and then leaned into him giving him a long kiss where their tongues danced, and he felt his body become alive. They made out for what seemed forever, and they shed their clothes. Together they made love. Dean finally felt like he was getting in control of himself. His heart beat hard and his release was more intense then anything he had ever experienced.

She rolled out of bed and stared at him as she dressed. Dean liked her green eyes and how the auburn color of her hair seemed like a natural accent. She made love with more passion than he had ever known. His wife hadn't been his first lover when they married but she had been his last until now. Rochelle made him wish for a tomorrow.

"Tomorrow will never come for you my dear," she said.

He sat in the bed already dressed as was she, standing right in front of him.

"See," she said, "no exchange of bodily fluids. Walk me to the door?" She asked.

He stood to accompany her out. She peered into the bathroom as they went by and paused in the small foyer.

"It might be better if you moved the desk chair to right here," she said.

"Okay."

She went to open the door, and he could not help but think of the cameras out in the hall. How they would pick her up leaving, and how they saw him come into the hotel with Esther and herself. She turned back to him as she opened the door.

"The cameras have been off all night until we stepped foot on this floor. Funny thing is, I don't reflect in a mirror or show up on a recording of any type."

He wanted to seize her and live the false memory, but he appreciated it was never going to happen. She left and headed down the hall. He stuck his head out to watch her depart. She glanced back at him.

"You're okay with just killing me," he said.

"Yes," she said, "don't fear the next step and enjoy your shave. Be sure to nick both sides." She disappeared right before his eyes as the others had just a few hours before.

He closed his door and went to the desk to grab the chair. He placed it where Rochelle had suggested, and he went into the washroom where he turned on the shower. As the room heated up the top of the mirror misted. He brushed his teeth and kept the sink water warm as it ran.

Dean lathered up his hands with shaving cream and applied it to his cheeks and neck. He then rinsed off the razor and began his shave along his neck in strips. With each stroke the lather disappeared showing his smooth skin. On his fourth pass, he dug in a little farther and snagged his skin. It didn't cut deep enough so he took an extra blade from his bag. He viewed his reflection as he sliced where his razor had marked the spot.

He struck the correct spot. The first spurt of blood hit the mirror. He caught the other side of his neck with the blade.

His heart rate increased at the sight but he calmly placed his hand over the wound but didn't clamp down to stop the bleeding. He stepped out of the bathroom and sat on the chair he placed just outside the door. Where he dreamed of another moment with Rochelle and sat until he collapsed. The blood didn't clot but pumped out of him with each heartbeat, where it pooled around the chair.

Black Harvest Moon

Terry Stock

Jake floored the accelerator of his pickup and we hit a hundred heading east on 84. My hands reached for the belt and I snapped it home as Jake took us around a dozen vehicles littering the interstate, tyres shrieking, truck lurching. I gripped the door and seat and breathed Christ. We hit a clear stretch and made one ten. *Christ.* We came up on a semi that spanned the width of the highway and our speed didn't drop. I said Jake, take it easy. He said shut up in a flat monotone and we were on top of it. It filled the windscreen and I shouted *Jake!* and he said shut up in a flat monotone as he went left and screamed past the cab across gravel and earth. The back slid out from under us and I thought the tyres would blow and we'd roll but they gripped and we ripped out of the scrub and back onto the hard top. Jake pushed it up to one twenty. Christ, *Jake.* He said shut up.

We blew through American Falls and I said wait, let's check it out. Jake didn't take his eyes from the road or his foot off the accelerator. I said slow the fuck down and he told me to shut up in a flat monotone. He didn't drop below ninety, weaving in and out of abandoned cars. There was a line of them a mile long outside Chubbock and Jake ran his truck up through the scrub beside them, trailing dust. I shut my eyes and held on tight as we bounced through potholes and clipped vehicles, waiting for my window to shatter in my face. He tore by everything with all he had.

It was another hour before Jake said more than shut up. He said there he is, there he *fucking* is. I stared stupidly at the empty road, it was clear, there was nothing and he pointed off to the right a hundred yards ahead of us. There, he said, in the ditch. I saw a red Ford lying on its right side and before I could identify it as Tom's, Jake was leaning into the brakes and we skidded to a halt just beyond it. While it still rocked on its springs Jake had released his belt and leapt from the truck, pulling his gun. I fumbled with my belt, shouting Jake, wait, be careful.

I got out of the truck and ran after him, reaching for my gun. Jake was crab walking around the front of Tom's car, his gun held in both hands at arm's length and pointing at the windshield. It was still intact and he was trying to peer through it, didn't take his eyes from it as he barked I can't see him. I said he's there and pointed past Jake at the field behind him.

Jake swung around and saw Tom making his way up a hill, three hundred yards away, hurt and hobbling, walking slowly through tall grass in a dogged fashion. Jake set off after him at a run, his gun raised. I raced, tried to catch him and shouted, told him to stop, told him to please just stop. He ignored me, ran up the hill, his gun aimed at Tom's back. Bigger than me, older than me, he left me for dead and I shouted Jake between gasps, shouted don't through ragged breaths.

Tom never turned, just kept walking, made the top of the hill. Jake got within ten yards of him, shouting his name, and Tom still didn't turn and I saw his hands were empty, he wasn't armed and Jake stopped and aimed and emptied his gun into his back.

Jake dropped his gun and bent over, one hand grasping his side, gasping for breath, saying thank God, I got him, I got him endlessly, repeatedly.

***

Trent leant into Jake's face again, got in real close, said, 'Why did you kill him?' Jake retreated another step and Trent said slowly and carefully, 'If you move one more time, if you move from that spot by an inch, I *will* have your eyes.' Trent looked questioningly at Jake as he waited for his response, his head cocked to catch every word. When there wasn't one, Trent closed the gap again and Jake found the heart to stand perfectly still as Trent put his face within inches of Jake's and said softly, 'Why did you kill him?'

In a voice I could barely hear, Jake said, 'Self defense.'

Trent didn't remove his face from Jake's and said very slowly, 'You shot him in the back. How does that work, Jake? Because I don't think it does.'

Jake took his time. Closed his eyes, his mouth working silently as he formed his response. 'Had no choice.'

Trent said, 'I counted eight. Eight rounds you put in his back. Doesn't look like self defense to me.'

Jake opened his eyes, tried to see past Trent who was still in his face but had nowhere to look and said in a weak voice 'You weren't there' and there were small groans from amongst us.

Trent smiled broadly. His unrelenting pressure had resulted in a response that he could take as insolence. Insubordination. His juices were beginning to flow and he stepped away from Jake and looked at us.

It was nearly midnight and we were gathered in the college car park. Every one of us lit up by our own vehicle's headlights. Nowhere to hide as we waited with a sick sense of dread in expectation of the punishment beating. All that was left to be decided was the victim and that could be any one of us. An arbitrary, incomprehensible lottery.

I stood beside Abby and she had Cathy in her arms. Her daughter was tired, restless and I breathed, 'keep Cathy's head up.' Abby didn't need my warning, had stiffened and tried to control her trembling as she gripped her child tighter, said quietly, 'c'mon sweetheart. watch the man.' Trent demanded attention. There were no exceptions. He stood alone and the rest of them encircled us in the dark, watched us, noted our reactions. Nothing escaped them.

Trent looked at us, taking everybody in, no more than three dozen left now. His eyes settled on me and he said, 'No. But Rob was, wasn't he? Hey Rob, why don't you come up here? Bring Cathy with you.'

I turned to Abby who stifled a moan and I said, 'It'll be ok. I'll bring her right back.' I tried to take her from her arms but she wouldn't let go and I started to panic. 'Abby, please. Don't give him a reason. I *will* bring her back.'

Abby's grip loosened a little but she was still unable to let her daughter go and her eyes found mine and they were pleading, terrified. I pulled Cathy out of her arms and found I couldn't talk. I shrugged her grasping hand off my shoulder as I moved through the group that made way for me, leaving her behind. I stepped around Tom's corpse and stood before Trent.

He only had eyes for Cathy, smiling happily as he studied her, said, 'Hi. Wow. You're adorable. It *is* Cathy, isn't it?' Cathy tried to wriggle free and looked back for her mother and I looked at Trent whose smile hadn't dropped. There was no reason for hope, it meant nothing. I said, 'She's just tired. It's late, you know?' I aimed for conversational and it came out desperate.

Trent's left forefinger reached out and laid itself along Cathy's jaw line and gently turned her head to face him. She stared at him in silence with as much courage as any of us had ever managed. He was death and plague and horror and Christ, please don't kill her. I held her tight, saying, 'S'okay, play possum, remember?'

Trent stared into her eyes for way too long and I didn't like what I saw. He looked at me for the first time. 'Is Rob a good friend, Cathy?' Cathy nodded slightly, her gaze still caught up on Trent. 'I *bet* he's a good friend. I bet he wouldn't do anything to hurt you.'

Trent's hand dropped and he turned his attention back to the child. 'We're going to play a little game. I'm going to ask Rob a few questions and if he doesn't get them right he'll have to pay a forfeit. That means he'll have to pay a price but don't worry, I'm not going to hurt Rob. I'm not going to touch *him* at all.'

From behind me I heard Abby start moving through the crowd, heard her say, 'Rob, I'm taking her home.' Trent looked at me, still smiling, enjoying himself, said, 'Tell her to stay where she is, Rob. And I mean now.'

I turned and she wasn't far, moving fast, and I snapped 'Abby' sharply with a desperate edge of warning in my voice. 'Stay there. Don't move. It'll be ok.' She managed to stop despite herself, her eyes pleading with me. Cathy said 'Mom' and I saw tears appear in Abby's despairing face. Jean stepped towards her, put an arm around her shoulders to comfort her but her grip was tight and firm and I could see she wouldn't let her go. I said, 'Abby. You have my word. She'll be ok.'

I turned back to Trent and Cathy wriggled to be free, called for her mom. He said, 'Hold her tight, Rob. Keep her quiet. We need to talk now. I don't want her interrupting us.'

I looked at Trent, my chest starting to heave with panicked breaths. I said, 'Trent...'

'What is it, Rob? You told your sweetheart it was gonna be ok. You gonna let her down?'

I turned to Cathy, whispered in her ear. 'Cathy, give me five minutes. Sit still, be good, be quiet. Five minutes and we'll go home with Mommy. Ok? Be good and we'll go soon.'

Cathy looked at Trent. Understood more than I could bear. She wrapped her arms tightly around my neck and hid her face from him behind my head. I rocked her a little. 'Good girl.'

Trent looked at me with a warm, thoughtful smile. 'Ok. Five minutes. I promise.' He looked at Jake who hadn't moved, staring doggedly at a point on the ground before him and Trent appeared satisfied. He looked back at me.

'Rob, let's go back to this morning. When did you realise Tom was gone?'

'Like Jake said. Around nine.'

'Nine?'

'He hadn't showed up for the work crew so Jake sent Howard and Paul round to his place. He wasn't there.'

'What did you think when you heard this?'

'Same as everybody else. His car was gone. We knew he'd taken off.'

Trent adopted a puzzled surprise. 'You *knew*? How

did you know?'

'I... just did. We all did.'

'Why?'

'Why what?'

'Why did you automatically assume he'd run? Did you know he was going to do this? Had he told you?'

'*No.*'

'Then tell me why you thought he ran if you'd had no reason to suspect him.'

I stared at Trent. Saw the challenge. Took a breath. 'We had no choice but to make that assumption. If Tom was still in town he would show up. If Tom had fled and we didn't get him back by nightfall we would be in breach of the rules laid down by your council and punished. Severely and arbitrarily. We had to assume he'd run in order to avoid disciplinary action. Retribution. Death.'

Trent smiled and wagged a forefinger in my face. I tried not to cringe or step back. 'Clarity. That's all I ask. Keep that in mind.'

He looked at Jake again who still hadn't moved, taken Trent's instructions literally and with good reason. He had a semi-automatic 9mm on his hip. I had a Browning. Neither of us would even think of touching them. Trent watched him until he saw him start to tremble and his eyes flicked back to me. 'So you didn't find out he was gone until nine?'

I said, 'Yes.' Nodded for emphasis.

'You think he skipped at first light?'

'It makes sense.'

'So you gave him a couple hours head start?'

'We gave him nothing.'

'You gave him plenty. You split up?'

'Yeah. Sent out search parties.'

Trent looked past me, into the group that watched,

waited. Any of them might be called up next and I knew any number of them were praying it wasn't going to be their blood spilt tonight. They were silently begging it would be mine. Or Jake's. Or Cathy's.

'And you and Jake took the 86 Northeast.'

'Yes.'

'And you found him.'

'Yes.'

'Convenient.'

'It's just how it went.'

'Then let's hear how it just happened to go.'

'It wasn't so hard. It was Jake's idea. He figured Tom would go for the border, try and get as far as he could as fast as he could and he was right. We were just this side of Shelley when we saw his car. He'd lost control, must have hit something, I don't know, ran into a ditch and tipped over.'

Trent's attention shifted to Cathy, still hiding from him behind my head. He said, 'Cathy. Look at me.' Cathy didn't move and I felt her arms tighten around my neck.

I said, 'She's tired, you know?'

Trent said, 'She's scared.'

'We're all scared, Trent. Let me give her back to her mom. Please.'

Trent reached out, placed his left hand gently on her right shoulder. As if claiming his property. 'What happened next?'

Cathy's face burrowed deeper into my neck, her arms gripped even tighter and she began to tremble, just like Jake, and her heartbreaking fear rolled through me and what courage I had failed me. I said, 'I don't know' and I wanted to plead with him but he said, 'Yes, you do. C'mon, it's nearly over. Not far to go now. What happened next?'

I tried to swallow, felt nausea surge and said, 'We didn't even have time to get out of the truck. It was... Tom came out from behind his car and started shooting at us. Blew the cab up. The whole clip, seven, eight shots. I don't know how we weren't killed.'

Trent's grip on Cathy's shoulder tightened and she gripped tighter, her nails digging in to me and she cried out. I heard Abby shout 'Baby' and 'Let me go.' Trent looked at me and said, 'That's what I've been wondering.'

I looked at him, unable to formulate a response, the world becoming the weight in my arms, a weight I couldn't bear.

He said, 'What happened next?'

I thought, Christ, what did happen next? 'What?'

'He blew the cab to pieces, remember? Neither of you had a scratch. What happened next?'

'He ducked back behind his car to reload and we got out.'

'Ok.'

'I stayed with the truck and Jake went around the back, trying to get behind him. I distracted Tom, tried to talk to him but as he came back out to fire at me again, Jake had got around behind.' I saw Trent's face had darkened and my throat thickened and I breathed raggedly through an open mouth. 'Shot him.'

'Ok. How far away was he?'

'I don't know. Fifty yards?'

'You're asking *me*?'

'Thirty, maybe.'

'And Jake, he's what? Two hundred and fifty pounds?'

'I don't know.'

'Ran between your vehicles like some ghost ninja?'

'Yeah. In the confusion.'

'Tom didn't see him coming?'

'I figured it was concussion.'

'Ok. You can't judge a guy's weight but you can diagnose concussion. What did you say to him?'

'To Jake?

'*Tom*,' he spat.

'Nothing. He was dead.'

'*Before* he died, Rob. What did you say to distract him?'

'I said... I said...'

'Yeah?'

'I can't remember. Anything.'

'Just bullshit?'

'Yeah,' I said. 'Just bullshit.' The words dying on my lips.

Trent tensed and I braced myself. He still had a grip of Cathy's shoulder and I fully expected him to pull her out of my arms. Behind me I could hear Abby's sobs, she said, 'Rob, you promised me.'

Trent said, 'Doesn't add up, does it, Rob? Even she can see that. Seems to think you're willing to sacrifice her daughter's life. Probably wondering why you're choosing Jake over her little girl. I guess we're all thinking that.'

My heart started to hammer and in desperation I almost shouted at him. 'Christ, Trent, I'm not lying, do you think I'm that fucking stupid?'

'I really fucking do. In fact, I think I need to spell it out to you. You're about to choose between this sack of shit over here and your girlfriend's daughter.'

'Fuck *no*.'

Trent laughed, a barking surprised snort. 'Fuck *yes*. Have you been lying to me, Rob?'

'Trent.'

'Answer the question.'

179

'I can't.'

'Your choice. Answer the *question*.'

'I *can't*.'

'Last chance. Yes or no?'

'Trent, *please*.'

'Yes or no.'

Trent stared hard at me and in those eyes I saw his intent. I said, 'No.'

Abby screamed and Trent pulled Cathy out of my arms. I let her go, didn't resist, her nails dragging across my neck and throat. He set her on her feet and said, 'Go find your Mom.' Cathy ran back into the crowd and Trent smiled at me, leant in to me, made sure no one else could hear him and said, 'Looks like you won your bet. Now you can tell your girlfriend how you did it. Good luck.'

***

I headed home and let myself in. Abby hadn't bolted the door and I tried to take some comfort from that as I moved through the house, softly calling her name. There was no response. She'd left all the lanterns on and I pocketed my torch. Heading upstairs, the silence confirmed all my fears and on entering our bedroom I found her curled up with Cathy in the bed. I stayed in the doorway, suddenly afraid to cross the threshold, held in place by her empty stare.

I found some courage, said, 'Is she ok?' softly, not wanting to wake Cathy.

Her eyes drifted from me and she said, 'I don't know' in a quiet, beaten voice. In the silence that followed she said, 'She's going to sleep with me from now on.'

I said, 'Oh. Yeah, of course. I'll take the spare

room.' I waited, said, 'Abby, what just happ-'

She said, 'I'm tired.'

'Ok.' I backed out, said, 'Goodnight' and shut the door behind me.

***

I woke from a dream of trees that were too far away and trembled. I lay with my heart racing, still reaching for her hand.

I made my way down to the kitchen at dawn and found some chips and a candy bar, shoved them into my pockets. Grabbed a couple of sodas and closed the front door quietly behind me. Five minutes later I pulled up beside Tom and got out, wrapping my jacket tight around me against the chill. I dropped the tailgate, sat on it and ate my breakfast, waiting for the day's work crew.

The guys arrived in three pickups and pulled up before me. They clambered out and Jake said, 'You coming?' I nodded and we got Tom into the back of Ethan's truck, bundled up in a tarpaulin. We took him out of town on our way out west, found a spot that was easy digging and rolled him into a two-foot-deep hole. A traitor's grave, prey for coyotes. Mason said, 'Anybody want to say anything?' and nobody did.

After an hour or so we pulled into Filer and assigned the details. I nudged my way into the gap beside Jean, aiming to work with her, hoping to talk to her about Abby, about Trent. She met my questioning look with a nod and a smile and I thought I was going to be scavenging in a house-to-house search for the day but Jake said, 'Hey, Rob, I want you to come with us.'

I was surprised, said, 'Me? I don't hunt.'

'We know. You need to learn.'

'Today?'

Jean leant into me, bumped my shoulder, said, 'We'll talk tonight. Come round.'

We both knew something was up and there was no avoiding it. I shrugged pissed acceptance and Jake and Mason climbed into Ethan's truck and I followed them north while the others took up their grid search of the city.

At the State Park we got close to the river and we pulled off the road. I took a deep breath as I got out because Jake wasn't the thanking kind and saving his life last night would be the last thing on his mind. All three of them lined up opposite me and I said, 'Jake, is this about your truck? I'll get you a new one.'

'It's about last night.'

'No shit.'

'It's about how long do you think we can go on like this?'

'As long as we have to.'

'They're going to kill us, Rob. Tonight. Tomorrow. We're all going to die.'

'They *need* us. They can't afford to.'

'This whole thing's breaking down.'

Mason said, 'The only reason nobody got hurt last night was because Trent wasn't in the mood.'

'No. Trent got exactly what he wanted last night. He fucked me over.'

Jake said, 'Maybe. But the next time he wants to fuck you over it could mean Cathy's head on a spike. And he'll say here Rob, hold this for me. Do a lap of the town and while you're at it sing the Star-Spangled Banner. And you'll do it. Because that's what we do. Obey their every goddamned word.'

'What are we supposed to do, Jake?'

Jake turned to Ethan, hooked a thumb at the truck. 'Show him what we've got.' Ethan leant into the cab and as tired as I was I suddenly got a whole lot more. He brought out hellfire and damnation with a broad grin and bible reverence.

I said, 'That looks like army issue.'

Jake smiled. 'And you'd be right. M240. Belt fed machine gun. We got M4's, AR15's, grenades, shotguns. Pulled them out of some army trucks in Clover. *We're* the military now.'

'You gotta be fucking kidding me.'

'We can do it, Rob. We got all the firepower we need.'

'Those army trucks in Clover you found. How'd that go with all their guns?'

'I'm guessing they didn't end up like cattle. Waiting to be hogtied and butchered.'

'You'll get us all killed.'

'Then we'll die with some dignity 'cause I can't live with the humiliation.'

'Nobody is going to die if we stick to the rules.'

'Tom's dead. Look what their rules made us do.'

My mouth dropped open to snap a reply but I didn't have one. There wasn't one. All I could do was concede his point and then the argument was lost. He had me and he knew it.

He said, 'Trent is pushing too damn fucking hard. That psychotic piece of shit is losing it.'

'Beth won't allow it. She's still in charge around here.'

'No. No, she ain't. Where was she last night? When was the last time we saw her? Those two are at each other's throats and if Trent wins it's game over. That fucker will kill every last one of us and it looks like he's winning to me. And I don't know what it is, Rob, but he doesn't like you and I'll be damned if I don't know why you're not dead already.'

Once again, I just stared at him. Every word he said couldn't be denied. Only this time he didn't press home his advantage, just watched and waited. Knew he had me every which way I turned. I said, 'Who else knows about this?'

'Just us. You got the balls and we need your smarts. I figure the rest can know when they need to. Too many hear about this and it'll get out.'

I counted three breaths, said, 'We need a plan.'

'Yes we do.'

'A good one.'

'A bad one ain't gonna do it.'

***

That night Trent had Elijah take roll call, had him bark out our names and we replied prompt and loud. Jake thought Trent was winning control of them and I didn't want to believe that but I saw that more and more of them were willing to do what he said. Jake was right again and that was happening a lot lately. I was starting to think he was smarter than me as well and that stung.

Trent's eyes kept returning to me and more than once I met his gaze, dropping it immediately, adopting submissive compliance with an ease that had long since failed to shame me.

Abby held Cathy tightly in her arms at the back of the group, as far away as she could get from either of us. And I knew that if Trent tried anything she would simply run. She wouldn't have him near her daughter ever again. And she wouldn't look to me for help. Trent saw it all. He dismissed us and I watched Abby hurry away. I let her go and headed in the opposite direction, out into an empty part of town.

The sky was clear, the moon was almost full and I

didn't need my torch, didn't need to attract any undue attention. I constantly checked behind me, stood patiently at corners and waited. I saw nobody, human or otherwise. At my destination, I slipped through a waist high chain link gate and went into a single storey house that could have been mistaken for a garage. I stopped just inside the front door and saw a pale light in the back.

I went through to the kitchen which was lit by a single lantern and found her sitting in a chair at the table, fingers tapping lightly at its worn and scarred Formica surface, her eyes on the floor. I stood in the doorway and waited but she didn't move, didn't open her mouth, didn't even raise her head to look at me. I stared at her, said, 'Where have you been, Beth?'

Her fingers stopped tapping. 'Around,' she said quietly.

'I needed you last night. Trent threatened Cathy.'

'The child?'

'Yes, the *child*.'

'Did he hurt her?'

'No.'

She lifted her head and looked at me. 'Then what's the problem?'

'He's getting worse. You need to do something.'

'Trent's ok. Don't worry about him.'

'Trent is not ok. He's fucking everything up.'

She studied me, said, 'What happened with Tom?'

'I don't know. He ran.'

'What did you know about it? Did you suspect anything?'

'I would have told you.'

'You haven't had a lot to tell me recently.'

'There's nothing to tell.'

'There's always something, Rob. You taught me that. What have you got?'

I paused, matched her steady gaze. I said, 'Trent's pushing us too hard.'

'I'm not interested in Trent. Tell me about your friends.'

'We're trying not to get killed.'

'Meaning?'

'Meaning we are doing everything in our power to satisfy your psychopathic demands including killing each other. If I hear anything that jeopardises that position I will tell you.'

Beth's fingers tapped lightly on the table, weighing my every word and her eyes pinned me to the back of my skull. 'I always knew when you were lying to me, Rob. You used to get a little spot of colour in your cheeks. Like you were ashamed. Like that time I first met your parents and I asked you if they liked me and you said they loved me and your face burned. But you don't do that no more and now I can't tell. So what is it? No more lying or no more shame?'

I remembered. She got upset. Thought she'd let me down somehow, ruined everything. She broke my heart every time.

Quietly, I said, 'Beth. Please. Talk to Trent.'

She pulled her cigarettes and a lighter out of her jacket pocket and lit one. Smoked it leisurely down to the butt. In silence.

***

I knocked on Jean's door and she greeted me with a can of beer in one hand. I accepted it gratefully and she led me through to her kitchen, lit by a couple of lanterns and the warm scent of a stew simmering on a camping stove on the counter. I surprised myself by finding a smile. 'Please say I'm invited to dinner.'

'Anytime.'

I fell into a chair at her kitchen table and she sat opposite me, a glass of red before her. I said, 'I never had you as a wine drinker.'

She raised the glass and saluted a world of absent friends. 'My husband introduced me.' She took a drink, placed the glass back on the table and smacked her lips loudly. 'Great with fries.' She laughed, said, 'Did that every time I wanted to yank his chain. He never let me down. How'd it go with Jake?'

I shrugged, said, 'The strangest thing. Had this idea he should thank me for, you know, saving his life. So we wandered round the woods all day looking for something to shoot. I guess his debt has been paid in full.'

'I didn't think Jake was the thanking kind.'

'Well, you'd be surprised.'

'Yes, I would.' She took another taste of her wine, set it down in front of her and said, 'He did the right thing, you know. Killing Tom. If you'd brought him back here alive they would have taken all night to do the same thing and we would have had to watch. And even though he ran and one of us would have had to pay the price if he got away, I can't find it in myself to judge him. Or any of us when it comes to those animals. Not you. And certainly not Abby.'

My throat tightened. 'You've spoken to Abby?'

She nodded. 'I've spoken to Abby.'

'Is she ok?'

'No. She's pretty fucking freaked out right now.'

'What did she say?'

'About you?'

'Yeah.'

Jean paused, lined up her thoughts. 'She's got a lot to deal with. She needs time, she needs space.'

'I need to tell her what happened.'

'But she saw what happened. You need to leave her be, Rob, because you can't put it right.'

***

Jake emptied the M4 into the tree forty yards away. Bark flew and chips of wood peppered its base. I stood behind him, staring hard, my anger boiling to rage. The gun clicked empty and he lowered it. In the stunning silence I said to his back, 'Turn around, fucker. *Talk* to me.'

He didn't turn. He removed the empty clip, tossed it aside, continued to ignore me. I started to shout as I lost control, a white heat pressure in my head threatening to burst. 'You stupid piece of SHIT. *You murdering ASSHOLE.*' He slotted home a new clip. 'Tom wasn't enough, was he? You enjoyed it, didn't you?' He raised the gun to his shoulder. 'I've never seen anybody run so *fucking* fast. I couldn't keep up with you, *you fat FUCK.*' He fired the gun and the roar of it ripped through my head and I kept shouting obscenities at his back. My ears buzzed and I was screaming uselessly and I turned away as the weight of the Browning on my hip began to draw my hand.

I stormed towards Ethan and Mason who watched me coming with an expression of casual disinterest as their grip tightened on their military issue. I practically screamed at them. '*You're gonna listen to this stupid motherfucker? You're gonna do what this fucking psycho fucking says?*'

Mason shrugged, said, 'You want a ride back or what?'

***

Cutting out a cancer, that's all it was. Saving mind, body and soul. Trent wasn't around at roll call and it ended without incident. Anna, third grade Anna, taking a silent head count and dismissing us with a string of invective. I headed north, back to the house where cancers are cut out, the moon hidden behind banks of racing clouds and I found my way in the pitch black without a conscious thought. Couldn't remember how I got there. Thinking about Jake and Ethan and Mason. I'd given them a chance, the time to realise that nothing they'd come up with could possibly work. In their frustration they doubled down and it was out of my hands.

I entered the house, felt my way through to the back, calling her name. The kitchen was empty and I shouted, swore, made my clumsy hazardous way back out to the front. She was there, standing in the street in strobing moonlight through tattered clouds, still and remote.

Relieved, scared, sick to my stomach, I said, 'You're late.'

'Trent wanted to see me. He has something in mind.'

'Like what?'

'He has plans for you. Stay away from him.'

Fear shot through me and my mouth tripped over the words. 'How am I supposed to do that?'

'I don't know. Think of something.'

'You're supposed to help me.'

'No. You're supposed to do as you're told. That's all this is.'

***

I sat in the back of Jake's new truck. It was a good ride, he'd chosen well. He was behind the wheel and

Mason was beside him. Ethan was following and we made good time to the river.

I'd got to Jake's by nine, pulled up in front of his old truck he'd left across the street. It was minus the windshield I'd made him shoot out, the cab peppered with rounds. On the way back we froze in the buffeting wind with Tom's corpse bumping around in the bed.

As I crossed the street to his front door, it opened and he stepped out, watching me darkly. I held up two six packs, one in each hand. 'I come in peace.'

He stood and contemplated. 'Not fucking good enough.'

'I know.' I went to the back of my pickup and dropped the gate. He ambled up and ran his eye over the six cartons. 'Take them. I feel like an asshole as it is. Don't make it worse.'

He looked at me, said, 'Is it an apology or a bribe?'

'Shooting the town up isn't going to work. Taking them on is suicide. If we do anything we got to run, separate, take our chances. And maybe the border isn't the border anymore. Maybe they just kept going and killed everyone and there's nowhere to run to like Trent says. But I'd still take that chance over fighting him. With a little luck I think most of us could get away. So let's get ready and let's get out of here. How does three days sound?'

'Like two days too many.'

'Tomorrow?'

Jake grabbed the beer. 'Tomorrow.'

At the river we got out and went to recover our stash of arms, planning on sharing them out in the morning at the crack of dawn after outlining our plan to everybody else. I let them get ahead of me. I casually fell behind. Just a few yards. I had a gun in my jacket pocket, I had a gun on my hip and a hunting knife sheathed in the small of my back. I took my gun from out of my jacket pocket and it didn't catch, slid smoothly free and I eased the safety off. No one heard a thing, no one turned. Having guaranteed their deaths, I took the gun off my hip. With the safety catch released I shoot Jake first, empty every round into his stupid fucking head and do us all a favor and when Ethan and Mason start to turn I spare the time to empty the other gun into their faces before I take the knife and cut Jake's throat, cut out his tongue, just shut him the fuck up and I cut out his heart and fucking shoot that and despite my lack of sleep, the uppers, PTSD, the loss of everything I ever had and six months of interrogation, humiliation and waiting to die at the hands of demons, I manage to snag a thought in the haze and I pocket my weapons.

I was going to need him.

***

At roll call I hovered at the back of the group. Trent barked out our names as he watched me and I stared into the space before me, reasoning that it could not possibly offend any predatory psychotic. He finished and in the silence that followed Mary's 'here' we all knew there was blood in the air. We weren't dismissed and we stood waiting and Trent said, 'Rob, come up here.' I took a breath and walked in a straight line towards him as the crowd parted for me, nobody meeting my eye. As I passed Jake I felt a small pat in the back. It was as much encouragement as he dared.

Trent pointed at a spot on the tarmac three yards in front of him and I took up my position there. I kept my eyes on his feet and he clicked his fingers impatiently. 'Up here. Look at me.'

I reluctantly raised my eyes and I saw his hunger,

191

his intent and I found I couldn't swallow.

He said, 'I can't deny it. What you said the other night. I can't let it go. All I wanted to do was establish the facts around Tom's death, no more, no less. And your refusal to cooperate, your manipulative lies undermines what we're trying to achieve here. If we can't establish any trust, any mutual understanding, this entire project is doomed.'

He paused, said, 'Any thoughts?'

I thought that it was just as well he was going to kill me before he drove me insane. I shook my head and blank comforting spaces appeared in my reason.

'Your silence confirms all our fears. I believe that every one of us here identifies you as the cause of our discontent. I feel that I speak for all of us when I say that if we don't act now, your future conduct will only ensure further unrest.' He paused and stepped away from me, took in everybody that watched. 'If anybody voiced any disagreement I would be surprised and shocked but everybody here will get a chance to tell us as this procedure will require a public vote.' He looked at me, smiled. 'You're about to be tried by your peers. A fair and democratic process. Any objections?'

I stared silently at him. Any response would be futile, possibly suicidal. He could interpret anything as an invitation to cut my throat. Just waiting for the opportunity. Of course, my silence could be taken as all the reason he needed. My head continued to dissolve.

He stood before me again. 'I'll take that as a no.' He looked happy, like he'd waited too long for this. 'Let's start, shall we? Please indicate you recognise the authority of this court and your willingness to accept its findings.'

I stared at him and I found I couldn't open my mouth.

'A nod will suffice.'

I nodded stiffly.

'Good. I propose your execution here and now on the grounds that you're a lying asshole. Does anybody object to the motion?'

I said, 'Trent.'

'Shut up.' He watched the group, allowed the silence to ring loud and clear. 'Anybody want to come up here and defend him?'

I said, 'Trent, please.'

'Shut the fuck up. How do you expect me to hear anybody leaping to your defence?' He paused, surveyed the group one last time. None of them met his gaze, none of them moved. 'Looks like no one gives a shit.' He turned to me, said, 'You're out of luck, Rob. Out of time.' He gripped my right shoulder and held up his right index finger. 'I'm going to start by taking out your eyes. But you know how this goes. We only have nine hours til dawn so we better get started.'

I felt my knees start to give and in a rush of desperate horror I said, 'Trent, we need to talk.' I spoke urgently, barely above a whisper. 'There's something you need to know.'

He smiled as his index finger felt its way around my left eye. Said distractedly, 'What is it?'

'Not here.'

I closed my eyes tight as his finger applied pressure to my eyeball. 'You'll tell me *now*.'

'It's Jake. He's going to kill you.'

I felt his finger pull back and I dared to open my eyes. I stared into his face and all his good humor had evaporated.

I said, 'He's going to kill you. Mason and Ethan are with him. They've got everything they need, believe me.'

Trent's eyes flashed and he turned angrily to the crowd, releasing me, searching for Jake. He found him, saw Jake understanding and a numbing horror come over him. Trent said, 'Jake, get the fuck up here.'

Everybody around him moved away, cleared a large space and Jake found himself alone, looking about him.

Trent said, 'Ninja ghost, I want to talk to you' and Jake's legs acted independently of his body, betraying him. He approached us and he looked at me. I saw disbelief, a mute appeal. I have no idea what he saw in mine.

Trent said, 'Want to guess what Rob just told me?'

Jake shook his head, stuttered, 'I have no idea.'

'He just told me that you're planning on killing me.'

Jake's eyes flicked to me and I saw terror. 'Liar. Like you said. Always lying.'

Trent looked at me, made sure I had his attention. 'That's the least of it. Did you know Rob works for Beth?'

My heart froze and I breathed out slowly as I tried to grasp the scope of her betrayal.

'They go way back. Long before this shit show got going. But I don't suppose he told you any of that. He's been spying on all of you. Running back to Beth with every little whisper. Remember Paul?'

Jake stared at me, nodded.

Trent said, 'Course you do. He was a buddy of yours, wasn't he? Rob told Beth he'd been sowing discontent amongst the masses. Union talk, I'd wager. Fight back, he said. So we killed him. Here in front of you. Like Amy. Like John. Who else was there? I've lost count.'

Trent looked at me. 'You remember, don't you, Rob? How many?'

My voice, weak, whispery. 'Seven.'

'*Seven*. All dead. Because they trusted Rob with their plans. Their *lives*. But I find it hard to believe all those people were that stupid. Maybe Rob just didn't like them. Wouldn't surprise me if they were entirely innocent and Rob thought he'd just get rid of them.'

Trent reached out and turned me towards everybody and I met their eyes. 'Now Beth wants nothing to do with him anymore. This little cockroach even turns her stomach. I don't know, could be a lovers tiff. But old habits die hard, just can't stop himself signing your death warrants, so here he is, in front of all of you, getting Jake killed. But if he expects me to kill you at his bidding he's in for a surprise. Rob isn't going to pull my strings. This lying piece of shit thinks he can play me. So for everybody here, and for all your dead friends, I will tear his head off. It'll be an honor.'

Trent turned to me, tightened his grip on my shoulder. My knees buckled under the pain but he held me up and clamped his right hand under my jaw and prepared to push and tear. 'Pucker up.' I stared into his gleeful eyes and my hands gripped his forearm and pulled helplessly at it. His grip under my jaw tightened, my tendons stretched as he pushed my head back and up. My spine at the base of my neck was compacted, twisted and I started to choke, thinking my jaw would tear off before my head as his fingers dug in and I couldn't scream and I could feel something coming apart and he released me. I backed away gasping for breath, watched Trent in anticipation of resuming his attack but he turned his back on me and I was aware that the group immediately retreated. Jake joined them, trying to get as much space between us as they possibly could, their escape cut off by the creatures encircling us.

It was then that I saw Beth. She was standing beyond Trent, watching him as he straightened his back, hitting his full height, his arms braced at his side. He looked as primed for violence as Beth looked relaxed.

Trent said, 'Been talking to your boy.'

Beth stared.

Trent said, 'You still fucking him?'

Beth stared.

Trent said, 'I'm going to kill him. I'm going to kill anybody who tries to stop me.'

Beth spoke. In a language I'd never heard before. A rich, complex phrasing that multiplied sinuously.

He barked at her viciously. 'In *English*.'

Beth ignored him and she spoke again in that alien tongue, her voice husky, honeyed and sweet.

A furious Trent uttered a short phrase in what I can only imagine was meant to be the same language. Crude and guttural, it died in his throat. He tried again, more growls that died an ugly death.

Beth said, 'You're only fit for pulling the wings off flies.'

Trent marched towards her, his shoulders bunching, hands clenching and becoming fists. He stopped within inches of her and looked down on the slight figure before him. She was at least eight inches shorter than him, weighed half as much and yet his arms remained at his side. He didn't even raise a hand to her. I thought, *he's afraid of her*, and my racing, ragged breath caught in my throat.

She met his fury with calm grace, patiently waiting for his inevitable capitulation. Her authority crushed him, dismissed him with casual ease, and he conceded with a helpless shriek of '*FUCK*'. She said, 'It's over. You'll leave them be.' He stared at her and she held his gaze until he finally broke by averting his head. She turned and walked away.

Trent roared at her back and turned to me, came at

me like a freight train. He picked me up by the front of my jacket and I stared into the promise of death. Humiliation was a new experience and it cut him deeper than he could reach. He said something I couldn't understand in that language he could only butcher and snarl and I knew I was marked.

He threw me to one side and by the time I got to my feet he was gone. All of those creatures were gone.

***

I pulled my Browning and levelled it at Jake's head, right between the eyes where the heart of his fucking stupidity festered. I said, 'Say it, I *fucking* dare you.'

Jake said, 'You murdering fuck.'

I fired a shot, cleared his head by six inches. Found the urge to empty the gun into his face overwhelming as a white raging light took hold of me. 'They would have got us all killed and so would you so don't you *fucking* dare. *Any* of you. The only reason you're standing there giving me shit is because I sold my fucking soul to keep you alive. I know what I've done and what it cost me and trust me, you have no idea.

'You owe me every precious breath you take. Those stupid fuckers would have put you in the ground. I did it for you and *fuck* knows why.

'And now you're free. You can run. And that's down to me as well. So don't you *fucking* dare.'

***

I woke in a haze of vertigo, falling to the ceiling. I was in a bed and I didn't know where. My head ached, my neck and jaw was bruised and stiff. Every movement sent bolts of pain through me.

I staggered to my feet, bitching and groaning, and stood at the window in the pale light and I dug in my pocket for my keys. They were there and I had everything I needed.

I drove round town, stopped at Abby's, went by Jean's. Everybody had gone, they'd wasted no time in clearing out.

I remembered music. Beth.

**

At noon I pulled into the college car park. I sat on my dropped tailgate, huddled into my jacket under grey skies against the chill and waited for her. Again. Always her.

At midnight I said, 'Hello Beth.'

'Robert.'

'You need a ride?'

'Where you heading?'

'Where do you want to go?'

'East. Over the mountains. I've heard a lot of interesting things.'

Clear as Dae

Sam Fletcher

Six of us sat circled on the rooftop of some apartment building downtown. It hadn't rained for a few hours, but large puddles remained all around us.

We hadn't spoken in a while. I felt tense; wasn't sure why. My fingers wrapped tight around the grip of my revolver. I pulled it from my hoodie pocket, held the barrel to my temple.

And all their eyes were on me. Still, none of them spoke.

So I pulled the hammer back.

All of them—especially Summer—had that worried look on their faces, but I knew they weren't. A smile crept slow on my lips, and I pulled the trigger.

The shot rang out. My blood stained the tiles as my head smacked onto them.

The last thing I heard was her gasp. Then, my ears ringing.

I blinked a few times against my blurry reality, then

sat up once I had the composure. The words fumbled from my bloody lips.

"I've always wanted to do that."

No one was amused. "Fucking lunatic," Caleb said, could hardly look at me now.

They moved to the building's ledge. I stared at the moon, lighting all of us. Right. *Luna*.

From my other pocket I pulled out a flask with a shaking hand, almost unable to pour its contents into my sunken jaw.

I managed to swallow a large gulp of—merlot, I've been calling it. The teeth-stainer. It didn't heal the gaping hole in my skull, but it helped.

I mocked the others to myself as they stared out unto the night like gargoyles. The city was dampened by fog. I don't know how any of them could see a thing.

As blood crusted over my face, I crept over and joined Caleb. He continued to surveil the city.

"Are we feeding for ourselves tonight?" I asked him. "Or—"

I took his silence as the 'or' option.

"*Why*?" I asked. Like a whiny child, probably. "Miksa is plenty capable of serving themselves."

Caleb peered over at me as if I were a moron. "Miksa is a *thousand* years old," he said. "For a thousand years they've studied the mystic arts. To get a drop of Miksa's knowledge is a blessing. If you don't understand that, there's nothing I can do for you."

I looked at the others, who were quiet and tense as Caleb said this, staring out among the mist. They were restraining their thoughts, I could tell. Miksa could be anywhere, always watching. No way their servitude was as willing as they made it seem.

I cut their focus with delayed laughter. "Vratislav practically ruled all central Europe in the 11th century," I said. I'd done plenty of research on Miksa's relatives. "Edward the Third had the greatest army in the Hundred Years' War. George Washington was the commander and chief of the revolution. And Miksa has—us?"

Nobody laughed, just kept staring into the fog like cowards.

"What do we need them for?" I asked Caleb. "How old are you?"

"178," he said.

"Right, Union soldier," I said. "What about you guys?" I looked to my left. Everyone's feet dangled off the roof ledge.

"134," said John. "I transitioned during—we called them Asiatic exclusion riots—not too far from here." He looked to the others. "Anthony and Cameron are married, ain't that right? How old are you now, 50?"

"Man, shut the hell up," Cameron said, sitting on his skateboard now. Anthony's was sticking up from his backpack.

"49 and 51," Anthony said.

"What do you mean, married?" Summer asked.

"They transitioned during the same event," John said.

"Which was?" I asked.

"Rodney King," said Cameron.

The age disparity still confused me. Caleb did look the oldest, but only by a couple years. Really, we all looked about the same. Hardly old enough for facial hair.

"I suppose you and Summer are married too," John said.

We didn't look at each other, her and I. I could tell they all were thinking about last fall, the circumstances that led to us being bit. Me by Caleb, her by Miksa.

"We all transitioned during war," Summer said.

"People are most honest then," I said.

Caleb shook his head. "War's around us always. Race wars. Class wars. Strong versus weak, weak versus strong, it never goes away." He nodded his head to the street over. A guy in a jacket, flat brim, sunglasses, and COVID mask walked into the corner market. "And neither do soldiers."

"Who's that?" Summer asked.

"Caleb's been watching him for months," John said.

"I like this guy," Caleb said. "*He* makes people honest." He looked to Summer. "Watch what happens; tell me who you'd pick."

Summer held tightly onto the rain gutter. A tattooed python spiraled down her arm.

The minimart had glass doors and big windows on both sides. The guy got in line and waited his turn.

"I don't want to prey," she said.

"That's why we *pick*," Caleb said. "Shut up. Watch."

When he reached the cashier, the man palmed a gun to the counter.

Everyone else in the place fell to the floor when they saw, the second cashier too. The robber and the first cashier talked for a bit, but I couldn't hear them.

From the kitchen behind the counter, a knife slid across the floor to the cashier's feet. He seemed to notice it immediately but didn't want to rouse the robber's suspicion. He clenched the knife between his shoes.

"Him," Summer said, "the cook. If I *have* to."

Caleb shook his head. "You don't want a hero."

The cashier casually reached for the knife but couldn't grab it without bending down more. He danced in this awkward tension before opening the register and unloading the cash.

The robber snatched it desperately and stuffed it in his pockets.

"The villain, then?" Summer asked.

Below their dangling feet, a girl emerged from the fog and entered the alley. Caleb nodded her way.

"She was behind the guy with a can of iced tea," he said. "When he pulled out the gun, she ducked down and walked out the back with two weeks of groceries."

John, Cameron, and Anthony leaped down onto the fire escape.

Summer and I took after them, dropping from platform to platform. Caleb simply scaled down the bricks like some douchey spider.

It didn't matter, anyway. The girl was already through to the other side. Cameron and Anthony hopped on their boards and followed.

The two of them caught up first, obviously. They grabbed her by the arms and dragged her back into the darkness as she flailed and screamed. Her tea rolled across the asphalt. All of her groceries spewed about.

She was poor, I could tell; I wished I could tell her she wouldn't want the food much longer.

Caleb pulled a rope from his pack and struggled to tie her hands behind her. She kept screaming; almost all of us helped fasten the rope between her upper and lower jaw.

Summer held back. Having flashbacks, perhaps.

Even with the rope around her head, the girl wouldn't shut up. She kicked and kicked until her legs were tied. Sometimes we don't have to do that.

And then, the darkness was stolen from us. Red and blue painted the bricks. She screamed loud at the siren's echo.

This pissed me off. I'm not afraid of pigs, but I'd prefer not to talk to one.

I put my palm over the girl's mouth, sealing the parts the rope couldn't. Huh; my black polish was almost completely worn off. She screamed into my hand. Even muffled, easily they could hear it the street over.

"Just—sleep!" I yelled. Lost my cool for a second.

And she did. Knocked unconscious, like nothing.

Everyone dropped her, and we looked at each other. They all looked at me, more like.

"That's… unusual, isn't it?" I asked.

I'd only ever seen Caleb impressed by Miksa. "You've been practicing?" he asked me.

"Practicing what?"

Squad lights kept dancing across everyone's irises. We all put a hand on her and carried her out the other way, back into the dark.

Caleb's pick-up was down the block. He slung the girl over his shoulder. "Split her six ways?" I asked as we ducked into another alley.

"We're not biting her six times," Summer said.

"Fine. We'll rotate. I'd rather one of us gets her than Miksa."

"Enough, Dae," Caleb said. "We're due." He threw her into the bed of his Ford; Cameron and Anthony hopped in back too.

I put in headphones on the way to the chateau while the others talked. It was an hour drive, out of the city, up a mountain. The old rig was loud as hell; I was sick of hearing it.

Caleb puttered up the steep cliff until the trees cleared. Miksa's turrets were perhaps the only things that stood above them. The fog was even thicker up here.

A pack of wolves guarded the property, but they must have finally learned to recognize our headlights. They didn't bother us so much anymore.

Cameron and Anthony carried the girl, but all of us walked through the haze to the front door. Caleb, of course, clanked the door knocker.

They dropped the girl to the stone porch, and we waited for a moment. Bats scraped at the eave above us.

To my surprise, the door creaked open. Moonlight revealed Miksa's chiseled features, their clean face above long, dangling arms and tucked batwings. If they weren't hunched over so, they'd stand clear above the doorway, a good ten feet at least.

They stooped even farther and sniffed the offering. Chin nearly touching the floor, their pupils shot up at Caleb. "Is it dead?" they asked.

He shook his head. "Dae knocked her out."

Miksa sprung up, eye level with me. "Then you will carry it to the basement for me. Come in."

I picked the girl up. It wasn't as hard as it used to be.

"All of us?" Caleb asked.

"No," Miksa said, harshly. Once I was in, the door slammed behind me.

I'd never been in Miksa's main entrance before. They led the way, walking with their long, hairy arms as crutches and their legs trailing behind. Their black wings nearly blended with their cloak.

Candles lined the walls and long rugs the floor. Miksa hobbled over to a large wooden door and slid it to the side, revealing a spiral staircase. As I followed them down, a red glow took over.

The basement was hot, smelling of sweat and blood. All the lights down here were red. When Miksa stepped in, a wall of bodies came alive, rattling against their chains, angry, trying to break free. Wall to wall of this sauna prisoners were locked in, nude.

I dropped the girl to the concrete floor when I saw. Still, she didn't wake.

"Why keep them alive?" I asked over muffled grunts. The odor only worsened. Miksa's head whipped in my direction.

A thin smile grew slowly across their face. "Everyone's blood tastes different, I'm sure you've found that by now." They slid their long, black nails down a man's cheek. His chest heaved up and down as they did it. "I like to know truly who my victims are, know truly how worthy they are of this power.

"And—" Miksa spread their wings and danced to the other side. They looked deeply into a woman's eyes. "I like them to know truly who I am too." Their voice fell deep as they said this.

"A freak?"

They ignored this and shrunk back down to observe the fallen girl. "You pistol-whipped her, is that right?"

I crinkled my brow. "No."

They stood to meet my eyes again. Next their icy hand brushed my cheek. "I know you didn't," they said. "Why carry it, then?"

"It's a toy," I said. "Like a squirt gun to a child."

"Do you not trust your power, Daemon?"

"My power?"

"Is—*unfathomable*." That low voice again. Now high. "Does that scare you?"

I eyed them up and down. "I don't want to look like a bat."

A reptilian smile grew up their face again. They began to shrink, down to my height, as did their wings into their arms. Their face broadened; their hair retracted.

"Of course not," they said. "You want to be a strong man."

What was left *was* a man—more masculine than I had ever seen Miksa. The man was so familiar, recognized mostly from photos. It was my dad.

Catharsis hit like a bullet would in the old days.

Miksa could tell. I didn't know they could transform this way. Didn't know how they knew what he looked like.

"I don't want to be that piece of shit," I finally said.

As Miksa knelt to pick the girl up by her wrist, their feminine features reemerged. They looked like themself again, but more human than I knew they could be.

"Stop carrying his toys, then." Miksa sounded angry, as if I disappointed them. They chained the girl to the wall, snug between two squirming bodies.

Miksa seemed to take note of my headwound before falling back into the darkness of the staircase. "You call me a freak, but we're the same and you know so," they said. "'Outcast' doesn't cover half of it. You were excluded always, weren't you? Left outside until the inside was blinding."

I nodded, deciding if I should engage. But they were right. "As if I'm trapped in a movie, and all of my frames are opposite everyone around me," I said. "We appear in the same scene, we interact, but they can never truly see me. There's something off, always."

We wandered back through the hallway, to a second set of stairs. Miksa continued to ascend, and I followed. "I know what that does to a person," they said. "When you're young, you do everything you can to belong. But you matured, didn't you Daemon? And what did you learn?"

"People treat loneliness like a curse," I said. "But it's a power only few will really know."

Miksa unhinged the latch of the door and opened it to their terrace. "You've only scratched the surface of this power," they said. We stepped out onto the roof, the turret's cones the only things above us. Blurry trees made their shape through the fog. "When you cannot connect with anyone, when no one cares truly, nothing is to stop your wildest, darkest fantasies from coming true."

"Not caring is passive," I said. "What I felt—what I've always felt—is active. People went out of their way to push me out, push me to this freedom."

"How do you think I ended up all the way out here?" Miksa asked. They stretched their back, chin pointed up at the veil of moonlight cutting through the fog. They howled, and their pacing canines all howled back.

They looked at me, amused, but I wasn't. "Here's what you don't understand, Daemon." Their smile faded. "This role you've taken, the perverted jester, it only works when death is on the other side. It works because everyone around you is afraid of death, and you aren't. That puts you above them.

"Jest to the mortals all you want, but you also must learn to behave. *Everyone* around you now is as lonely, as broken, as strong."

I shook my head. "I feel no closer to the dead than I did to the living."

"Of course you don't!" Miksa put their arm over my shoulders, positioning me toward the hazy horizon. "Close your eyes. Tell me what you see."

I did as I was told. "Darkness."

"I can't remember seeing anything but," they said. "So, tell me what you see in the darkness."

I took a deep breath, thinking this was stupid. But as I let it out, I understood. Immediately. Caleb and the other goons had almost made it back to town, but Summer wasn't with them. Summer fled. She stayed on the mountain, alone.

Not everyone was free as me. Summer was just now feeling loneliness's sting. Her whole family knew she died. They were still mourning. Still looking for her body, maybe. She hadn't truly made it to the other side yet.

But I felt more. Thousands more. Flying through the sky, hopping shadow to shadow, hunting, lurking, hiding, being. Unending gangs of the undead, just like mine. All touched by fog, all touched by Miksa.

I opened my eyes, pulled back from their embrace, looked at them. They were right. This was a power I didn't understand.

"You are different from all of them," they said. "A body is dropped on my doorstep each night, gallons of fresh blood at my disposal, because none of my servants can truly escape the fear they think they've embodied. Not as you have."

Miksa stared into my eyes. "You've never served anyone in your life, have you Daemon? That's what makes you special. That's what makes you like me. But if you want to taste this power truly, you must *behave*."

Miksa saw me, unflickering. I nodded.

"I'm all you have, all you will *ever* have. Do you understand?"

I nodded once again.

"Good." They smiled. "Because those who cannot see through the fog—" They squeezed their long, pale fingers into a fist, and a terrible screech came from above. A loud, awful scream rang out through the sky. Something was being tortured.

I looked up, wincing, seeing nothing but mist.

Miksa opened their palm, and a lifeless bat fell into it. "—get consumed by it."

They dropped the bat to the stone floor, freeing their bloody hand to brush my cheek. "You'll be just fine. You simply need a bit of clarity."

Just as they said the word, the fog thinned all around us until the night was clear.

I looked out through the trees; I could see the ocean now. Miksa walked out in front, appreciating too the unending starry horizon.

I wanted to learn this power, and serving Miksa seemed beyond fair. But I didn't feel like it right now. When they turned around, I disappeared.

Gone into a fog that enveloped them once again.

Rain came down as I flew. Was Miksa doing this? What a stupid thought. They're not Thor.

I had no idea how I was moving this way, but I felt nothing doing it but Summer's sadness. It pulled me in from down the mountain, consumed my every thought and emotion. Nothing compared to the feeling, but it was proof enough that Miksa was lying. There were other powers out there. The hell Summer was doing in a literal cave was anyone's guess.

I could hardly see her as I solidified on the cave lips; I must have appeared as a silhouette at most against the mucus outside.

She looked up from her folded arms, sniffled. "M-Miksa?"

"It's Dae," I said.

She stood and moved closer, slowly. I couldn't wait. I tugged her by her wrist the rest of the way and kissed her. Her lips were salty, but soft. I pulled back before I could enjoy it.

"We're not married," I said. Water dripped from my hair. "We don't have to see each other again, even."

"You've—always wanted to do that?" she guessed.

"Married doesn't mean anything," I said. "Neither does vampire." I turned around just a little to listen to the wind whistle against the rocks. It was growing louder. "You're free," I said, not looking at her. "That's really what I came here to tell you. What you need to understand. Genuinely—*free*."

My back was now to her. There would be consequences for being here. But when I took a step to the opening, I felt her cold hand latch tight to my wrist.

Curse of Avalon

Anthony Regolino

The fog had lifted earlier that morn, allowing the travelers to proceed more easily. England's weather had proved to be a hindrance to so many of their journeys and tourneys as of late, and this fortuitous break was most welcome. The sun even visited their skyline and remained unblocked and in view for most of the time, lighting their path readily and seemingly intent on sticking around till at least their afternoon's repast. It dried the ground and evaporated any mist that threatened to remain from earlier, which further assisted them in their travels.

But if the climate was fairer than usual, the volatile conditions of the land's people remained unabated. They still pounded the earth as they pounded each other, turning the island into a nest of angry hornets, with too many "kings" vying for control of it. The goal of forming a united realm was in everyone's heart, but the notion of who should wear the crown differed in every county—

sometimes in every house.

The constant warring was finally wearing away at not only the bodies but the souls of the people, and even the kings realized that a kingdom would be nothing without a populace left to fill it. After many trials and debates, one king proved himself to be virtuous enough for the role of leadership over all the isle's peoples, but by his own actions he put his worthiness in question when he allowed his base, humanly needs to come before those of his subjects.

This man was Uther Pendragon, and he brought strife back to his domain for the love of a woman that was not his. With the aid of his royal magician—an aged seer named Merlin, who claims to have lived for centuries—King Uther replaced the woman's husband and made her his own wife once her spouse was fatally dispatched.

Even were he not intimately acquainted with the possible fates that awaited them, Merlin could clearly see that this king would not have the loyalty of his people for long. He conceived of a plan to save the realm, but it would not necessarily save this king from his destiny. Before he agreed to help the king attain the object of his passion, he gave one condition—that the product of the king's union with the wife be given to him, so that he may take the newborn away until the young heir was ready to assume the throne himself.

The babe was placed in a house, far from any courtly intrigues, so that when Uther's indiscretions finally resulted in his own demise, his immediate descendant would be safe and unable to be found and snuffed from existence by those who would wish to ensure the end of Uther's line of succession. Not even the child, nor those in whose care Merlin placed him, would know of his birthright.

The next step was to find a way to announce the next high king, and to this end Merlin hit upon the notion of a test. Before the inevitable could happen to Uther, he convinced the king to help him set the way for his son to replace him. Giving up his sword, with which he had proven his mettle time and again in both battle and contests, Uther did as Merlin bade him. This was done none too soon, for it was shortly after that Uther was poisoned and his body laid to its eternal rest. When his sword was sought out to lay on top of his body in honor and respect, it was nowhere to be found.

Thus the realm was committed to a period of unrest for nearly two decades. During that time, Merlin had retreated to seclusion, convincing the masses further that dark times had forever fallen upon them. They had lost their sovereign, and they did not even have his mystical advisor around to help guide them and tell them what to do.

So when he finally did return, it was a cold reception that awaited him. And when he expected people to accept a young man who had not even attained knighthood as their new king, he was suspected of using trickery to achieve his own ends. Eventually he was able to convince many of the youth's right to succession, but there was still a long way to go before that title could be held without challenge. Which leads to our travellers and their mysterious quest, of which none but one understand.

The weather may have brightened, but the land was still rough on the route they had taken, and only one of them knew their destination, leaving the troupe to silently bemoan the conditions of the course they were forced to take. For the final leg of the journey, only two proceeded onward, the old man and the young king.

Wishing he had stayed home to better get to know

his new bride, Arthur—the sequestered offspring who grew up to pass the test and become king—tied his steed to a tree and numbly followed the old man who had changed his life so greatly. They approached a body of water, on which Arthur saw no fishing boat or larger vessel. Wondering why he had been dragged out on this fool's errand, he gazed casually over the water's surface.

There was something under the water. That much he could tell, but he could not make out what it was. As Arthur inched further along a rocky promontory that extended outward from the lakefront almost to the point where the shimmering image persisted, he fought to keep his footing. Slipping and stumbling as he struggled to avoid sliding into the water, he wished he had first removed the armor he now wore. It may protect him from unseen foes, but it made his careful steps more treacherous and would endanger his life should he take a misstep and plunge into the mysterious depths.

He hesitated—no, he froze in place—glancing about and searching for a safe place to put down his foot next, but to the wizened figure watching him from the shore it must have looked like he was giving up. Merlin called out to him, encouraging him to proceed, and if it were any other man Arthur would have yelled at him in fury. But Arthur had too much respect—and admittedly fear—for the mystic, to speak to him in such a way.

Opting for a more cautious approach, he dropped down to his knees and managed to creep along to where he was in reach of the submerged object. The sparkling reflections of light on the water faded as a cloud blocked the sun overhead, and as he waited for it to pass he turned back to let the warlock know what he thought it could be.

"I think it's a sword," Arthur said disappointedly, "plunged into the sandy bottom."

"Can you reach it?" Merlin asked, with hope and eagerness in his voice.

"What's the point?" Arthur uttered with disgust, the closest he'd ever come to raising his voice to the sorcerer. "It's surely rusted to uselessness by now."

"Not if it's enchanted, as I believe it to be," came the reply. "Recall the one you drew from the stone, the one that helped you attain your kingly status. If this is the one I expect resides in this location, it would do even more to assure your position."

Arthur looked back at him with an expression of doubt that was apparently clear to see despite the distance between them and the shadow cast by his helmet's raised visor. But if this weapon was in some way imbued embued with a mystical charm, as the one Merlin mentioned had turned out to be, this could be the answer he was looking for.

Arthur's true father—Uther Pendragon—placed that other sword into a rock, and there it remained under Merlin's spell. Whosoever could remove the sword from the secure hold of the rock (actually, of the magic binding it) would lay claim to his title as king of the Britons. Everyone who was considered worthy—and some who weren't but insisted anyway, using might over right—attempted to lift the sword out, but always to no avail.

When Arthur's heritage and direct lineage to Uther was revealed by Merlin, even Arthur himself doubted the old man's words. He was allowed—mainly through Merlin's intimidating insistence—to try to pull the sword from its resting place, and he did so with such extreme ease—much to his own surprise—that many of those present were convinced they were in the presence of majesty.

But not everyone accepted his birthright or claim to

the title, and feuding began, threatening to prevent Arthur from uniting the land and protecting its people, as the king of the Britons was prophesied to do. If that one mystic act wasn't enough to win over his adversaries, perhaps another would do the trick. After all, they could discount one incident as a fluke or an outright accidental mistake—a slip in the spell's power perhaps—but if Arthur were to be *twice* blessed to retrieve a magical item intended only for the king, how could they then deny it, or him. An item such as . . .

"Escalibore," Merlin spoke reverently, in answer to the young king's unasked question.

Arthur's eyes darted back to the spot where the sword was buried. He waited for the sun to peek out again, and when it did he questioned his senses—his sanity even—for what he then saw. The sword was not alone. Below it was a shape, and whatever it was held the sword in place just as the rock did that secured his father's sword in place. Removing his helmet, for its faceplate constantly threatened to fall from all his bending forward, he leaned closer to the surface to ascertain what he thought he saw.

"It's held by a woman," he muttered in disbelief, and the old man behind him had hearing as sharp as his vision.

"The Lady of the Lake," Merlin breathed in awe. "I myself had thought her a myth. Now surely we know that sword to be the one. Escalibore it is, or I'm not worth my salt as a soothsayer."

"Nimue," Arthur whispered to himself, for he had heard the legends as well, and upon hearing the name the female opened her eyes, fixed them upon his own, and bestowed on him the most beatific smile he could ever hope to see.

His heart melted. He had to know more about her.

Why was she under all that water? How could she live there in this way? Who had put this curse upon her, and how does one break it to set her free? Some of these questions managed to escape his lips, and Merlin offered what little he knew in response.

"She bears the sword of kings. I have heard her described as both its guardian and its prisoner. It keeps her in place—I know not how—and she in turn keeps it for its next rightful owner. A king, of course, but not just any. It is meant for the one who is destined to have it and use it to save and protect the realm. To unite the land and bring peace unto its people. It is a time anticipated with great expectation—second only, perhaps, to the Second Coming itself!

"Of the Lady herself," Merlin continued, "she will be freed when the sword's owner comes to claim it. I believe this to be you, Arthur."

The king could not take his eyes from the beauty below. She seemed to lie flat on the lake bed, the sword perpendicular to her as it stood with its hilt inviting him to grasp. He marveled at how her golden hair and soft white gown managed to sway with the motions of the water, but without appearing to be soaked or even slightly damp. More enchantment? How else? What else could explain how she yet lived when she never seemed to take a breath?

Her eyes beckoned to him, the sword seemingly held out, proffered, to him. Memories of his reaching out to take his father's sword from the stone it was in returned to him, but this would not be as easy, given its location. He wondered if he could even reach it, and if not could she hold it out a bit more. Forcing himself to break eye contact with her so he could look down at the sword itself, his blood suddenly turned cold.

She could not hold it out further. She wasn't handing

it up to him. The sword was planted in the sandy lake bottom, and its blade went straight through the maiden's midsection, staking her in place as well. *She* was the stone this time. Without a second's thought, he dove his gauntleted fist into the water, leaning over as much as he dared so that he could take hold of the weapon that pinned her down. He felt its handle against his palm, wrapped his fingers around it, and yanked hard.

He stumbled back as it came free, and only then did he worry what this may do to the girl. There had been no blood in the pool of water before; would this suddenly release all that she held? He began scrabbling back from where he fell and was about to return to the water's edge when he suddenly saw something emerge from it. Climbing out of the lake, her head down as she crawled on all fours, the Mistress of Escalibore, Nimue, was finally freed from her watery grave.

She made her way to him in this fashion, her hair hanging forward over her face. It was now fully soaked, as was the cloth that clung to her frail body. Arthur reasoned that the spell had been broken, and that she must be chilled and in need of warmth. He would have rushed to her but he was still in a sitting position, and before he could begin his efforts to rise in his full armor she was already upon him.

Merlin was saying something, trying to get his attention, but he could wait. This waif required his full attention now. He spread his arms to embrace her, despite the fact that his body heat was being blocked by the metal suit he wore. He wrapped his arms around her, noting how thin and small she was. The clinging clothes let him count her ribs, and he decided she needed food fast. He told her as much, and asked her to let him rise so he could lead her back to shore where he could provide something to satisfy her hunger. But she would not let go, and she lifted her face till it was mere inches from his own.

The effect upon meeting those eyes was overwhelming. He didn't see a near-drowned waif any longer but a voluptuous creature who emitted life and vigor. Her hair didn't even seem damp, but was somehow soft and luxurious, curling waves of grain falling in yellow ringlets about her neck and shoulders. He could not see beyond her full bosom to tell if her ribs were protruding or not, and when he returned his gaze to her face he saw that her lips were even painted in rouge. She was the very picture of life itself. Had the spell returned? Maybe she was still bound to the sword in some way, and her proximity to it restored her enchantment.

The slippery rocks made it impossible for an old man like Merlin to traverse, but he made the attempt anyway, since Arthur could not hear his words. He made his way as quickly as he could, but his footing was unsure and he was forced to repeatedly stop and reassess where his next step should fall. He saw the drenched being in Arthur's arms and the way he was looking at her. He knew he had to save the king from himself.

As for Arthur, he was lost in the water nymph's eyes. Her lips parted, inviting him to taste, and he thought of how different those full lips were from . . . there was a name he couldn't quite place. And her hair, so light, not like that of . . . again, the name eluded him.

He wanted to drown in her eyes, devour her mouth, but something held him back. It was with great effort of will that he did not crush her to him and ravage those lips. In truth, it was the sword that he still wielded which allowed him to resist. It drew upon his nobility and righteousness and focused these so that the line where intention meets action was not crossed.

And yet, he could not look away or release her, or push her far from him as he should. Instead he watched the tip of her tongue as it tenderly swept over her top teeth. There was something not right, but he couldn't decide what it could be. Something about her teeth, perhaps. Their length or shape.

As he tried to figure out what it was that looked wrong, their appearance altered before him. They seemed to grow longer, but rather than simply extending out further they tapered off to points, giving the impression of an animal's fangs.

He sensed her next action just slightly before she made it, and the small sideways motion he was able to perform saved his life, for her thrusting mouth hit upon the metal of his armor rather than his neck. Grateful that he had never removed his suit as he had thought about doing earlier, he brought up a hand to protect his neck from a second attempt, then realized that his other hand was holding something.

Escalibore! He had forgotten all about it in his entrancement. He moved his hand away from where it guarded his neck and pushed her away so he could have enough room to use the sword. With one motion Escalibore's blade sliced the creature's head from her body, and he watched as it fell with eyes still open.

Its eyes suddenly turned to focus on him, and he panicked that her gaze might capture him again in its spell when something suddenly came between them. Merlin's robes offered the barrier he needed, as the wizard bent down and lifted the severed head so that it was facing away from both of them.

"No blood," the king observed, finally realizing that nothing had spurt forth from either head or neck.

"It may have a little bit within," Merlin commented, "giving it enough power to compel and exert its will. It probably made you see it as some magnificent angel."

"Yes," Arthur informed the mage. "I saw the most beautiful vision I could imagine. I felt it willing me to submit, to give in to desire, and thus exposing myself to its feeding frenzy. But Escalibore gave me strength to fight back."

Merlin wrapped the head within folds of his robe, asking Arthur to help him get back to the shore, where they could find a sack to place it in and some vines to tie around it for added protection. When asked what he would do with it, Merlin replied that he would get a blessed wafer of Holy Communion and place it inside its mouth, then burn the head for good measure. "The body you could just push into the lake," he added before they left the rocky platform.

"The blood remained inside," Merlin elaborated, "because it doesn't actually *flow* throughout its veins. There is no beating heart to pump it, no pulse to drive it along. It probably just lies in the thing's belly or some other organ that animates it. It isn't alive, as you and I know of life. It takes no air into its lungs and doesn't take nourishment from food. It lives on the blood of others, and considering how long it must have been under there it must have been starving for more."

"You know of these . . . *things*?" the king asked of his mentor.

"I'm familiar with legends about them," the ancient wizard acknowledged. "Stories really. Never expected to actually meet one, and certainly didn't expect the Lady of the Lake to be one of them. If anything, I would have thought her to be a water nymph, not a siren."

"Is that was she was?" Arthur asked with interest. "A siren?"

"I'm not sure," Merlin admitted. "There are so many things she could be. From what I've heard Greeks speak of, she could have been a gorgon or vrykolakas. A mermaid isn't out of the question either. And long ago my travels brought me to lands that feared a thing called the strigoi, which seems to be what this thing was. Then again, they may all be one and the same, or close cousins to each other."

After rolling the lifeless body into the water, Arthur eyed the rolled-up bundle warily. Merlin chided him, telling him not to give it another thought, and remarked with a dry chuckle, "At any rate, like never before, you have *earned* the name Pendragon that your father once claimed." Arthur considered this, recalling how the appellation's roots were quite literally "head" and "dragon."

The young king helped the older man back to the shore, and further back to the trees where their horses were tied. Arthur was relieved to find that both their animals and supplies were not stolen—always a good thing, finding your horses and goods untouched. Not wanting to put it down, Arthur took one last long look at the prize in his hand before securing it in a saddlebag. He wouldn't wear it in a scabbard out here; it was far too precious for that. Escalibore was meant to wield when charging into battle, or when presenting at formal functions. For scaring off bandits or wild beasts, a lesser weapon would suffice.

They set up a site for a campfire, and as the younger man hunted for rabbits to eat, the wizened one used his mystic arts to start a fire in a way others would not recognize. As they feasted, neither could stop thinking about what had transpired that fateful afternoon.

"I wonder what king staked her down there," Arthur wondered aloud, to which Merlin speculated that it must have been one from a time long ago—perhaps even as far back as when he himself was a youth—for it was likely to have been done when the lake was more shallow.

After some more thought on the matter, Merlin suggested that they not reveal the true nature of the mythical Lady of the Lake when they return, preferring instead to keep alive the blessed impression everyone had of her. "Besides," he added, "what would sound more impressive when presenting your new possession, that you slew a monster for it, or that it was accorded unto you by a handmaiden of the Divine?"

Arthur mused over this, weighing both options in his mind before agreeing to the false account. He was completely against the idea of lying, and he knew Escalibore would not approve either, but he also didn't like the idea of dispelling what in fact was nothing less than a sacred belief held by so many of his people, of tainting the image of a woman who was held in no less esteem than the Lord's Mother herself. He couldn't do that to them. Besides, there wouldn't really need to be any actual lying involved. He *did* receive the legendary sword Escalibore from the Lady of the Lake. *How* was not important, nor was the true nature of the sword-keeper herself. Let both remain a mystery. As it should be. As it always had been before.

The sun was beginning to set by the time they finished feeding themselves and set off on their mounts. Its blood-tinged rays turned the lake crimson behind them, but neither man looked back at it. Their bellies full, they now had their minds on the future, no longer on the past. They met up with the royal guard at the spot where they had separated and he had ordered them to wait, and together they proceeded on their way to Camelot, Arthur with his treasure and Merlin with the remains of a cursed wretch whose ultimate end would be delivered posthaste.

Feeder
Rose Strickman

*W*hen are the clients coming? Claire paced back and forth, turning near-invisible in the beams of sunlight through Anna's bedroom window, only to come into focus again as she passed into the shadows. Her insubstantial hands worried and pulled at the dress she'd died in.

Anna barely looked up from applying blush. "Don't pester me, Claire. They only ever come after dark. Don't want their wives catching them. You should know that by now." She straightened her low-cut gown in the mirror, admiring the glass brilliants sewn into the bodice.

I'm hungry! Claire's voice took on a high-pitched whine, like a mosquito back on the farm.

"When are you not hungry?" Anna demanded, more impatient than ever. "You'll just have to wait." She concentrated on her mirror, trying to put up her hair. But it was hopeless: her slick blond locks just kept sliding away. She cursed as the braids slipped yet again and wished, as she had so often before, that Claire was still capable of helping with her hair.

Ask Betty to help, Claire said. She tossed her own ethereal curls smugly. Even now, she couldn't stop showing off her golden tresses, much brighter and thicker than Anna's. *She's got a way with even your hair.*

"Betty's probably getting ready herself." The afternoon was waning, and all of Mrs. McMaster's girls would be readying themselves for the evening's work.

Well, no harm in asking, is there? Come on, you look like a haystack right now. How are you ever going to entice good prey like that?

Anna sighed, but stood and made her way to the door and out into the poky, narrow corridor. Behind closed doors, women's voices rose in chatter, and soft thumps sounded as the rooms' inhabitants moved around, preparing for the night's work. Claire accompanied Anna down the corridor, as she accompanied her everywhere, flitting invisibly behind.

Anna knocked on Betty's door. "Betty? You in there, honey?"

"Yeah," came the reply. "Hold on, Anna, just getting my dress on…"

"I can help with that."

"Oh, would you? Come on in then!"

Anna opened the door onto Betty's messy room, scattered with shoes, stockings, petticoats, hats, cosmetic boxes, fancy chocolate boxes, painted Chinese fans and artificial flowers, along with a million other glittery items, spread in glorious disarray. Anna picked her way through the chaos. "Lord love us, Betty, don't your clients object?"

"To my room?" Betty chuckled. "Honey, they only come in here for one thing, and my décor ain't it. Lace me up, would you?"

Anna took up position behind Betty and hauled on the laces; Betty liked it nice and tight. Betty fluffed out her hair and smiled at her reflection: a small, curvy, colored woman, eyelids painted gold, lacy dress flounced, bare shoulders glittering with cosmetic dust. "Thanks, honey. Want me to take care of that disaster on your head?"

Anna couldn't help laughing. "Thanks." She delicately removed a crumpled handkerchief and a half-empty cosmetics box from the stool and sat before Betty's perfume- and underwear-strewn vanity. Betty's dexterous fingers set to work.

Anna couldn't see Claire in the mirror—her sister had no reflection—but she could hear her humming as she toured Betty's room, bouncing around from floor to ceiling. Claire loved Betty's chaotic, glitzy mess. Anna closed her eyes under the slight, soothing tug as Betty braided her hair back. "How do you have such a way with hair, Betty?"

"Used to do up my mistress's hair all the time." Betty's voice went clipped, as it always did whenever her past was brought up. "Your hair ain't that much more slippy."

Anna sighed, melancholy settling on her as she thought of Betty's past, and her own. "Betty…do you sometimes wish that things were different?"

"What things?"

"Just *things*. Life. The world."

"Sure I do, but the world don't change, honey." Betty flicked her bare shoulder with a fingernail. "And besides, if you want unfair, try being a Negro."

"Fair point," Anna admitted. She sat still while Betty finished up. "This looks amazing, Betty." She gently touched the crown of braids on her head. "Thank you."

Betty winked. "Too bad it'll only get torn down again tonight."

I can't wait, Claire added, rushing over Anna in a wash of cold.

***

Night fell over the city, broken only intermittently by dim gaslights. Houses and apartments fell silent, with few lit windows. Thieves prowled, smugglers worked the docks, and robbers lay in wait at the mouths of filthy alleys, truncheons in hand. Still the night's revelers crept out: men and sometimes women, discarding their respectable daytime identities to don cloaks and dominos, picking their way along the dung-lined streets to taverns, fight clubs, cockpits, rat pits and, of course, establishments like Mrs. McMaster's.

Anna finished another song on the ill-tuned piano, tipping her head back to applause and catcalls from her audience. The main parlor was, as always at this time of night, a jovial, well-lit place. Gas lamps shaped like flowers glowed on the papered walls, and girls and clients alike lounged on divans and chairs, feet buried in the plush carpet, the air freshened by potted plants and cut flowers in Chinese vases. Betty sat snuggled against her client's side, laughing at something he'd just said, while on his other side Josefina the Mexican also giggled: Mrs. McMaster was famous for the wide variety of her girls, from ice-blondes like Anna to the darkest of hues. Wouldn't the clients be amazed if they knew how *truly* varied the girls were, Anna reflected as Claire flitted overhead. Her sister floated like an insubstantial vulture, watching the herd with a hungry eye.

A long hand slid over Anna's bare shoulder. "Hey, miss," said the client. He was already slightly drunk, swaying on his feet, but he was rather more good-looking than most of the other men, with lustrous dark hair and dark eyes against his pale skin. "How about a duet?"

"Certainly, sir!" Anna smiled and slid over on the piano bench, letting him sit down. She flipped through the music book until she found a suitably easy duet. Together they began to play.

The client was actually a rather good piano player, and his voice rang so melodiously that several couples broke off their conversations, falling silent to listen. The music also attracted Claire's attention. She drifted over, and her eyes lit with that familiar, hungry light.

She swooped over Anna, shadowy body fluttering with eagerness, to hover over the oblivious client's head. Anna bit back a sigh. *Him?* she mouthed.

Him. Claire nodded hard, incorporeal eyes shining with avarice.

Anna hoisted a professional smile onto her face and turned to the client. "Well done, sir!" she said, and gave him a kiss on the cheek as they finished the duet. Applause and congratulations rang out, and Anna stood to give a deep, showy curtsy, prompting laughter. "Now how about we have a drink and give someone else a turn?" She drew her client to his feet and guided him to a nearby drinks stand. "I haven't seen you here before," she said, pouring him a bourbon. "Too bad, because you're certainly good-looking!"

He laughed. "Thank you!"

"What's your name, if you don't mind my asking?"

"Not at all. And it's John Zeeman." Zeeman knocked back his drink with practiced ease. "I manufacture gunpowder."

"Really?" Anna was genuinely intrigued. "How is business going?"

"Oh, very well!" Zeeman laughed. "What with this new gold rush out in California, we can't keep pace with orders!"

"I suppose all those miners do need plenty of gunpowder. Have you considered going out West yourself, sir?"

Zeeman sipped his bourbon. "Perhaps. It might be good to set up another factory in California Territory itself…But it would be difficult to get all the supplies we need. Better to stay put."

"I sometimes think I'd like to go out West." Anna's voice softened as she thought of it. A new territory. A new life.

"Perhaps one day you will," said Zeeman. "But where are my manners? What's your name, miss?"

Anna pulled herself together. "Anna Bloedel, sir. I currently manufacture explosives myself…of a sort." Zeeman laughed, voice cracking in the crowded parlor.

Overhead, Claire hissed. *Get on with it!*

Anna poured Zeeman another drink. "Do you enjoy your work, Mr. Zeeman? Even if you can't set up another factory in California?"

"Very much. Do you enjoy yours?" Zeeman leered at her over the glass's rim.

"Well enough," Anna lied pleasantly. "But we were speaking of *you*, sir." She laid a gentle hand on his sleeve. "Tonight," she said, giving him her most dulcet look, "is all about you."

Zeeman flushed, looking suddenly as bashful as a boy. Anna had mostly given up on feeling guilty these days, but she felt a stab of regret now. She bit her lip. Overhead, Claire narrowed her eyes at her. *Don't go soft!* she hissed. *You have to feed me. It's your fault I'm like this.*

And didn't Anna know it. With a faint scowl at

Claire, she continued chatting up her client.

After some more conversation, Zeeman and Anna put down their drinks and crossed the hall to join the dancers in the second parlor, revolving to the music of a fiddle and harmonica. Anna could tell what Zeeman really wanted, though: his eyes were burning on her, and his cock hard against his trousers. She knew what Claire wanted, too: the ghost of her sister flitted like an impatient fly around them, muttering and swearing with desire.

Hurry up! she snarled, throwing herself at Zeeman so hard a slight breeze blew off her passage.

Zeeman paused in his graceful dance. "Did you feel that?" he said, frowning in confusion.

"Probably just a draft," Anna said, cursing her sister's recklessness. "Come upstairs. My room is perfectly sealed…against drafts, anyway."

Zeeman chortled at this as she led him off the dance floor and into the entryway. There, Betty's client had braced her against the wall and was sucking on her neck, hands roving over her bodice, thrusting in among her breasts. Unnoticed by him, Betty peered over his shoulder and grinned at Anna. *Good luck,* she mouthed. Anna felt Betty's eyes on all three of them—woman, client and ghost—as they headed up the carpeted stairs.

***

"You have a nice room," John Zeeman said, looking around Anna's chamber.

"Thank you, Mr. Zeeman." Unlike Betty, Anna kept her room clean and tidy, with a few tasteful prints on the walls and lacy curtains at the window. Her bed was a white confection, the sheets crisp, colorless and, not so coincidentally, easy to clean. Anna indicated the heavy leather chair, an anomaly in her otherwise dainty, feminine room. "Care to sit down, sir?"

With a grunt, he sat, and Anna knelt down in a puddle of skirts before him, to untie his shoes and ease them off. She ran her hands up his legs and over his lap, and he moaned as she handled him, his head tipping back.

Anna made no protest as he pulled her to her feet and into his lap: she always preferred to entertain her clients in the chair rather than the bed, where, after all, she had to sleep. To her surprise, however, he sat her sideways in his lap and held her in a near-chaste embrace. "Call me John," he murmured. "And how did you end up here, Miss Bloedel?"

Anna fought down another sigh. She hoped he wasn't going to turn out to be the preaching type, out to save the poor fallen whore's soul—especially not with Claire hovering behind his chair, eyes glowing like starving stars. "That's a long story, Mr. Zee—I mean, John." She tried putting her arms around his neck and kissing him.

He craned away from her embrace. "Tell me," he insisted. "I want to know."

His brown eyes were warm and earnest. Like he really did want to know. Anna found herself moved.

"I came from a farm upstate," she said at last. "A farm with too many kids and not enough work for them all. And my stepmother wasn't any too kind to us after Papa died. My sister and I came to the city to seek our fortune." She bit her lip, realizing her mistake. Behind the chair, Claire hissed.

"Your sister?" Zeeman looked startled and intrigued. Unseen by him, Claire rushed back and forth in agitation. "Is she here too?"

Shut up! Claire buffeted Anna's head with icy,

nonexistent hands. *Don't tell him!*

Anna scowled at her sister and turned back to her client. "She's dead," she said to Zeeman, and Claire gave a long, silent howl.

"Oh. I'm sorry." Zeeman shifted in the chair, rocking Anna slightly. "How did she die?"

Claire folded her arms. *Going to tell him that too, sister dear?*

"Trolley accident," Anna said, shortly and untruthfully. "Horses trampled her."

"All too common a fate." Zeeman shook his head. "But she's in Heaven now."

"Yes," Anna lied as Claire flattened as a shadow on the wall, keening with bitter rage. "She's in Heaven."

"But we're here on Earth, aren't we?" said Zeeman, face going eager. He pulled down Anna's bodice and nuzzled into her breasts, mouth hot and wet.

"Yes," said Anna, stroking a hand through his hair. "We're here now."

She reached down to undo his necktie, grinding her crotch against his hard cock. He tipped his head back again, groaning, and Anna bit back a sigh of exasperation, impatient to have it all over and done with.

She scooted back to undo his buttons, pulling aside his clothes to free his erection. Men's cocks certainly were ugly, she reflected as it sprang out: that was one indignity she just couldn't get used to in this job. Then she pushed the thought aside and got to work.

Anna pulled up her skirts and guided him into her. She sighed in pretended pleasure as he began to move, rocking back and forth in the chair. Zeeman groaned and yanked on her bodice again, so her breasts flipped free. And the power started to flow.

Claire's eyes grew brighter and brighter, her essence trembling, growing more solid and substantial, as she drank in John Zeeman's life, flowing from him into her sister and then transferring to her. More and more the starving ghost pulled into herself, gulping down his strength and vigor, his *life*, appeasing the yawning void of hunger that Claire carried with her always, as a dead woman trapped in the land of the living. And Anna felt that power too, vibrating and flowing through her even as Zeeman moved inside her. The power fed her too: she could feel it burning through her, strengthening her, cleansing her, bringing life and power and vitality to her, just as it did to Claire.

For this was the bargain between the two sisters: Claire would feed, and so would Anna. And the client would return again and again, feeding the sisters, slave to the lust inspired by the first experience, until he lost all strength and wasted away and died. As had happened to dozens of other men, during the last three years, ever since Claire's death.

But not this time.

Zeeman gripped Anna with sudden firmness, and she gasped as the power began to—retract. Eyes alight, face set in a rictus of concentration, John Zeeman thrust ever harder against Anna, ever faster, and she screamed at the sudden weakness, the coldness, as he sucked his energy back from her, and from Claire.

Stop it, stop it! Claire beat around him with her icy hands, but her undead essence simply passed straight through him. Zeeman let out a strangled laugh.

"You have a hungry ghost haunting you, don't you?" he gasped to Anna. "I could tell right away, even if I couldn't see her. Your sister wasn't killed by a damn trolley. She was killed by someone like me. A Feeder."

Anna couldn't respond, but only brace herself on his shoulders. Her vision was blurring, and she felt like her bones were turning to liquid, sucked down through her body into Zeeman's. Somewhere far away, Claire was screaming.

"That's what happens when we feed too fast," Zeeman whispered. "But you—you have so much *strength*! The lives of dozens of men you've fed on. Oh, it will last me such a long time…"

Anna collapsed against him. She didn't have the strength to hold herself upright anymore. Chill weakness spread through her like frost, and Zeeman let out a triumphant laugh, thrusting even harder. *He's killing me,* Anna thought through the growing haze.

Then he yelped, jerking, as a pair of dark, slender hands yanked his head back. His grip loosened, and Anna fell back, crashing to the floor, head spinning. Claire fluttered around her in worry, but all Anna could do was stare through a dim blurred veil as Betty held Zeeman's head and locked her mouth on his. Zeeman fought—his legs kicked—but he could not break away, could not resist, as Betty drank and drank, his life flowing into her—

Just before the darkness closed in and Anna lost consciousness, Zeeman went still, limbs going rigid before crumbling into bone-colored dust.

***

When Anna came to, she was lying on her bed. How had she gotten there? The room was lit by her dim lamps still—clearly not much time had passed—and she was shivery and weak.

A rush of cold air, and Claire hovered over her. *Are you all right, Anna?* she asked, voice thin with anxiety, eyes huge in her ghostly face.

"Yes." Anna started back as Betty loomed over her from beside her bed. "How are you feeling, Anna?"

Anna gave a thin, hoarse cough. "Like shit."

"Good." Betty sounded relieved. "If you can talk, you're probably going to recover. Come on, sit up…"

Anna somehow hauled herself up as Betty rearranged the pillows. She looked around her room. It was empty but for her, Betty and the ghost. "Where's…Mr. Zeeman?"

"Collapsed into dust," said Betty. "I drank him up too fast. Don't worry, I've already cleaned up." She gave a strange little shiver. She was looking very—bright, Anna thought. Every part of her was sleek and healthy, glowing with vitality, from her hair to her fingernails. "My Lord," Betty murmured. "But I haven't fed so deeply in *so* long."

Anna stared at her. "You're…like him, aren't you? A Feeder, like he said."

"That's right," nodded Betty. "More powerful than that fool, though. I don't need to have sex to feed, not anymore." Her eyes shifted to Claire, and the ghost trembled. "Hello there. You're Anna's sister Claire, aren't you?"

How can you see me? Claire demanded, outline vibrating in agitation.

"Usually I can't," Betty shrugged. "But I've just fed, so I can both see and hear you. For a while, at least, until the power fades again. I could always tell you were there, though, right from the start. I can always sense a hungry ghost." Her eyes flicked between Claire and Anna. "I have to say, I admire your little scheme. Your sister feeds through you, Anna, and you share the power, don't you? You both benefit."

Benefit! Claire flew at Betty, silent and furious. *Do you know how we even ended up like this?*

"You were killed by a Feeder, weren't you?" said Betty. "You went with a Feeder who fed too much and killed you. He turned you into a hungry ghost. Into a Feeder, like him."

"Yes." Anna slumped down on her pillows, defeat and exhaustion surging through her. "And…it was my fault." She licked her dry lips. "I…I made her go with that man. That Feeder. We were homeless and starving on the street, and I—I made Claire go with the Feeder when he offered. I didn't see how else we were going to survive…"

And look what happened! Claire shrieked, sparks flying out of her eyes. *I'm trapped here on Earth, unable to move on! Forced to feed on the living, just as* he *did.*

"Ain't fair, huh?" said Betty with a singular lack of sympathy. "Thank your luck: you have a sister who can feed for you." Her lips twitched in a humorless smile. "Not many of your kind can say the same. If they don't learn to feed for themselves, they starve."

"And you?" Anna eyed her warily. "What about your kind?"

"My kind?" Betty's eyes shone bright with secret laughter. "Those of us born with the hunger? Those who must feed on the lives of others, even while we're still alive?"

"It's evil," Anna cried out. She wasn't sure why this was coming out now, of all times, but all the thoughts and feelings she'd been repressing for three years were suddenly overflowing. "It's a power from the Devil! You're damned for it—we're both damned for it—"

"*I'm* damned?" Betty rose to her feet, face a mask of rage. "Want to know how I discovered my power, Miss Bloedel?" She struck herself on the breast. "When I was thirteen, my master sold me to a passing peddler who raped me! I took all his life for myself that day—I had no control over my hunger, over my feeding. He's a hungry ghost now, just like your sister, but don't tell me he didn't deserve it! Or any of those other men, all of our *clients*, those rich, spoiled white men who come and take what they want, and to hell with what any of *us* think or want or feel about it!" She took a moment to regain control, breath ragged. "I used the power I took that day to escape," she said in a lower tone. "I came North, and ever since, I have been feeding on men like that peddler, like my master. And if you're asking me to feel *sorry* for them, well, you're asking the wrong girl."

Silence fell, broken only by the distant chatter from the parlors below, and the pants and thumps from various other rooms on their floor. Even Claire hovered quiet, struck dumb. Anna found she couldn't meet Betty's eyes.

"I've got to get back to work." Betty turned away, twitching her skirts. "And you'd better get back to work too, if you don't want Mrs. McMaster to throw you out." She glanced at Claire, smirking. "Or your sister to throw a hungry ghost hissy fit."

She was halfway to the door when Anna spoke. "Betty," she said, "thank you. Thank you for saving me. And…I'm sorry for what I said."

"Apology accepted," Betty said. "And you're welcome." She reached out to take the doorknob.

Wait! Claire swooped down in a rush of cold air. *Don't go! I've got an idea.*

Betty looked back, raising an eyebrow. "What idea?"

Remember what Anna said? About things being different? Claire fizzed with excitement. *Well, why don't we make a bit of difference for ourselves?*

Betty and Anna looked at one another. "What do you have in mind, exactly?" Anna asked at last.

***

As the clipper sailed into San Francisco's harbor, the sun came out from behind the clouds in a dazzling curtain, illuminating the town. It was a sprawling, untidy place, but its harbor was busy with ships, and Anna could practically feel the energy pouring off it. It was busier and more crowded every day, she'd heard, with more miners coming in all the time, landing at the harbor before setting out for the interior. Gold miners, and those offering services to them. Fresh prey every day, and no Mrs. McMaster to take half their earnings. Anna shivered in anticipation.

Betty, heavily veiled, came up beside her. "That's San Francisco?" she said. "Not much of a place, is it?"

"Not yet," said Anna. "But more miners are coming all the time, you know."

Yes, said Claire, hovering in the shadow of the mast, leaned forward, an eager predator. *A lovely new feeding ground, all to ourselves.*

And the three women exchanged knife-edged smiles as their ship carried them closer in. "Happy hunting," whispered Betty, watching their new territory with hungry eyes.

Identity Theft
Elaine Pascale

The day I had been sent to market, I hid the scroll in the statue in the old library. The library had been abandoned. There was no need for reading in a world covered by a curtain of darkness.

No one was sent to market without a cadre of Familiars to guard them. This prevented attempts at escape. I didn't want to escape; I had a different plan. Part one of the plan had been installing the scroll, which I did by pretending to trip as we made our way past the structure. I had grabbed the statue for balance, overhearing a Familiar snicker, saying "she is not able to see her own feet." The Familiars had an odd jealousy of me and the other Snacks. While the Familiars were spared our torture, they seemed to wish that the same desirous gaze was bestowed upon them.

In the before times, I had grown accustomed to being looked at lasciviously. I knew I was a tasty morsel. As a child I had been kept from the sun so that I would not gather spots or freckles. The result was an enviable milky complexion. I am nearly as wide as I am tall; I have been told that I have curves that could keep eyes entertained for days. My wife, Mercy, and I could make heads turn when we would go out. She mirrored my stature but was caramel colored with dark freckles. I loved to kiss her spots, telling her that each had a different taste.

Mercy. The last time I saw Mercy had been before the blindfolds; before the night screams.

The second part of the plan would require more time.

***

We are kept blindfolded, even in the dark of night. The Predators believe their faces would frighten us to death. Our blood is tastier when we are alive: alive and scared.

Even without seeing, I know the Predators look at us with hunger. I can feel their eyes move slowly over my body, delighting in the surplus flesh. They feed us well. They keep us sated and scared.

The Predators recycle our identities. It is a way of dehumanizing us, which is ironic as they aren't human. They use adjectives for our names: delicious, scrumptious, succulent. My real name had been etched on the scroll hidden in the statue outside the library. I had also written the names of those I loved. Mercy's name was large to match her spirit. I had made the scroll by sticking together candy bar wrappers with caramel. I had written the names with a sharpened stick that I had burned at the tip. The Predators do not fear stakes as they don't have hearts to pierce. The Predators are empty, just like the meaningless names they call us.

They don't allow us to have matches or a lighter, so

I have become good at starting fires by primitive means. In the before times, I had enjoyed camping. I had enjoyed being in nature and learning about plants and animals. This knowledge will come in handy for my plan. Not having access to matches or a lighter does not bother me. Those who smoked in the before times were told to suffer through the pangs and withdrawals. They were whipped if caught biting their nails or otherwise trying to satisfy their oral fixation with anything besides food. The only smoking allowed were Snacks roasting on a spit. The smell of burning human flesh is indescribable.

***

"Tasty," they called me over. They had summoned the Familiars to bring me. I was one of six "Tasties." The only good thing about another Snack being consumed was it meant the name they had given you became a little more special as it was shared by fewer.

They gave the Familiars hand signals once I was in front of them. They didn't realize I could still see some things despite the blindfold. They underestimate how smart we are.

They were seated in front of a fireplace that was ablaze. They love to have a fire when they bring us to visit with them. They cannot feel it, as their blood is coagulated, and their tissues hardened. There is nothing that could warm their cold skin.

The fires are nostalgic for them. Centuries ago, they would hunt by picking off the small tribes that gathered around fires for warmth and protection. Those had been tough meats, not sweet and tender like our flesh. Processed foods have led to the evolution of the perfect Snack.

And processed foods led to the Predators realizing that they no longer needed to hunt. In the new, darkened world, they fostered a food industry that allowed them to simply consume.

"Be a good Snack and tell us about your creepiest encounter in the before times."

"Creepiest? I guess that would be the man on the bridge." I clasped my hands behind my back so they would not see that I had been pulling the threads from the clothing around my wrists and waist. If they noticed, I would attribute it to my clothing growing too tight. They would love to hear that.

They won't want to know that I am picking at threads. Not because they are anticipating my plan, but because they want as little movement from us as possible. They don't want muscles to develop, not even on our fingers. When they want to make us scared, they tell us what part of us they plan to eat first. I have had several Predators mention the skin between the thumb and forefinger. That seems to be the sweetest spot.

"The bridge?" I knew their love for structures would hold their interest. All Snacks were aware that the Predators buried our bones when they were finished with us. They had started by burying Snack bones around the factory where we were kept. They had enough bones to branch out to the surrounding buildings. They placed bones around the factories that contained the livestock— the livestock fed the Snacks which fed the Predators. They placed bones in the town which was now empty as all homes had been given a shakedown and all people had been sorted.

The Predators that had taken over other towns followed suit.

They believed our bones would guard the structures, that we would become devoted Familiars to them after sating their hunger. They would use our spirits after they had devoured our bodies.

The Predators' metabolism is very high. They can eat and eat but remain wraith-like in form. Their hunger had allowed them to overtake and kill the biggest and strongest of us. As with all apex predators, they now focused on exerting the least amount of energy in order to obtain the energy they consumed.

"Tell us about it," they urged with a quiet confidence, their voices constantly synchronous. "What were you wearing?"

"A blouse and a skirt. Wedges. I had had a pedicure and wanted to show it off." I knew they wanted details about my feet; they liked feet.

"And the blouse…it was tight? The man on the bridge, he could see, you know, your size?"

"It was dark, but I am sure he could see my outline. There are lights on the bridge."

"That is right," they seemed to be speaking to each other and also in unison. "Snacks don't see well in the dark." They sighed happily, "But the man, he could see you despite his deficits. There is enough of you, too much to hide."

It was difficult to keep talking because I hated them so much. I had been told that Mercy's bones were buried behind the room where I stood. I had been told that by Familiars who wanted to taunt me.

"Was it too dark…could he see your skin?"

The Predators liked my complexion. I had become practically translucent since we were kept from the sun at all times. I could hear them smacking their lips as they looked at me and I wondered if it was now my time, that I would not get to see my plan to fruition. They were trying to make me afraid, and fear came before eating.

"I am not sure. When I looked behind me, I could

see him. He was under the light."

"And what was he doing?"

"Staring. At me." I tried to keep calm. I didn't want them to hear my heart beating. That sound was like a dinner bell to them. The story was not scaring me, it wasn't even true, just some nonsense I was telling them because they expected it. Sensing their hunger was scaring me. "I could see he had a knife in his hand."

"Was the knife…large?" Their words were thick with desire.

"It was large. I did not look at it for too long, as I needed to get away. But I could hear him take the blade and run it along the bridge railing."

Their breath quickened; I could hear soft panting. "What did it sound like?"

"Like a squeal."

"Like…like someone in pain?"

"Hmm," I could hear the saliva dripping from their mouths, triggered by my words. "The knife did sound like a person, I guess. Like a high-pitched scream."

I could make out movement. They gestured for a few Familiars. My stomach dropped.

"He was a stalker, a nightmare," I said, and then I did the only thing I could think to do. As the Familiars grew closer to me, I shit myself. Shit had saved me this time, and it would save me again later.

***

I had managed to secretly stockpile manure from the cows they kept in the factory beside ours. I took one patty each time I was let outside for fresh air and hid it in the bedding inside my cage. We were only allowed out at night; the Predators wanted us on their schedule. The Familiars encouraged us to urinate and defecate in select spots that were blissfully obscured by trees and near the animal factory. They hated having to clean our cages. The darkness made it easier to hide things from the Familiars who also had the bad habit of losing interest in watching us. They often joked and flirted with each other, and this provided the opportunity to sneak the dung. Luckily the Predators never entered our rooms and the Familiars entered and exited quickly to highlight their disgust at our very existence, so the smell did not give away my intentions. The rendering of both the livestock factory and the Snack factory worked to create an overall stench that masked the manure, as the factories assaulted olfaction so that no other scents could find their way in.

I also collected the fat drippings from the cows and pigs that were slaughtered. While I felt a sympathy for them that was on the level of kinship, I understood that they were dispatched in a much less brutal fashion than we were.

On Mercy's last night, I swore I heard her say my name amongst her screams. Some of the other Snacks assured me that there was no way I could tell it was her screams: torture makes everyone sound the same. But I knew. I knew how she sounded when she was filled with delight, I knew how she sounded when she was sick, I knew how she sounded hung over. I remember the early days when my name hung on the lovesick lyrical notes she whispered/sang. Over time, that tone deepened, and the cadence hardened with loyalty.

I would recognize her sound anywhere.

***

Mercy and I had shared a wardrobe. We mixed and matched clothing and even mixed and matched pieces from clothing. We sewed a sleeve from one of her garments onto one of my shirts. We took buttons from my dress and applied them to her jacket. Our clothes blended together as well as we did.

I sent my mind into this happy memory while I tore off the loosened hems of my cotton clothing. It made my outfits look raggedy but unless I was closely inspected, it was difficult to notice that swatches of cotton were missing.

"You are planning something," Yummy said to me. I knew his voice despite the blindfold. He once told me his real name was Cade. I liked Yummy, so I had written "Cade" on the scroll I had hidden. I kept imagining a better world, a world *after*, when someone would find the scroll and know that we had all been here. They would know what had happened to us.

I began to nod but remembered the blindfolds. "I am."

I could hear a smile in his voice. "I am sure any plan from the girl who shit herself alive will be spectacular."

***

When the Predators took over, they separated us into Snacks and Familiars. Anyone not sorted into one of those groups had been exterminated. They wanted our numbers manageable, and they wanted the bones for protection. Children automatically became Snacks so they could replace us once we were consumed. The Predators had been studying animal husbandry with the livestock they fed us, and one could only assume that they would begin breeding their own food once our numbers dwindled.

While the Predators worked to remove our identities, so we were nothing more than food to them, we Snacks told each other facts to distinguish ourselves. These were not the scary stories that we were forced to tell the Predators, these were personal identifiers. We did not have the luxury of saying more than a few words to each other as we were rarely out of ear shot of the Familiars when we weren't sleeping in our cages. We would whisper our real names, where we had gone to school, where we had worked, how many children we had, anything of burning importance. We would repeat the short phrases to the same Snack, like a mantra. We hoped that at least one of us would live to record the details.

I had become famous for shitting myself out of becoming a meal. Many Snacks wanted to share their identities with me, but I always partnered with Yummy/Cade. He told me that his wife's bones were buried near Mercy's. He assured me we would all be reunited someday.

"My wife was Mercy," I whispered.

"My wife was Dee," he whispered back.

We said these names often to each other. So often that my mind now repeated "Mercy Dee" as I fell asleep and when I awoke.

One day, Yummy/Cade whispered to me, "They removed our pictures."

This was said at dinner, and I pretended to lean over my food so that my ear was closer to his mouth.

"In my house," he continued, "I was the last one dragged out." He paused and the next words were spoken around mouthfuls of food. "The blindfold slipped when they dragged me. They had taken our family pictures off the walls."

"No trace of us," I mumbled from behind a soda can. My clothing had become so tight that I would no longer need to pull threads; they would snap on their own. Still,

I kept eating because there was nothing else to do until the plan was enacted. We all kept eating because that had become our job and we had been accustomed to having a purpose in the before times.

"Not even our bones," he added.

The Familiars brought us table-side smores. The Predators thought this type of dessert would inspire fireside urban legends. The Predators also liked to force the Familiars to serve us painstakingly particular foods as a way of keeping them in their place. I could feel the flames even though I could not see them. I imagined the marshmallows roasting on sticks, sticks similar to the one I had used to write the names on the scroll. I grabbed the burning marshmallow I had been handed, scalding myself in the process, and stuffed it into the now empty soda can. I would secure the can between my thighs at the last minute, not wanting to have it scorching my skin for longer than necessary.

As I ate the remaining chocolate and graham crackers, I thanked the marshmallow for having a usefulness beyond the way it tastes.

***

Familiars entered our bunker after we had dozed off from all of the turkey they had fed us.

I could hear their feet pacing. I knew they were sizing us up.

They opened a cage and dragged someone out. I could hear the body falling to the floor. It has become difficult for some of the Snacks to move on their own. The joke about not being able to see our own feet over our large stomachs was no longer a joke. I wasn't resentful of the extra weight; I saw it as additional force. And, if the worst happened, I hoped they would choke on my fat.

There was some sobbing followed by a woman's voice saying, "Don't take me, I don't have a story to tell them."

A Familiar snorted and said, "Make something up. You must have watched TV in the before times. You must have seen some scary movies."

"N-no. I didn't watch…I don't like scary things."

A few Familiars laughed at the irony.

As horrible as the thought was, I was hoping they would take her and leave quickly so that my stash of ingredients would not be discovered.

A stony sounding Familiar insisted, "It is an honor to give back to the Predators after all they have given you. They have provided for you and now you provide for them. I suggest you think of something between now and when you are in front of them. It will be easier on you if they are not angry."

I could hear them dragging her from the room and locking the door behind them. Shortly after there was the sound of struggling, followed by a Familiar yelling, "What did she put in her mouth?"

There was some additional struggling and then the announcement, "She had rosary peas. She is trying to poison the Predators!"

"You can't poison the Predators," another Familiar said in a tone that was meant to be calming.

"But if she kills herself before they eat her, then they are eating death."

Screams filled the air along with the distinctive sound of the whip. This continued and a harmony of kicks and grunts were added. Eventually, the screams died, and later the whipping stopped.

The door was unlocked, and the Familiars hoisted another Snack from a cage. "No cleverness from you," the Snack was told. "We will be watching closely."

This last part seemed to be meant for all of us.

***

I have learned to ignore the night screams.

I have also learned to stop searching for Mercy's bones.

When they called me to them this time, their bellies were extended. Full of Snack meat. An undergarment had fallen into the fireplace, discarded as one might discard the wrapper from a candy bar. It smoldered on top of the flames, refusing to succumb. It burned the final commitment of my plan into my brain, of my refusal to succumb.

"Tasty, what would you say you weigh now?" They asked, even though they routinely weighed us.

"My last weigh-in, I was 284 pounds." I held my head high as I said the numbers. I was nearly ready to enact my plan, but if they wanted to take me now, I would not give them the satisfaction of whimpering.

"And when was that?" they asked in unison. They always spoke as one.

"Last week."

"Would you say it is possible you weigh more now?"

"Of course. I have been eating as I should." I moved close to the heat of the fire, so close that I scalded my hands, but I needed to trap an ember for my plan to work.

"And your menstruation…. your cycles…is your body clean?"

"I have not had a period in months," I answered. I pretended to cough and bent over, scooping a tiny coal into a piece of aluminum I had stolen from our feeding station. "I stopped at around 240 pounds."

"But you cough. Are you sick?"

"No, just the smoke."

"Then you must step away from the fire. You are too close to it. You will roast." They laughed at the irony of their joke. "Tell us, Tasty…do you care for anyone in here? Any of the other Snacks?"

I paused. I presumed they were asking this as a means of torturing me. The first name that popped into my mind was Yummy and I could imagine them forcing me to watch what they would do to him.

"I did, but she is gone," I answered. "I have no one or nothing left that concerns me."

My statement seemed to suck the energy from the room. Their full bellies and my lack of fear kept me off the menu one more time.

***

"The others are ok with whatever you have planned," Yummy/Cade whispered when we were supposed to be eating.

"Even if it might go terribly wrong?" I asked, stuffing packets of powdered coffee creamer into my pockets. It would be a useful part of my collection. We had come to know where all food would be laid out on the table, as we ate blindfolded. I always made sure to sit strategically close to something of value.

I swore I could hear his shoulders shrug when he said, "What could be worse than this?"

***

"Tasty," they called me over. "Tell us a story that haunts you to this day. What are your nightmares made of?"

It was great luck that they had singled me out again. Normally, that was a bad sign. Their interest meant a shortened life, but I was ready for my plan now. In fact, I had already enacted it.

I pretended to think. I was really estimating how long it would take for me to reach the fireplace.

"My worst nightmare began when the before time ended."

"You do not need to tell us of our treatment of you; we are the masterminds behind it."

I shook my head vigorously, and the motion allowed the blindfold to slip slightly so that I could see the fireplace.

"No. What you do to me now pales in comparison to how I got here."

I could hear their sandpaper-like tongues run over their protruding teeth. "Tell us about that…which ruse were you?"

"The electrician," I answered, and they laughed. "The power went out, like it is now, like it has been since…"

"Since we took over," they finished for me. "You had no idea then, right? You thought it was simply a black out."

"Yes. I called the housing office. They told me that the electrician who normally is sent on calls had left for another job. They said they would be sending someone new."

"And you suspected nothing?" they asked excitedly.

"No. I had no reason to. The electrician came and he worked in the house for a while. Then he told us, he told my wife and me…my wife, Mercy," I enjoyed saying her name in front of them. "he told us that he would have to return later. Something about the fuse box and needing replacement parts."

"You must have been disappointed," they said happily.

"Very. We had made plans to watch a movie that night and I wasn't sure he would be able to fix the power in time." It was difficult to recall a time when a small inconvenience felt like a large problem.

"And he didn't come back."

"No. he did. What we hadn't realized was that he had tampered with our windows. He and several…friends—"

"—Familiars don't have friends," they insisted, and I wasn't going to argue. It didn't matter anymore anyway.

"He and some other Familiars came back when we were asleep. They beat us and blind folded us and…" my words got caught in my throat.

"And what?" Their drool began dropping to the floor like dense rain drops.

"They touched us, Mercy and me. They did things while we were tied up and blindfolded."

There was a sharp intake of breath. "The Familiars should not be defiling our food."

"No," I agreed, "They should not." I maintained a poker face, even though I was internally delighted that everything was going according to plan.

They called the Familiars into the room, which I had anticipated. I knew how they hated for their food to be impure in any way. This is why they had asked about my cycles.

"Which one of you touched her?" They asked the Familiars in raised voices.

The question was met by silence which only seemed to anger them more. "You are well aware of the rules," the Predators continued angrily.

The only problem was that angry Predators were

focused and hard to defeat; hungry Predators made mistakes. I needed their attention back.

"If I had known what was coming, if I had known…"

I could hear a few calming, deep inhalations. They liked to make noisy breaths, even though they were only mimicking breathing. "Continue, Tasty. If you had known how horrible things would become, what would you have done?"

It was my turn to take a deep breath. A real one. "I would have burned down the house with us in it."

I knew their eyes would be glazing over with blood lust. "You would…you would have burned yourself? And the one you loved?"

"Without a second thought."

The Predators began snapping their fingers at the Familiars. This must have been a cue to begin my undoing. Just as suddenly, the snapping ceased, and it sounded as if the Familiars stopped moving. I squinted against my blindfold and could see the Predators looking at the window. It was the darkest part of night, so the flames coming from the factory could not be ignored. Even I could see the flickering heat against the black backdrop that was my constant view.

The manure patties had lit easily. I had made char cloth using the soda can and a few of my cotton swatches. Yummy had acquired some dryer lint from the laundry where they launder the clothing of the deceased so the Familiars can wear them. The lint was used as kindling. We had managed to toss the lit patties into the corners of the rooms, furthest from our cages but closest to the windows. The other Snacks and I were calculating how to escape once the Predators or Familiars would become aware of the fire. Them calling for me had provided the others the time and opportunity if they were able to take it. I was holding the Predators captive, and the Familiars had been preparing for the feast that would include me.

If all else failed, the Snacks were prepared to fall prey to the fire. It was preferable and they knew their bodies could not be used by the Predators once they were dead.

Through the blindfold, I could see the Predators stand. I had never seen them at their full height, only seated. Their lankiness was exaggerated when they were fully upright. They resembled the twig I had used to write names on the scrolls. I hoped that, like the twig, they would be easy to ignite.

The lard I had wrapped in torn scraps of my clothes had been tucked in my hands. I used these as make-shift wicks and dipped them into the fire from the fireplace. I then thew them onto the Predators closest to me.

Their baggy clothing quicky caught fire and their screams were a register I had not yet heard. Torture does not make us all sound the same.

A few of the uninflamed Predators moved toward me. I threw the confiscated creamer packets into the fireplace and at the burning Predators. They quickly exploded, shooting a fire ball into the room.

The smell of the burning Predators was decidedly worse than the smell of burning Snacks. Centuries of death and decay made for a horrible flambé.

The Familiars ran about the room, trying to extinguish the Predators with their hands and aprons. It was no use: the undead burn quickly. There is little of substance to burn, and an inhuman amount of time-consuming others causes them to be rapidly consumed.

I appreciated the Predators' obsession with bones once I saw that the ones that I had lit first crumbled into ash. There were no shards or pieces as there were when

Snacks were burned and we always want what we cannot have. The Predators' bodies nearly evaporated and would have appeared completely ephemeral if it were not for the screams. The screams and screeches echoed in the room even after the bodies were mostly disintegrated.

Sparks flew and soon all of the Predators were engulfed in flames. I laughed at how easy they were to kill. My laughter was nearly as loud as the screams.

The Familiars fell into a pile on the burning Predator pyre. They did not make a noise; their loyalty continued inside of the flames.

Knowing my name was secure in the statue, I lifted the blindfold to watch it all burn.

The Vampire Lord of the Wasteland
Holly Saiki

Liam gave a bark of triumph as he speared the rat running across the desolate, grey landscape. The skeletal trees and scraps of rusted metal the only things he could see. He opened his jacket and took out his pocketknife and a glass jar filled with blood. He opened the jar, putting it down on the ground. He picked up the rat and cut its throat with the pocketknife, squeezing every little bit of blood into the jar. After Liam finished, he replaced the lid.

"Hey there, what brings you out to the wasteland on this fine day?" a friendly voice said from behind Liam.

Liam jumped in surprise, giving out a small scream as he nearly dropped the jar, the blood inside sloshing furiously. He took some quick breaths before turning around to see the stranger.

The stranger was a dark-skinned young man with short kinky hair dyed a bright orange red. He had a long grey duster like what Liam wore, with two pouches strapped to each side of the duster in an X pattern. A pair of oversized goggles lay on top of his head. A shotgun strapped securely on his back. A long white rayon scarf wrapped around his neck, a slight breeze causing it to flutter gently.

"Woah! Don't scare me like that," Liam said, "I almost had a heart attack."

"Sorry about that," the stranger said, "I usually don't see anybody else out here. Coming across you is quite the surprise." he stuck his hand out in a greeting, "I should introduce myself. My name is Nelson, what's yours?"

"My name is Liam," he replied, grateful for the friendly contact. It had been months since somebody had touched him in a gentle manner. "What are you doing out in a place like this?"

"Blame it on a good old case of wanderlust," Nelson said, putting his goggles on and adjusting them. "I've always wanted to travel around the world. I'm not going to let something like a nuclear apocalypse stop me now. Some of the world's landmarks may still be intact." his eyes became sadly wistful as he reflected on it, "Still, I wish the war never happened. So many wonderful places and lands were destroyed."

"Man, that does suck," Liam said, looking at Nelson with sympathy. Five years had passed since the war ended, but the emotional wounds were still fresh like it had happened yesterday, "I'm hunting animals so I can gather blood for my master."

"Wow, that's sweet," Nelson said, breaking out into a big smile, "I'm sure he's touched he has such a loyal human servant."

"I wish it was the truth," Liam said, shaking his head sadly. His shoulders slumping as he looked down at the ground in sadness, "I'm the only human servant who didn't succumb to radioactivity because of a magical symbol. He only values me because I clean his lair."

"He let the rest of his servants die horribly?" Nelson said, eyes widening in horror, "Why didn't he protect them?"

"Because their job was basically to be glorified walking blood bags for him to suck on," Liam said, his eyes becoming bitter as he scowled. "I begged him to do it, but he said 'There are plenty of other juice bags where they came from. Why should I worry about getting prepared for some silly nuclear war the humans don't even have the balls to carry out'? Well, you can see how it turned out." Liam gave a short, bitter laugh before resuming, "That's why I hunt down animals. I don't tell Vlad about where the blood comes from because he hates animal blood."

"You're basically lying to him about where the blood comes from?" Nelson said.

"Yeah, but I wonder sometimes if he knows the truth," Liam said, "After all, he's about five hundred years old. I'm sure he knows the difference."

"Wow, I'm amazed he hasn't killed you," Nelson said, sounding a little surprised.

"I agree with you," Liam said, "But he hasn't hunted in an awfully long while, so he completely relies on me to do it for him. It's the only reason I'm not dead yet."

"Your master seems like a total idiot," Nelson replied, giving Liam a sympathetic look. "I wonder why you're still serving him?"

"My magic sign sends painful shocks if I rebel against him," Liam said. "Believe you me, if I had the opportunity, I would've escaped."

Nelson stood still, not certain what to say to make him feel better. After a few awkward moments of silence, Nelson cleared his throat before he spoke.

"I'm not sure what I can do to help you," Nelson

said. "I'm tempted to go with you and kill the asshole, but we would either be killed or I would also get turned into a vampire slave. I can't just abandon you either."

"Don't worry about it," Liam said, "I know what makes him happy and what pisses him off. Besides, I'm still a good janitor, even in this post-apocalyptic wasteland."

"I want to be able to help you in some way," Nelson said, putting his hand on his chin as he thought about what to do. A minute passed before Nelson broke out into a big, silly smile.

"I know," he said, "Why don't we have weekly visits here? We can use that old, leafless tree there as a meeting place." He pointed to the nearby titular tree. "Whenever your master acts like a total douchebag, you can come here and vent your problems to me."

"Thanks," Liam said, blushing faintly. "I really don't want to be a burden on you, especially since you're a wanderer."

"Don't worry about it," Nelson said, grinning as he took a medallion out of his coat and waved it in front of Liam. "I've learned a few magical tricks of my own. This little trinket can magically transport me to any place I've ever been without traveling through the actual distance. It was a gift from an elderly mage when I saved his life from a motorcycle gang."

"I don't know what to say," Liam said, "Thank you for being so kind."

"Think nothing of it," Nelson said. "I do have one question."

"What?"

"How come none of the vampires and other supernatural creatures were able to stop a nuclear holocaust?" Nelson asked. "You'd think with all of the power they have in their fingertips, they would be able to prevent this from happening."

"I'm not an expert on supernatural creatures," Liam said. "My master believed humans were weak creatures incapable of the strength of his kind. When I told him about the nuclear war, he said humans didn't even have the balls to start it. I'm guessing the other supernatural creatures shared his belief and didn't do anything until it was too late." He gave a short round of bitter laughter, "Well, I guess we showed him."

"Yeah, I guess," Nelson said, with a hint of sadness in his voice. He paused for a moment as he opened his duster and took a gold watch out and popped open the lid. His eyes bulged a little as he looked at the time. "Holy crap, I promised the old mage to come by his house. I better go at once, or he's going to chew my ear off."

"I understand," Liam replied. "So when do you want meet? Would next week be good?"

"Sure," Nelson replied. "What day and time would be suitable for you?"

"My master lets me take Fridays off," Liam said. "It's his way of making sure I don't 'keel over from peasant work.' I can go wherever I want as long as I come back to the manor by midnight. If I'm late, he'll use his mental powers to give me a magical shock again."

Nelson winched in horror. "That's terrible, how do you even cope with a horrible master like him?"

"Well, I do enjoy my job as a janitor," Liam said. "My snarky sense of humor also keeps me from going insane."

"I guess you have to do what you must to survive," Nelson said, looking up at the sky with a wistful look on his face. A second passed before he opened his duster again, putting the golden pocket watch back and getting out a small silver baseball bat.

"I usually don't give out magical trinkets to total strangers," he said, "but I have seen too many humans brutally killed by supernatural creatures. I'm worried your master will kill you someday, so I'm giving you a weapon that will harm him. The bat senses when you're in danger and grows so you have a ready-made weapon with which to defend yourself."

Liam opened his hand and accepted Nelson's gift with pleasant surprise. "I don't think it'll happen," Liam said, "But thank you anyway."

"You're welcome," Nelson said. "Well, I better get going. The mage is going to chew my ear off if I'm late. Goodbye and take care of yourself." He held up the medallion in the air and said something in Latin. Liam had to close his eyes so he wouldn't be blinded by the flash of white light.

After the green spots in his vision faded, he slowly opened his eyes. As he turned around in a circle and scanned with his eyes, he saw there wasn't any trace of Nelson throughout the whole gray area of the wasteland. He had effortlessly vanished along without any footprints.

"Crazy travelers and their magical trinkets," Liam said, smiling to himself as he walked towards home. Making a new friend lifted his spirits a bit, although it couldn't completely get rid of the anxiety building up in his stomach as he drew closer to the mansion. It was an old Victorian style, two floor building with a black rooftop. Every one of its windows had broken panels and shutters hanging loosely by one hinge. The roof was missing half its tiles and the lawn was a mass of weeds and overgrown grass threatening to overshadow the mansion. Smudges of dirt decorated the panels of the outside of the building, contrasting sharply with the faded white paint.

He stared at the crumbling mansion, taking a few deep breaths to gather his courage. *It looks like Nelson's words had more of an impact than I thought*, Liam pondered, idly rubbing the charm he gave him. *I'm really worried about my master trying to kill me in a fit of rage.*

Liam kept staring at the building for a few more minutes, struggling to decide whether to enter or not. He gave out a huge sigh, his arms sagging as he released the tension from his body. Standing around wasn't going to make his master happy, so it was best to face the situation and go inside. He squeezed the charm tightly as he walked up and opened the door.

The inside of the house was dark, the furniture beginning to build up a light layer of dust. He also spotted a spider's web on the left-hand corner above the door. A cool breeze drifted through the hallway, causing Liam to shiver a little. He took a quick scan of the front room to see if there was anything else needing his cleaning expertise.

It looks like I'll have to do some cleaning this weekend. Liam thought, sighing as he took another look around. *I really wish Master would find another servant to gather blood for him. Having to do both jobs is starting to wear me down.*

A high pitched scream, like a bat screech, reverberated down the hallway, Liam jumped backwards. He took a few deep breaths before taking out the jar of blood, sloshing it around to make sure it was real and in his hands. He then looked forward, getting ready for the inevitable storm coming his way.

"Human!" a raspy, deep voice said from the opposite end of the hallway, "Where is my blood? My throat aches for the bittersweet elixir of warm, hot life! I will rip you limb from limb if you do not give me my food."

Liam dashed through the hallway, not wanting to run the risk of having his master break his arm in a fit of anger. The blood in the jar moved wildly, mirroring the turbulent fear rolling in his stomach. As he neared the dining room, a bright light shined in his eyes. He put his shoulder to his eyes to protect himself from the glare while he waited for his vision to focus.

The scene in front of him was a macabre sight. His master was sitting at the head of the dinner table, with the corpses of his willing blood slaves occupying the other tables. They were little more than mummies, their dry, withered skin stretched tight over their bodies. Their eyes were nothing more than black pits of emptiness, their mouths pulled back to show the dead's classic rictus grin. A few wisps of hair floated on their bald head, like ethereal lines of ghostly energy. They were all dressed in Victorian finery with a few anachronisms, like sunglasses for the male corpses and 18th century jewelry for the woman.

Liam turned his attention from the elegantly dressed corpses to his master, Vlad. He could've been easily mistaken by somebody for one of the corpses. He wore only a black smoking jacket with dark red trim and a pair of black, silk pants on his withered, bony frame. A rusted silver crown with all the jewels missing adorned his bald head, the remaining wisps of ash blond hair hanging over the crown. His black eyes with blood red irises were a hint he wasn't a lifeless body like the others surrounding him. His eyes had immediately opened when Liam walked near him.

"Hey there, Master," Liam said, putting the jar of blood right in front of him, "I got you the blood. I worked hard to make sure there was enough. Although considering how old you are, I bet you don't need to consume as much."

Vlad gave him a dirty look before focusing his attention on the jar of blood in front of him. He placed one hand on the lid and the other on the jar so he could steady it. Vlad then quickly yanked the lid from the jar with one sharp twist of his hand. The force of the movement caused the lid to fly into the air and land on the floor with a loud clatter. Vlad ignored the noise and stared intently at the jar like it was an odious object before he leaned his face towards the opening.

Loud sniffing sounds filled the air as Vlad was smelling the contents of the blood, making sure it wasn't laced with drugs or magical chemicals designed to weaken and kill the undead. He had once foolishly drunk the blood of a person high on LSD and gotten high as a result.

Vlad sniffed at the blood for a few more minutes before he raised his head away from the jar. His face scrunched in disgust as he stared at the jar in his hands. He leaned backward, like he was holding something gross. Vlad turned his head around and stared at Liam with a frightening intensity.

"Where did you get this blood?" he said in a soft, polite tone. Liam moved an inch back, knowing the tone revealed the rage bubbling to the surface. "This carries the fetid odor of rodents and who knows what else?"

"I had a tough time trying to find human blood," Liam said, "The ones still alive are either dangerous motorcycle gangs or hiding out in underground bunkers. I had to scrounge for animals in the wasteland."

"You took that long to get animal blood?" Vlad said, leaning forward to take another look at the blood in the jar. The environment became tense as Liam nervously waited for his master's response.

"You wasted valuable time getting animal blood, I

want human blood, goddamn it!" Vlad threw the blood at Liam with all the force of his anger. Liam expertly dodged the liquid projectile, a lifetime of surviving Vlad's angry rages embedded in his muscles.

When Vlad saw Liam avoiding it, he threw the jar at Liam. Liam ducked to one side, letting it slam into the wall. A loud shattering sound echoed through the room as the jar exploded into a million pieces. The pieces scattered throughout the floor, some reaching as far as under the table.

Liam turned around, looking at the mess for a few minutes as his territorial instincts kicked in. He shook his head, clicking his tongue in disapproval. He turned around to look at his master, a stiff smile plastered on Liam's face with his cheeks raised and eyes wide open. He had to keep a pleasant demeanor even though his anger was bubbling underneath the surface.

"It really wasn't wise for you to do it," Liam said. His happy tone could barely hide the emotional stress he was feeling now. "Now I'll have to go get more blood. Although I'll need to clean up this mess first."

Vlad bolted upright, the chair legs scraping on the floor. Liam gritted his teeth at the screeching noise it made. But before he could make a snarky comment about it, Vlad glided across the floor and grabbed him by his collar. Specks of red tinted saliva fell on Liam's face as Vlad hissed at him.

"I am sick and tired of the bloody swirl you give me," he said, his voice a raspy whisper filled with malice. "I do not care what you have do in order to get it! You get me human blood!"

All Liam could do to respond was mumble incoherently, his ability to speak washed away in blind animal fear. Vlad stared at him in contempt, leaning in closer to increase the fear of his servant. He paused, catching a whiff of a scent unfamiliar to him. He eased his grip on Liam's collar, focusing on the strange smell on his servant. Vlad moved around Liam's body, sniffing loudly so he could catch every detail of the strange scent. He continued the search for another five minutes, the horrible, raspy noise ringing in Liam's ears.

"I knew it," Vlad said when he stopped smelling Liam, pulling back, and looking accusingly at him. "There's the scent of another human. Why didn't you kill them and drain them of their blood?"

"I wasn't expecting another human to appear when I was finishing my duty," Liam said, trying to remain calm despite knowing his master was about to lose his temper. "I didn't want to waste the blood I had gathered. Besides, he was a nice guy. I didn't want to kill him."

"That's the most pathetic excuse I've ever heard in all of my unlife," Vlad said, grabbing Liam's collar in an iron grip only the undead could master. "You know very well what I do to disobedient servants."

"What do you do sir?" Liam said rhetorically, his voice an agonized high-pitched whine as he tried desperately not to succumb to his fear. He had seen first-hand how Vlad brutally punished those servants who failed to obey his orders.

"It depends on how I'm feeling that day," Vlad said, his voice taking on a creepy gentle tone. "If the servant has done a minor mistake, I am content to merely give a harsh beating. However, I am inclined to think that what you did today was a major one. And you know what happens to those who fail me in such a horrible manner."

Liam shook his head, unable to speak with the icy grip fear had on his heart. He wanted to keep at least a modicum of dignity even though he had to be careful of what he said to his master. Vlad had ripped the heads off the servants who made snarky comments towards him.

"Today," Vlad said, "I will just drink your blood, since I tend to maim my servants when I torture them. I do not want to irreparably damage my janitor, who would clean my mansion then?"

Vlad ripped open Liam's shirt, exposing the latter's neck. His mouth opened wide, a soft rattle issuing out as his fangs extended. The smell of rancid blood hit Liam right in the face. A cold wave of fear radiated throughout his entire body as Vlad took his time moving toward his neck. A vision of his dead body slumped against the wall, blood spurting from his torn neck flashed right before his eye.

Liam was never able to fully remember what happened next, feeling like an out-of-body spirit watching things through a thick fog. Somehow, he managed to get Nelson's charm out of his pocket without Vlad noticing. A bright silver aura glowed as the bat grew in length, shining on both.

"What the hell?" Vlad said, before Liam slammed the bat right into his head. He fell to the floor with a sickening crunch, as his bones had become weak with the lack of fresh, healthy blood.

Liam bent down and swung the bat again, running purely on a raw survival instinct screaming at him to finish the monster off. Black blood decorated his clothes as he smashed Vlad's head into a gooey paste, the squishy, crunchy noises ringing in his ears. He never noticed his arms aching from the strain of the bloody deed or the blood drying on his face. All he noticed was the blinding desire to live at all costs, even if it meant betraying his master.

However, Liam was a mortal man, not a vampire; so even he began to feel the fatigue welling up in his body. His arms slowed down, the bat's blows getting gentler until it was lightly tapping the pulpy mass of Vlad's head. As Liam grew tired, his awareness came back to him in increments. He stared at the blood covered silver bat, glowing brightly with its magical aura. Liam couldn't remember taking out the bat; in fact, he could barely remember killing his master, it felt like he watched those memories through a blurry haze.

The silver bat dropped out of his hands when he fully realized what he had done. A flash of light temporarily blinded his eyes as the weapon turned back into a small trinket. When he opened them again, he stared in bone chilling horror at the pulpy remains of Vlad's head. A large pool of blood underneath. Liam tried to scream, but what came out sounded more like a death rattle.

He slowly backed away from the corpse, as if it would rise again and try to kill him for his betrayal. Liam hit the wall with a soft bump, his eyes opened in mild shock. He then slid down the wall, still staring at Vlad's corpse as he sat down. He continued to look for about two hours, trying to prevent an emotional overload as he realized what he did.

What do I do now? He thought as he achieved a fragile mental balance. *My entire life revolved around my master. I thought I would live the rest of my life serving Vlad, not killing him with a baseball bat.*

Liam spent the rest of the day staring at the corpse, taking deep breaths to strengthen his emotional equilibrium. When the sun finally set, he slowly got up, walking upstairs with a zombie like gait. He went to the bathroom and washed his face before going to his bedroom. He stripped down to his boxers, flinging his clothes on the floor. Liam fell face first on his bed, wrapping himself up in blankets and hoping sleep would give him the peace he desperately craved.

Liam's dreams were plagued by blood covered

silver bats bearing the face of his master. Vlad called him a vile traitor and other horrible names as he swung himself at Liam, breaking every bone in his body. Liam woke up in a cold sweat, pulling the blankets tightly as he shivered in horror.

***

Nelson hummed a cheery tune as he flew a kite near the old, gnarled tree in the wasteland. He had explored the ruins of a city and had stumbled upon the decaying corpses of a family sitting around a dinner table as he explored their home. The mold covered food on the dinner plates indicated their death took place at the beginning of the nuclear apocalypse. He was able to bury the bodies, but the horrific scene still lingered in his head. He flew a kite to help him forget about the whole thing.

This was a great idea. He thought, smiling as he saw the kite doing a crazy figure eight against the grey sky. It was a splash of bright red standing out amidst the background of dark clouds, showing how moments of beauty and joy could flourish even in a bleak wasteland.

A noise of shuffling feet jolted him out of his happy thoughts. He turned around and saw a familiar face slowly walking towards him. Nelson's mouth opened in delight as he furiously wound the kite line on his stake kite winder, very handy for killing feral vampires who ambushed lonely travelers.

"Liam," he said, noticing the heavy, dark bags under Liam's eyes and the wrinkled clothes hanging loosely on his body, "It's great to see you, but you look like hell. What happened?"

"I killed my master," he said, sounding like he had a stressful day at work instead of killing another person, even if they were a blood sucking corpse. "He wasn't happy about the animal blood I gave him and tried to drink my blood. I instinctively attacked him with your magical bat and bashed his brains out."

"Woah! I'm not surprised you attacked him," Nelson said, his face scrunched with disgust. "Still, killing a person must've sucked; even if they were an abusive, bloodsucking vampire." He put a hand on Liam's shoulder, gently petting it in sympathy.

"Thanks," Liam said, giving a tiny smile despite the emotional turmoil he felt now. "I fled the house the next day. I couldn't stay there after what I did. I know all of Vlad's friends died when the nukes were launched, so I'm safe. But the house brought up way too many painful memories. I figured I would ask you for help in finding a new home."

"Wow, that is pretty bad," Nelson said, mulling over what happened to his new friend. "What can I do to help?"

"Do you know anybody who needs a janitor? Cleaning services are in short supply in a post-apocalyptic world after all," Liam replied, nervously laughing to control the overwhelming fear of becoming useless. What if Nelson told him he didn't know anybody who wanted a janitor? He couldn't see a life not doing the job he loved so dearly. "If there isn't anybody you know who needs one, I understand."

"Hold on for a second," Nelson said, holding up his hand before pondering about it. He put his hand under his chin, making it into a fist. His brow scrunched up.

A few minutes passed; Liam's stomach clutched in nervous anticipation as he watched his friend in deep thought. Would there be a miracle for him, or was fate playing a cruel trick on him? He was sorely tempted to shake Nelson and tell him to hurry up, but he couldn't do it to somebody who had showed him some actual kindness. He took a deep breath and suppressed his impatience.

Nelson darted his head straight up, giving out a burst of happiness as he finally got an idea. He had a huge grin on his face, his eyes lighting up with boundless joy. His fist uncurled and dropped to his side as he spoke.

"I think I found a way to solve your problem," he replied. "The old mage who is mentoring me has a really messy home with stuff all over the place. Heck, the last time I went to the bathroom, there was a thriving eco system in there."

"No way," Liam said, eyebrows rising in suspicion. "I've seen hundreds of horrifically messy bathrooms. But it's impossible for an ecosystem to thrive there."

Nelson suppressed the urge to roll his eyes in disbelief. "It does when the owner of the house uses his magic to create it from the dirt in the bathroom."

"Wow," Liam said, surprised. "Your friend is a handful like my late master was."

"Don't worry," Nelson said, "He can be grumpy at times, but he's a decent guy. He'll be grateful for your help."

"It's great to know nice masters exist," Liam said, the weight in his stomach lifting away as his future became brighter. "I've been with Vlad for so long, I forgot there were masters who do treat their servants well."

"You definitely need to serve a better boss," Nelson said. "Vlad got you believing abusive bosses were normal. No self-respecting worker uses the term 'Master'."

"My master ripped the heads off of anybody who showed the slightest disrespect," Liam said, chuckling nervously. "I had to do what I did to survive."

"You won't have to worry about it anymore," Nelson replied. "I'll make sure no supernatural creature ever hurts you again." He put a comforting hand on Liam's shoulder, the latter smiling gratefully.

Nelson gently took his hand away after a few seconds, thinking for a moment before another idea came into his head. "Anyways, why don't you join me today in kite flying. Considering how haggard you look, you need a break." He held the kite winder in front of Liam's face, like it was a magical gift he wanted to share with his friend. "Besides, my hands are getting tired."

"Are you sure?" Liam said, looking at the winder hesitantly, "What if I accidently damage the kite?"

"Don't worry about it," Nelson said, patting him on the shoulder. "I can easily repair the kite with a few pieces of scrap paper. I've damaged the kite myself."

"Well, okay," Liam said, giving a small smile as Nelson handed him the kite winder. "Thank you for everything,"

"Think nothing of it," Nelson said, taking his duster off so he could sit down on the ground. "I'll just rest up and watch you have fun." He laid it right in front and sat down, looking up at the sky.

"Okay," Liam said, "I've never flown a kite before, so tell me what to do if I can't control it."

"Sure," Nelson said, gently laughing as he watched Liam flying the kite. It zigzagged hesitantly across the sky. "Just make sure you don't accidently hit any angry, marauding biker gangs."

"I'll do my best," Liam said, laughing before becoming quiet, content to watch the kite flying lazily in the sky.

Ilona
Gregory Von Dare

Part One: WHITE RIBBONS

"Don't let the Russian soldiers take you," my mother said. "Do anything. Run till you drop, but do not let them take you. Understand?"

I whispered that I did, but I didn't really. I was only fourteen years old, a foolish girl who lived in a backward part of Moldavia. I thought all soldiers were the same—heroes with big moustaches.

"They will ruin you," she said. "They will do terrible things to you, my little dumpling. Then they will cut you in two with their bayonets and let your blood soak into the ground. You must live for your country, not die for it."

I didn't want to be cut in two, so I nodded.

Mother took my face in her hands and kissed me on the forehead. She was a small woman, her mouth wrinkled and her back bent. Her hair was gray and wispy under a stained babushka. One of her eyes looked cloudy as a winter day and when she smiled, several teeth were missing. She was old long before her time. I promised myself that I would never be such as she was.

I heard a booming noise like thunder. "Will it rain, momma?"

"No little one, those are French cannon."

"What is cannon?"

Her eyes grew wide and she smiled sadly. "It is like a hollow log and from one end comes fire and smoke, then far away a building falls down."

"No! How can that be?"

"You will see very soon. The French are coming this way and the Russians are leaving. I cry for those souls who live on the main road, for they will feel the Russians' anger. Here on the rump of Balaklava we should be safe enough."

"I hope so."

"You are a good girl, Ilona. Now, watch the soup while I run to market. I thought I had carrots. If the soup boils, swing the pot away from the fire, yes?"

"Yes, momma."

She rushed out and had taken no more than five steps when the whole world exploded and everything turned black.

I woke up, covered in dirt, dust and pieces of brick. Someone was feeling my legs. I hoped it wasn't a Russian soldier. Fearful, I opened my eyes. To my great surprise, it was a nobleman from my own country. The nobleman had a thin face with much curly hair near his ears and large brown eyes like a deer. On his upper lip he wore a tiny, waxed moustache with upturned ends. He had a dimple in his chin.

"Where's my momma?"

The man took his time and looked at me sadly. He

was dressed in a tight red velvet jacket with a flurry of lace at his throat. His boots were polished and shiny and he wore riding pants the color of honey. I hoped he wouldn't blame me for the house falling down. He gently brushed some dirt off my forehead. He touched my cheek with the back of his hand. His hands were pale with long, thin fingers like a frog's.

"I'm sorry little sparrow, your mother is dead," he told me. "She was walking where the French shell hit and it blew her to tiny pieces. You barely survived yourself. No broken bones at least. I have given you a drink that will bring back your strength."

"Momma is dead?"

"Yes and she can't be given a proper burial for there isn't enough left of her."

I cried without shame, "Where will I live? Who will take care of me?"

"Don't worry, little bird. I will take you in and look after you. You are a very special girl and the good God has brought us together."

So it began.

***

His name was Count Teodor Moldau and he lived in a gigantic house on the Chernya River. He owned a carriage drawn by four horses and had stables behind his house with many other horses. He had servants!

Some of his ways were odd, but I never met a member of the nobility before, so I knew nothing of their customs. He treated me as his own daughter and bought me beautiful dresses in cream, sky blue and yellow. His housekeeper showed me how to tie the white ribbons in my hair that signified I was unmarried and innocent.

Count Moldau practiced a strange ritual every night

and I joined him. We sat at a long table and each of us drank a goblet of duck's blood, freshly drained by the cook. It tasted sweet and meaty, like one of the dark red wines Moldau kept in a chilly cellar below the house. After we had drained our cups he would wish me goodnight and go riding on his black mare, Fenrir. I would dance in front of the fireplace for hours while the groom played Romani music on his ancient violin.

I stayed with Moldau for a year, while the war raged outside. I learned the countries of Europe and could now read a map. The Count told me stories of the world and of distant places he had seen. He taught me many things: how to eat and have manners, how to dance the waltz and how to appreciate art and music. He was a wonderful, gentle, thoughtful man who demanded nothing of me. Every girl should have such a father.

One morning in September of 1855, French soldiers attacked the house and forced their way in, killing several of the servants. They ran up to Count Moldau's bedroom and brought him down to the great room. It took eight brawny men to subdue him, despite his thin arms and legs. While they held him still, one of the soldiers read something from a parchment. I understood nothing. Not a word.

Then a priest came from behind them holding a mallet and a sharply pointed wooden stake. While Count Moldau raged and cursed at them, the priest placed the point of the stake over the Count's heart and with a single heavy blow, drove it clear through his heaving chest.

I screamed and fainted.

This time when I awoke, no one was caring for me. There was no one to be seen. A pile of ashes marked the spot where the count had been killed. As I ran, sobbing, from room to room I realized the servants had fled. My arms and legs were bruised and dirty; my undergarments torn and bloody. I remembered what my mother said so long ago. The soldiers had ruined me, stolen my innocence while I was unconscious. In a fury, I tore the white ribbons out of my hair and threw them into the fire.

I went down to the kitchen and ate bread and cheese and meat. I drank pints of foamy ale. I slit the throat of a duck in a cage and swallowed its hot, salty blood. Karlovy, the groom who played the violin, emerged from a cabinet where he had been hiding.

"We must go," he said, his hazel eyes wide with fear.

"Yes," I agreed.

I knew where the Count kept his secrets. Although the soldiers searched the house and had stolen many things, the Count's hiding place was untouched. It contained stacks of money, jewels, letters of passage, a pair of pistols and many valuable items. Karlovy and I packed three carpet bags with the Count's treasures. I changed my undergarments and dress, then put on the Count's trousers, riding boots and his heavy coat. I told Karlovy to get the carriage. He bowed to me and said he would be my servant for as long as he lived.

We were going to Sebastopol and would find a ship bound for England. The Count once talked of sending me to school there and said there was a man in Oxford who would understand my needs and help me. But first we had to leave Moldavia and the Crimean War behind us.

Part Two: DARK STOCKINGS

She knew it was only a matter of time until they came for her. Despite the Nazis fascination with all things occult and forbidden, they could be very prudish and her "tastes" were well known in the Berlin underground. Any day might bring that knock on the door, any hour.

Well dressed and elegant, she moved at ease through the late afternoon crowds on *Unter den Linden*, Berlin's main drag. With a casual glance behind her, she stopped at the American Express office near Wilhelmstrasse.

"Hello," she said to the telegraph clerk. "Anything for Ilona Moldova?"

The young clerk replied, "Just a minute," and withdrew to page through a hundred envelopes. Due to the increasing violence and danger in 1938 Berlin, people from around the world tried to contact loved ones and make sure they were all right. Some were, some weren't. It made for a heavy volume of telegrams.

He came back with two pale yellow envelopes and held them out with a cocky smile. "Here you are, doll."

She took them and slid a 50 pfennig coin across the counter.

The clerk gave her a crooked smile. "Hey, thanks, sister."

Ilona walked quickly to a small café on Glinke Strasse and ordered a coffee. With growing excitement, she tore open the two envelopes and unfolded her messages. The first one was from her banker in New York saying that all was well with her account, which had grown considerably over the years.

The second one, the one she wanted, was from the Theosophical Society in California. They admired her book about obscure blood rituals of Eastern Europe. They would be glad to sponsor her lecture tour in America. But they could not be of assistance in getting her exit visa from Germany. Such things were very difficult these days. They looked forward to meeting her and hearing firsthand of her many amazing exploits in the Carpathian Mountains.

She hit her thigh with a tight fist and cursed quietly.

Then she called the waiter back and ordered a double schnapps. She downed the fiery liquid in a gulp and ordered another.

As the sun set that evening, Ilona strolled toward her apartment, feeling dark and defeated. She knew she was on a list and getting a visa would be next to impossible, no matter how much she paid out in bribes. Not far from her building, she became aware of a man walking behind her, following her. Their footsteps sounded in unison along the sidewalk, like the dancing feet of Fred Astaire and Ginger Rogers. As she slowed to take out her keys and slide her Walther pistol into a pocket, he caught up to her. The man was tall and broad shouldered, had brown hair and eyes. He wore a belted trenchcoat and fedora hat. His shoes were scuffed.

With a tight smile, he said, "Pardon me, Miss Moldova, it's important that we speak."

"Oh is it?" She sighed in relief: an American.

"Yes, ma'am. I think I can offer you a way out of Germany, in return for a little favor."

"How do you know I want an exit visa?"

"I think we should talk in private."

"Do you have a name, cowboy?"

He almost smiled. "Colonel Drew Preston, ma'am. U.S. Army."

"Perhaps you're a masher who tries to talk his way into women's apartments?"

Preston reached into his pocket and Ilona tightened her grip on the Walther. He took out a leather case. Inside it showed his picture and a United States Army ID.

"I'm on the third floor," she said.

***

Ilona threw her coat across a chair. "May I give you

a drink, Colonel?"

"No ma'am. And you can call me Drew."

"All right. Well, sit down Drew; take a load off."

He removed his hat and trench coat. He wore a chestnut-brown, double-breasted suit with a white chalk-stripe, a white shirt and maroon tie. And…

Ilona almost wet herself. She shrieked with laughter, her face grew red and she bent double. "Oh," she said. "Oh… really…"

Around Drew's neck like an impossible and gauche necklace was a string of garlic cloves threaded with coarse twine.

He actually blushed. "They told me…"

She shook her head in amazement. "What? That this would protect you from the big, bad wolf? My people are less understood than the Gypsies! We live surrounded by myth and lies. Please, take that ridiculous garnish off and leave it in my kitchen—while I make us a drink. I will tell you a few things to set the record straight, yes?"

Drew nodded and went into the kitchen while Ilona walked to a drink cart, near the front bay window of her apartment. She uncorked the gin and made two strong, dry Martinis. When he returned, the garlic was gone and he had the sheepish look of a man who had fallen for a prank.

"Much better," she said, handing him a drink and gesturing him to the sofa, while she sat in an overstuffed armchair. "Now, this is the truth. Certain people, when they drink fresh human or animal blood become… supercharged like a race car. Out of millions of people, only one or two are made this way."

Drew held up a hand. "But, I thought—"

"Please," she said, "let me finish and it will be easier for us to talk."

The American nodded and took a big drink of his

Martini.

Ilona made herself comfortable and sighed. "We are not immortal but the aging process is slowed down to a crawl. Say five years to one. So we live a very long time but not forever. We do not turn into bats or wolves… or turkeys. That is part of the peasant legend surrounding us. Somehow, we can recognize each other. We actually need very little blood to nourish ourselves. Some of my kind, however, are compulsive and will drain a human or animal dry. They are like alcoholics among your people, unable to control their craving. I drink a single cup of animal blood every night and it sustains me. Nor are we superhuman, although we have unusual strength and endurance. We also have great strength of personality and can often bend others to our will. But so can many normal humans. Look how Hitler has hypnotized a whole nation!"

Drew nodded again. "Yes, truly. And that brings us to why I'm here."

She leaned forward in her chair. "Go on."

Drew took another drink. "You make a damn fine Martini, I'll testify to that."

"Please," she said. "Go on."

Drew reached into an inner pocket and took out a small photo. He handed it to Ilona, watching her carefully. "Do you know him?"

The photo was of an older Slavic man with a sharply pointed goatee, wavy hair and deep set, intense eyes. Ilona studied the picture for a moment and then looked up at Drew. "Of course I do. This is Jan Rashevsky, Hitler's occult advisor. I have met with him several times. But you already know that."

"Yes, I do." Drew reached out and she handed the photo back to him. He stared at the face on the print for a few seconds. "I want you to kill him, to drain his blood.

I want you to make it obvious that this was a vampire killing—"

"Oh," she whispered, "that word."

"—and then my people will get you out of Germany. You can go anywhere you want, England, the 'States, South America, Australia. You name it."

Ilona smiled sadly. "Why do you wish him dead?"

"On two separate occasions, Rashevsky has correctly foretold the future for Hitler. It may be a fluke, a random coincidence. But if it isn't, if he truly can see the future, then he becomes a weapon. One that could guarantee the Nazis victory if, or rather when, war breaks out. We believe that if he is killed in this fashion, it will keep the Nazis from looking into the matter. They will accept that Jan went too far with his occult contacts and fell victim to… one of your people."

"And if I refuse?"

Like a man with a sour stomach, Drew's face contracted. "Then, I will denounce you to the Gestapo. And we both know what that means."

Ilona put down the Martini glass and stretched out her long, shapely legs, covered in silk stockings the color of espresso coffee. "You don't give me much choice."

"I'm sorry," he said. "But Rashevsky must die. You are the best way we can think of to make it happen."

"You are right about that. He knows who and what I am. He will see me. But I will drink no more than a cupful of his blood. I have a delicate stomach. The rest must be spilt some other way. I'm sure you can invent something."

"Then you'll do it?"

"Yes. But when I leave Germany, I want to take my servant with me. Karlovy."

"All right. That can be arranged."

A few long moments passed in silence. Drew put his

glass down on an end table. He stood and took his hat and trench coat from the back of the sofa. He had the melancholy air of a man who knows when the evening is over. "I'll call and let the phone ring twice and call back. Then I'll give you final instructions. We'll use the password…dark stockings."

"Yes." Ilona stood and held out her hand. Drew stared at it dully for a moment, then gingerly shook it.

"And good luck," he said. "It's been amazing to meet you." With a nod, Colonel Drew Preston turned and let himself out of Ilona's apartment.

She sank back into her arm chair and couldn't help a small moan.

Karlovy entered from his room. "Are you in pain?"

She looked over at him. "No, and you better start packing. After I kill a man, we're going to America."

"Why not back to Oxford?"

"No, I wore out my welcome over that music student. Remember, the blonde girl who played oboe? We'll go to Chicago. They slaughter a million animals a week there. Rivers of red flow down the streets. I can bathe in it if I like."

"As you wish, madam." Karlovy made a slight bow.

"And bring my goblet of blood now," she said. "I'm exhausted."

Part Three: OVER FIFTY

It would be a senior-singles event, said the email, hosted by allTogether.com.. Meet at Casa Caliente on Taylor Street in the western Chicago suburbs. A night of dancing and mingling. There would be live music. I decided to give it a try.

Picture it. Innocent fun. A little clumsy flirting; maybe a crude joke or two. Some talk about the grandkids and vacation time-shares. Mentions of dead or absent spouses. A bit of unsought investment advice and dire predictions about this year's pennant race. After a few drinks, someone laughs too hard and wets their knickers.

Casa Caliente had high ceilings and colorful murals of Acapulco cliff-diving on the walls. It smelled of cumin and a bit of spoiled meat. The lights were very low. I sat down opposite a nice-looking brunette in a sparkly strapless dress. Her dark hair was lightly streaked with gray and her handsome face was smooth, wrinkled only at the corners of the eyes. I smiled my killer smile. She looked away. Shy, I thought. But there was a kind of music, a poetry in her eyes. They were very powerful and deep, those eyes.

We exchanged names. I am Heller, she's Ilona. I'm from Swedish ancestry, and she seems to be an import from Eastern Europe. That's not unusual for the Midwest. I told her that I had been an executive in the insurance industry. She said that she liked to travel and meet new people. I invited her to dance when the band of senior musicians played a Foxtrot but she declined.

"Perhaps," she said, "if they play a Polka?"

But they didn't.

She asked my age and I told her. "How about you," I said. "Are you over fifty?"

"Well over fifty," she whispered, with a wink. She did not look it.

It seemed we didn't have much more to say. I was about to write the whole evening off as a loss when my empty wine glass tipped over and broke with a melodic *tink*. I'm not sure how it happened, but it did and Ilona looked at me with a raised eyebrow. I gathered the shards together and tried to put them in a pile. In the process I brushed my hand over a sharply curved piece of wineglass and got a surprisingly deep cut on my thumb.

As the ruby drops of blood appeared, Ilona grew disturbed, or excited; I'm too old to know which anymore. Her face flushed and her eyes opened wide.

"You are bleeding," she said in that peculiar accent of hers.

"Yeah," I replied. "It's nothing."

"Oh, no!" she said. "We must take care of it. At our age, a cut can become infected with many bad things. Perhaps I can help you?"

"How do you mean?" I asked, naively.

She stood up, her eyes never leaving the gathering stream of red on my thumb. "Come," she said and took my hand. "We'll fix it."

She led me into the darkened kitchen and found a quiet corner near the walk-in fridge. "You see," she said, "when wild animals are cut or injured, they lick the wound because there are elements, chemicals in saliva which sterilize a cut and help it to seal off, to stop bleeding. I know it must sound strange, but I can lick this for you and make it stop bleeding… if you like?"

She still had my hand in her grasp and held it rather firmly.

"Can't we just take a napkin and tie it around?"

"No!" she said forcefully. "These napkins are not clean as people think. And look, it is still bleeding."

"But we're in a kitchen. People get cut here all the time. They must have a drawer with bandages and iodine or something like that."

"If you let me lick your wound, you can touch my sexy parts, right now. What do you say?"

It was an intriguing offer. "All right," I told her. "Even if you're just kidding. You've made me smile and that's worth something. Go ahead."

With a strange, triumphant look, she raised my cut

thumb to her mouth and drew it in between full, soft lips. An expression of profound ecstasy came over her face. I actually wanted to look away, it was a moment of such extreme and private pleasure. I was almost sure she had an orgasm just then, the way her body trembled. She sucked on my bleeding thumb and rolled her tongue around it as, I thought, a prelude to other delights.

After a long while, she took my thumb out of her mouth and there was but a thin red line where the glass had sliced me.

"As I told you, she said, "bleeding has stopped."

Then, she lifted the hem of her sparkly dress and slid my hand down into her brief, see-through green undies. I felt the compression of the nylon fabric on the back of my hand and the crinkly roughness of her pubic hair on my fingertips and palm. I didn't need instructions for this part. Soon, another spasm shook her body. Moments later, she cried out in a foreign language.

"Please," she said after calming down a bit, "please let me lick your thumb again. To seal off the wound."

I could hardly say no at this point. I withdrew my hand from her mons and raised it to her face. I was shocked by the passion with which she took it, smelling as it now did of sex, and pulled it toward her mouth. As she opened her lips, I had a glimpse of sharply pointed teeth. The next moment, I felt a stabbing pain like a dagger when she bit down hard on my inner wrist. As I watched in awe, she sucked up the blood that poured from a double puncture there.

I was sure I was dreaming and don't remember her saying goodnight.

But, next day at the hospital, the doctor in the emergency room told me that I suffered a very unusual injury. "How did this happen?" he asked, completing some delicate stitching on the muscles and tendons of my wrist.

"I cut it on a broken wineglass," I told him. And smiled at his look of surprise.

You know, once my hand heals up, I think I'll try another of those senior-get-togethers. Maybe Ilona will be there. I liked her.

Jump Scare
Loki DeWitt

In the early hours of June 6, 1944, before the sun had even risen over the beaches at Normandy, over 13,000 United States paratroopers descended into France. This effort was not without significant cost as several complications rose to make their difficult job that much more so. By the time all was said and done, many soldiers' lives were lost and a multitude went missing in the chaos of war, never to be found again. This is the story of what happened to one of those soldiers on that fateful night.

It didn't matter how loudly the engines of the C-47 roared, Charles Campbell could hardly hear them over the sound of his own heart pounding in his head. The war against the Axis Powers had raged for years and showed no signs of ending. War had a funny way of making people think outside the box, and that is exactly what some of the brass had done. They had formulated a plan that would either turn the tide against the enemy or lose ground that they might never regain. To set this plan in motion, they needed volunteers. As a red-blooded country boy from North Carolina, Charles jumped at the chance to take part in this radical strike. After several months of training, the time had finally come and now he was in a perfectly good airplane flying above a small town in France, and he was about to jump out of it. His eyes had been locked onto the red light near the rear entrance of the plane since it had lit up. He was hooked up to the jump line and even though he was nervous, he couldn't let that show. The light flashed from red to green and the plane full of still soldiers suddenly set to motion. One by one, they leapt out of the safety of the plane. As they jumped out, the hook pulled their parachute from its pack and sent them sailing through the night sky.

Charles had expected to land under the cover of darkness, but the volley of shells exploding all around him like fiery thunderclaps saw to it that he wouldn't be getting the luxury of stealth. As the artillery bursting around him revealed the truth of the situation, Charles pushed back the panic that was threatening to overtake him. Instead, he closed his eyes and took a deep breath. While things were far from ideal at that moment, he had spent months training for it and had absolutely zero intentions of letting his country down. The sound of an artillery shell whistling past him caused him to snap his eyes back open. While he was still doing his best to remain calm, the near miss served as a stark reminder that he had to keep his wits about him, even so far above the ground. His eyes darted around, trying to take in everything unfolding around him. Besides the sounds of the artillery shells whizzing to take out the planes that soared through the air, he could see numerous parachutes drifting downward. Occasionally, one of those bright lights would stop short and make one of the parachutes vanish from sight. The panic tried to take over again. Charles couldn't continue to watch his fellow paratroopers be snuffed out by the onslaught, because each one he saw did nothing but remind him that the next one to be snuffed out in midair could be him. So, he looked to the one place he hadn't yet looked; down. He had expected to see the town coming into detail below him. Instead, he saw nothing other than small flickers of light. The panic was becoming nearly impossible to push back, so Charles did the one thing that always brought him comfort: he prayed. As the words of the Lord's Prayer left his mouth, he closed his eyes for one brief second, silently hoping that the Lord wouldn't see fit to call him home in the middle of his petition.

When his eyes opened once more, thick fog had enveloped him completely and obscured his vision. He could only make out the bright flashes of the continuing hail of shells and the occasional shadow of his fellow paratroopers. Though he could still hear the battle raging, there was something about the haze that helped to calm his nerves. While the fact that he was essentially blind should have heightened his terror, the removal of so many of the visual reminders of near certain death seemed to have the opposite effect. Things seemed to slow down as he continued to drift through the mist. He took a deep breath and sent a short thanks Heavenward. As he continued his descent, he tried to put his focus back where it belonged, on the mission that awaited him on the ground. He knew that regardless of how everything else had unfolded up to that point, the endgame was the most important part of everything that might happen that night. As he thought of how nice it would be to strike back against the sinister forces that had caused so much pain to the good, decent people of the world, he couldn't help but smile. "God bless America." The words escaped his lips effortlessly and galvanized his resolve. In fact, his simple statement of patriotism had stoked the embers of his focus back to a fire. As that flame rose inside him, he yelled the words out into the fog to push away any fear or doubt that may have been lingering in his heart. "GOD BLESS AMERICA!" The words cut through the German thunder and rallied his fellow soldiers, with several returning his cry. In that moment, he felt truly invincible. His heart pumped with pride as the flashes of light continued to cut through the fog. Even though he was still descending at the same speed, everything had seemed to slow down in the fog. In his mind, he went back over what he was supposed to do as soon as he was safely on the ground. He glanced down, past his boots toward the ground he could not see. As he did, a shell cut through the fog, providing a moment of light. That was when he saw it. Someone was below him. Sure it was another paratrooper, he shouted out the inspirational cry. The words were cut short by the explosion of another round. This one flashed just as brightly as the ones that had come before it. It even illuminated the area around him once more. With his eyes still cast downward, he saw that whoever was below him had somehow done something that should have been impossible: They had risen.

He squinted his eyes as the light faded. Surely his eyes were playing tricks on him from the sudden brightness that appeared in the fog. After a few moments, another shell sheared through the fog, bringing the slightest moment of illumination along with it. As the light passed through the shroud, this time, Charlie saw nothing below him. He chuckled lightly and shook his head. Clearly, between all the chaos and the stir of emotions rushing through him, he was just seeing things for a moment. The fog made the air thick, but Charlie drew in a deep breath. The sounds of explosions continued to come from seemingly everywhere, but the lights seemed to not be as close. A smile came to his face as he exhaled. Maybe all his panic earlier had been for nothing and he was going to survive this after all. A loud noise ripped Charlie from his thoughts. This time, though, it wasn't the sound of German launched explosions, it was the sound of a blood-curdling scream. The scream continued to ring in Charlie's ears, somehow drowning out the barrage of artillery that had so easily dominated only seconds earlier. Panic shot through Charlie's body again. Every time one of the shells found a target, there were no screams as the bright death seemed to snuff out its victims quickly and without mercy. This scream was something altogether different, though. It was a mixture of terror and pain. Whoever was screaming was clearly in a great deal of pain. His eyes darted back and forth to see if he could detect where the screaming was through the seemingly impenetrable fog. "Where are you? What's wrong?" Charlie knew the words were most likely useless given the current circumstances, but he spoke them out of instinct. The questions were answered by the continued sound of the scream. His heart raced in his chest as he continued to look around. Suddenly, the scream went silent. As much as the sourceless sound of pain had sent chills up his spine, the silence that replaced it only seemed to make things worse. Though he wasn't sure what he expected to see, Charlie's eyes continued to scan across the fog. The moments of silence surrounded only by fog were agonizing. Then his eyes finally caught something. Something was drifting through the dense mist and came right toward Charlie. He squinted his eyes to see if he could figure out what it was as it came closer. It took a few moments before it finally came into sight. The thing coming toward Charlie was a large piece of white cloth that was stained with several splatters of crimson. The piece of cloth nearly blew past Charlie, but he reached out and caught it. With it firmly in hand, he brought it close to his face so that he could get a better look at it in the fog. As his eyes focused on it, a cold chill swept up his spine. The cloth in his hand was a piece of parachute. His body trembled as his mind put together a sequence of terrifying thoughts. He wasn't sure how, but someone was up there with them, someone who clearly had no problem cutting them out of the sky.

He let go of the cloth, and it floated away, disappearing into the fog. His hand reached for the one weapon he had that wasn't tied to his leg, a combat knife. The knife had been left in reach in the event that he had somehow been caught up in something while landing, but it had become his lone defense against whatever had attacked the other soldier. The knife exited its sheath with a slight scraping sound. The sound hit Charlie's nerves and nearly made him jump out of his skin. With his weapon now firmly in hand, Charlie swallowed hard and waited, hoping that whatever was out there wouldn't find him next.

The moments continued to pass as they had earlier, but now they seemed like an eternity. Charlie could barely hear the shells any longer, as the pounding of his own heart banged loudly in his ears. He continued to take short, shallow breaths as he kept looking all around him. Another scream ripped through the mist. This one didn't last as long as the one before it. That didn't matter to Charlie though, because while it may have been shorter, it was also closer. His whole body trembled as the fear fueled adrenaline coursed through him. "Our Father, who art in Heaven….." The prayer came from his lips nearly instinctively. He had already called out to the Lord once, but somehow, this petition was that much more urgent. Another shell exploded into the night sky, but as the artificial thunder faded, another sound took its place, a predatory screech. Charlie's head snapped in the sound's direction. The lights from the continued barrage provided the slightest reprieve from the fog. The faint light was just enough to reveal what Charlie feared the most. Whatever was up there with them was coming right at him.

Charlie lifted his knife, but the thing was supernaturally fast and was on him in mere moments. The impact of the thing caused Charlie to jerk sharply through the fog. With the monster now on top of him, he could finally get a good look at it. It was an unholy abomination, a wicked combination of man and bat. Its eyes glowed red in the fog, and its mouth was filled with two rows of razor-sharp teeth that were already stained crimson from its previous work. What Charlie was looking at was impossible, yet there it was. He had read stories about these kinds of things when he was younger, but never for a moment thought that they were real. Yet the monstrosity that was now moments from taking his life proved that they did indeed exist. Charlie had been so worried about the Germans, never once considering that his life might end at the cruel whim of what he had previously thought to be just a myth. The creature opened its maw wide and moved to plunge the mouthful of daggers into his flesh. Charlie quickly moved the knife and the steel blade collided with the teeth, narrowly stopping the impending death that they promised. The creature bit down on the blade as it let out a growl. Its red eyes flashed with anger as they met Charlie's. Still afraid, Charlie knew he had to move fast. He quickly yanked the blade out of the clamp of the creature's jaws, slashing its cheek open as he did so. The creature shrieked again, but this time it was one of pain. It pushed away from Charlie and flew back far enough to take stock of its wound. Charlie did the same. The cut opened up the creature's cheek, nearly back to its jaw. Charlie took in a quick breath. Something told him that this creature wouldn't be so easily beaten.

The creature let out another primitive cry as it soared back toward Charlie. As it collided with the paratrooper, a shell exploded somewhere in the fog, punctuating the struggle that was hidden from most eyes by the enveloping mist.

The creature moved to tear into Charlie's flesh with its jagged teeth once more. Between the training and the adrenaline, Charlie responded without hesitation and delivered the tip of his knife hard into the jaw of the creature. This time the creature didn't flee, though. Instead, it dug its long talons into Charlie's ribs. As the creature's fingers tore into the paratrooper's soft skin and scraped the bone beneath, Charlie let out a yell of pain. The agony of his insides being explored by the creature was nearly unbearable, but just as it had been since the moment he leapt out of the plane that brought him here, Charlie was determined not to die. He pulled the blade from the creature's face and stabbed at it repeatedly. The steel punched into the creature's face and neck repeatedly, causing its black blood to spill out into the air. The two continued to fall through the air, locked in a life and death struggle.

Charlie pulled the steel blade free from the creature's neck and went to plunge it back in once more. As the knife headed toward its target, the creature twisted its head. Instead of finding the neck of the bat thing, the knife landed in the open mouth of the creature.

The rows of vicious teeth closed down immediately on the knife and the hand that held it. Charlie howled as the jagged teeth shredded his hand to pieces. Between the claws still digging in his side and his only manner of defense being torn to shreds, Charlie knew he had to make some distance between himself and the bat creature. He lifted his foot and kicked the monster hard in the stomach. The impact served its purpose and violently pushed the creature away from him, freeing him from its viciousness, if just for a moment. In that same moment, though, the creature's teeth had also done their job. Charlie looked down at the bloody stump that used to be his hand and let out an anguished cry. Not only was he missing a hand, but he was quickly losing blood while still falling through the air. He lowered his head as he tried not to look into the fearsome face of the creature that had caused him so much pain. As he did, he caught sight of something he had nearly forgotten about in the struggle, his leg bag. It would be difficult, but if he could get into that bag, then he might get out his gun and put an end to the creature once and for all.

The paratrooper kicked the latch on his leg bag, causing it to go sliding down his leg and dangle just past his feet. With the bag now off his leg, Charlie rocked back and forth. His whole body swayed as he gained momentum. The creature spit the mangled remains of the knife out of its blood-soaked mouth as it watched its prey carefully. Charlie did his best to ignore the fearsome visage of the creature. He knew that he would only have one shot at what he was attempting, and any distraction meant failure and failure was death. The creature shrieked and rushed back toward Charlie. Seeing that he had to move immediately, Charlie kicked up with all his momentum. The bag came flying up toward Charlie. A small smile somehow appeared on his face as he saw the olive-green duffle sack coming up toward him. He reached out his still intact hand, prepared to catch the pack that held the only weapons he had left to fight with.

The bag never landed in Charlie's hand. Instead, it landed in the creature's grip. Charlie looked at the creature in disbelief as it looked down at the bag. "NO!" Hot tears streamed down his face as the finality of his fate settled into his mind. The creature eyed the rope at the end of the bag. Charlie screamed out again, but the creature didn't seem to notice. Charlie shook the leg that was still attached to the rope to get free from the binding. The bat thing looked up at Charlie, and with its rows of teeth, it smiled cruelly. The creature soared upward, the bag still in hand. The sudden shift in momentum turned Charlie upside down. As his parachute turned inside out, his drift toward the ground stopped. He hung there, suspended in the air by only his leg. The tears stung in his eyes as he tried to lift and get a look at the creature. It took every bit of the energy he had left, but he finally glimpsed the creature just in time to see it let go of the bag.

Charlie's life flashed before his eyes as he hurtled toward the ground. He was still so young and had done so little. From Holidays with family, to playground scuffles, all of it came flooding back. Eventually, memories of moments earlier played in his mind. He knew that the risk of death was part of being a soldier, but never in a million years had he expected it to be at the hands of some…... vampire. He didn't even have time to consider the madness of it all before he felt intense pain shoot through his entire body before everything turned black.

"Hello American." The voice had a heavy German accent. Charlie wasn't sure how he heard it. After all, most people who fell out of the sky died immediately. It appeared as though fate wasn't quite done with Charlie though. He tried his best to open his eyes, but doing so caused him intense pain. Instead, he just lie there, agony shooting through his entire body and listened to the voice continue. "You are going to die." Charlie would have scoffed, but that would have required that he be able to move. "But that seems like such a waste. You see, American, you are a worthy foe. That is why I am going to give you a choice. You could lie here and die, a warrior forgotten to time, no one ever knowing what truly happened to you." Charlie wasn't sure where the voice was going. He was fairly certain that what it described was exactly what was going to happen. "Or, I can make it where not only will you live through this, but I can also make it where you never fall from the sky again."

The body of paratrooper Charles Campbell was never recovered.

Lilitu

Helen Mihajlovic

When Reina Feldman grew weary of a troublesome world, she escaped it for a while. She liked to walk through the city late at night, when the crowds were gone, enjoying the silence of the empty streets. She spent hours gazing at architecture, a source of inspiration for her designs.

The urban high-rises appeared identical, oblong shapes that filled the skyline, but among the ordinary structures stood a majestic building. It had a Gothic facade with two grotesquely carved creatures perched on sandstone above the entrance, glaring down at her.

The moonlight streamed through lancet windows and when she put her face to the glass and peered through – as she had done many times before – she marveled at the vaulted ceilings and the grey Corinthian columns with gilded acanthus leaves.

The building had not been used for any commercial purpose for years and she had heard an unknown buyer had bought the property. It remained dark inside, but occasionally Reina would see a light in one of the windows on the top floor. But she had never seen a person enter or leave the building.

Reina craned her neck to the sound of a violent flutter. She could make out two large, crooked wings on the rooftop. It appeared that a large bird had landed on the tower and its feet were of a Corvidae. Sharp claws gripped the tower's iron lace trimming.

The bird soon disappeared, and a chill ran through her. As she turned to leave, a sign in the window caught her eye.

Room for Lease. Enquire Within.

"Good evening."

Reina started; she had not heard anyone approach. She turned to a tall man in a navy-blue suit. He had long dark brown hair that extended down his shoulders, thin square glasses that framed pale blue eyes and a long, trimmed and pointed beard. "Are you looking for a place to lease?"

"Yes," she said.

"I am Bradley Elrod. It's a pleasure to meet you." He stretched out his hand and shook hers.

"I am Reina Feldman. I am looking for a place to work from. My lease expires on my flat in a week."

"What sort of work do you do?" he asked.

"I'm a freelance architect."

He stroked his long beard. "The basement is for lease and the owner is providing an option to sleep at the property for a little extra."

"Aren't you the owner?" asked Reina.

"No, the owner isn't in at the moment,"

"Shall I come back during the day?"

"You can come back at the same time tomorrow night. I will tell her you want to discuss the lease."

Reina nodded. "I will come."

"Good night," he said.

Reina felt intrigued as he entered the building through the side door. She thought herself fortunate to have found a new place to live. She quickly ran back to the station to catch the last train home.

***

The following night, Reina stood before the front door admiring the black, iron foliage that curled on the wood. The lease sign had been taken away and this was the first time she had seen the lights shining through the windows on the first level.

Reina grew puzzled, she noticed there was no doorbell or knocker. A security camera looked down at her from above the door. She felt watched.

A few moments later, Bradley opened the front door, wearing the same navy-blue suit.

"Welcome Reina," he said. "Come inside."

When she walked in, a musty smell filled the air. Her gaze rose to the imposing height of the hand-painted ceiling decorated with gold leaf. A mirror hung over a marble fireplace, with a velvet sofa by its side and her feet sunk into dark red carpet.

"Is that a Rococo mirror?" asked Reina.

"Yes, the owner bought it during her travels abroad."

Reina admired its ornate frame with exquisite scrolls.

She followed him to a staircase descending to the basement and a dusty hallway with a few narrow doors. She held back a sneeze.

He opened one of the doors and they walked inside a dark room.

A moment of fear crossed her as she stood with Bradley in the darkness. As her eyes became accustomed, she saw another person at the other side of the room.

A thin woman stood near the window, moonlight beaming through the glass pane behind her, and she appeared as a silhouette. The woman switched on a tiny lamp on the table, only adding light to the immediate vicinity. Reina could finally see the woman's face: dark brows arched over large eyes that held a deep solemn look, her long hair had a slight curl at the ends and a fringe brushed away from a narrow face. She wore a black dress, with long draped sleeves and a high neckline. She appeared fairly youthful in the dimness of the light, but Reina could not guess her age.

"I'm Lilian Laurier." She was softspoken and languid in her speech. "I have been told you are interested in leasing the basement."

"Yes, I'm looking for a place to live with a workspace."

Lilian shot a glance at Bradley, who nodded in response and exited.

"Who else lives on the property?" asked Reina.

"I am the only one who lives here," said Lilian.

Reina looked around the room. An ebony oak table sat near the window with a finely carved chair, a pair of bookshelves and drawers near the side walls.

"How much is it?"

"I am leasing it for six hundred dollars a month," said Lilian.

Reina nodded with approval. Her eyes darted in search of a light switch; she couldn't see one. "It's a bit dark in here."

"I can bring a desk lamp to give you enough light to work with."

Reina looked outside the small, barred window and saw a couple of people walking by on the street.

"The panes are tinted, they can't see you, only you can see them," Lilian said. "If you require more furniture, I will ask Bradley to bring something down from upstairs."

"This is ample," said Reina, looking pleased.

"Let me show you the bedroom."

Reina followed Lilian down a hallway, where she was shown a bathroom and small kitchenette. They then walked to a tiny room with quaint furniture at the far end of the basement. A cast iron single bed was in the center and on each side was a French provincial antique drawer. Two paintings hung on the walls; Reina recognized one painting as Gustave Moreau's Venice. The room had no windows and Reina felt slightly claustrophobic.

"I live on the top floor," said Lilian. "But I am a very private person and do not want anyone to enter that area."

"I understand."

"Bradley has told me you are an architect by trade."

"Yes, that's right," said Reina.

"He has seen some of your designs online and was impressed," she said. "I have been searching, for some time, for a skilled architect to design a Gothic home for me in the country."

Reina's eyes lit up. "Gothic architecture is my forte. I would be very pleased to help."

But Reina felt a sudden moment of doubt when Lilian's lips curled into a cold grin.

***

Reina moved into the building a week later. The haunting interiors of the stone basement, the dark chambers, arched doorways and narrow staircases, inspired her as she began sketching Lilian's Gothic country home.

Whenever Reina designed a building, she always thought carefully of the owner's character and how it would influence the materials used to build it, the walls, the roofs, and foundations. Lilian clashed with the modern world she lived in. She had an old-world charm, her hair was long and flowing like Rossetti's Proserpine, her clothes were made of antique lace that draped the floors, and she surrounded herself in decor from a bygone era. Lilian had assigned her to not only create a home, but a world that was suited to her.

Reina's food was delivered to her weekly and Bradley was assigned to run errands for her, allowing her to focus on her work.

During the day, she did not hear even a footstep in the old building. At times she wondered if she was on her own and Lilian spent the days out, or if she was a late sleeper. But there had always been faint groans at night. She put it down to the wind howling through the rooms as it made its way through the fractures in the house.

***

Reina had been working steadily on Lilian's country home for a fortnight and was almost finished. She looked up at a crack of thunder as it temporarily distracted her from her sketching. When her gaze returned to her sketches, she flicked away a cockroach crawling on the sheet.

She continued working while fierce rain battered the windows.

Suddenly she stopped when a shadow cast across the table. Reina turned to find Lilian peering over her shoulder. In brighter light, Reina could see fine lines etched across Lilian's pale forehead and a curl of grey at her temple, a contrast to her otherwise ebony hair.

"Have you made much progress on the design of my country home?" Lilian asked, in her usual languorous manner.

"I've nearly finished the sketches." Reina shuffled through a pile of papers on the table. "I'm old fashioned, I like to sketch the designs by hand first before they're turned into a computer model."

Reina picked up a smaller sheet with sketches of the building's exterior.

"As per your specifications, the Gothic manor will be made of bluestone and will have six towers, with gargoyles near the front two towers," said Reina pointing to them. She presented a large sheet with a floor plan. "The manor will have fifty rooms: a master bedroom, a loungeroom with a coffered ceiling and an elaborate dining room for dinner parties. There will be large bay windows and a fireplace in nearly every room, with spiral staircases through all three levels."

Lilian's dark eyes fixed on every detail as Reina discussed the sketches.

"I have included three studies and two libraries. At your request I added a private library with a dome ceiling near your bedroom."

"Your skills have exceeded my expectations," said Lilian.

"I've designed an elaborate home as you asked me to," said Reina. "My sketches will be completed by this evening. Bradley has taken my old laptop and mobile phone today to trade them in for new ones. Once he returns, I will have these designs uploaded for your builders."

"Perhaps you will consider designing another home

for me in the future. I intend to have a home built for my overseas travels."

Reina was pleased to know her work was so well appreciated, but as Lilian's gaze remained on her flesh, Reina became slightly nervous. She felt a chill as Lilian left the basement.

Reina worked past midnight and headed to bed satisfied with what she'd accomplished.

When sleep overtook her, a weird noise woke her not long after. The noises seemed different than she had heard on the other nights.

Her limbs trembled as the noise grew louder. Screams echoed through the hallways and seeped through the walls. As she lay in the cold bed, she felt a strange unease creep inside her. She wrung her hands and wondered what lay ahead of her.

***

The following day, Reina dismissed the screams as part of her wild imagination. It was nothing else but the whistle of the wind, she thought.

She shivered as cold air entered through the cracks in the walls. The heat of the lit fireplace upstairs usually found its way to the basement, but she had not felt it for a while.

She grimaced and made her way to the floor above, knowing upstairs the chill in the air

would be gone.

Her face brightened at the magnificence of the gothic revival room with its cavernous space and intricate carvings of foliage that she had seen when she first arrived. She had spent years studying dark interiors and often dreamt she would explore the inside of the Gothic building when she had quietly admired it from the walkway.

Her sense of wonder led her up the marble staircase to the second floor. The walls were a blood red, the stained-glass panes reflecting a myriad of colors, and a vintage chandelier hung from the ceiling.

She succumbed to the temptation of an open door nearby and walking through it found a burnished wooden staircase. As she climbed the stairs, she was mesmerized by the mosaic patterned wall of a double-headed serpent. It continued up the stairs and through the hallway on the top floor. The further she entered the hallway, the dimmer it became, until the walls and rows of doors were barely visible.

She grew nervous when she suddenly remembered the instructions that Lilian had given her: she was not to enter the top level. Turning back towards the stairs, Reina heard a groan behind a door. She became worried that someone was hurt. The noise grew louder, and she anxiously peeked through the keyhole of the chamber.

A woman knelt on a bed. A toss of ebony hair revealed the side curve of a naked, slender back and the white skin of a long neck. Red lips kissed her male companion who lay naked underneath.

Reina withdrew slightly when she realized she had seen an intimate moment between Lilian and a lover.

But her heart beat faster, and even though she was thinking she must leave, being deprived of many desires lured her back. She would remain. She looked through the keyhole once again.

The male had a red flushed face, a slim frame and his lips parted as he let out a groan. Lilian's tongue tasted each part of his body and her motion on him was wild.

As Lilian explored his body with her hand, his eyes shut with a look of pleasure. Reina watched as Lilian's feet morphed into a shape akin to a Corvidae and a large claw appeared on her finger.

Lilian's claw tore at his flesh and his screams penetrated the keyhole. Reina watched on in horror as Lilian ate his flesh with an uncontrollable hunger.

Reina covered her mouth to hold back a scream and ran for the stairs, the floor creaking in her haste. She glanced over her shoulder, hoping Lilian had not heard.

Reina's blood pulsed as she rushed down the stairs. She headed to the front door of the building, but it was shut. She tried each door – they were all locked. Sobbing, she hurried to the basement. She reached for the bars on the windows and shook them in a frantic attempt to escape. A cold hand reached from behind and grasped her arm. Reina gasped. She turned her head and Lilian's dark eyes stared at her.

As Lilian touched Reina, a vision came unbidden. A naked woman – who looked like Lilian – lay on verdant grass, a serpent slithering beside her. Her dark tresses brushed against her white skin as she turned towards a tall man standing before her. She rose, walking past the tall man to the towering tree, where crimson fruit with an alluring aroma delivered a temptation, yet she resisted.

She craved for freedom above all else.

"Lilith!" called Adam after her, as she left the garden.

Reina felt the sharpness of Lilian's claw as her vision continued. She heard the screams of men running on a cobblestone road on a stormy night as they were chased. In the dark skies a winged creature with feet of a Corvidae and sharp talons soared above the village.

The men attempted to hide in vain.

"Lilitu!" They screamed, pleading for their lives as she broke down the doors of the medieval cottages.

She goes by many names: Lilith, Lilitu and Lilian,

thought Reina.

Reina was overwhelmed by fear and collapsed.

***

Reina woke in a cold bed, shivering. She didn't know if the visions were reality or dreams. Her anxious mind could be playing tricks on her.

Did I really see Lilian kill a man? she thought.

Reina rose from her bed and began to pace up and down the basement, kicking a cockroach out of her way. She covered her ears when she heard more screams.

Reina desperately made her way to the front door and in vain she tried to open it, but it was locked again. She heard a thumping noise and she snuck up to the next floor. Her lips trembled as she saw Lilian dragging a male's limp body up the staircase and a trail of blood was left on each step. Lilian shot her a deadly look, but then continued to drag the man up the stairs.

Reina assumed Lilian would feed on him. She grabbed her head, shook it and descended back to the basement. She began to scream.

"Murder!"

But she knew that no one from the outside world would be able to hear her.

***

Reina spent the next two nights shaking in her bed, watching the door for the monster. But when her body could no longer resist sleep, she shut her eyes.

After a while, Reina woke to cold lips kissing her mouth and she looked onto Lilian's white face. Reina froze.

Lilian's arms weighed against Reina's shoulders

and her naked body wrapped around Reina's torso. She was a prisoner within Lilian's limbs.

Lilian appeared like a spectral figure, who at times had the wrinkled face of a hag, and at other times had the silky skin of a maiden. Her wide eyes were hypnotic and had a look of evil, a Medusa like stare.

She felt Lilian's long yellow tongue taste her neck and find its way back to her breast.

Reina feared for her life, feared she would become Lilian's prey. But she also felt a strange desire at the touch of Lilian's hand. Petrified with fear, she could not move. With a final kiss, Lilian left Reina's petite frame and crawled out of the room. Reina's limbs were tired, and she drifted back to sleep.

***

Reina sat in the corner of the dark room on the cold floor for a period unknown to her. She grinded her teeth and clenched her fists, beating them on the ground. The moonlight beamed on her greasy, unkempt hair as she sat there surrounded by cockroaches crawling on the cold ground.

She glanced to the table where she left her sketches, but it appeared emptier. She stood up, lifted her books from the table and shifted papers, searching for her design of Lilian's Gothic country home. But her sketches were gone.

She let out a scream of mental anguish and grasped her hair.

When she heard voices outside the building, her head jolted up. Two people were talking near her window and the man's voice was familiar. She saw the navy-blue trousers that hung loosely on long limbs. It was Bradley, with a young woman in red stilettos standing by him.

"I am Bradley Elrod. It's a pleasure to meet you."

The young woman let out a flirtatious giggle. "I'm looking for a room to lease."

"There's a basement for lease and the owner is providing an option to sleep at the property for a little extra," continued Bradley.

Reina's mouth fell open. Have they hung a sign on the building advertising the space? But what are they planning to do with me?

She watched as they parted. As Reina shook her head, she saw her reflection on the pane: the hair on her temples had grown white, her eyes encircled by dark shadows and her skin had become a pasty color.

***

The next day, the building was silent, and Reina had not seen Lilian. She lay in her bed, crippled by her mind, unable to move. When she heard a rustling sound outside her room, she hid her face behind trembling hands. The doorknob turned with a screech.

"Reina."

She slowly dropped her hands. Bradley towered over her.

"It's time for you to leave," he said. "I will help you get out of here."

"Yes, Bradley," she said, letting out a sigh. "I don't think I can manage living here anymore. I need to get away from Lilian."

He reached for her bony hand and led her to his car outside.

Reina opened and shut her eyes in a melancholy stupor, while Bradley drove for a long time on an unfamiliar winding country road.

When the car stopped, she looked up to a large, grey building with tiny, barred windows and a clocktower in the center. They walked down an empty corridor with the smell of disinfectant and screams of madness could be heard behind the rows of doors.

She followed him, in a trance, to a tiny white room with a bed and a small chair in the corner. Through the barred windows she glimpsed a large Gothic manor in the distance resting on a hill.

"Where are we?" she asked.

"We let you stay with us till I found another place for you to live," said Bradley.

An asylum! She thought.

"You've served a purpose," he continued.

Reina looked puzzled.

"The lease is always given to people who serve Lilitu's purpose." This was the first time he had referred to Lilian by another name.

"What purpose did I serve?" Reina's voice shook.

"It's your skill as an architect that is of interest to us," he said.

"But the designs I did, they were lost."

"No," he paused. "I took them while you slept."

She raised her brows. "The manor I designed was never built!"

He pointed a long finger outside the window. "That grand manor on the hill is the Gothic manor you designed."

Reina looked out the window in horror. Dusk was falling on a building with six towers and gargoyles near the front. She knew it was her creation.

"When you are better, Lilitu will need you to design another home."

She heard the bang of the door, the key turn in the

lock and Bradley's footsteps grew faint down the corridor.

Reina's lips quivered; her gaze remained fixed on the manor.

From that day forth, Reina's screams could be heard at nightfall as Lilitu flew over the dark sky to seek her prey.

Dedicated to my brother Bill © 2022 Helen Mihajlovic

Love and its Sacrifices
Kay Hanifen

Daddy and I found her by the side of the road. Whoever she was, she was wealthy, rich enough to own a car that she had crashed into the cornfield. The Model T was on its side, and the new moon made it so dark that I almost didn't see it from our buggy. We were on our way back from administering last rights to Bertha Reinfeldt—a girl my age who had fallen ill suddenly—when a movement in the darkness caught my eye. The wheel of the Model T turned lazily in the starlight, and there was a pale hand on the ground.

"Daddy, stop," I said, not even waiting for the buggy to come to a halt before leaping out the side and approaching the owner of the pale hand. It belonged to a woman with an equally pale face obscured by dark hair. She wore fine clothes, finer than my flour sack dress, and a massive diamond on her ring finger. I turned her over to get a better look at her injuries, only to find the most beautiful girl I had ever seen. Her lips were a cherry red, and her long lashes fluttered open, revealing a mesmerizing ice blue that seemed to glow in the darkness. I felt like the Prince Charming to her Snow White. She opened her mouth in an attempt to speak, revealing long canines. I froze, staring at the vicious fangs, but then her eyes fluttered shut in a faint.

I cautiously prodded her lip, but she didn't wake, and her teeth were normal. Perhaps it was just my imagination. Daddy never liked me reading those Penny Dreadfuls. He said they invited darkness into my heart.

"What's wrong with her?" he asked.

I jumped, having half forgotten that he was there. "She's unconscious. We should take her back to the house and call Doc Perry in the morning."

I moved aside to let him pick her up and carry her to the buggy, but the moment he touched her, she cried out and struggled against him. Despite her injuries, she managed to beat him back. Now, my Daddy isn't a small man. He may be the town Preacher, but he's also a farmer, and years of hard labor have made him strong. There was no way this tiny girl could overpower him, but she did.

"God bless it," he swore, stepping back.

"Can I try?" I asked. I'm no waif either and she didn't seem too frightened by my touch earlier. I approached softly and said, "Miss? My name is Laura, and I'm not gonna hurt you. I swear. But we need to get you back to our house so we can call the doctor." She made no protest when I threw her arm over my shoulder and bridal carried her to the buggy. The horse, Buttercup, snorted and danced at the extra weight, but we were close to home, so she just had to bear it.

I held her to me and was struck by just how cold she felt. It was a late summer evening—one of the last warm ones before the autumnal chill—but she was ice. Though unconscious, she seemed aware of that fact and nestled in close to me as though seeking warmth. The heat in my face alone should have been enough to warm her. Finally, we reached the farmhouse. I carried her to the guest bedroom while Daddy lit the candles. We hadn't had a guest in a long time, so placing her on the bed stirred up enough dust to make me cough.

Daddy brought a candle into the room, and we checked her over. She had a bruise on her temple, and superficial cuts and scrapes. Most likely, it was the shock of what happened that kept her from waking.

"You go on to bed, Daddy," I said, "I'll keep an eye on her."

"Just be careful. I've never seen her around before, and strangers don't just wander through town unless they're looking for trouble."

I stared pointedly at her small, thin frame. "I think I can manage."

He smiled, and I could see the pride plain on his face. "Of course, you can. My little girl's growing up into a woman as kind and brave as her mother."

My cheeks warmed again, and I studied my muddied church Oxfords. "Goodnight, Daddy. Love you."

"Goodnight, Laurabell."

With that, he left me alone with the strange, beautiful girl asleep in our guest bed. I pulled Mama's cross necklace out from under my dress and took the crucifix from the wall. I felt silly doing so, but better safe than monster chow. As the candle burned low, I began to drift in a half-asleep stupor. Between this stranger and watching death pluck a young life like a spring flower, I felt physically and emotionally wrung-out.

I was awakened by movement and a hiss. It was in the grey area between night and dawn where the world itself seemed reluctant to wake. But the woman in the bed was more than awake. She was alert and glaring at me. "Where am I? What do you want?" she asked, speaking in an accent I didn't quite recognize.

"Our house. My name's Laura, by the way—" I offered my hand to shake, "—and I don't know about where you're from, but in this part of the world, we thank the people who rescue you from the side of the road and open up their homes to you."

"Why would I thank a couple of fools?" She sat up and then hissed, her hand coming to her temple. I reached out to examine her, but she batted my hand away. "You shouldn't have brought me here. It's too dangerous."

"Why? Because you're a vampire?"

She froze, looking up at me in shock.

I shrugged. "You're super strong, really pale, feel as cold as ice, and have long fangs. It doesn't take a genius to put two and two together and make four."

"So, I'm a vampire. Now what? Will you hold me here until I starve? Drive a stake through my heart and burn my body?" Her icy glare struck a primal fear within me. She was the predator and I the prey. If she wanted to, she could tear out my throat…but I didn't think she did.

"Well, that depends. Do you plan on eating me or my Daddy? Because you look like you need some help, and we don't have much, but we'll spare what we can."

She tilted her head and moved closer, cat-like. "Oh, I see now, you don't want to end the vampire's reign of terror. You want to redeem her." I sat frozen and mesmerized as she brushed a lock of my blonde hair from my shoulder, exposing my neck. "The clever peasant girl who tames the monster." Her fangs grew longer as she approached. I willed myself to move, to fight back, to do anything, but I was locked in my own body. "You wish to be the beauty that breaks the curse of the beast. Unfortunately, I prefer being a monster." She lunged for my neck and I gasped as her fangs stopped short, just barely grazing my throat. "There's no girl left to save. Only the monster remains."

"Then kill me," I said.

She jerked back. "What?"

I forced myself to meet her eyes instead of staring at the needle-sharp fangs in her mouth. "If you're such an irredeemable monster, then kill me." My voice never wavered, and an emotion I could not quite read crossed her face.

After an eternal moment, she burst into laughter, which turned into a wince as her hand moved protectively to her ribs. "You're brave, Laura, I'll give you that. Foolish, but brave. War hardened soldiers and explorers of unknown lands have begged for my mercy after a single glare."

"Hard to be scared of someone who snuggled with me on the ride here," I replied with my own laugh, though it was quite a bit more hysterical.

The vampire averted her eyes, and, if I didn't know better, I'd say she was embarrassed. "Right. I suppose I haven't thanked you for your kindness. So…thanks. Though it was stupid for you to do so. Call me Carmilla."

"So, Carmilla, what brings you to the Middle-of-Nowhere, USA?"

She returned to her bed and pulled her knees towards her chest. "It's a long story, and better that you don't get involved. I've put you at enough risk just by being here."

I crossed my arms. "Well, you're not going anywhere until Doc Perry at least takes a look at you."

"And how do you expect me to explain my lack of a pulse," she said.

"So, maybe not Doc Perry, but you're still too hurt to travel. I won't force you to tell me what you're running from, but please, stay here and recover." I took her freezing hand, and she stared at me like I was an exotic animal. Hopefully, not one she would eat.

She shook her head. "You are such a fool." With that, she laid down and turned her back to me.

"One more thing."

"What?"

"Do you eat human food?"

Enough eggs and bacon for three sizzled on the skillet when Daddy came into the kitchen. The sun had barely risen in the east, and he sniffed the air like a bloodhound that caught a scent. "Don't mind if I do," he said, grabbing himself a plate, "I heard you and the girl talking. How's she seem?"

"Better than I thought. Will probably be fine after a couple days of bed rest." *And a pint or two of blood,* I didn't add. I took my portion, another for Carmilla, and added a small bowl of cereal in case she didn't like bacon and eggs.

"That's good to hear. The conversation sounded intense." He had his back to me, so I couldn't read his face.

A wave of fear crested over me, but I kept a careful mask. "She was confused. I would be too if I was knocked out in a cornfield and woke up in a bed."

"Of course," Daddy replied. "Did you find out anything else about her?"

"Her name's Carmilla—" *and she's a vampire* "didn't learn much else." I almost told him that she was running from something but decided against it. He was already suspicious of her and didn't like that we brought her into our home. No need to make him even more wary

321

of her. "She was a little in and out. A mild concussion, I think. Nothing serious, but she needs to sleep it off." I picked up her plate and forced myself to walk slowly to the guest room. I knocked softly. "Carmilla?"

"What?"

"I brought you something to eat." Without waiting for a response, I opened the door to find a massive lump hiding under the quilt Grandma made when Mama was expecting. I set it down on her bedside table. "I know you don't need a lot of food, but I thought you might feel better with something in you. I even undercooked the bacon."

"Thank you, Laura," she said curtly, "I truly do not understand you."

I shrugged. "Only doing what I hope someone would do for me if I was ever found by the side of the road."

Carmilla chuckled. "I'll admit that your good Samaritan tendencies are rather charming. So kind, but so naïve to the way the world works."

"Well, we stopped for you, didn't we?" I asked, crossing my arms.

"You're right, you did." Her voice was soft and awestruck as she seemed to have an existential crisis over the fact that some people actually do care enough to help an injured woman by the side of the road. She averted her eyes, instead separating out and counting each individual corn flake.

Choosing not to comment on it, I patted her shoulder and got to my feet. "I've got some chores to do, so if you need help, just holler. You shouldn't get into too much trouble alone in your room."

She smiled, a glint of mischief in her blue eyes. "Trouble has a habit of finding me."

"It better not," I replied, shutting the door behind

me. I nearly ran into Daddy as I turned the corner.

"She sounds better," he said, eyeing the shut door. His tone set my heart racing. He only ever used it when he thought I was up to some mischief—fooling around with some boy or reading my penny dreadfuls when I should be working.

I gave him my most innocent smile. "She's a fighter. I've only had a couple conversations with her, but I can tell you that much. I thought I'd let her rest while we got our chores done."

As the days passed, we settled into a routine. I'd get up, make breakfast, and eat it with Carmilla while Daddy ate in the kitchen. I'd invited him to eat with us, but he muttered something about me needing to spend time with girls my own age, and that was that. Carmilla would tell such fascinating stories of her travels around the world—of Mattie, her sister and daughter of Mansa Musa King of the wealthy kingdom of Mali, Viennese balls where the women all wore dresses that glittered in the candlelight, the gossip of the French courts and journeys through the Amazon Rainforest and along the silk road. Sometimes, she'd get this odd look on her face and tell me all the ways I can protect myself from vampires: crucifixes, garlic, wild roses, and, if I ever needed a quick getaway, pour out seeds or millet, because vampires are compelled to count each individual grain.

I'd never left the confines of my small town, not even to visit the city where I knew Mama had some relatives. My only escape had been in books, so hearing this girl's centuries of stories filled me with wonder.

On her third day of convalescence, she stopped mid story of a man she met on Coney Island that taught her to swallow swords and let out a self-deprecating laugh. "How terribly rude of me. I've only talked about myself.

Talk to me about you and this quaint provincial life you lead."

"I feel like I should be insulted," I retorted. She said nothing, but the amusement in her face spoke volumes. I smacked her arm before continuing. "It's really nowhere near as interesting as your life. Mama died of the Spanish Flu, leaving Daddy to raise me. He's a preacher, so I've helped him prepare the church on Sunday along with most major ceremonies like baptisms, death rites, and my favorite, weddings. Those are always the best."

She studied her hands folded in her lap. "I imagine you have plenty of gentlemen courting you."

My breath caught in my throat. I had…unnatural desires. No man had ever caught my eye, but nearly every pretty girl walking down the street set my heart thrumming like a hummingbird's. Daddy had set me up with a couple potential suitors, but the thought of marrying any of them made me sick to my stomach. "I…uh…yeah, I've had a few."

Her head shot up, icy blue eyes meeting mine and piercing like a sword through my chest. "Do you…desire any of them?"

I shook my head, not daring to speak through the lump in my throat. I knew her darkest secret, so she should be allowed to know mine. "I don't fancy men, to be honest."

She took my hand in hers. I studied her long, elegant fingers comparing their cold softness to my own warm calluses from a lifetime of hard labor. With an aching slowness, she brought my hand to her cold lips and pressed a kiss to my knuckles. We didn't speak. What was there to say? We were both already damned.

A few days later, Daddy and I went to the general store to pick up food. Carmilla had grown lethargic during her stay, likely because she wasn't eating, but when I offered my blood, she refused.

As I lingered by the penny candy, the door opened, and a tall man who looked to be in his fifties strode in and approached Mr. Vordenburg who runs the store. "I'm looking for a girl," he said in an accent like Carmilla's as he showed Mr. Vordenburg a photograph. "She looks to be in her late teens, early twenties, and has a few aliases. Marya Zaleska, and Mircalla or Millarca Karnstein."

Mr. Vordenburg shrugged. "I can't say that I've seen her."

"Are you sure?" he asked, leaning in closer, "It is imperative that I find her. I believe that she may have had a hand in the death of Bertha Reinfeldt." I nearly dropped my bag of groceries.

"Well, I'll ask around, Mister…"

"Van Helsing," he replied with a smile as though it was a private joke.

I had to get back to Carmilla. With a forced casualness, I brought my groceries to the till and danced from one foot to another as he slowly rang them up. Carmilla couldn't have killed Bertha, could she? She was a vampire, but she was also sweet and funny and had shown no desire to feed on me or Daddy.

With the groceries paid for, I sprinted the three miles home, arriving breathless and sweaty. Daddy would just have to take the buggy home once he was finished with his business in the town. I carelessly dropped the groceries on the counter and opened the door to Carmilla's room. "Did you kill Bertha Reinfeldt?"

She looked up from the penny dreadful I had leant her. "Well, hello to you too. Did you run all the way here?"

"Answer the question."

Carmilla put down the book with a sigh. "I don't

know what you're talking about. The last person I fed on was three towns over. I left her alive and paid her for her contribution."

"Then why was a man asking for you?"

If it was possible, her face turned even more pale. "A man was looking for me? What did he look like? Did he say his name?"

I crossed my arms. "He was tall, fifties, dark hair, and said his name was Van Helsing. Who is he?"

She buried her face in her hands and let out a noise between a laugh and a sob. "It doesn't matter. We're already dead."

I sat down beside her on the bed and entwined her cold, delicate hands in mine. "Tell me anyway. I have a right to know who would kill me to get to you."

"His name isn't Van Helsing. It's Count Dracula. His use of the name of an old enemy as an alias is a private joke. The old Dutchman may have defeated him once, but he won their war simply by outliving him." She sniffled, wiping her eyes. "He's ancient and powerful and always gets what he wants. The lesser vampires all pay a tithe to him, whatever he desires that they have. And when it came time for Mother, my sire, to pay her dues, he wanted me to be his new bride."

With a bitter laugh, she curled in on herself. "Mother isn't cruel, as vampires go, but she's coldly practical. She knew that he'd rain hell upon us if she refused, so she agreed for the sake of her clan's survival. I had no choice…until Mattie gave me one. She secretly booked passage for me to travel to America while she fled to greener pastures. She would have come along, but you know how Americans treat her people. It was best she found a safe harbor elsewhere. I landed in New York and began a circuitous journey to the west coast, so he couldn't find me. But apparently he did. And death will be a mercy."

I couldn't hold myself back any longer. I pulled Carmilla into a hug. A wet patch formed on my shoulder, but I didn't pull away, instead savoring her cold touch like the final meal before going to the electric chair.

She was the one to break the embrace, only to press frozen lips to mine. It stole my breath like she was the wind whipping through a winter storm. I'd never been kissed—never wanted to kiss a man and had no opportunity to try with a woman—but I'd never felt more alive than I did in that moment in the arms of a dead girl.

The door burst open, and we separated with a yelp. Daddy was in the doorway, red in the face and shaking with rage. "Laura," he said with a dangerous softness, "get away from that monster."

I stood up, drawing myself to my full height as I stood between him and Carmilla. "Daddy, you don't understand."

"I understand plenty. This Carmilla is a vampire who seduces young girls and turns them away from the Lord."

"I know she's a vampire, but whatever you may have heard—it isn't true."

"Eh," Carmilla added, doing a so-so gesture with her hand.

"Not helping," I muttered through gritted teeth.

"I only take what's been freely given and compensate my blood bags very well," she said, ignoring me. "You'd be surprised how many are willing to give up their lifeblood to put dinner on the table for their families, especially in this economy."

Daddy looked between us with abject horror and disgust. After all those years of keeping my head down and my desires silent, having it all in the open tore me apart from the inside like swallowing shards of broken glass. "You're already too far gone. Laura, move, I have to rid this evil from my house and free you from her spell."

I took a breath, forcing myself to meet his eyes with my head held high. "No."

"No?" he repeated, his face turning almost purple in rage, but I stood my ground.

"You'll have to move me, because I'm not going anywhere."

"Laura," he warned.

"The angry mob with the torches and pitchforks is here already, aren't they? I imagine they've covered all the exits in case I attempt an escape," Carmilla said, swinging her legs off her bed. When she stood, she swayed slightly, and I resisted the urge to steady her.

"Carmilla, please don't do this," I said.

Ignoring my father in the room, she caressed my cheek, wiping away tears I did not know had fallen. "It's my turn to be the good Samaritan, Laura. It's for the best. I'd sooner die than watch you come to harm or return to Dracula's clutches. I've been around for too long anyway." She turned to my father. "So go ahead, stake me and let me rest in peace."

Daddy laughed, a maniacal glint in his eyes. "You think it's gonna be that easy? We're making an example of you, girl. Let all other vampires know what happens if they cross us."

"Right, and three guesses as to who suggested I be made a warning. It wouldn't happen to be the mysterious stranger with the overly long canines, would it?"

"Enough talk, demon." Daddy tried to pass me, but I stood my ground. "Laura, move."

I stared up at him, jutting out my jaw defiantly. "I said no."

"And I said move." I should have seen the blow

coming, but Daddy had never so much as laid a hand on me. So, when he slapped me across the cheek, I wasn't ready, and he sent me stumbling to the ground as stars and fireworks bloomed in my vision.

"Laura!" Carmilla exclaimed as she fought Daddy's iron grip. Ordinarily, she would break free easily, but she'd been injured and starving for days, and therefore no match for the man who worked the fields all his life.

I struggled to my feet as he dragged her out the door, locking it behind him. I banged fruitlessly against it as the sound of struggle increased and then a gurgling cry, followed by yells and more heavy footsteps. I desperately wished I could see what was going on, but the only other exit was the windows, and the rest of the crowd was gathered there, erecting something made of wood. I swallowed my nausea as they dragged her out.

She cried out in an unearthly howl as they tied her to the wooden structure and pulled it upright. They'd crucified her, and all I could do was watch helplessly as her porcelain skin bubbled and burned, her screams piercing my heart like daggers.

Bile swelled in my throat. I bent over the small trash can at her bedside and vomited all that I had eaten today. I needed to free her, but between the ancient vampire and the angry mob under his spell, I was woefully outmatched. That didn't mean I couldn't try.

I fingered the cross necklace Momma gave me. Even around Carmilla, I never took it off. She had talked about the vampire's weaknesses. They were less powerful in the daytime; abhorred crosses, silver, and garlic; spilled seeds or millet…

A very dangerous, very stupid plan began to form. Figuring that Dracula and the mob were distracted by the torture, I opened the window and slipped out, landing behind the entranced crowd. Seemingly unaffected by the parody of a crucifixion before him, Dracula was transfixed on Carmilla while the crowd's stared blankly ahead. Hugging the walls, I slipped along the side of the house until I reached the back door. Like always, it was open with the storm door closed to let in the summer breeze. There, I grabbed a knife, a stool, and a bag of cereal.

"What do you think you're doing?" With a gasp, I whipped around to see Dracula standing in the doorway. Dark amusement sparkled in his eyes. "Are you trying to rescue your lady love? Foolish child, she cares nothing for you. Why should she? You are nothing but a moonflower blooming for one night before dying at dawn. She is long lived like the ancient cypress."

I shook my head. "I don't care." With that, I poured out the cereal. "Have fun counting, Count."

While he stumbled to his hands and knees to count the cereal grains with a frustrated cry, I sprinted past him and into the yard. The mob hadn't moved, standing like toy soldiers as they watched Carmilla's agony. They didn't react at all as I set down the stool and began sawing at the ropes binding her feet. Then I stepped up and cut her first arm free, catching her as she sagged forward, hanging on by one wrist. Somehow, I got her other wrist free, and we both sagged to the ground.

"Laura…" she said weakly. The burns on her back had charred and blackened, and I knew what I had to do to heal her.

"Here, Carmilla, drink." I cut open my wrist and pressed it to her lips. She latched on, and a warmth spread through me like drinking hot cocoa after spending the day out in the snow. I soon grew lightheaded, darkness edging in from the corner of my vision.

Ironically, Dracula saved me. Apparently finished with counting cereal, he yanked her off me, his eyes red and burning. With her hunger sated, she turned on him, aiming a kick to his chest and breaking free. She rolled out of the way, transforming into a giant black cat, which then lunged for his throat. He became a wolf, and, expecting for him to be at his normal height, she leapt over him.

The world devolved into the animalistic sounds of hunters fighting to the death. My wound still bled, and I was vaguely aware that I should try to stem the flow, but thinking was like walking through a field of molasses. I forced myself to sit up, and nearly fell back over as the world swirled around me. Blinking the fog away, I grabbed my wrist and searched for the vampires.

Carmilla and Dracula were human again, their clothes torn as they battled with the ferocity of tigers. But she was flagging, and it was only a matter of time before he got the upper hand. I slowly got to my feet as he pinned her to the ground and took off my cross necklace.

"You thought you could disobey me? Now, you're going to watch that little pet of yours bleed out and squeal like a slaughtered pig, begging for you to help." He was so focused on her that he didn't notice me approach until I had the cross around his throat like a garrote and pulled it tight. Undead flesh sizzled and charred as it dug in deeper and deeper. His cries were choked off by the white hot chain of my mother's necklace, a dual symbol of love antithetical to his nature. Though my hands burned, I didn't stop until his head was separated from his body.

Vaguely, I heard Carmilla call my name as the darkness finally overtook me.

I woke at night in a field of wildflowers with Carmilla by my side. "Am I in Heaven?" I asked weakly.

She snorted, shaking her head. "I'm afraid Heaven isn't in the cards for either of us."

It was then that I noticed the needle-sharp canines in my mouth and unnatural thirst. "You turned me?"

Immediately, her eyes filled with tears. "I had to. You would have died, and I'd be—" I cut her off with a kiss. After a few moments, she pulled away. "You're not angry?"

"Of course not," I said, pecking her lips, "An eternity with you is worth the damnation."

She gave a shaky smile and took my hand. "Then the road to Hell awaits."

No Man's Land
Stephen Patrick

July, 1916
British Front near Amiens

"You want to know what scares me?" The flame from Private Burns' cigarette danced in the dim light of the earth and wood dugout. "What I think about at night in this godforsaken place?" Burns exhaled a cloud of smoke and rested his quivering hand on his knee. "I don't want to die all alone out here."

On the other side of the table sat Private Abner Wilkens. A smile tore across his face as Burns spoke. A thin white plume of smoke trailed out from his yellow teeth. "Bloody hell, boy, there's a thousand boys beside you every day, afraid of the same thing. In the trenches, you never gonna die alone. There's always some poor bastard beside you giving up his ghost. The only thing that matters is to take one a theirs before they get you."

Private Joseph Taylor was (or sat?) calming his fears

with a warm bottle of wine. Taylor took a swig and joined in. "I ain't gonna see the one that gets me. That's what I'm afraid of. I wanna meet my maker face on, eye to eye."

"Bollucks, you never see it coming," answered Wilkens, still looking at his cards. "That's why we're here while the rich boys stay home. Ain't that right, Sergeant Price? Guys like you belong back home, making up laws and such to govern us poor wretches, not slogging through mud and blood like this."

In the corner of the dugout, Sergeant William Price wiped down his rifle. "You want to know what scares me?" Price reached into his left breast pocket with practiced ease and pulled out a brown-tinged photograph of a demure brunette in a frilly school dress. "I'm afraid of letting her down."

The photo made a quick trip through the hands of the other three soldiers. Private Wilkens lingered over the picture, devouring her image. "If I had a gal like her, I'd keep myself outta harm's way. Hide when I could or slop beans at the chow line. No sense playing out those foolish stunts of yours and leave your wife for another bloke."

"I promised Lucy I'd make her proud and that's what I intend to do."

Wilkens crushed his cigarette and tossed the butt into the dirt. "Lissen up, boys. You want to know what scares me?" His answer was lost in the shriek of an incoming mortar shell. Price and the two young privates dove for cover, but Wilkens simply ducked his head, covering the playing cards with his hands.

The shell exploded above them, rattling the wooden beams of their dugout. Dust dropped from the ceiling, adding a layer of filth to each of them. Price and the others picked themselves up from the ground, but

Wilkens, still seated at the card table, was still talking. "It's not easy to explain." His eyes narrowed. "There's this thing out there, what's hunting. It's always hunting and always hungry. I never seen it with my eyes, but I've seen what it does."

"Sure you have," interrupted Price. "I heard stories like that when I was a kid. I didn't believe them then and I ain't gonna believe one out here. There's enough around us to be scared of without making up a story."

Wilkens grabbed Taylor's wine and finished it in one swallow. He continued, oblivious to Price's comments. "It walks out here in the mud, feasting on torn and tattered bodies. The lucky ones, they die outright. The others, I'd rather not talk about."

"The reaper," added Burns, ashes dripping from the cigarette between his quivering fingers.

"No. The reaper takes you away. This demon, he keeps you here, stripping away flesh and blood 'til you're trapped in this hell. Bent and broken, you're stuck in this land of corpses looking for a life you left behind. When the moon is up, you can hear him slinking in the shadows. In the morning, the stink o' his breath in the air tells you he's been by."

Taylor leaned back, a smile cutting across his face. "I guess it's better to be afraid of something that don't exist than something real, like the bullets and bombs that seem to keep finding us every day."

"Boy your age should listen to the folks around him. Might keep you out of trouble,"

Price intervened. "Everyone's got a right to be scared, but we'll all do our duty, no matter what's out there."

A tiny rap came at the entryway to their dugout. A French boy stood in the doorway, his body blackened by soot and dirt. His blue jacket was that of a French soldier and was three sizes to big. The sleeves were cuffed several times over and hung down over his fingers. A small collection of buttons and beads hung from his lapel, a colorful arrangement that made him look like a general in formal dress. Some were familiar to the men, the standard flashes or insignia of British or French soldiers while the other bore eagles and some other unfamiliar symbols. His pants were torn open at the knees and had been hemmed with rough stitches above the top of his boots.

"I mean no disrespect, but I have some items that might be of interest to you."

Wilkens was on the boy in an instant. "He's a goddamn vulture, robbing the dead!" Wilkens drew his bayonet and held it to the boy's throat.

Price raced to the boy's aid. "Wilkens! Stand down, he's just a boy."

The boy remained calm despite the gleaming blade against his skin. His dull chestnut eyes looked up at the raging Wilkens.

"I am sorry, sir. C Company said these things might belong to your men."

The boy held out his arms. He held a tiny locket containing a photo of Private O'Grady and his mother. O'Grady had been killed three days earlier when a mortar round landed at his feet.

"You're a bloody thief," screamed Wilkens as he snatched the locket from the boy's hand. "How many have you kept?"

"None, sir, I am…my family was…" The boy, stammered, searching for the right words. "I am too small to fight, so I do the only thing I can. I read how, in ancient times, women would strip the dead and return their possessions to their families. I want to honor those who fall, to make their sacrifice known so they can be properly mourned. I meant no offense."

Wilkens took the other things from the boy and fingered through the familiar items; Sgt. Halloway's diary, Cpl. Saunder's engraved wrist watch, even the bible that belonged to Private Wolf, who had been the only voice of God in this Hell.

Price stepped between them and handed the boy his canteen.

"Take a drink, son. I…we…appreciate what you're doing, but a boy your age should not be here."

The boy took a small sip and wiped his mouth, leaving a clean streak across his face. "It's OK, sir. I am small and weak, but I do my work at night when the soldiers try to sleep."

"What is your name, son?" asked Price.

"Francois, Sir. Francois Dumond."

Price held out his hand to the boy. "My name is William."

***

The next day began with a dawn barrage that shook the ground beneath their boots. The Germans were on the offensive. Price led them through the foggy, smoldering trenches that they had taken, lost and recaptured twice in the past week. They crawled to the edge of the trench and looked out into no man's land through the sights of their rifles. The morning haze hung in front of them like a curtain, hiding the advancing Germans behind a lingering white cloud.

"Wait 'til they hit the wire. Don't waste your bullets while they're running."

A terrible battle raged until nightfall. The Brits repelled two German assaults before launching their own, which was also turned back. After nineteen hours,

Price's squad ate and slept in the same dugout, defending the same series of trenches they had defended for the past month.

In such a setting, individual valor was hard to define. Survival was the only indicator of victory, but Price had been carving out a name for himself. His courage made him an object of scorn from the veterans and admiration from the young soldiers. The veterans had begun to dismiss him as a man with a death wish or someone too stupid to know better. The green soldiers learned to admire him, but their mimicry of his actions sent many home or to the grave.

Only Francois seemed to understand him. They shared boundless courage. Price's exploits to save the lives of other soldiers came under fire. Francois' came under nightfall to save the memories of fallen heroes left behind on the battlefield. Although the men hated Francois' reason for visiting, his appearances became a welcome routine.

A few weeks later, Francois came across Price writing a letter to his dear Lucy. Francois devoured a piece of Price's chocolate rations and sat beside him.

"She means a lot to you?" Francois asked through brown-tinged teeth.

"She's everything to me," answered Price, still scribbling his letter.

"You love her and can't wait to go home, so why risk your life here every day?"

"I could never face her if I turned away from a fight or let another man take a bullet for me."

"I may be young, but I see a lot. Some men cry for their mothers and others would betray their closest friends for another second of life. I think Lucy would understand."

"You've seen too much, my friend. Boys should

never see such things."

**

The next attack was supposed to be a cake walk. A twelve-hour artillery barrage would destroy the German trenches and the infantry could walk across no man's land and take them. In front of them, dirt and smoke hung in the air and made it difficult to see. Like always, Price was the first one up the ladder. The others scrambled up behind him and over the pock-marked French countryside. As Price moved forward, a solid wall of men walked beside him. They moved deliberately, maintaining their steady lines.

After fifty yards, they heard the staccato pulse of German machine gun nests coming to life. The British advance cracked and soldiers fell like corn before a scythe. The German positions had survived the barrage.

Price found cover in a crater torn open by an artillery blast. Wilkens and Burns followed him. Taylor was twenty feet behind them, clutching at a crimson stain on his chest.

"Cover me!" screamed Price as he raced toward Taylor.

Wilkens and Burns fired over the edge of the crater, but were immediately overrun by the German counterattack.

Price skidded to a stop beside Taylor, but he was dead. Price never saw the bayonet until it was too late. A German soldier drove his bayonet through the small of Price's back. Price tried to turn and defend himself, but the pain was too intense.

The crimson blade jutted out of his belly for a moment and then it was gone. He fell to his knees, only to feel the blade cut through him again, driving through his upper back and stealing the breath from his lungs. Satisfied that Price was finished, the German withdrew his blade and ran toward the British trenches.

Price fumbled at his shirt pocket, longing to see Lucy's face once more. His entire body went slack and he fell face first into the mud. He groped through his memory, trying to recreate her face, so that he could die with her image in his eyes. After a year of carrying her photo in his pocket, he died without remembering what she looked like.

***

The dull tug of death pulled him away from no man's land. The pain was gone, replaced by a faint sense of weightlessness. He struggled to feel his hands or feet but could not find them.

Suddenly, he felt heavy, like he was sinking. He fell down and down until he slammed hard against something. Shells exploded above him and explosions thundered on both sides. It was dark and he was alone. His belly was whole again and strength flowed through his limbs.

"Welcome back, my friend."

Price followed the voice to his left. Francois knelt beside him. A tiny trickle of blood ran over his chin.

"What happened?" asked Price.

"You died."

"Is this heaven?" The horrible screams and acrid smoke told him otherwise.

"Heaven is an illusion, where people are taken away from the things that mean the most to them. You have seen how I save things from the battlefield to be remembered. You are too valuable to rot on the ground. I have saved you, my friend."

"You brought me back from the dead?"

"Not exactly. My gift allows you to ignore the ravages of time and of death. Two hundred years ago on another battlefield, I was given the gift that I now offer to you. It is a kindness you truly deserve."

"What kindness? Another life?" asked Price.

"Not another life, but another chance. A chance to return to your Lucy."

"What about the others?" Price stood up, looking around for his men.

"They do not concern you, now. Your worries are beyond the trenches and the war, beyond living and dying. I have freed you from them."

"You're the demon that Wilkens was talking about."

"I am no demon. I simply do what I must to survive and try every day to make the world a better place. I ...hunt… among the bodies for the life force that sustains me. It keeps me here. You are like me now, free to explore all that the world has to offer. You are beyond death."

"Beyond death?" Price's eyes were filled with rage.

"You deserve this gift. To return to her."

"You've cursed me. Don't you see that?" Price turned away and slammed his fist into the dirt. "You've turned me into a monster."

"I've given you a chance to see Lucy again. How can that be a terrible thing? My gift is not to you, but to your love for Lucy. Return to her, make her proud of the man you were."

"Not like this. Don't you understand? I can't return to her. I'll never see her again. Lucy died three years ago from tuberculosis. It is only her memory that drives me."

"But what about the letters?"

"They let me talk to her until I found my way to heaven beside her. But you took that away from me."

Price stood up in the mud of no man's land. He looked to the west and saw the trenches of the British front line. To the east was the German line. He turned his back on Francois and headed north, away from everything he once knew, and out of no man's land.

Wolfsbane
Greg Patrick

Night had begun to cast its moonless pall on the red aftermath of battle.

The anticipated and aspired moment of winning knighthood that I had envisioned would be one of radiant euphoric glory was grim and marred with blood and groans instead. I saw myself mirrored in the varnished armour of my lord king when I was bade kneel for my accolade. I suppressed a shudder at the touch of the sword, weapon that made men kings and kings monsters. The battlefield stretched before me in a terrible vision of red and black as gorging ravens swarmed the carnage in aerial revel. Raven feathers fell like black tears shed for my soul in sardonic mirth.

My eyes were met and transfixed by a pale she wolf, her face and bared fangs were encrimsoned as she fell on a slain knight. The crimson gore was striking against her ethereally pale pelt. Her impossibly glacial blue soul-delving eyes never left mine. I had felt a kindred lycanthropic rapture when I had stood over my first slain enemy who had nearly sheathed his blade into my king's chest.

The blood had flowed down my face like red tears or tribal warpaint as I screamed a wild battle cry.

She did not recoil from our presence as most of her kind would. Her stare smoldered red in the weaving torchlight as the grim search to identify the slain commenced. The she wolf raised her head in a ghostly battle cry over her kill, yet it seemed eerily human somehow as if the banshee bemoaned the souls of the slain. The cries of distant packs drawn by the aroma of carnage answered in chorus. Her cry shivered through my soul.

"I admire her spirit," the young king smiled.

"I admire that pelt even more," he continued.

He reached for a bolt to load to his crossbow, yet when he looked up the haunting magnificent beast had eerily vanished…inconceivably so. But the terrible ordeal of battle could play its trickery on a man's mind.

He fancied he'd mount her head at the court amid tapestries ordered to commemorate the battle. That would be a trophy fit for a royal hall.

The battle had nigh been lost that day. The scimitars of the enemy felled our knights inexorably. We faced the prospect of being completely vanquished. Our allies from beyond the distant range of mountains made their belated entrance with the twilight…but they did come. And no warrior could withstand their lances and blades. No sword it seemed could touch them as they tore through the enemy like a maelstrom of steel. I could see their dragon emblazoned banners flowing against the sunset, yet they remained aloof from our euphoria and mourning.

They had taken some pitiable remnant of the enemy alive.

Some of the high-ranking enemy commanders had every expectation of being ransomed. Impatient ravens swarmed around the bound enemy commander as he writhed at the stake. I could see no master among them curbing their excesses. I turned my face from the grim spectacle of tortures inflicted. Their screams would haunt my nights.

Silhouetted against the vermillion splendour of the twilight a knight clad in striking dark armour and astride a great black warhorse dismounted. The knights of the dragon banner stood down as the dark malevolent figure strode to the bound figure whose turbaned head slumped down as he shuddered spasmodically. The figure seemed mauled rather than tortured. The black knight leaned in as if to whisper a final gloating mockery and ravens rose as an agonised scream rent the air. A luxuriant cascade of hair spilt like wine from a chalice. A woman? Some trick of the dwindling light surely but her eyes seemed to smolder emberously like a beast's. I knew our king had made a devil's bargain for that victory. What he had vowed in return I knew not nor wanted to.

We drew back to our lord's castle, marching under frayed banners as night fell and I cast my eyes to the myriad of stars dreamily. For where else had man to avert his eyes and lift his mind when stupidity on earth was astronomical? In the nights leading to the victory banquet the king was hosting for our knights and allies I was haunted by strange dreams. Yet I was a knight now of an esteemed company and found some solace and pride. Rumours swirled about the anticipated debut of the princess of the mountain court. That eve as tapestries to commemorate the victory were unveiled and toasts rose, the court feasted on venison and boar.

I felt flushed, almost feverish and I sought the chill air of the battlements.

The cries of wolves haunted the night. More than I ever heard in eerie choir as if they were heralding something that only the beasts could sense. I returned to the hall as a carriage drawn by white-plumed horses and escorted by an entourage of knights approached. The troubadours played raucous ballads called out for by the retainers. Suddenly the hands stopped at lute and harp mid-song. Yet I could hear music as she made her entrance announced by the herald. The Countess of the Northern realms. She was gowned resplendently in ethereal gossamer and white silk adorned with spangles.

The albinism of her features seemed rendered all the more melodious by torchlight that seemed to sigh in crimson homage at her presence. It seemed Midsummer eve's moonbeams were granted radiant form and face.

Her eyes in their impossibly saphiric mystique were silence set to nocturne.

A cascade of hair caught the light and breath like pale gold as if by an alchemist's art. A vision of captivating beauty gracing the hall behind enigmatic impossibly blue eyes.

Those eyes cast their spell like the vexing maddening light of the sanguine moon. No witch or warlock would have dared aspire towards that maleficence.

I stood before her as she seemed to glide rather than stride down the stairs.

She seemed to usher in the moon-haunted night. I kissed the graceful silk-gloved hand in courtly fashion. The king stepped arrogantly between us, not about to let a lowly novice knight usurp the object of his desire. She looked up at me over his shoulder, the glacial blue of her eyes smoldered crimson in lycanthropic rapture and blood trickled from her lips. She smiled sensually. She leaned in and whispered.

"Just another trophy to an ambitious lord."

Her voice was venomed honey and lips like a wound reopening. Her voice caressed my heart with a ghostly touch. Her features lost something of their pallor and her façade rejuvenated. The courtiers and knights all ceased their movements as if they were taxidermized rophies in a huntress's hall. She gestured to the ballroom floor. Her gaze whispered its soundless intoxicating incantation.

I felt the sensation of flight in the turns of our waltz. It seemed I danced alone for she could not be seen in the reflections of varnished shields on the wall. The candles merged to coils of fire around us. The rebel angel soul in me felt granted wings in her embrace and dance and like a castaway swept overboard in a maelstrom I felt the sensations akin to dark Lethean waves draw me down into fathomless darkness... drawn down further by the Endorean bewitchment of her eyes...then uplifted as if to the stars, radiant and immortal as her.

The blood-chant of my heart quickened like ritual drums as a dark rite reached its climax. Her eyes read my dreams, desires, and nightmares like an unsealed diary.

She held my arms even as I tried to draw the blade reflexively as dark figures appeared at the thresholds and blades were unsheathed like bared fangs.

Screams were heard amid the clatter of silverware and broken platters. The crimson-frilled jester raised his head from a secret jest and chuckled like a hyena, his eyes shimmering red and baring serrated fangs. In the eye of a red storm as carnage swirled kaleidoscopically around us.

I felt her breathless lips on my neck. I closed my eyes in expectant ecstasy.

"Join me then. Together we will rule the night."

The talisman of a silver crucifix entwined with a rose slipped out of my collar.

She recoiled from me then beckoned to me hungrily. I brandished the crucifix and she seemed struck by a ghostly fist. I pivoted and fled. Taking a horse from the stables I rode from the causeway, feeling her watching eyes burning into my back. My horse reared, nearly throwing me as the vampire jester hung upside-down from the gateway. Like a carnivorous hybrid of rose he seemed, in his red frills and bared fangs. I drew my sword and its consecrated steel shimmered in his unhallowed presence. I struck him aside and rode explosively into the night. The Countess stood on the battlements and languidly raised her arms like a stage illusionist in the act of conjuring. Bats swept past her in a torrent like an eruption of underworld fire.

Like rapidly shifting maelstrom formations gathering form, the swarm morphed into a horde of knights astride dark horses. I heard their shrill echo-locative cries as they sought me in the cauldrenous dreamscape of mist and the cries of wolves like hounds of a dark huntress leading a royal hunt. I fell, chest heaving in the shadow-haunted ruins of a remote pilgrim's shrine. I beheld their shadows circling and pacing, their torches casting crimson splashes that glowed in their eyes. They were held at bay by the consecrated ground. I heard the silvery siren's song of her voice beckoning and I rose like a somnambulist to answer. Blades were drawn in expectation. The silver talisman held me forcibly back. Writhing from the red visions of nightmare-haunted sleep I rose with the dawn, and I rode as a landless knight to seek service in the courts of distant realms…

Yet my dreams were always haunted by the eyes of wolf and princess and knew somewhere in the night our dance would be finished.

The Precarious Politics of Modern Vampirism

Stephen Loiaconi

Bobby Pickett and the Crypt-Kickers boomed from the speakers as the roar of the crowd echoed through the hangar. Even inside Malcolm Roth's campaign jet, the excitement was palpable. Ten thousand cheering Americans fearful of the future and desperate for the kind of change only a white man with no relevant experience can promise.

My kind of people, that is to say.

The crowd outside was doing the mash – the monster mash – when Roth stepped from his private office into the main cabin of the jet to greet me, my campaign manager, and his other honored guests.

"I don't know what it is, Colin," Roth said to me, surveying the audience through the tinted glass of one of the windows, "but these people really love that song."

"Well, it is a graveyard smash," I offered, and he laughed distressingly hard.

"Graveyard smash!" he repeated. "I'm going to use that."

This trip was the first time we met in person, and he looked pretty much exactly like he did on TV: chalky alabaster skin, thinning silver hair, bags under his eyes like he hasn't slept in a month, suits at least a half-size too small. And yet somehow exuding unshakable self-confidence.

I noticed an aide pouring Coke into a Diet Coke can with a funnel.

Roth peered through a window at the stage. A projector played a grainy copy of the 1931 "Dracula" against the wall behind the podium. A "Roth for President" banner hung above. Folks in the audience held up signs with slogans like "Vampires Suck" and "Go Back to the Shadows."

He checked his watch. The event was scheduled to begin nearly a half hour earlier.

"You gotta make them wait," he said.

Like most people, I always thought Malcolm Roth was a joke. A washed up 80s synth-pop star who had been eagerly forgotten until he made a foray into politics. His first presidential run was a disaster. He dropped out after a humiliating primary debate performance where he froze for over a minute when pressed about his education plan.

This time had been different, though. After a rash of high-profile vampire crimes, he glommed onto a wave of sanguivoriphobic sentiment that had been building in America for years. He came forward with the harshest invective a mainstream politician had ever hurled against vamps and a raft of wildly draconian policies no party had seriously considered putting in their platform. To the surprise of virtually everyone, that approach resonated. He had led public opinion polls for months, and his endorsement could make or break a candidacy.

Even for a bloodsucker like me.

My race for a House seat in rural Pennsylvania had proven surprisingly competitive. The novelty of what was quickly – and unfairly, I might add – branded as an "anti-vampire vampire" candidacy had already faded, and primary opponents were crawling out of the woodwork. An even tougher fight loomed in the general election. Getting on Roth's good side was my clearest path to Congress.

That imperative put me on this plane, cozying up to a man who might be the next president of the United States. For Roth, a visit to Lancaster County shored up support in a key swing state. For me, an endorsement would bring a flood of small-dollar donors, a smattering of earned media coverage, and a significant social media signal boost.

"Worthy, can I have the boys fix you up something?" Roth asked, gesturing at his staff. "A clamato juice, maybe?"

I glanced at the handful of staffers milling about the cabin. Some consciously tried to avoid eye contact. Others offered a polite nod. One young woman made a sign of the cross.

"I'm good, thanks," I said.

I flashed a fanged smile.

"You sure?" Roth took a sip of his soda through a metal straw. "Don't want you getting peckish during the show, if you know what I mean."

"I do." Of course it's rude to assume a vampire can't keep his teeth to himself for 45 minutes, but I was not going to be the one to push back on his perceptions. "And I won't."

Roth shuffled through several pages of notes. Before I met him, I had assumed his performances were just off-the-cuff rambling about whatever sprouted to mind. There was a method to it, and considerable preparation was needed to make it all feel spontaneous. He put the papers down, took his suit jacket off a chair, and slipped his arms in.

"So level with me," he said, as we waited for the OK to deplane from his security team, "this vampire shit. What's real and what isn't?"

This was a conversation I had become accustomed to having in recent years. The answers were always greeted with a twinge of disappointment. Every debunked legend is inevitably somebody's favorite.

"Most of the lore has some basis in fact, to be honest," I told him. I waved to myself in the mirror behind the bar. "Though, obviously, our reflections show up in mirrors."

"What does it take to kill you?"

"Crosses, holy water, sun, that stuff can legit hurt us." Again, a common question, but man, every time, you can't help feeling like the person asking has a sharpened hunk of wood behind their back that they're hoping to plunge into your chest. "Anything else is pretty iffy."

"Garlic?"

"I mean," I shrugged, "too much gives me heartburn, but that's about it."

My campaign manager, Denton Rawlins, stewed silently by the cockpit, reading and responding to emails on his phone. He had made his displeasure with Roth more than clear to me for days, even if he didn't dispute the political benefits of aligning with him.

"You coming?" I asked him.

"Hell to the no," Denton said.

Roth's assistant opened the door to the gangway and waved us forward.

"Would a stake through the heart kill you?" Roth asked, looking back over his shoulder as we descended the stairs.

"A stake through the heart would kill most things, wouldn't it?" I responded, though I realized my words were drowned out by a burst of wind.

***

Dina Rogers, Philadelphia Enterprise-News: Colin Worthy, thank you for taking the time to speak with me.

Colin Worthy, House Candidate, 11th District of Pennsylvania: Thank you, Dina, and thank you for accommodating my admittedly unconventional schedule.

Rogers: I understand you are somewhat nocturnal.

Worthy: That is certainly a way of putting it. I'm a vampire. You can say it.

Rogers: You are a vampire, but you've become very outspoken in support of policies that most of your people consider discriminatory against vampires. Why is that?

Worthy: Look, Dina, I know what Americans think of when they hear the word, "vampire." We've all seen the movies, watched the TV shows, read the books. Some of that stuff is accurate, some of it isn't. But there's no reason anyone should be afraid simply because we're here.

Rogers: Don't curfews and coffin bans perpetuate those fears?

Worthy: First, it's not a coffin ban. Anyone can own a coffin. My proposal would simply limit how they can be used and the circumstances in which one can sleep in them.

Rogers: By banning it.

Worthy: That's an oversimplification. Now,

second, as I said, some of the horror movie lore is based in fact. We do drink blood, often human blood. Vampires have been known to kill people. I believe the best way to ease Americans' minds is by demonstrating we can restrain ourselves, comply with rules, and assimilate with society.

Rogers: What would you say to those who consider that abandoning your identity?

Worthy: Okay, seriously, being a vampire is not an identity. It's not a race or an ethnicity or whatever. It's a thing we were turned into – more often than not, against our will. There is nothing natural about it. Our very existence is a tragedy.

Rogers: A lot of vampires see embracing their, um, nocturnalness as a way to overcome that tragedy and reclaim their sense of self. Are they wrong?

Worthy: I'm not here to tell anyone else what to think or how to feel, but yes, they're wrong. I understand what they're trying to do. I one-hundred-percent do. But this isn't like gay pride or Black power. This isn't a thing to be proud of. It's a burden to shoulder.

Rogers: Some would say that's an unhealthy attitude.

Worthy: Drinking blood and sleeping all day isn't what most would consider healthy either, now, is it? Come on, I know what the vamp rights activists say about me, but I'm not some self-loathing traitor. I'm fine with who I've become. If I wasn't, I would have given myself the old Tallahassee Sun Tan years ago.

***

Fifteen minutes after taking the stage, Roth was in his groove and building to his big applause lines. It was barely 40 degrees outside, but his face was dripping with sweat.

"We need to build a great big wall of light along the East Coast," Roth declared. "Massive UV spotlights every 100 feet. Fences with garlic butter smeared on the bars."

I stood to the side of the stage, bundled up in my coat, clapping along with the crowd.

"It's true what they say, isn't it?" he added. "Sunlight is the best disinfectant."

My eyes scanned the hangar. To say the least, this was not the kind of crowd I usually drew. People drove in from several counties over just to see this. Most probably didn't even know who or what I am.

"These unholy bastards are literally sucking the lifeblood from our nation," Roth stated. "Taking our jobs, committing crimes, collecting government benefits. And let me tell you, you don't want millions of immortals becoming eligible for Social Security and Medicare."

For the record, vampires are not immortal, per se. It's a good line, though. You learn to live with the misconceptions pretty fast. Trying to fact-check every slur and insult can be exhausting, not to mention pointless.

"Now, it needs to be said, if only so the so-called journalists in the back report that I said it," he gestured toward the press pen in the rear of the room, triggering a wave of boos from his adoring audience, "not all vampires are bad. Some are fine, trustworthy patriots. They love their mothers. They love their children. They're not stalking you through the cemetery at night. They leave us alone and they want to be left alone. And I'll tell you, I have no beef with them."

Whether I actually agreed with any of this was entirely incidental. It was my platform and my public persona. Nobody needed another run-of-the-mill politician or nauseatingly earnest activist feeding them focus group-tested talking points. They wanted a well-honed patina of authenticity.

"Let's be honest with ourselves, though. Let's not delude ourselves," Roth said. A bright stage light spun over me. "Vampires like my very good friend over here, future Congressman Colin Worthy, are the exception that proves the rule. Just look how much abuse he gets from other vamps and their media allies. You'd think he was pissing holy water, the way his own kind run away from him."

He gyrated and swung his crotch around, as if the joke required a visual aid. Some in the crowd laughed and cheered. Others stood awkwardly and uncomfortably.

"Meanwhile, they're out there pleading for leniency and protection for criminals and illegals," Roth said once the crowd calmed. "Defending unfettered immigration from Eastern Europe without any blood testing. Tell me something, why is it that the other guys always want to let the wrong ones in?"

Vampires had been living out in the open for decades across the world. There was no reason beyond antiquated stereotypes to focus fears in any one region. Still, people like to feel like they're doing something.

"You don't want to know what this country is going to look like if they get into power." He held a hand out as he painted the picture. "Blood banks on every corner. Bats blotting out the night sky. You're not going to be able to step outside after dark without a steel neck gaiter."

I hear it a lot. Vampires tell me I should be ashamed of turning my back on my people. They accuse me of saying whatever I have to say to get elected. But see, the thing about power is, once you have it, it doesn't matter all that much how you got it.

"It's going to be just like when those werewolves got loose in London," Roth shouted. "Drinking pina coladas and mutilating little old ladies."

Roth pulled a folded sheet of paper from his jacket pocket, as he does at most of his rallies. The page was wrinkled and the ink was probably faded, but I'm sure he knew the words by heart. It might seem obvious that Warren Zevon's "Werewolves of London" isn't based in fact. I have to imagine most of the audience knew that. But it doesn't matter. They were practically ensorcelled as he read the lyrics with dramatic flair.

When he got to the chorus, the crowd howled along.

***

Rogers: Does the name Santino Rialto mean anything to you?

Worthy: I don't think so. Should it?

Rogers: I'll come back to it. Now, you have backed Malcolm Roth's campaign for president.

Worthy: I have.

Rogers: Roth is perhaps the most anti-vampire candidate we've seen in this country since the 1970s. His rallies, one of which you just attended, are filled with hateful rhetoric, irrational scapegoating, and what, frankly, can only be described as blatant lies about the vampire community.

Worthy: I'm sorry. Is there a question in there?

Rogers: The question is, why would you support a candidate who so clearly hates your kind, whose base would gladly watch you burn at sunrise, whose entire platform is dedicated to marginalizing and persecuting people like you?

Worthy: Gosh, Dina, tell me how you really feel. No, I understand where the question is coming from. I don't agree with the premise, but I get it. Let me tell you about a fellow named Roderick James. You've probably seen him. He's the guy holding up the "Vamps for Roth" sign at so many of the rallies. I spoke to him a couple weeks ago. Now, Roderick was turned as a child nearly four decades back, in the days when vampires were literally being hunted in the streets at night. Today, he's got a job, a family, a pension. He pays his taxes, donates money to charity. And he sees those other vampires out there breaking the law, sucking blood, terrifying people – hell, he's terrified. He's got human kids and he doesn't want those kinds of vamps coming anywhere near them. He hears what Malcolm Roth says and it makes sense to him. He said to me, "I would sleep better during the day knowing Mr. Roth was in the White House." See, I don't have kids of my own yet, but if I did, I expect I'd feel the same way.

Rogers: I'm sure you know this, but crimes committed by vampires against humans are relatively rare, particularly compared to gun violence or drug overdoses. Aren't there bigger problems you could focus your energy on?

Worthy: Bigger problems. You know, when it's your husband, your wife, your daughter, your dog that's lying there drained of all their blood under a full moon, skin all shriveled and pasty, vampire violence feels like a pretty big f***ing problem, Dina. Excuse my language.

Rogers: So you resort to extreme tactics that violate basic human rights?

Worthy: Key word: human. Our founders were smart men, brilliant men, but they never contemplated beings like me who aren't even human anymore. Nobody can tell you how the Constitution is meant to apply to, let's say post-humans.

Rogers: Isn't that why many states have passed laws conferring rights onto vampires?

Worthy: And others have restricted them. States can do what they want, within reason. Welcome to federalism.

Rogers: And woe to the vampires living in the states that want to lock them away?

Worthy: You don't like it, you can move. Personally, I'm more than willing to give up a little freedom in the name of safety for my community.

Rogers: Benjamin Franklin said, "Those who would give up essential liberty to purchase a little temporary safety deserve neither liberty nor safety." Isn't that exactly the trade-off you're calling for?

Worthy: Well, contrary to popular belief, Franklin was defending the right of the state legislature to tax the wealthy. It might not come as a surprise that he and I don't see eye to eye.

***

"I'm going to be a president for Pennsylvania, not Transylvania," Roth declared as the crowd roared with excitement.

This was the climax. It was so familiar by then, they sold it on t-shirts.

"For freedom-lovers, not blood-suckers!" he added. "For patriots, not parasites!"

Chants of "U.S.A." filled the hall. Roth stepped back from the microphone and let the energy wash over him. After just a few months on the campaign trail, these people would follow him through hell, and he knew it.

"God bless America!" he said. "And God damn the monsters."

Roth waved to the crowd and pumped his fist a few times before retreating from the stage. He climbed down the stairs and gave me an aggressive, theatrical hug.

"Smile for the cameras," he whispered in my ear.

Once he released me, he motioned for me to follow him back to the jet. Onboard, a staffer handed him another Diet Coke can.

"So, what do you think?" Roth asked. "Greatest show on earth, am I right?"

"I can certainly see the appeal."

Waiting by the door, Denton rolled his eyes so hard, I was surprised Roth didn't hear them spin. Although I guess he wasn't listening to anyone but himself.

"And I owe so much of it to you," Roth said, putting an arm around my shoulder. "Well, not you personally. But you people have been such a gift for me. I don't know what I'd be talking about out there if people weren't utterly terrified of vampires."

"Tax policy, health care…"

"I know, right?" he chuckled. "Can you imagine?"

He sat down on a cushioned seat and stretched his legs.

"You sure you don't want that clamato juice? Maybe some fruit punch?" he asked, seemingly convinced any red liquid would sate my thirst. "When we're in charge, Colin, I guarantee you're going to have a seat at the table. When we meet at night, at least."

"I appreciate that, Mr. Roth."

He looked down at his left wrist as if checking a watch, which he was not wearing.

"Will you look at the time," he said. "Places to go, people to do."

An aide ushered Denton and me off the plane onto the tarmac. He was silent as we watched Roth take off for his next event in Ohio.

"That was…interesting," he said when we turned toward the parking lot.

"I know what you're going to say," I replied. We had argued about my pursuit of Roth's endorsement many times in the previous weeks. "I don't disagree, but we need his support."

"This isn't the campaign we wanted to run."

"We wanted to win, didn't we?"

A cacophony of car horns out in the lot.

"We wanted to make a difference," Denton said.

"And how are we going to do that after we finish third in the primary?" I sneered. "See, the thing about power is, once you have it, it doesn't matter all that much how you get it."

"You keep saying that like it's a fact," he said, turning and heading toward the exit.

A traffic jam clearing out a venue like this is inevitable, and post-rally crowd control is never the highest priority for campaign cash. The time we had spent arguing on the tarmac practically guaranteed we would be on the tail end of the long line of cars meandering back to the highway. Denton and I worked our way through the sea of people and vehicles. I heard some whispering and muttering, caught more than a few people pointing and staring, but I tried to tune it out.

The first garlic knot bounced off my shoulder.

This had been a thing since the 70s, when the public first became convinced vampires were real. Holy water wasn't that easy to come by and pelting fangers with crosses felt borderline sacrilegious, so sanguivoriphobes armed themselves with garlic instead. Never mind that it doesn't actually do anything. Garlic bulbs, garlic knots, garlic bread – those garlic supplement pills from the drug store – whatever they can get their hands on.

Generally speaking, it's little more than a nuisance,

but the lingering smell does tend to rack up dry cleaning bills. So I can't say I was surprised some yahoos who listened to Roth's screed might take aim at me, but it was frustrating just the same.

"You alright?" Denton asked.

A garlic bulb bonked me on the forehead. "Peachy," I said.

"Don't do anything stupid."

Don't flash your fangs or threaten anybody, is what he meant. I brushed aside a hunk of bread lobbed from a couple of aisles over and hastened my walk to the car, trying not to draw too much attention. That's difficult to do when you've just been singled out in front of a crowd of thousands as the thing they distrust and despise most in the world. Denton raced to keep up.

I ignored the insults and deflected the garlic as I walked. I tried not to make eye contact with anyone, but I could sense a small scrum gathering around us. By and large, people like this don't want a confrontation, don't really want to get their hands dirty. They just want to feel big and tough, convince themselves and their friends that they're not scared of something that quite obviously terrifies them.

At least, that's the bet I was making.

We made it to the car without further incident and slipped inside. As Denton started the engine, I realized we were essentially surrounded. He shifted into drive and inched forward, counting on them to step out of the way rather than get run down. Most did. One man banged repeatedly on the hood as I passed. As we waited to clear out of the lot, Denton watched the clock closely. He needed to get me back to the campaign office for an interview in an hour.

"You sure you're ready for this?" he asked.

"Talking to a local reporter?" I shrugged. "Yeah, I

can handle it."

"Dina Rogers is one of the best investigative reporters in the state." Keeping his eyes on the cars and the crowd in front of us, he wagged a finger in my general direction. "Don't underestimate her."

"Denton, unclench. It'll be fine." I flashed my fangs. "I eat local reporters for breakfast."

"Not funny," he sighed. "Are you sure you don't want me to tag along?"

"I don't need a babysitter."

"Okay, but please resist the temptation to make any 'Interview with the Vampire' jokes."

I made no promises.

***

Rogers: I want to talk about your, well, your origin story, if you will.

Worthy: How I became a creature of the night.

Rogers: How you did, yes. The story I've heard you tell is that you were walking home from work late one night – this was when you were a mechanic in Lancaster, Pennsylvania – and someone swooped down and dragged you off the road into the woods, drank your blood, forced you to drink theirs, and then you fought him off and pushed him into a tree, where a protruding branch pierced his heart and turned him to dust.

Worthy: That's the gist of it.

Rogers: It sounds terrifying.

Worthy: It was.

Rogers: So the thing is, I've been digging into this for weeks, I've filed record requests with the county, I've spoken to law enforcement officials, and there's no record of any of it. Can you explain that?

Worthy: Well, there wouldn't be a record. I didn't

call the police. I didn't go to the hospital. It's hard to say this, but I was ashamed, embarrassed. Not to mention afraid. It took me a while to come to grips with it all. By then, there wouldn't have been any evidence left. I realize this kind of skirts the law, but I didn't even register for several weeks after my transformation was complete.

Rogers: Still, it shouldn't have been difficult to identify the vamp that turned you. All vampires are registered and tracked, precisely so the government can identify them and anyone they turned.

Worthy: Not all vamps.

Rogers: Illegals? It seems awfully convenient that the one who attacked you was unregistered and that you managed to dust them before you blacked out.

Worthy: It would have been much more convenient, all things considered, if he hadn't attacked me at all.

Rogers: That'd be one way of looking at it. Another is that being a vampire who hates vampires is the kind of branding money can't buy for a congressional candidate.

Worthy: What exactly are you accusing me of?

Rogers: I'm not accusing anyone of anything. I'm just asking questions.

Worthy: Then ask the question. Go ahead. Ask the question you came here to ask.

Rogers: Did any of this really happen?

Worthy: I think we're done here.

Rogers: Santino Rialto was an unregistered vampire. His brother told me he was murdered a few nights after he was paid to provide a blood sample for you to submit to the federal registry.

Worthy: This is ridiculous.

Rogers: Mr. Worthy, are you a vampire?

Worthy: This is why nobody trusts the media

anymore.

Rogers: That's not an answer.

Worthy: What do you want me to do, Dina? Suck your blood right here and now?

Rogers: I don't think you can. Those aren't even real fangs, are they?

Worthy: I have to get back to my crypt.

Rogers: You can't run away from the truth.

***

One thing you have to appreciate about vampires, it's real easy to dispose of their bodies if and when the need arises. You get yourself a sharpened pencil and a dust pan, and you're all set. Hell, a few minutes of sunshine and a stiff breeze can do most of the work for you.

Humans are messier, as I quickly learned.

Blood trickled from the wound on Dina Rogers' forehead, seeping into the rug of my campaign office. I stomped her digital recorder to bits and prayed it didn't upload the audio to a cloud somewhere. It was late and the office was mercifully quiet, but it wasn't going to stay that way forever and I had no idea what to do next. I imagined there were YouTube videos I could watch about how to deal with this situation, but web searches for "how to clean up a murder scene" are the type of thing that inevitably turns up as evidence at a trial.

Four years earlier, I had been working in a garage, racking up debt, and drinking myself to sleep most nights. I knew there was more out there, but I wasn't sure how to get it. Every direction seemed like a dead end. When I caught the guy who worked the overnight shift draining a hooker's neck behind the dumpster, I saw an opportunity.

I watched enough cable news and listened to enough talk radio to know the world was changing, a backlash was brewing against efforts to mainstream bloodsucking monsters, and blue-collar Americans like me were taking their country back. There was a political wave worth riding if you could hitch onto it before it crested.

So Santino and I made a deal. And I know it's hard to believe, but I really had nothing to do with him getting dusted soon afterward. The guy didn't exactly have the healthiest lifestyle.

Anyway, Denton knew all this. We had been friends since high school and he was my first phone call when I decided to get into politics. Smart, idealistic, but just morally malleable enough to do what needed to be done to get ahead. It took a little convincing once he found out what I wasn't, but he signed on as my chief adviser pretty quick, and he was the one who prodded me to aim higher than state politics.

I was struggling to roll the body up in the rug and trying to game out whether I could clear this up without him finding out when I heard his familiar nasally voice over my shoulder.

"You got something you want to tell me?"

The rug slipped from my arms and unfurled. Dina Rogers' lifeless face stared up at us. "Not especially," I said.

Denton shuffled back toward the doorway and grimaced with disgust.

Once he regained his composure a bit, he said, "I take it the interview didn't go well."

"She knew everything," I told him. "I didn't know what to do."

Denton stepped around the body and the blood, coming closer to me. His eyes darted around the room, and I hoped a plan was taking shape in his head.

"We get her out of here, we clean up this mess, and we deal with the rest later," he said, hurriedly and not quite as confident as I would have liked. Still, I stood and helped him try to roll up the rug without getting any more blood on myself. It went much smoother with a second set of hands, but Denton's discomfort was obvious.

"This is going to keep happening, isn't it?" he asked.

"I don't know," I said candidly.

We lifted the rug together and made our way out of the office, struggling to avoid knocking anything over along the way.

"If a two-time Local Emmy runner-up figured it out, others will too," Denton said as we entered the stairwell. "What do we do?"

"I don't know," I repeated.

We started navigating down the stairs carefully, but a human body wrapped in a rug is heavier than television and movies might lead one to believe.

"If any of this comes out," he asked, "can we survive?"

"I don't know," I snapped, attempting to shrug my shoulders.

However, in the process, I lost my grip on the rug. It slipped from my hands, and Denton couldn't maintain his hold on his own, so it slid roughly down the rest of the steps. One of the reporter's high-heeled shoes fell out.

Neither of us said anything for a moment, and I could tell by the strain in Denton's eyes he was running through the same scenarios I was. No matter how well we cleaned this up, I was going to be a prime suspect once people figured out Rogers was gone. I could deflect some scrutiny by playing the persecuted vampire card, but that only goes so far. The reporter's editors and family would be looking for her. I'd be the last person to have seen her. Her car was parked outside my office. She surely left some notes somewhere about her investigation.

"I hate to say it, man," Denton said with a tinge of embarrassment in his voice, "but we might not be smart enough to pull all this off."

I began walking down toward the body.

"What, exactly, is the alternative?" I asked.

"Get caught? Give up?"

"Well, we're not doing that," I picked up the shoe and pointed it toward him, "but I'm open to other ideas."

Denton remained at the top of the last flight of stairs.

"You just killed someone, Colin." Before I had a chance to protest, he added, "This has gone too far."

"Or – and hear me out on this – you could make an argument it hasn't gone nearly far enough," I prodded. "The lies, the pandering and posturing, the cover-up. Sucking up to Roth. All these sacrifices."

I tried to lift the rug by myself and simultaneously prop open the door to the parking lot. It was a heavy door. Blood was starting to show through the fabric of the rug. Times like this, I kind of wished I did drink the stuff.

"This can't all be for nothing," I said.

Denton stared at me, alone and desperate at the bottom of the stairwell, grasping at a dead body, my jacket stained red.

"Of course it can," he said.

He walked back up the steps.

Steel and Fangs
Josh Darling

The Disappearances

The news freaked out everybody. The conspiracy nuts had three answers. It's lizard people. It's aliens. It's the government. They muttered the same wrong bullshit all day. I'd be bringing them coffee, and hear pieces of their bullshit. They'd grab my ass, and I'd do my best to not slap them. You'd think in a place as liberal as Vermont, and after #metoo, they'd get the idea it was time to stop but they didn't. I hated working there. I was 19 and only wanted to work the lunch and dinner shifts. They kept screwing me and putting me on the graveyard shift. The late nights felt creepy, and the tips didn't cover all my bills. I'd debated moving to Albany or Boston and stripping. Everyone said I had the body for it. I didn't know how my parents would handle their daughter getting naked for money. I didn't know how to pole dance, and it'd take me time to save up to move to either place. The cash would be off the books, and I'd still be able to get financial aid for school. At the same time, living with my parents in Stonefield, I didn't have to pay rent. The people that came into the Starlight were all truckers passing through. This was one of the few places serving food 24 hours in the entire state. It might be the only place outside of Burlington open around the clock. I have no idea why it was in Stonefield.

The news channels, even Fox, were all the same. Entire populations of towns in the middle of nowhere America were vanishing. Small towns in the deserts. Places on the borders of Canada in Wyoming and Maine. It was happening worldwide, with a heavier concentration in the US. Stonefield was small, being in town overnight creeped me out.

What the disappearances had in common was they happened at night.

The feeling of paranoia was the same as at the beginning of Covid.

With Covid, people would say things like, "It only kills the old and the weak."

With this, nobody knew what to say. They jumped to conspiracy theories. It didn't help the government and investigators had no answers. The politicians put together Special commissions to figure it out.

After 2 weeks, the country was in uproar, panic, and mourning.

The TV over the counter looped, "The story of the hour is what some are calling "The Great Disappearance." Experts want to know, why do these disappearances only happen at night? The world is baffled as..."

I couldn't take listening to it. I headed through the kitchen.

Hernando, the cook, flipped burgers on the grill.

"*Qué haces mami*?"

"I'm going out for air."

"I didn't know you smoked?"

"Only when it's free. Right now, I can't keep listening to the TV. It's that same loop over and over. And those three fat ass truckers out there talking about aliens and Jesus. And then theirs the guy with the greasy black hair who doesn't talk, but nods." I didn't addthat he was watching me with hungry eyes, and had about two-hundred pounds on me.

"Oh, that's Mouse, he's a local boy. His *familia* lives here, but he don't live in town. He comes in here every three, four weeks. He works with people in wheelchairs or some shit."

"It's nice to know I won't have to see his creepy face every night then. But yeah, I'll be back in a few when you've got those orders up."

The summer night air was too hot for Vermont. I leaned against the outside wall of the diner as far from the dumpster as possible. The light back here shone on the pavement. It filled the distance between the building and the forest. There were 10 more miles of Vermont forest. Then it became New Hampshire forest.

In the darkness, something growled. It was a sound I hadn't heard before. Bass with a clicking staccato…Headlights washed over the trees and the shadows. The creature in the darkness retreated. A white van stopped between me and the wilderness.

Mouse sat in the driver's seat. He raised a tablet with his right hand. His left arm hung out the window.

The writing on the tablet started in large letters, "Help me, I'm mute," but got smaller. I had to get closer to Mouse to read the rest. Mouse lurched toward me. Grabbing my ponytail, he slammed my head into the side of the van's door.

Seconds later, I came to on the floor of the van.

I screamed, "Help."

Handcuffs cut my wrists. The van started. I wobbled to my feet. The front of my head throbbed. Coming to, I felt like something rattled inside my skull.

I screamed again.

I tried standing, but a chain limited my stretch upward. Padlocks secured a chain connecting handcuffs to the floor.

As the van pulled forward, Hernando ran from the back of the diner.

He yelled, "Get back here motherfucker."

A man jumped down from the trees. The man pinned Hernando to the ground and bit into his neck. The two figures diminished as Mouse gunned down the one-lane highway.

I tried reasoning with him, "You don't have to do this," "I won't tell anyone about this," and "My name is Bailey. Please, talk to me."

I thought it was important to say my name. If he knew my name, he might register that I'm a person.

***

Mouse pulled off the highway onto a gravel ditch leading to a river. This put the van at a steep angle. Mouse got out of the van. Opening the rear doors, he pulled a knife. The blade was a foot long.

I started crying. I started listing all the people I knew. Starting with friends and ending with my parents. I thought about how my death would hurt them.

"Please, don't kill me," I said.

With his left hand, he undid my pants. He threatened me with the knife in his right.

"I don't want to die. Please, my parents will miss me. My name is Bailey. My best friend will be heartbroken.

I'm an only child. I'm all my parents have. Please..."

With my jeans undone, he pulled them down to my ankles. With a flick of the knife, he caught the front of my shirt. He climbed into the back of the van. Using the cut in my shirt, he ripped it open.

Air never felt so cold on my skin.

He undid his fly.

I worried if I fought back, he'd kill me.

Even if I resisted, even if I killed him, the chains would still hold me to the floor. Killing him, I'd starve to death in the back of his van.

There was no part of this I enjoyed.

It hurt when he entered me.

As he raped me, I stressed he was giving me a disease. If he got me pregnant, I'd need an abortion. I'd do it myself if I had to. There was no way I'd have this piece of shit's child.

I focused on the wall of the van and cried while he fucked me.

He didn't make any sound.

He pulled out and came on me.

He poured bleach on me.

He got back on top of me.

He pinned my arms in front of me with his fat legs.

He dangled the knife over my face. He'd lower the blade closer to my eyes and then pull back.

"No, don't kill me… please, don't…"

I remember these images clearer than anything else. I remember them because they are the last things I'd see.

He forced open my left eyelid with his thumb and forefinger. He stabbed the knife deep into my eye socket. There was a flash of color as he hit the optic nerve, and then nothing.

I screamed, shaking my head back and forth. I kicked, I tried grabbing him. I felt wetness sliding along my temple.

I don't know how long I writhed. That fat fuck lay on top of me, pinning me in place. He held my other eye open. His large hand held my head in place as he stabbed my other eye.

The pain distracted me from noticing he'd removed the cuffs. With a few hard jerks, Mouse ripped my clothes off. Seizing my leg, he yanked me out of his van. Naked, the rocks on the ground winded me. The throbbing holes where my eyes had been was so intense, I didn't hear the van start. I knew he drove off when his tires spun out, spraying me with gravel.

Crawling, I headed upward and made it to the road. I couldn't escape the smell of bleach.

Years later, the smell of bleach still incites memories of the back of the van.

***

Blindness is not darkness. Not seeing is not seeing, darkness isn't the same.

I don't know how long it took for someone to stop their car and help me.

Coming to, I felt the bandages around my head. The day after, my head felt worse. I wanted to pull them down, but I was in restraints. They reminded me of handcuffs. I thrashed in the bed. From the antiseptic smell and gossip in the halls, I figured I was in a hospital. When a nurse finally came in, she told me a doctor would be in soon. For hours, nurses stopped in and told me that. I kept asking about my parents. The hospital staff didn't want me getting out of bed. The catheter did not add comfort. I felt so alone. The nurses turned on the TV I could not see in my room. No one came in and talked to me. I didn't have my phone, so I couldn't reach out to anyone.

A day had passed when the doctor came to see me. He undid my restraints. I positioned myself on the edge of the bed.

The doctor said, "You'll be blind for the rest of your life," like it was nothing.

I didn't cry. I was in shock.

Crying came later.

"When are the police coming? I was sexually assaulted," I said.

"In the next day or so, right now they're overrun. The disappearances started in Vermont about two days ago."

I just realized how long I'd been unconscious.

"Oh God, where?" my pulse was up…

"Deerfield, Glastonbury, Stonefield—"

"I'm from Stonefield. My parents are in Stonefield, please, let me call them."

The state police were there within the hour. They had questions for me about the man attacking Hernando. They said people from the government would be there to ask me questions.

One of the detectives said, "You know, in a way, you're lucky, everyone from there is gone."

He was the first person I'd ever hit in my life.

Blindness didn't matter. I struck him dead on.

"I should arrest you for assaulting an officer."

"You said I was lucky I got raped."

A woman's voice said, "I apologize for the Detective's comment. He didn't realize his lack of sensitivity. You were telling us about a man who jumped out of the woods and bit Hernando Vasquez in the neck?"

"Like a vampire," I said, expecting them to laugh at me.

They didn't.

The Becoming
Being blind sucks.
The first week, I wanted to die.
I'd been violated.
I'd lost my sight.
I'd lost my parents.

The man who raped me and took my vision was loose. He could be in the room next to me. The cops did a rape kit, but they didn't care. They asked me the same questions about what I'd seen from the back of the van in Stonefield.

They didn't care about me.

The people who cared about me were gone.

After 4 or 5 days, the hospital's social worker said they were transferring me to The Lake Placid School for the Visually Impaired. It's a live-in facility in upstate New York. Its goal is to help the newly visually impaired adjust to life "differently-abled."

The car ride there felt like forever.

This time of my life was confusion, loneliness, and fear.

I didn't know how to read braille or use a Jitterbug (cellphone for the blind.)

Arriving, someone opened the van's door.

A woman's voice said, "Bailey, I'm so glad to meet you. I'm Rose Dittersdorf. I'm the head administrator here at Lake Placid." Taking my hand, she helped me out of the van, "You don't have a cane?"

"They don't hand those out at the hospital."

"I've got a variety of canes you can choose from in my office. We'll see if we can find one that suits you. Many of our students have more than one cane."

In her office, I tried out canes. I half ignored her as

she went over the rules of the facility. Once a week, I had mandatory therapy sessions with a psychologist. She said she'd been informed of my *situation*. Because of disappearances, the woman working as one of the institute's two psychologists left. She's with her family in Pennsylvania. The remaining doctor was Rashid Patel.

Later, in therapy sessions with him, I'd talk about losing my family. I didn't feel comfortable talking about the lead-up to my blindness.

I had a room and a roommate, Teresa. She smelled weird. She was clingy and would say stuff like, "Don't forget your cane."

The dorm room had its own bathroom. In college, the showers were public stalls. Not that I minded. I knew I was hot when I didn't have sliced-up eyes.

I adjusted to hearing where things were fast. They told us that some people had developed a sense of hearing so sharp they could tell the difference between a square and a sphere by the sound echoing off it. They also told us about a blind guy in England who rode a bicycle by making clicking noises and hearing the echoes off of trees and cars.

The staff loved their *See what blind people can do* inspirational stories.

I hated Teresa. She was a morning person. She was a real Pollyanna. After what I'd been through, I didn't need her telling me this was part of "God's plan." She didn't like it when I asked if it was "God's divine cock in me when I was being raped?" But it did shut her up about Jesus for the day.

I spent my awake time thinking about what happened to my parents. Had monsters attacked them? Men like the one who bit Hernando's neck? I dreaded the idea of psychos breaking into my home and ripping their throats open.

The cops didn't laugh when I said, "Like a vampire…" was that it?

Were they killed by fictional creatures?

Sleep was a nightmare –no joke.

Every night, I tried staying awake.

Every night, Mouse raped me.

Every night, I woke up screaming.

The psychiatrist said I had "PTSD."

Really? I mean, like derp.

Dr. Patel recommended a cocktail of drugs.

He said, "70% of blind people have trouble sleeping due to an inability to sync their circadian rhythms."

After three weeks of that failing, I gave up. I needed to work fast. I had two hours while Teresa would be at her *The Bible in Braille* class. With a length of wire I stole from my *Understanding Tactile Input* class, I was ready. On my knees, I tied one end to the bathroom door handle. Looping the other end, I slipped it over my head. Leaning forward, my feet held the door in place. This was the best way I could think of to off myself.

A man said, "Shit!"

I thought, *fuck,* as he pushed me back.

He kept saying, "No, no, no…" repeating it over and over…

He had big hands. He smelled of cleaning supplies, triggering bad memories. I assumed he was one of the orderlies.

He got the noose off my neck.

He leaned me against the door.

"Please, it's what I want," I said.

"You're so beautiful, and you deserve to live. Especially with all the stuff that's happening."

"I've lost everyone I love. I've lost my sight, I'm fucked in the head, why can't you people let me die?"

"I know you've heard this before, but suicide is a

permanent solution to a temporary problem."

"My problems are permanent. I'll be blind for the rest of my life because some bastard stabbed out my eyes. I've got nightmares –probably for the rest of my life, of that guy stabbing me in the eyes. My parents are dead. I can't get in touch with any of my friends because I lost my phone. I can't get on social because I can't see a screen –for the rest of my life."

"You need to catch a break. I know a guy who might be able to help you."

"Fuck off, if you're about to say Jesus."

"No, he's a guy who teaches Krav Maga to the blind."

"I don't know what that is."

"It's kind of like Kung Fu. Knowing how to protect yourself could reduce your stress. Let's get you to your feet, and get this wire out of here."

"What's your name?"

"Joe."

"Joe, do me a favor, leave it here. If you're Kung Fu therapy doesn't work, I don't want to struggle looking for another way out."

***

It was a Thursday evening when Joe got a bunch of us into the school's van and drove us to Krava Maga lessons. I'd later find out this was not his idea. Dr. Patel arranged it. During the ride, all I could think was I'd been in a van like this, only without seats in it.

The other students in the van talked about the disappearances. There were reports of "blood-drinking creatures" and "monsters" attacking people. Did they know those theories came from the last things I'd seen?

There were blind and sighted people in the Krav

Maga class. I didn't know how much the blind got picked on. You'd think people would have evolved beyond this kind of nastiness. Our instructor was Simcha Rosenblatt. He'd studied Krav Maga in the Mossad. He did more than teach fighting. He'd say stuff like, "Street fighting Jews developed Krav Maga to fight Nazis in Germany during World War II. Every time you punch, swing like you're punching a Nazi. Nazis killed the blind, they killed the Jews. Throw every punch like your life depends on it --it does. These creatures are killing towns. You must be ready to stand against the coming evil. Anything destroying life is evil."

Simcha was intense. He did his classes on Thursdays and Sundays to make it to Friday and Saturday synagogue services. He also taught us how to grab a gun out of someone's hand and break their finger while doing it. Sometimes, he'd lean into me and say, "When I was in Mossad, I did this to a man."

He said it when teaching me how to rip someone's throat out, and I chuckled.

He said, "Bailey, you're a very sick girl laughing at that, I like it."

I got good at Krav Maga.

It took the edge off the nightmares. I still had them. I still had Teresa poking me awake, or I'd wake up screaming the edge off, they didn't go away.

After six weeks of training, I sparred against a sighted opponent. Ryan was a teenager going to the local high school. Before this, Simcha had us learning moves and how to take a hit.

He started off the fight by clapping and repeating, "Now. Fight. Now. Fight." he didn't stop.

I couldn't hear shit over his clapping and shouting.

The first guilty punch got me in the ribs. I knew he felt weird hitting a blind person. The punch felt more like a tag than a punch. Ryan retracted his fist before I could catch his hand.

"Hey Simcha, let me learn to fight when I can hear my attacker before you start doing this nonsense?" I said.

"No. Bailey. Must. Learn. To. Fight. When. She. Is. Surrounded. By. Distracting. Noise. Life. Is. Not. Easy. Life. Is. Hard. Now. Fight. Now. Fight."

He was right.

Life is not easy.

Life is hard.

I felt the mat shift under my feet. This let me know where he was –he was moving toward me. I caught him with a right cross in the center of his chest.

Ryan hit the floor wheezing.

"Shit stop!" Simcha shouted.

"He should have blocked. Next time, come correct when fighting a blind girl," I said.

"Bailey, this is sparring, not killing your opponent. Can you breathe?"

Ryan coughed out, "Yeah."

Over the next few months, Simcha would throw different scenarios at me. He'd blare music while I sparred. He'd bang pots and pans. He'd throw balled-up pieces of paper at me.

I hated him for it.

During this time, one-third of the population of the earth was gone. In America, 100 million people were missing.

Later, I'd be grateful for all he taught me.

***

Some of the students in the school left. With so many people gone, their families wanted them at home. Some of the instructors left as well.

Unfortunately, Teresa didn't leave.

One afternoon, I awoke from a nap, "Flick your bean while you're in the shower."

Teresa said, "I would never…"

"I can smell your cooch. I don't care that you're touching yourself. Everybody does it, but not when I'm in the room. That's weird."

"I wasn't touching myself."

The waistband of her panties snapped as she pulled her hand out of them. She sat up. Grabbing her cane, she tapped out of the room.

As she left, Joe entered.

I could tell it was him by his strained breathing.

"Hey Bailey, how you doing?"

"I'm awake."

"I'm making a fire outside, wanna join me?"

"Sure…"

***

The October air was crisp. When I first showed up, Joe was building the fire pit behind the school. Every few nights, students and staff gathered around a fire. The mid-day fire was random, but I enjoyed it. The radiating warmth felt kind. The smoke was intense. Coughing, I backed away from the heat.

"Why are you still here Joe?" I said.

"What do you mean?"

"Why not be with your family? You know, before they're gone with the rest of the human race."

"They're already dead. They lived in New Hampshire."

"You have my condolences."

"It's okay, can I tell you something?"

"It's never good when someone says, *Can I tell you*

something? it's like saying, *we need to talk.*"

"It's not like that. You know how you said you were sexually assaulted? My father molested me. My mother knew but didn't do anything about it. After years of saying 'I didn't see anything' she blinded herself. Later that year, she killed herself."

"Oh wow, I'm genuinely sorry."

"They weren't part of the disappearances. My dad overdosed on OxyContin a few years ago. I wanted to tell you because I feel close to you. I feel like I need to care for you."

"I'm pretty sure my barbecue is canceled because my grill is busted."

"I don't get what you mean?"

"Someone stabbed out my eyes. I have a nice body, but I'm sure you can do better than a blind girl. And that's even with one-third of the women in the world missing."

"You're the most perfect creature ever. I want to take care of you. I want you to know that I'll forever be here to serve you. Let me worship you at your feet. I shall tend to you as your steward."

"That means a lot to me."

I didn't know what else to say.

Joe's vibes were sniveling –not romantic.

The War

The knock on my door was hard, a cop's knock.

"Who is it?" I said.

"You tell me?"

"Come in, Simcha."

Paper rustled in his hands.

"I wanted to see you before I leave," Simcha.

"Leave?"

"I'm going home to Israel."

"Oh."

"I might be back, I don't know. Sighted or blind, you're one of my best students and I wanted to bring you a gift before leaving."

He handed me a long straight object. Wrapping paper crinkled around it. My body slumped toward him as he sat next to me on the mattress.

"This isn't hard to use," he smiled.

How do I know he smiled? When people smile, their lips make a tiny pop as they lift off the teeth.

I unwrapped it.

He took the paper from me.

"Oh great, you got me a wooden cane. What I've always wanted, thanks Simcha. What a consolation prize for my only friend going across the world in a time of global crisis."

"Cane? It's not a cane. Run your thumb down it about eight inches. Go slow."

The wood had a natural finish and felt smooth. I sniffed it. I knew the names of the typical wood scents like pine and cedar. I didn't know the name of this one. I felt a tiny indent that went around the cane…

"Put your hands on both sides of where it separates and *carefully* pull it apart," he said.

"You mean, the crease I'm feeling?"

"Yes, *carefully*."

The cane expanded, telescoping in my hands, "Shit, did I *carefully* break it?"

"No, the blade is out."

"Oooooooooh … it's not a cane," I said.

I kept pulling, waiting to feel the blade loose, "This is a pretty long knife."

"It's not a knife, you ever see the Zatoichi movies?"

"Nope, and I don't think I'm going to," with my arms outstretched, the blade was free.

"I got you a cane sword."

I put the blade on the mattress next to me.

"Holy shit, thank you," I hugged Simcha and kissed his cheek.

"Now, let me show you how to put it back in the sheath."

"*Show me?*"

"Don't give me a hard time."

I had to practice finding the blunt side of the blade to guide it into the sheath.

Simcha and I talked more before he left. He thought I should do competition fighting if the world ever went back to normal.

"I have to go," he said. The mattress under me lifted as he stood, "One more thing, don't trust Joe. You can't see it, but he's a schmuck and a half. The way he looks at you is unsettling –at best."

That was the last time we talked.

***

The smell of death preceded them. I woke thinking it was a gas leak. The odor brought me to consciousness before my PTSD nightmares.

I didn't tell anyone about my cane.

No one needed to know.

Sleeping with it next to me made me feel safer.

I sat up.

I put my sneakers on.

Solid footing is important when fighting.

It was before Thanksgiving. The night air in the room was cold enough to make me wonder if there were flurries outside. I heard the wind. Lots of wind rushing on the glass. The smell came from outside. I headed for the door.

"Where are you going?" Teresa said.

"Don't follow me, they're here."

"What's here?"

"Death."

I exited the room and slammed the door behind me.

I wanted them to know where I was.

I'd been kidnapped.

I'd been raped.

I'd lost my parents.

I'd lost my eyesight.

I'd lost my future.

I wasn't about to lose anything else –but my life.

Teresa came out of our room.

"What are you—"

I poked her in the middle of the chest with my cane, "Go get in your bed and pull the covers over your head for safety."

She sucked her teeth and did as she was told.

Their footfalls came from the first floor. Down there were all classrooms. The second and third floors were the dorms. There were more buildings on the campus. I guess they figured they'd start killing the easy targets first.

I would.

A finger clicked on the elevator button.

The elevator's motor whirred, heading down to them.

Ding.

They got in.

Voices echoed in the elevator shaft.

One of them said, "I'm so hungry…"

Another replied, "My master hasn't allowed me any blood, tonight I'll gorge myself …"

The elevator stopped. The doors rolled open.

They walked out.

I tapped my cane on the floor… *I'm here.*

"Food!" one of them shouted.

"Bleed the bitch dry," another cried.

Fighting is about understanding what resistance means.

When jabbing outward and the blade stops, you've hit something. If the blade keeps going, it is muscle. If the blade wiggles like you're fishing and you've got something on the line, the blade has hit bone.

I kept swinging, cutting through them.

There were screams and splashes. Rot filled the air.

There was no way anything living could smell that bad.

They made wet slapping noises on the tile floor.

The elevator whirred…

…more came.

This was my night. Hours of cutting rotting flesh to pieces.

When morning alarms sounded, they stopped coming.

Every muscle in my body felt like it was ready to give. I'd never exerted myself this hard before.

The elevator dinged. Its doors opened. By the heavy breath, I could tell it was Joe.

"Bailey, I'm so sorry."

"For what?" my hands trembled with fatigue.

"I'm supposed to take care of you, but I failed you."

"It's okay, it's not a big deal."

I couldn't figure out what I wanted more, to take a shower or sleep.

In the notes of the smell of decaying flesh was something earthen. I opted for the shower. I didn't know what type of mess was on me. My BO aside, I smelled rank.

From the shower, I heard Joe stuffing body parts

into bags. Then came the squeak of the mop bucket. The first time Joe mixed bleach in the water, I had flashbacks. I'd told Rose about my PTSD and the smell of bleach. He switched to a pine-scented ammonia cleaner from then on.

While shampooing my hair, footsteps entered my room. Someone was being stealthy about opening the bathroom door. The inner parts of the door handle sounded off when rotated. The door opened with enough care the hinges didn't creak. The draft is how I knew it was open.

I put my hands over my breasts.

"I can hear you breathing. Don't come in here again while I'm bathing Joe."

He gasped and ran.

***

Dressed and out of the shower, I got into bed.

The knock at the door was a test knock –asking *Are you sleeping? I can come back later…*

"Come in," I said.

Chanel No. 5 filled the room: *Rose Dittersdorf, I presume.*

"I'm dead tired. What's up?" I said.

"What you did tonight was amazing. You're like a superwoman," she said.

"Thanks, I guess. I was fighting for my life."

"We figure you killed thirty vampires in the hallway. It's hard to tell. They're in pieces."

"Vampires?"

"They're dead things with fangs. What else should we call them?"

"Vampires it is."

The Offer

Every night they came. Sometimes by the dozen.

Every night I cut them into pieces.

There was comfort in fighting.

A Zen awakening came with the awareness of perfect victory after perfect victory.

I couldn't count how many of them I killed.

I had no idea.

The first people to show up at The Lake Placid School were a family.

We sat at the dinner table in the mess hall.

Joe made them soup and bread.

They smelled like homelessness. It was a mix of BO, rotting leaves, woods, fire, and a touch of frost. The Man did all the talking. Their breath wreaked of stomach acid –they'd been starving. They came to the school looking for food. The Man said they'd seen people with fangs and rotting bodies devouring towns. The military was losing the battle. Cities like DC and New York had fallen. They attacked at night and disappeared during the day. They drank blood, leaving the corpses exsanguinated.

"Joe, did you know anything about this?" I said.

"Everybody knows about the creatures," he cleared his throat.

"I'm fighting things that are killing off the army? Did you know the army has fallen?"

"You've been fighting them?" The Man said.

"No, I've been killing them."

Bullets don't do much to them. Cutting them to pieces is the only way to stop them.

Over the next few weeks, more people came to the school.

At night, I'd fight droves of the undead.

When it got dark, I'd wait outside for the vampires.

The leaves were not raked and stayed on the lawn. Their russeting made it easier to hit the vampires.

After the first snowfall, impacting snow became my cue noise.

The sighted said they'd never seen anyone move as fast.

People would ask, "How do you fight them?"

"When I swing my sword, it's only moving air. Hell, if I could see them, then I'd be afraid too."

***

We had our New Year's Eve Party during the day. Sixty or seventy people lived at the school now. Half of them could see. During the day, they'd scavenge for food. At night, I protected them from the vampires.

The night of New Year's Eve was different.

That night, they didn't come for me.

Outside, rotting flesh and frost wafted through the air, but they didn't attack.

A single person/vampire approached. From the light crunch of footsteps on the ice, it sounded like a woman.

"We should talk, I'm Neith."

"Come closer, I can't hear you very well…"

"I'm good here. While your sword won't work on me, I'm not up for getting stabbed right now."

"Why won't my sword work on you?"

"I'm a real vampire."

"I've killed hundreds of *real* vampires."

"No, you haven't."

"So, all those dead vampires—"

"Dead *familiars*."

"What? Like witches' cats?"

"Not quite. You've never read Dracula?"

"I skipped it in high school, and I don't think it'll happen at this point."

"It might."

"You can give me my sight back?"

"I can do a lot of things, and that's one of them, but we need to know you're going to stop killing our familiars."

"How do I know I can trust you?"

"Because I haven't killed you."

I braced myself to cut her down.

There was a tug at my cane. Panic hit me as I realized I no longer held it.

The blade *shushed* sliding from its sheath.

"You haven't encountered a vampire. Fighting us is not something you can do. We have our weaknesses, but that's not a discussion for now. I want you to think about having your sight back, take the day and consider it."

She pressed my cane into my hand, "Here."

Then she was gone.

Inside the front doors, one of the new people said, "Why aren't they attacking?"

"We have a truce for tonight."

***

In my bedroom, I got out of my winter gear. I lay in bed wearing a sweatshirt and wool socks.

I ran through all the memories of the things I'd seen since childhood until I saw the knife coming at my pupils.

How could a vampire restore my vision? They were committing genocide.

It had to be a trick.

She moved fast enough to kill me before I could get my blade out. Why didn't they attack? Why was I special?

I couldn't sleep...

I was too excited.

Sweat covered the front of my shirt. Teresa jacked up the thermostat before starting her snoring and farting routine.

It was more than the heat.

It was enthusiasm and happy-nervousness.

What if it was a lie? Or a dream? Or a hallucination?

I assumed this meant she'd turn me...

Would I come back here and kill all the vulnerable people?

I didn't know if I was okay with that.

Well, maybe Teresa and her deviated septum.

Teresa might have to die.

***

I waited in the snow in the same place as last night. On the edge of the property, I kept my hands on my cane, ready to draw.

Their smell trailed on the wind.

They were here.

"You smell like earth, freezer burn, and rot."

"I don't," Neith said.

Silently, she was inches from my face.

Her body odor, gardenia.

Her breath, fresh-cut meat.

Her last meal, blood.

She said, "What'll it be?"

"Do I lose all my free will and become a blood junky? Will I kill everyone in there?"

"No, you'll be a vampire. And we're slowing down the culling. When we started the first part of our plan, we were building an army of familiars. Humans fucked up the planet, and we have to live here too. We made the decision to reduce your numbers. The thing about familiars is they rot away and die. They're also weak and like us vulnerable to sunlight. We needed an army of fifty million of them to take on the one point five million that make up the US Army."

"This whole thing is because of the environment?"

"Yes. We need to be able to live on this planet without humans destroying it. We're taking away your nuclear bombs too."

"Why are you offering this to me?"

"Because we don't want you killing any more of our familiars. You're more dangerous than a team of Navy SEALS. Those guys are trying to fight us with guns and haven't figured out how to make a dent in our numbers aside from dropping bombs on cities and towns. They do more for us with their collateral damage. I figure eyesight and immortality are a good trade to get you to stop hurting our numbers. Also, you protect the weak, that's important to us. We're not monsters. Humans are."

"Last question, will I get my sight back?"

"Yes, more than you'll ever know."

"How do you know I won't turn against you?"

"You won't."

She ripped open the front of my jacket. Her bite felt like a sucker-punch to the neck.

Weakness overcame me.

I crumpled in her arms.

From the school, I heard a rifle cocking. Their hero was dead to them. They were preparing their last stand.

The shot echoed. The bullet shattered my spine, cut through my heart, burst out of my sternum, and hit Neith.

She let go of my neck, "No, no, don't die… drink and know life eternal."

Her bleeding wrist pressed against my lips. Her

blood was the flavor of cotton candy orgasms.

"Good girls swallow," she chuckled.

I saw her entire life…

Childhood drawings, the fertile valley, lover's bodies, sunsets, ships, mountain ranges…

I smelled everything she'd known…

Piss, incense, death parents' funeral pyre, rats on ships, perfume, ejaculate…

I heard her life.

Cooing parents, fights with lovers, instruments in the desert, Mozart conducting operas…

I tasted everything…

All the foods she'd consumed as a human, the taste of woman's sex, and the ecstasy of blood…

I felt everything…

Orgasms and suffering, pleasure and torture, the high of blood and the agony of sunlight…

The Rebirth

There was a sensation in the front of my skull. My eyelids fluttered open.

Neith was hot sex on a platter. Aside from fooling around in high school a few times, I'm not into girls. Seeing her made me reconsider. She was small but built like some cross between a supermodel and a sex goddess. The cold winter air didn't affect her Egyptian cinnamon skin. Her eyes were huge and black. They reminded me of a teddy bear's eyes. I wanted to kiss her. I couldn't explain my lust for her.

"Now she understands, after I turn you, you fall in love with me… just a little."

"Yeah, just a little."

"It's not real, it'll fade in a few years. I'm not the kind to take advantage of the newly reborn."

My eyes were working.

I could see!

A gunshot hit me in the back of the head. My eye exploded out of my head. The back of Neith's head exploded.

I fell into the snow.

My good eye watched –I was seeing again! As my blood and flesh in the snow tracked back to my body.

The rifle cocked again.

It was on the third floor of the school.

The puzzle of blood and bone that was Neith's head solved itself.

With my twice-healed eye back in place, I got to my feet and ran.

I'd never moved this fast before, and I was seeing…

I had to think about where to go and I'd be there. That's how fast I moved. I stood next to the shooter on the third floor.

"I'm taking this, okay?" I threw the rifle out the window.

I'd never seen him before…

I'd never seen anyone at the school before.

I went to the first floor, where everyone waited for me to return from battle.

Every ounce of high and excitement drained out of me.

Mouse stood there. He was gigantic in his winter clothes. I recognized the students and sighted people standing around him by their smell. It made sense, for him to work here. Did he blind me hoping I'd wind up here? Maybe his victim selection was random, and I was in the wrong place at the wrong time.

"You," I said.

"Are you okay Bailey?" Joe said.

I struggled with reality.

The man who raped me and blinded me was the

same man who cleaned the toilets and saved me from suicide.

"Joe?" I said.

"Yes," he said.

"Mouse?"

"Who?" he swallowed.

"Mouse, I can see, and the last thing I saw was your face."

"I wanted to protect you, I loved you and—"

Biting his face, his cheekbone caved between my teeth. He punched at my chest, my ribs, as his voice sang an unrelenting hymnal of anguish.

Drinking, I knew his life but felt nothing for it. I could see his molestation by his father. The beatings he suffered. The animals he tortured. The first things he blinded were squirrels he'd captured in the woods. He'd bring them home and care for them. His father would step on them in front of him. There were more women he'd raped in his van. The other women he'd left naked and in the middle of the woods. He'd never see them again.

I was the first one he'd dumped by the roadside.

He wanted me found.

He wanted a thing to care for too weak to leave him.

I felt inebriated. I didn't realize the sighted were trying to pull me off him.

My hearing still gets selective when I feed.

Neith's voice sliced through the panic…

"If this man hurt you, I have a better punishment."

Letting go of Joe, I drove my sword straight down into his knee and out the bottom of his heel.

He attempted to support himself.

"Bailey, what did you do?" Teresa said.

I didn't realize she was here because I didn't know what she looked like. I saw the disheveled thirtysomething snorer for the first time.

"Joe is the man who blinded me," I said.

"Oh God, how do you know?"

"I can see."

***

Nighttime is bright. Reflecting the moon, the snow illuminates the world. My new eyes see everything in contrasting shades of radiance. The cosmic light of the universe falling from the night sky borders on radioactive. Everything smells different. Where the humans had touched, where their life flows, their skin, their breath, their hair, the soap they use. Blinded, I trained my other senses.

Re-sighted, the world was reborn around the eternal I.

Neith walked down the hallway with her hands up.

The sighted who'd gathered at the school aimed weapons at her.

"Before you fail at killing me a second time, we should talk," Neith said.

Guns cocked.

Swords pointed.

Pitchforks raised.

Joe/Mouse cried in the background.

Neith sighed.

"What do you want?" Rose said.

"We're starting the planet over. For too long, we let you destroy the planet. We're sick of you polluting everything. The air doesn't feel right. In the Pacific Ocean, there's a swirling vortex of plastic bigger than the US. Almost every living thing on the planet has PFOA in it because of DuPont. You guys did a lot of damage over the last hundred years. These issues prompted us to reduce humans to manageable numbers. It's not a feeding thing."

"You're not going to eat us?" Rose said.

I wanted to bite Rose and drink-fuck the blood inside her so bad –an electrifying and ambiguous feeling.

"Occasionally. The things you've been fighting are our familiars. They'll be dying off from starvation soon. Your armies were destroyed by our familiar army. That's how we de-fanged you. We won't trust you with limitless access to technology again. Bailey has been doing a good job watching over you, we figured it would make sense for her to remain here."

"I want Mouse," I said.

"To do what with?" Rose said.

"I want to kill him for what he did to me."

"I didn't do anything. I only wanted to care for you," he said.

I started for him.

Neith hugged me, "Do you want to kill this man, or do you want him to suffer?"

"Please! Oh God, the pain, let me die!" he screamed.

"Suffer," I said.

***

Neith grabbed Joe/Mouse by the armpit and pulled him out of the floor with my sword in his leg. Running, she dragged him out of the school and hauled him across the field of snow. She kept sprinting through the forest and toward town. Keeping up with her exhausted me.

I felt like we'd been running for miles when we reached the construction site. It looked like it had shut down back when the disappearances built momentum.

Joe/Mouse screamed, hollered, blabbered…

She dropped him into a hole dug for rebars and

concrete supports.

Hands on my knees, I caught my breath.

"That's like the most intense Pilates class ever," I said.

"Your speed and endurance will increase over time. I'm going to show you an ancient torture. We used to do this to punish humans and sometimes for fun. Four thousand years ago, we stopped. People started attacking us during the daylight. That's when we went underground –so to speak."

Still catching my breath, I processed what she said. Despite running, the intoxication of blood continued. I didn't feel tipsy, but awake, powerful, and sensual.

I wanted more.

"Remove your sword from his leg. Step on his foot and pull it straight up. He needs to keep his legs."

"Fucking kill me! This is the worst fucking pain," Joe/Mouse screeched. Dragged for miles, didn't do much for his suffering.

Stepping on his foot, I pulled the sword straight out of his knee cap.

The distressing sound that came from him made me shiver.

A truck rumbled to a start.

Beeping, it backed up.

The chute for a cement mixer swung overhead.

"Hold him dangling over the hole," Neith said.

I tossed my sword out of the pit. Clutching his messy pulp of an ankle I jumped to the edge.

Neith hit a lever.

Cement flooded into the hole.

Joe bucked like a high voltage current was running through him.

Pleading for his life, he used all the variations of "Please, this is wrong," a person can come up with.

When confronted with death, a suffering coward will want to live. When the cement got to his face, he screamed, "Thank you for letting me die."

I wish he'd make up his mind.

It took a few minutes for the cement to cover up to his knees.

"It's important you leave his feet out of the cement. The sun will burn them in the morning, they'll regrow at night," Neith said.

As the cement hardened, his feet stopped moving.

"I think he's dying," I said.

"That's okay. I'm showing you this punishment because when people are horrible, this is how you deal with them. Until their society can learn kindness and they have forgotten about this."

Taking my index finger, Neith kissed the end of it and smiled. There was no sensation at the end of my finger as she pressed it to one of her fangs.

She squeezed three drops of my blood on the open wound of his foot.

"You have known awful suffering and loss. Every person who drinks your blood will know your suffering as they become us. Those who know three drops of your blood will become your familiars and will rot starving. They're too weak to break free of the concrete. In the spring, maggots will turn him to the bone. For now, he will suffer for months on end. Humans only understand barbarism. Can you administer this to those who cause needless harm to others?"

His foot kicked to life.

"Yeah, sure."

Stigmata

Ravenna Blazecroft

Damn you, damn you. We almost had you in Denmark. The other sisters think you're toying with us, but I sense your fear. I'll be the one to finally take you down.

"Mother Joan, he's too strong." Sister Chastity's well-known faith and courage make her outspoken about the limitations of the rest of us. "We must pursue the task that's right in front of us: helping those of us his victims that can still be saved."

I pace, frowning, at the front of the room. At twenty-eight, I'm the youngest Mother Superior in our Order's history—and not without reason. "While he corrupts more innocent souls with each passing day?"

She brushes back a strand of golden hair that strays out from her wimple. "We won't do much good if we ourselves end up turned."

Above the council chamber hangs an ancient crucifix, borne out of the Holy Land by pilgrims over a thousand years ago. "I can do all things through Christ

Who strengthens me," I quote, gesturing at the cross.

"Thou shalt not put the Lord thy God to the test," she counters.

"Sisters, please." The sweetest voice in the room: Sister Bernadette, our personal saint. At twenty-one, she's the youngest member of the Order of the Wolf of Gubbio; but her steadfast piety has been instrumental to destroying many of the Damned already. None of us would be surprised to see her bilocating, or bleeding mysteriously from her hands and feet. "Any quarrel that mars our charity, mars our sacred quest."

"You're right, Berna." Sister Terisa, the quick-thinking Neapolitan who once tricked an Enemy into drinking holy water. "Whatever we do, we do as one body with many members. Otherwise, we've lost."

I breathe in through my nose and close my eyes. They're right, of course. Here in Assisi, in the most sacred convent of St. Clare, we have precious days of safety in which to pray and plan. Exhaling, I turn my gaze back to Sister Chastity. "All right. Let's look for a way to weaken our primary target by undermining his network of slaves. That way, we advance two goals at once."

She nods vigorously. "Good thinking, Mother. If we—" She stops. "Berna? Are you all right?"

Berna's beautiful green eyes seem oddly glazed. Staring blankly at the wall, she says, "I warned you, Joan."

Her use of the familiar is unusual, but I take no offense. I know she'd never speak in wrath or pride. "Warned me? About what?"

"To stay away."

A glacial frisson slides from my scalp to my stomach. I found an old parchment in Copenhagen, inked with a flawless cursive: a message left by *you*. "Luckily for you, I have larger concerns at present. Stay away, and I'll spare your little troupe of nuns." I crumpled it, telling no one. "Sister Bernadette?"

Her lips move, and she speaks like one in a dream. "Guess again."

Well-trained muscles snap into action, even as my rational self is frozen in horror. My silver crucifix, blessed by the Pope himself, emerges from my habit; the sisters scatter as I brandish it in Berna's face. "Creature of Satan, I command thee! Begone from this child of God!"

Slowly, her eyes come into focus. They stare into mine, but they're not Bernadette's. In her melodious voice, I hear your cruel amusement. "I see I'll have to make time for you after all."

Gazing into your depths, I hesitate. I wish to call upon the power of Christ. I—I wish to—to—

In the silence of my mind, you whisper: *You want to know the Power of Lord Satan.*

Inaudibly, I murmur, "Yes."

Then Berna blinks and shakes her head. Her lovely smile returns. "My goodness, Mother, I beg your pardon. I think I dozed off for a moment. What were you saying?"

The others and I share a glance. Whatever our disagreements, we all cherish Bernadette—our own little saint, as we call her. "We were—ah—just about to adjourn, dear," Terisa says mildly, suppressing a quaver with admirable discipline. "Why don't you head to the chapel and start the Rosary?"

"Of course, Sister." Rising graciously, Berna bows to me and leaves the room with no sign of discomfiture.

The rest of us are grimly silent.

***

It's long past midnight. Cold rain rattles on the window, mixed with sleet; the stars are veiled. Tangled in my sheets, I've never felt further from sleep.

We've notified Bishop Burke of what happened. Tomorrow, he'll take counsel with His Holiness the Pope. We'll handle this. I haven't told them what you uttered in my mind—not because I couldn't, but I—I simply need time, that's all.

Clutching my crucifix, I lie flat on my back and keep repeating, "Hail Mary. Hail Mary." Pressing the cool silver to the skin between my breasts. "Hail Mary." Moving it slowly downward. Down the taut flesh of my midriff. "Hail Satan. Hail Mary." Down between my thighs. "Hail Satan. Hail Satan."

The breath is hot in my throat. What am I—what am I saying? My pelvis moves, yearning upwards, pushing itself against the blessed cross. Oh my God, it feels—so good—

"Hail Satan. Hail Satan. Hail Satan!"

No. My faith is the core of who I am. You cannot change it in a single instant of hypnosis. How can any pleasure be this strong? Please, Jesus, help me to resist. Oh my God, Lord Satan, it feels so fucking good.

I am a virgin for the lord—I *was* a virgin—he *was* my lord. The crucifix slips inside—a moment's roughness, momentary pain—then it's moving back and forth, the rapture mounting. Yes, oh yes, oh Master, Satan, yes! Let me know Thy Power, this I pray. Enter me, Lord Satan, fill my soul!

My back arches, my mouth stretches wide, every muscle strains; beads of sweat stand, quivering, on my naked skin. I feel my eyes roll up inside my skull; I feel my soul surrender to a new Messiah. No sound issues from my throat, but my head and heart are ringing with dark song as I climax in His Name.

Panting, I lay still. What have I done? What have you made me do?

I feel a smile on my lips. I'm not done yet: I've barely started. To feel His Power, to be truly one with Him, I have to share Him with another. I have to corrupt a once-pure soul.

Once again, my muscles react before my mind catches up. I'm on my feet, wrapping myself in a robe, and heading for the door. For half a second, I dissemble—*Where am I going? What's happening to me?*— but I know perfectly well where I'm going, and what's about to happen.

Her room's not locked, of course. We trust each other with our lives. Our souls. She's kneeling by her bed, her wooden beads held tight, mumbling her prayers to—him. That pale, impotent Nazarene. My smile becomes a grin. He can't protect her.

She looks up, startled. "Mother Joan! Is something wrong?"

Oh, the Power and the Pleasure! Stepping forward, I let the robe fall from my body and seize her by the hair. She jumps up, gasping; baffled and afraid, she yields to the passion of my kisses on her mouth and neck. You haven't even bitten me yet, but I feel your strength in my limbs. I drag her down the hallway to the chapel.

"Mother, please! In Christ's name, what are you doing?"

I slap her across the face. Cackling, I force her to her knees. You haven't even bitten me, but I feel your will in my gaze. Staring into her eyes, I command her: "Shut up. In Satan's Name, submit. Submit to me, and to Him."

Her mouth comes open, but no sound comes out. Bent by some force greater than her nailed-marked god, she bows to kiss my feet. Impatiently, I lean down, take her sweet face in my hands, and guide her mouth to the pulsing warmth between my thighs. "Yes," I moan, "yes Satan, yes Lord Satan."

But we're not here to worship me. I yank her to her feet and strip the cotton robe from her lithe, slim body. I mount the altar, going to my hands and knees upon the lord's table, and pull her up behind me. On her hands and knees, she begins to pleasure me once more. I shriek with rapture—but now I sense another presence.

Here you are. Here you are at last.

The saints have many gifts, including levitation; and you, Dark Saint of Satan, levitate before me with your throbbing manhood thrusting from your robe. As Bernadette continues her whore's work behind me, I thirstily pleasure you in turn. No hint of resistance remains, my Lord and Master. I am yours, I am yours.

A new sound behind me, at the other end of the altar: you are there as well. Glory to Lucifer, you have the saintly power of bilocation! Entering the once-saintly Berna from behind, you fuck her virgin flesh as she kneels beneath the stained-glass images above.

And now you rise up higher. Your feet are bleeding! Oh Master, I understand. That gift, too, is yours. I press my lips to the bloody marks in your body, receiving your Unholy Spirit.

Oh my God, Lord Satan, I am Your slave, Your whore, Your plaything. Kiss me, oh kiss me. Take my body, take my soul, take me to Hell and fuck me forever in the Darkness. I worship You, need You, ache for You. Fill me, Wicked Spirit, I beg of You. Ravish me, own me, possess me!

And now
—at last—
your fangs upon my neck.

Blood in Paradise – Quincey's Tale
Denise Ciencin and Dr. Chris McAuley

Prologue

The monster's strength was impressive. I had grappled with a grizzly bear once and been set upon by a wolverine when I had been out hunting in the north. Dracula's ferocity was easily equal, if not greater than those encounters. As I managed to draw my weapon, Harker had caught the Count unawares, and had sliced his throat in a single movement. Dark liquid flowed from his neck and a gurgling sound issued from the demon's throat. It was then that I decided to take my bowie knife and plunge it into Dracula's chest. I prayed to God that my aim had been true.

I got my answer when he disintegrated before my eyes. His body first catching flame and his skin melting like wax. I watched as he turned into powder and descended like grit upon the brown earth. Weakened by the lack of blood from my wounds, I crumpled into a heap and closed my eyes upon the world for the last time.

I fell.

Rather it felt like falling, a great descent which accelerated and made me giddy.

This sensation as well as the darkness which surrounded me, had me convinced I was going to hell.

I had done a lot of things in my life that I wasn't proud of.

Cheated at cards, played the fool with a lot of women.

I don't think my daddy, Elias would have been proud of me.

Maybe one good deed in my life could never make up for the mistakes of the past.

A light appeared below and as I headed through it, I was reminded of beauty once again.

"Quincey, you have not defeated Dracula but only delayed his plans. Even now, in his non-corporal state, he is communing with his dark masters."

The words made no sense to me but I remembered the voice that spoke them. Lucy Westenra. She was the great love of my life. The woman who did something no other could, she made me want to change, to become a better sort of man. Dracula took her innocent and playful soul and changed her; under our noses he took Lucy from the men who loved her. The foul bastard took her away from me.

I saw her then, as she was but filled with luminescence. Her hair still tumbled down onto her shoulders and although her face radiated joy, she had that look about her when she would brook no argument. I'm not sure how long it took, but as I held her gaze, I finally found the nerve to speak.

"Lucy, my darlin'. Am I in heaven? Did Dracula kill me as I done for him?"

Lucy moved closer and reached out to me, her ethereal hand touched mine and I held it like it was the old times.

"Yes, Quincey, this is a form of heaven, though not as you would understand it. There is great good in this world and terrible evil. I am asking you to return to the world. To become an ambassador for everything noble, to defeat Dracula and his fellow monsters. To stop his masters from achieving their aims and bring a thousand years of darkness into the world."

I nodded my acceptance, not really understanding the meaning behind the words which she had spoken. All I knew was that my Lucy was asking me to do something and with all the will at my disposal, I would undertake it.

Abruptly I felt the sensation of being pulled upwards, away from Lucy and back into the darkness. As this occurred, I remember a lingering thought. If this was heaven, why was I pulled downwards towards it?

Romania, December 1893
I was mobbed by returning senses.

I could hear the soft whine of dogs, distant murmurs of conversation and felt the bitter cold on my uncovered hands and face. All of this tumbled to and fro, my mind was lurching between a dull haze and a sharp awareness. As I desperately attempted to hold onto a sense of consciousness, I felt the weight on top of me give way. A heavy, earthy smell filled my nostrils. Something was strongly tugging at my exposed hands and feet. As for my body, I seemed to be wrapped up tightly in a blanket. It was over my face, a feeling which I could never abide as a child. My mama used to tuck me in like that at night, she claimed it was to 'keep out the bed bugs'. I groaned and flailed my arms up, attempting to remove the annoyance.

At this explosion of movement, the tugging abruptly stopped and the things, which now I could tell to be several dogs, moved closer and took long sniffs at me. They seemed confused, I reasoned at the time that they were assessing my level of threat. However now I know that they were trying to work out what they had found.

I couldn't tell how many of them there were but to judge by the sounds, several at least seemed to hold me as the focus of their attention. My head was still fuzzy and as it was night, it was difficult to truly focus on them. I immediately grew fearful as when the moon peered through the clouds to illuminate the trees, their aspect became clear to me. With a raw shock tearing through my nerves, I realized that these were not dogs but wolves.

In that instant, a level of panic swept over me, it cured the previous dullness of my senses and I was fully awake. I lay there in the freezing earth, in the full expectation that the creatures would start ripping into my defenseless body. I had lost my bowie knife when I plunged it into the undead heart of the fiend that we had traveled from England to kill. I was, for one of the few times in my life, truly helpless.

Moments passed and the curious sniffing stopped. The wolves backed away from my body. I attempted to swallow but found myself coughing up lungsful of dirt instead. My mouth was interminably dry and I decided to attempt to rise. It would be better to die on my feet rather than on my back.

As I pulled myself up from the pit in which I had been placed, scrambled memories forced their way into my head. Images of a shoot-out and then of grappling with the creature known as Dracula. He wounded me and then… Then I woke up here.

It was then that I realized that I had crawled out of the place which was intended to be my grave. My comrades must have thought me dead, it's hard to keep Mamma Morris' son down though. Many times, it's been assumed that I had an appointment to sit with my father Elias P on the pearly celestial steps. I always managed to beat the odds no matter how bad the situation. I couldn't be dead. I could feel and I was nearly attacked by wolves.

A voice in my head responded to that train of thought.

"Are you sure that the wolves didn't obey you and move off into the night. You wanted them to go away. Remember they helped you and dug you out of your dirt nap, Quincey."

I raised my hand; I wasn't sure if it was trembling because of the cold or because I was terrified at what I would find. I ran my fingers along the bottom and top rows of my teeth. Thankfully I could find no canines that were as pronounced as those of Dracula. Everything appeared and felt to be normal.

I couldn't deny that I felt differently however, as my head cleared and my eyesight, sense of hearing and smell seemed acute. As I observed the snow falling on my hands, which had turned blue, the second awful realization struck me.

My mouth was emitting no cloud of air in the cold.

I was not breathing.

The evidence was beginning to mount that I was indeed a revenant of some kind.

As I became lost in my reverie, the wolves returned. I came back to my senses to find dozens of them encircling me. I could hear their eager panting and the gentle click of their claws against the bare stones or crunching into the thick snow. This time I felt no fear, I stood my ground even as the pack leader approached me. He was a big fellow, where the other wolves' fur was comprised of shades of grey. This beast was black. He lifted his head into the midnight hued sky and howled. It was an eerie sound; it hung and lay among the thick branches of the trees and seemed to pierce my soul.

As the mournful sound continued, several of the other wolves accompanied it. One after another, they joined him, blending and weaving their many voices into a triumphant song. A melody whose phrases only they could fully understand.

As the leader stopped his chorus, he lowered his head and focused his huge green eyes upon me. When he did this, the other wolves continued to howl and wail at the invisible spirits and the light of the moon. I was taught in the prairies that it was dangerous to ascribe human characteristics to an animal but in this instance, I couldn't help myself. The thing looked not just interested in what he saw, but curious, in a manner that a human being would be curious.

The black wolf sat down on his haunches and a rolling darkness seemed to come from within the creature's body. It blurred the details as I watched bones and joints soundlessly shifting, the muzzle and fur retreated and the skin became swollen. It rose on its hind legs and kept rising until it became a match for me in height. The crooked legs straightened and thickened until they became the legs of a man. A tall lean man dressed in rags. Only his bright green eyes remained the same, and when his red lips thinned into a smile, I clearly saw the hungry wolf lurking beneath the surface.

When the man spoke, it was with a deep baritone. His quiet voice carried across the snow and forest with ease.

"Mr. Morris. We have been waiting for you. You must have many questions, come with us and perhaps we can provide some answers."

I'm usually wary of accepting a stranger's invitation, it comes from being raised in a place where thieves and bandits waited behind every rock or bush. When I assessed my options however, I realized that I didn't have much choice. So, I nodded my acceptance and the man smiled with those thin lips of his and we traveled on.

The wind picked up as we continued to walk westward. I felt everything keenly, it seemed that every sensation in my body had intensified. I could see farther and clearer, even in the darkness which surrounded us. I could hear the gentle step of the company of wolves as they walked beside us. Their paws padding the soft snow. Oddly I felt warm enough, even though I was hardly dressed for the circumstances.

My new companion never spoke a word and in that same vein I kept my questions to myself. I knew that it was more sensible to bide my time in situations such as these. Every so often I would catch him looking at me, perhaps to check that I was still standing upright. Eventually we came to a clearing. It looked like a camp had been set up, a fire was going and a makeshift spit was hung over it. I imagined all kinds of meats on that wooden pole; rabbits and hog roasting slowly over the fire. At these mental suggestions my stomach made a growling sound. I gave a half-hearted gesture to apologize but my new friend waved those politeness's away.

"We shall feast soon; my brethren shall hunt for us as you and I attempt to discover the mysteries of your past."

With that instruction, the wolves moved through the clearing and back into the forest. My friend introduced himself as Barnabas. He bade me sit by the fire and began to prepare a mixture of some sort. He gave a form of explanation as he moved between the tents, bringing out powders and leaves.

"Sometimes we require a little aid to help us stir the hidden things in our mind. I do not come from these parts as you may have guessed from my manner of speech. I was drawn here to aid your return and to assist you in the journeys to come. This is a form of tea which will draw you into yourself. I was taught this by the Shamans of my tribe, it is how I remembered my own true nature."

As the water boiled in the pot, it released a bitter scent into the air. I had heard of these practices from some of the men on the reservations in Texas. The young native men would go on a form of spirit quest before they were granted the status of warriors in the tribe. At the look of disgust on my face as the smell of the tea enveloped me, Barnabas laughed.

"If you think it smells bad, wait until you taste it!"

As the first sips of the liquid touched my tongue, I had to agree with him. This was the foulest tasting concoction I ever had the displeasure of imbibing. I thought my uncle's sour mash whiskey would always have that honor. I managed to get a quarter of the potion down before I retched a little. Barnabas took the bowl from my hand.

"That should be enough. Too much and you may never come back."

All at once I felt dizzy and cold. I was as weak as a kitten and allowed Barnabas to lay me on the ground. He wrapped me in thick blankets and muttered a chant as he did so. The rhythm reminded me of the lullabies that my mamma would sing as she rocked me to sleep as a boy.

Everything got really quiet and, in the distance, I could hear my name being called. It was a voice that I never thought I would hear again. Rosaline had been a lady whose acquaintance had brought me much joy. She was the first real woman that I had been with. She brought me from boyhood to become a man. Teaching me how to read better and how to love a woman better. Guiding my mind and hands to do a little of both each day.

I was brought back to my final night with her. She unleased a passion that had never been unequaled to this day. A storm had been raging all night and as the wind howled and the rain hammered at the roof and window panes, she took me again and again. I was at the point of exhaustion when I recall that she bit me. This wasn't a love nip either, I still carried the mark of it on my shoulder fifteen years later. Though now as I recall it, there was the sound of howling mixed with the rain outside. The potion which Barnabas had given me had made the memory clearer somehow. Although I was experiencing that night from my body, I could also look outside it.

I could see Rosaline outlined by the flashes of lightning as she used my body. Her eyes seemed to take on a yellow tint and she almost growled my name over and over again. Then something happened which didn't come from my memory of the event.

Her face elongated, morphing forward into a bestial snout, vicious teeth sprang from her lips and her howls of pain and pleasure became mixed with my cries of terror. Her throaty barks of my name became indistinct but every so often I could almost hear an extra word being expressed.

"Remember, Quincey... Remember."

At this Rosaline vanished and I found myself in a new place. Somewhere that I had experienced the unexplained for the first time. When Professor Van Helsing had told us that Lucy had come back from the dead as some kind of monster. I knew it to be possible. I had encountered the undead before, eight years ago.

My memories had pulled me back to that place.

They had pulled me to New Orleans.

New Orleans, August 1885

I stepped off the river boat onto the cracked and weathered wooden planks of the port of New Orleans. The air stank of rotting fish and the steamy, sultry air clung to everything. But even with the oppressive heat, this was a town which understood what a man needed in this short life—good food and drink, obliging women and great music.

Unfortunately, I wasn't here to enjoy myself, at least not at the moment. I had received a letter from an old sweetheart, Dodi O'Brien. A little slip of a thing with thick auburn hair and eyes the color of the deepest emeralds who deserved far better than a scoundrel like myself. Her father, who was an inveterate gambler, had incurred debts to one of the local Voodoo priests who had decided to make an example of Robert O'Brien so everyone would know what debts were owed would be paid in full.

Dodi had begged me to help her father and arrange the repayment of the debt. She had some valuable jewels which belonged to her ma she'd kept hidden from her father. It would leave them with nothing but at least her pa's debts would be paid and they'd both be alive. That was enough for her. But it wasn't enough for me. I would help her pa deal with these heathens but I'd be damned if I'd leave her destitute because of his weakness. Mother

Morris would bar me from entering heaven's gates if I treated an innocent girl in such a way.

I bought myself a horse and rode over to their home, Evergreen Plantation. The house was as formidable as I remembered. A large, white two-story with black shutters, and wrap around porches on both levels with twin staircases in front. The house was surrounded by an enormous green lawn as well as trees of every description.

The first time I saw this mansion was when I was driving Dodi home from a harvest ball held at a neighboring plantation for all the eligible men in the parish. Dodi had been striking in a green gown that matched her eyes and I had pursued her with a young man's passion with no thought to her reputation. Her ma had been alive back then and she had given me a stern warning about not wasting her daughter's time. Ma O'Brien was no man's fool, she had sized me up right enough from the moment she saw me swaggering up the walkway. The result was me on the next train from New Orleans for greener pastures and breaking a poor girl's heart.

I was greeted at the front door by an elderly black man who informed me that the O'Brien's had been forced to sell the property because of gambling debts over a year ago. Fortunately, he knew they were now staying at the home of James Gallier. The families had always been close and Mr. Gallier had taken them in after having to sell their plantation.

I rode over to the Gallier House in the French Quarter and arrived in the middle of absolute panic. I questioned one of the servants about what calamity had occurred and was informed that Dodi had disappeared from the house and couldn't be found anywhere. I joined the search and started with the outbuildings including the stables. It was there I discovered that useless piece of manhood, Robert O'Brien, hiding under a pile of horse shit and hay. I yanked him out of his hidey hole none too gently and threw him out into the crowded courtyard where everyone could see and smell him.

All the servants stopped in their tracks when they saw that no good son of a whore torn from his hiding place.

"Where have they taken her?" I demanded as he landed on the cobbles. "And you better not play me false!"

The coward shook with fear and covered his head with his hands waiting for the blows to begin but said nothing.

I reached down and yanked him into a standing position. "Tell me what you know or so help me, I'll whip you until you're dead!"

One of the servants from the stable rushed over to me and handed me a large whip. "Much obliged."

I could tell they were all fond of Miss Dodi, she had that effect on people. Everyone wanted only the best for her except for her pa that is.

"I'm going to count to ten… one… two… three."

"It's no use," the coward spat out. "What they are owed, they will be paid in full."

"Now there's a queer thing, cause from what I hear you're the one owes 'em, not your sweet gal. So, explain how you're here covered in manure and she's gone."

"She disobeyed her pa!"

This bit of scum dared to say this situation was her fault? I punched him hard in the jaw for that remark. "Try that again."

The slurred speech was difficult to understand. O'Brien tried to speak again but I could only make out one word. "Jewels."

I couldn't help laughing. She had refused to give her pa her jewels. That girl had more pluck than I gave her credit for! Couldn't be because she knew he wouldn't use them to pay off the debt, probably just use it to run away leaving her holding the bag. This creature didn't deserve a daughter like her.

"Tell you what you're going to do," I said as I tossed him towards a horse. "You're going to get up there and show me where they be and before you get any ideas of leaving me in the dust…"

I got him up on the horse, tied his hands to the stirrup and took hold of both horses reins before jumping on my horse.

A servant rushed over with a bag of food and a canteen of water. "Please bring her home safe, sir."

I nodded and rode off in the direction out of the city. On the way out, I stopped at a gunsmith's shop and purchased a rifle with enough ammunition to kill a herd of deer.

O'Brien finally realized he was not going to get out of taking me where I needed to go and he guided his horse with his knees and thighs in the direction of the Carondelet Canal and then past it into the most isolated areas of the bayou.

By the time we arrived at the Voodoo priest's place of worship, the sun had gone down and I could see torches being lit in a circle around a clearing. I climbed down off my horse and then helped the jackass down but kept his hands tied together. I tied the horses to a tree and gave them some oats to eat which I had in my saddle bags. I found a gap in the trees that surrounded the clearing where we could see but be unobserved. We crouched down onto the moist earth to get the lay of the land.

At the moment, young black men and women dressed all in white appeared to be setting up for a ceremony. While all this was going on, I took the opportunity to open the bag of food and the canteen to have a little supper before the night got busy. Inside the bag was a loaf of bread, some cheese, some apples and even a meat pie which smelled delicious. As I ate my fill -- and being a large man that can be a lot of food -- I noticed the ass staring at me with hunger in his eyes and drool forming at the corners of his mouth which was now black and blue where I had punched him earlier.

This waste of a man deserved no kindness from me, but I might need him in the coming fight, and so I tossed him a crust of bread and half an apple. He wolfed them down in a trice.

Once the food and drink were gone, I settled down to a long wait. I didn't trust that two-faced backstabbing waste of space to take me to the right place so I wanted to make sure that Dodi was here before making my presence known.

It seemed like hours had passed while various folks came and went from the clearing but these were different from the others, they weren't dressed in white. In fact, they were clothed in rags, their skin was gray and there were sores all over their faces, arms and legs… anywhere the flesh was exposed. Plus, there was a putrid smell on the air every time they came within view. They set up what appeared to be an altar made out of large tree stumps enveloped in an ornately decorated cloth covered in strange symbols. Once the altar was ready, the gray clan stepped back and hovered around the edge of the clearing, as if they were waiting for something.

Suddenly, I felt a cool breeze on the back of my neck, which should have been impossible in this August heat. I turned my head and I swear on my life I saw glowing yellow eyes watching me from the trees beyond. There were no wolves in Louisiana and no other had animals quite like those. I was just a bit jumpy from waiting for so long with nothing to occupy my time.

Then the drums started, slowly at first and then louder and faster. All the people clothed in white started dancing around the makeshift altar. Spinning. Waving their arms. Calling forth their gods from wherever they were. The dancing became faster and faster. The dancers appeared to enter a fugue state. A few collapsed on the ground, writhing as if they were possessed.

A man appeared on the edge of the dance, he commanded attention just by his mere presence. His skin was almost black in the firelight from the torches. A white skull was painted over his face, making his dark eyes appear to pop out of his skull. He wore only a pair of white pants. His lean, muscular chest and arms were bare. He spread his arms wide and the dancers opened a space for him to pass through their circle. Behind him, I saw what I had been waiting for… it was Dodi, dressed in a simple white gown, like a bride on her wedding day… but there was something wrong with her, her eyes stared out sightlessly, she was guided by a black woman on either side of her with a gentle touch on her arms.

I immediately wanted to race over, grab her and flee this profane dance but a hunter knows when to wait for their prey to be caught off guard. There were too many of them and it was too dark to find my way out of the bayou in a hurry. Elias P didn't teach his son to throw his life away.

Dodi was guided over to the altar and made to lie down on it facing up. I watched the scene with intense interest. What did any of this have to do with the Voodoo priest getting his money back?

My reverie was interrupted when O'Brien tried to wrestle out of the ropes which bound his hands and crawl towards the tree where the horses were waiting. Within a moment, I had him face down breathing in the soft earth then I quickly rolled him over so I could look him in the eye and whispered. "What the hell are you up to, you weasel?"

I'd never seen a man look more terrified.

"Zombie," he croaked.

"What are you talking about?"

He explained to me the priest's way of maintaining control over people who owed him money was to turn anyone who failed to make the payments into a zombie – a walking corpse who will obey any order that is given to it by the priest. The corpse is a walking warning to everyone until it decomposes and falls apart which doesn't take long in a Louisiana summer. That gray herd who set up the altar were zombies of others who hadn't paid off their debts or in other ways displeased the priest and needed to be made an example of.

"You were going to leave your daughter to this horrible undeath?" I hissed. Every time I think this man can't sink any lower, he sinks a few more feet. At the rate he's going, he'll be able to shake the devil's hand in no time!

"There's nothing that can be done," he begged. "We need to get out of here."

"You're not going anywhere," I said as I pulled him over to the tree where the horses were grazing and tied his arms up over his head to one of the lower branches. "If she dies, you're joining her."

I moved as silently as I could back over to the gap where I was watching the ceremony. The Voodoo priest had a knife in his hand and he was speaking some kind of prayer or spell over Dodi's upper torso as if he was preparing to plunge the knife into her.

I decided I couldn't wait any longer and I raced into the midst of the ceremony. The dancers attempted to rush me but I had worked for years herding cattle and I knew how to move fast. I reached the altar, gathered Dodi into my arms and raced towards the tree where the horses were waiting. I heard the Voodoo priest calling out something to his followers in a language I couldn't understand but the words 'Kill Him' comes across in any language.

I was surrounded by his followers and trying to decide how to fight my way out and protect Dodi, when, at the same time, there was a mighty crash and Pa O'Brien came riding through the clearing on his horse, shouting and hollering loud enough to wake the dead. He'd grabbed a whip from my saddle bag and was using it expertly. But then as I watched, they pulled him out of the saddle and proceeded to whip him to death. At least, he had the chance to atone for his cowardice and I prayed it was enough for St. Peter to take pity on him and let him into the pearly gates.

While everyone was distracted, I tore out of the clearing to my horse, lifted a confused Dodi onto it in front of me and then jumped up myself into the saddle. I kicked the horse to let him know that speed was required and said a silent prayer we were heading in the right direction out of the bayou.

I rode my horse hard for what seemed like hours, glancing behind me every once in a while, but there appeared to be no horses in pursuit. Perhaps they didn't have any horses, which would be an expected boon. The sun was starting to rise, turning the bayou a deep orange. Dodi stirred in my arms.

"Where am I?" she asked confused. She turned her head around and saw me smiling down at her. "Quincey. I was waiting for you and then… I can't remember. What happened?"

I told her as gently as I could about what had happened to her and her pa. She took it a lot better than I expected.

"At least, he's at peace now," she replied nodding her head slowly and then she started to yawn.

I realized we had been riding for hours and since our pursuers were obviously far behind us, we could afford to take a little siesta, as they call it in Mexico. I slowed the horse down to a trot for which he was very grateful and started looking for a place to rest.

After a while, I saw an abandoned barn on the edge of the bayou. I decided this would be a good place to catch our breath. We rode up to the old barn. It was derelict, the wood had turned gray, the roof had large holes in it and I could smell moldy hay along with rancid animal smells.

I gently lowered Dodi down off of the horse and then jumped down myself. I tied the horse to a nearby tree where it could graze on the tall, green grass.

Dodi stood where I left her, now in shock from the news she'd lost her pa. I doubt she even knew where she was. I carefully guided her into the barn and tried to find a spot that wasn't too filthy or putrid. I found a moth-eaten horse blanket and threw it over some rotting hay so she could at least sit down. She lay her hard back against the blanket and immediately fell asleep. Staring down at her in that white dress with her auburn hair hanging loose with a serene look on her sleeping face, I wondered why did I treat her so badly? Why did all the men in her life treat this innocent soul so wretchedly? We could have married and then she wouldn't be lying in this foul barn at dawn, an orphan with nothing to look forward to in this life.

I could marry her now, take her away from this hell hole but somehow deep in my soul, I knew she wasn't the gal for me. Somewhere, out in this great world, there was a sweet girl waiting to call me hers, to whisper my name 'Quincey' and until I found her, I would remain a bachelor.

I took the saddle off the horse so he could rest and got him some water to drink from a nearby stream. I went through my saddle bags and found the remains of the food and water that the kind servants had given me when I rode out to save Dodi. I brought them into the barn along with my trusted bowie knife as well as the rifle I purchased earlier. If anyone tried to sneak up on us, they would be in for a warm, Texas welcome. I decided to close my eyes for three winks. We'd rode hard since we left the clearing and with no horses, it would take them hours and hours to catch up to us.

It seemed like just a moment had passed when without warning, I heard an unholy caterwauling as well as an overripe smell coming from outside the barn. I took a look-see and had to shield my eyes against the bright noon-day sun. Stumbling towards the barn was the herd of zombies from the ceremony. The priest must have sent them to look for us and our little doze had cost us dear.

I reached over to where Dodi was still asleep and gently shook her awake. "Time to vamoose, my girl," I whispered into her ear. "We's got company."

Dodi's jade green eyes slowly fluttered open. She started to yawn and stretch so I pulled her close to me. "Not a sound," I croaked, my throat dry from breathing in dust and dirt. "They're out in the yard."

Dodi nodded and clung to my coat sleeve as if it could protect her from the devil himself.

In the bright light of day, I was able to see there was an upper level to the barn for storage that could be reached by a ladder. I instructed Dodi to climb up and then I hid the ladder under a pile of putrid hay.

Once the ladder was up, I concentrated on the task at hand and grabbed my rifle to hunt some zombies. I peered outside the barn door and the zombies were slowly making their way towards the barn, fortunately they didn't move very fast. There was half a dozen of them, all gray skinned, all men of one sort or another, but in the summer heat, their putrid smell was almost unbearable. I had to take out a bandana I carried around from my days working with cattle in Texas and wrap it around my nose and mouth to reduce the smell a trifle.

I fired my rifle at one of them and he quickly fell down to the ground, but in a trice he was back up on his feet, black blood oozing from the wound the bullet had made in his chest. I couldn't believe my eyes and without thinking I continued to fire my rifle at each one of the walking corpses with the same effect. The six of them continued to stumble towards the barn with dark blood oozing from the wounds on their chest, legs and in one case an arm.

Well, no son of Elias P was going down without a decent fight. Finding that the bullets had no effect, I switched to my trusty bowie knife then I spied an old ax which might prove useful in chopping off a limb or two. Hard to walk without legs. I stepped out into the yard with my rifle slung over my shoulder, my knife in my right hand and the ax in my left, and guided them away from the barn where Dodi was hiding.

"Come on," I shouted at them as I started to move towards my horse. "Here I am."

They turned towards me and started to slowly follow. I fought them for what seemed like forever. I cut off limbs and then they would just crawl towards me with the hands outstretched. I could tell hours were passing as I saw the sun continuing its inexorable passage through the sky. How do you fight an enemy who never tires or feels pain or even hunger or thirst?

I was nearly spent but they, even moving slowly, appeared ready to go until the world ended.

Out of sheer desperation, I drove the ax right into the skull of one of the corpses and like a miracle out of a bible story, it fell down and this time it didn't rise.

I stared down at the unmoving corpse in relief realizing that the brain was the weak spot. Destroy the brain and the monster returned to its dead state. With this new tactic in my arsenal, I dropped the ax. Putting the knife in its holster, I unslung the rifle, reloaded it and was ready for battle.

Now it was time to show these pagan corpses was Elias P's son could do.

"You had your little time in the sun," I called out to the five remaining zombies. "Time to amscray back to the earth where you belong."

Within a matter of moments, I had returned all the zombies to that state of true death from which they would not return. I checked my supply of ammunition, one bullet left. I smiled to myself, Pa would be proud.

The sun was starting to set. I was too exhausted to endure another all-night ride, especially in an area I didn't know. We'd have to rise with the roosters tomorrow so we could get back to the safety of New Orleans. I doubted the priest would dare follow us with his zombie servants into such a well-populated area.

I tramped towards the barn in the failing light, glad to see Dodi had stayed quiet during the entire fight. "Hey up there, it's all clear!"

There was no response from the girl.

I dug out the ladder, climbed up to the storage area but it was empty. Dodi was gone. I lit a match to search and all I found was a rotting piece of flesh…zombies. While I was battling the six, I had seen, there must have been others who took her while I was distracted.

"Damn, my soul to hell," I whispered under my breath. "Was there ever going to be a man who didn't fail this child?"

At least, I had a very good idea where they had taken her, back to the clearing so they could complete their ungodly ceremony to make her one of those undead monstrosities. I shook my head, I couldn't let that happen to her even if I had to kill her myself. I could at least save her soul from that torment. I can't wait for daylight; I needed to start heading back to before it was too late. Who knows what kind of lead they had on me?

I raced towards my horse, my hands itching to saddle the animal and to be away. I must atone for what I have done. It's my fault, she was taken a second time.

As I got near the horse, I saw a movement in the grass at the corner of my eye. It was Dodi. She was stumbling in the darkness. Her skin was gray and a piece of it had fallen off her arm, the piece I had found in the barn. Her eyes stared sightlessly.

Oh dear God, what have I done? I thought I had taken her before the ritual had been performed but I was wrong! It just took her longer to turn into one those soulless cadavers. A tear formed in my eyes. I felt so ashamed. What kind of man am I if I can't protect an innocent girl such as she was?

I pulled out my rifle, grateful at least for the one bullet I had left and prepared to release her from her torment. I closed my eyes briefly to send up a prayer for her soul, that it may find peace and join her family in heaven. She deserved so much better out of her short life.

I brought the rifle up, took aim, was about to pull the trigger when swiftly a hand reached up, grabbed hold of the rifle and stopped me from shooting Dodi.

I turned, relief mixed with anger, and in the light of the full moon, I saw a woman who was prepared for battle. She was tall, lean with dark brown skin, black eyes, and short cropped black hair. She was dressed in the clothes of a man going on a hunt. She had a rifle thrown over her shoulder and a large machete hanging from her thick leather belt. Around her neck was a large crucifix along with a leather necklace covered in beads, feather and amulets. She looked at home in this bayou.

"Your friend can still be saved," stated the woman with an authority I'd only heard from a battle hardened general. "The ceremony was not complete but it will take all of the strength and bravery you possess along with patience to bring your friend back from the abyss."

"I'd do anything to bring her back," I replied as I lowered my rifle.

"Anything? That's good to know," informed the tall black woman as she gently took Dodi's arm and guided her towards his horse. "Always understand what you are willing to sacrifice to the Gods."

While I saddled my horse, the strange woman disappeared and soon returned with a horse laden down with a myriad of amulets and talismans braided into its black mane and tail. She also carried with her two torches which she lit so they could travel at night and see where they were going.

Before getting on their horses, the woman took Dodi's hand and sat her down on the ground next to the torches so she could see Dodi's face clearly. It was painful for me to see her skin which once been like fine porcelain, now resembling ashes from a grate. The black woman took a small bag off of her large leather belt, opened it and removed a collection of several small glass vials and metal tins. Each was covered with some kind of arcane symbol. The woman started speaking what sounded like some kind of prayer. As she spoke the prayer, she opened each vial and tin in turn and put an ointment resembling oil or some kind of paint on Dodi's face. When the prayer was finished, Dodi's face was covered in arcane symbols. She also put some oil on Dodi's hands and feet.

I wanted to stop her, to demand to know what she was doing but I couldn't move, I couldn't speak. I could only watch as she performed whatever ritual she was performing on my sweet girl.

When the ritual was done, the woman rose. She made some strange motions with her right hand and suddenly I could move again. I reached over to grab her arm, to demand to know what was going on. She turned her face towards me and I got a good look at her face. I had not seen it close up in the torch light until now, it had been beautiful once but had been scarred by a horrible brand that covered most of the left side of her face. This was a woman who had known pain and knew how to fight to protect what she had.

There were a thousand questions in my head but I couldn't form a single one with my mouth.

She seemed to know exactly what I was thinking. "I have used a spell which will slow down the decay of your friend's body until we can reverse the ritual. We can talk as we ride, get on your horse."

Without thinking, I jumped on my horse and the woman handed Dodi up to me in the saddle.

The woman then mounted her horse and we started to ride, not towards the clearing where the ritual had taken place but instead towards New Orleans. "We'll find what we need in the city that is her home."

After a while, my head cleared and I found I was able to form words again.

"I'm sorry for enchanting you but I've run into many men who use words to control women so until I feel I can trust a man, I prefer to not let him use his words. You've proved your bravery, now prove to me you have a brain in your head."

I was going to argue with her but knowing how much I had failed Dodi already, I decided there was no defense for what had been done to her and she was willing to help.

"Who are you? Can you really help reverse the ritual?" Both questions came tumbling out of my mouth as we road in the darkness towards the Crescent City.

"Both are very good questions, young man," smiled the black woman as she rode her enormous horse through the darkness with only her torch to see by. "You can call me Huntress, although I've had many names in my long life. I hunt creatures like you fought tonight… zombies, werewolves, vampires and those who control them. There are monsters in this world, my handsome young man, and they must be fought tooth and claw. Sometimes I win and sometimes I lose but the fight goes on until I'm dead.

"As far as being able to reverse the ritual, it can be done with a counter ritual to bring the body back to life before the soul reaches the afterlife. She must be called back by all that she holds sacred. Do you know what that would be?"

I thought about Dodi, about her love for her family, her love for the church. "Yes, I know what she held sacred."

"Good! Then I'm glad I brought you along," she laughed. "You can help me obtain what I need for the ritual. It will be much easier with someone who knows her well."

I turned my head away from her in shame. "She loved the church and her family."

"Are you her family?"

I shook my head. "Her parents are both dead. Her pa died last night trying to protect her."

"We'll start where she lives," said the Huntress. "Take us there."

I was glad to have a task that I knew I could complete with ease. We rode through the night and arrived in New Orleans at dawn. We rode straight over to the Gallier House in the French Quarter. The servants were just starting their day and they were so very relieved to see Miss O'Brien returned until they saw her gray pallor and the markings on her face, hands and feet. One of them immediately started to wipe them off with her apron at which point, the Huntress stopped them with a crack of her whip.

"Don't touch her!" she shouted at them, making them all take several steps back. "Those markings are for protection."

She jumped off her horse, grabbed one of the female black servants and whispered something into her ear and then sent her on her way.

"First things, first, I need to take a piss and I need some food," stated the Huntress as if this was her home.

After the necessaries had been taken care of and everything had been explained to the Gallier family, the demanded to know who was in their kitchen eating their food. It was time to get down to business.

Dodi sat with them in the kitchen. Staring sightlessly. The markings that had been removed had been replaced.

"She has always been a devout girl," I stated when asked to talk about Dodi. It was something I admired about her but it also prevented her from giving me what I wanted without marriage. I admit that was the reason I left, knowing there were easier pickings elsewhere and I had no mind for marriage.

The Huntress nodded as she wolfed down her third beignet with a second cup of strong coffee. "That's good. She has a strong will. She'll need it."

I told her about how Dodi defied her pa, not giving him the jewels he demanded.

"Excellent," she stated as she licked the powdered sugar off her finger tips and glanced over at Dodi. "I like you more and more."

"She was also devoted to her mother who passed away last year."

"Does she have any special memento from her mother? Something that meant a great deal to her?"

I shook my head, no answer occurring to me but then one of the servants stepped forward.

"There was her ma's rosary made from mother of pearl," said the young servant. "She carried it with her every Sunday when she went to mass and kept it in her prayer book."

I saw a small smile creep onto the face of the Huntress even with the brand on her face, the smile lit it up and the lost beauty was briefly regained.

The servant girl that the Huntress had spoken to came into the kitchen at a run with a small package wrapped in a white linen napkin which she presented to her.

The Huntress nodded and told one of the servants to get Dodi's rosary and prayer book. Once she had them, she put her right hand over all the items, said a quiet prayer and pronounced we were ready to reverse the ritual.

I packed my saddle bags with food and a couple of canteens with fresh water for the trip through the bayou. I had also sent one of the servants to pick up some more ammunition for our rifles and make sure my bowie knife was nicely sharpened to a razor's edge.

Mr. Gallion insisted on Dodi having her own horse and to ride side saddle to ensure her modesty. He was horrified to learn that she had ridden on the horse of an unmarried man with no chaperone. I must admit I was horrified that after all Dodi had been through, this man was only concerned about decorum and her reputation! Her very soul was at stake as well as her life. I doubt zombies cared a fig about their reputation when carrying out their master's whims.

When everything was ready it was already afternoon and we needed to be off. I was impressed with how the Huntress handled Mr. Gallion's demands. It was amusing to see the spell worked on another man who was in the way.

We rode down the road and headed out of the city towards the bayou once again. I held the reigns of Dodi's horse and made sure she kept up with us. She seemed worse, more gray, more distant… as if her soul was slowly losing its grip on her body.

Once we were out of the city, we both felt it, the Huntress and I. The touch of evil, we were being watched by the priest's servants. This was not going to be an easy ritual to perform since it required us going back to where it was initially performed.

We kept expecting for them to make their move but for some reason they kept holding back as if they were waiting on something. Finally, after we crossed the

Carondelet canal, another much larger group of zombies made their move.

I stopped in shock when I saw the lead zombie. It was Dodi's father brought back from the dead by the evil Voodoo priest. He carried something in his hands which I couldn't see clearly at first. As he got closer, it became clear that it was the corpse of Dodi's mother which had also been made into a zombie, although she was so badly decomposed she had to be carried by her husband. It was the most horrifying and appalling sight I had ever seen.

I desperately wanted to prevent Dodi from seeing it even in her deranged state but it was too late. The horror had hit its mark. I heard Dodi's scream and it was as if all the torments of hell had been released on that poor girl's soul at the same instant.

She managed to pull the reigns out of my hand and climb out of the side saddle. She then jumped off the horse and raced towards her ma and pa in their zombie form.

I tried to charge after her but found myself surrounded by zombies. Attempting to pull out my rifle, I discovered it was tightly tied behind my saddle and I couldn't reach it.

All of a sudden, I heard a shots ring out and the heads of the zombies nearer to me exploded one, and then another. The Huntress had managed to get her rifle out and was firing with amazing speed at the zombies surrounding me, giving me the opportunity to reach for my rifle and start firing at the ones advancing on her.

When all the zombies were finally dispatched, we looked around and there was no sign of Dodi or her parents. They had disappeared but we both knew where the trio had gone. Back to where this started and where this had to end.

We whipped our horses to go as fast as they were able, we were now in a race against time to save Dodi's soul. Finally, we reached the clearing when it was full dark. It was again surrounded by a circle of torches. The dancers performed in their white garb. Everything was as it had been before, except this time, the zombies of Dodi's parents were sitting beside her on either side of the altar. Together again in a gruesome mockery of familial devotion with each parent holding one of Dodi's hands. She had been washed clean of the spells of protection.

The Voodoo priest came forward and stood before the altar, not yet starting the ceremony. Instead, he called out to us. "You there, out in the darkness! Do you dare put your souls on the line to save this child?"

Before the Huntress could stop me, I raced forward and offered to take her place.

The Voodoo priest laughed in my face. I wanted to shoot him but again I found myself unable to move.

The Huntress stepped forward out of the shadows and stood next to me. "What are you offering, priest?"

"I thought it was you, my little hunter," he smiled a large, wide smile. "It's been twenty years since we last met around this altar. You were so pretty then."

"What do you want?" the Huntress demanded.

"How about a test of power, little one? Your faith against mine. I remember when your family first came to New Orleans. The power was so strong in you. You were going to be stronger than even the great Marie Laveau. She wanted you to succeed her but then you ran from your destiny. Sad. So very sad when the young don't reach their potential don't you think?"

"What is he talking about?" I demanded of the Huntress.

"I hunt the dark things of this world because I was once a part of it. It destroyed everyone I loved -- my parents, my brothers and sisters. All of them were taken from me to test my loyalty to the darkness. Yes, I failed. When I had nothing left to lose, the darkness expected me to embrace it but I couldn't let their deaths mean nothing. I choose a different path and now I fight the darkness in all its forms."

The Voodoo priest laughed. "You never did understand that life and death are just two sides of the same coin, little one."

The Huntress glared at the priest; it was a look of such pure hatred, but he didn't even flinch.

"Is that a yes to my offer?"

The Huntress nodded her head. "I agree to test my power against yours. If I win, you will release all claims on the souls of Dodi as well as her parents, all debts are considered paid in full."

The priest twirled his sacrificial blade in his hand. "If I win, I keep Dodi and her parents' souls plus you and the soul of your erstwhile companion will belong to me, forever."

"Agreed."

I suddenly realized that I was part of this bargain and I had no say in it. I tried to speak and again could say nothing. I couldn't even move.

"Do you need a moment to prepare yourself?" asked the Voodoo priest. "It can take time to summon your Gods."

"My Gods are always with me," replied the Huntress as she opened the small white linen napkin she had been given. Inside was Dodi's rosary and prayer book as well as what the servant girl had brought her from the local church—a vial of holy water and a cross woven from the palm fronds from the last Palm Sunday.

All sacred items for Dodi, a devout Catholic and devoted to her family.

"Oh, isn't that charming," he said as he peered at the collection of items which the Huntress had placed on the altar next to Dodi.

"Let the stronger faith win the day," stated the Huntress and with that the battle began.

Watching the battle as a mere spectator, it can be hard to describe what was actually going on. I could see both the Voodoo priest and the Huntress saying prayers under their breath, making signs with their hands, pulling forth talismans and amulets from various pockets. Hours passed by, sweat poured from both of them drenching their faces and their garments. They looked exhausted and on the verge of collapse.

Unawares, Dodi regained some of herself, realized on some level what was happening that these two were fighting for her soul. She decided to join the fight. With one hand, she grabbed the items that were important to her, and she poured the holy water over them. With her other, she grabbed the Huntress's hand. She started speaking the Lord's prayer and the Hail Mary over and over again to give her strength for the battle at hand.

Dodi's strength turned the tide and the Huntress won the battle.

The Voodoo priest collapsed on the ground in a heap. None of his servants came to his aid, not even his zombies. He was a priest without a congregation. If he can be beaten by a couple of mere women then no one would follow him anymore.

"Release them."

The Voodoo priest ignored the Huntress' demand.

I finally could move again and took the opportunity to take hold of the priest and slam him face down into the dirt. "You do what the lady tells you to do."

The Voodoo priest said a prayer under his breath and then out loud said, "I release my hold on the souls of the O'Brien family." The corpses of Robert, and his wife Mary immediately collapsed, no longer animated by the priest. Dodi's color returned and she was now free of the zombie curse.

After helping to bury Dodi's parents, I stopped off at the Gallier House to say my farewells. Dodi had just returned from the doctor and learned that while she was good health after her illness, she had been left barren and would have no children.

I sat in the kitchen drinking a strong cup of coffee thinking about what Dodi had told me.

"We're all left with scars when we're touched by evil," informed the Huntress. "But that doesn't mean we're less than others, in fact, some of us become more than we could possibly imagine."

"She always wanted a family. We could marry. We could adopt," I stated with determination.

"And do you love her? Or do you just want to feel less guilty about what happened? Why don't you ask Dodi what she wants?"

Dodi stepped into the kitchen with her mother's rosary in her hands. She never went anywhere without it since her return home. "I've made a decision."

"Oh, have you?" asked the Huntress.

I had the strong feeling that the Huntress already knew what Dodi was going to say.

"I've decided to take holy orders," said Dodi with a serene smile on her face. "I always felt the calling but my family needed me. But now I'm free. Thanks to both of you for saving my family."

I walked with the Huntress to the docks of New Orleans.

"Where will you go?" I asked.

"Wherever I am needed."

I offered her my hand and received a strong handshake in return. She was like no woman I had ever met. I admired her strength and determination.

"You're good in a fight," said the Huntress as she watched her horse being guided onto the steamer. "If ever I'm in need of a strong arm…"

"I'll be there."

Quincey awoke, the fire had dimmed to embers and the breaking dawn was chasing all memories of his past away. That adventure in New Orleans had brought him to truly understand the old verse that his mamma used to quote. He used to think it was from somewhere in the good book. Later, as Lucy taught him a little more English 'high culture', he found out it was from the great bard himself, Shakespeare. He repeated the phrase slowly, his intonation one of understanding. A distinct difference to how his mother would utter it in exasperation.

"There are more things dreamt of in Heaven and Earth than are dreamt of in your philosophy."

Raising his head and taking stock of his surroundings, he found Barnabas and similar looking traveling folks packing up the camp. Instinctively he knew that these others were just like Barnabas. A form of shape-shifter, Skinwalkers.

Barnabas turned his head towards Quincey and smiled.

"I hope that you had some enlightening dreams, Mr. Morris. Soon it will be time to unveil a great truth about your new existence. Come and journey with us. There is much to learn on the road ahead."

Quincey examined his options. He was always a person who weighed the odds before making a decision.

You could blame his predilection for Poker for that trait. Nodding an agreement, he gathered up the blanket and moved to join his new friends.

Other titles from HellBound Books
The Lost Journal of Bram Stoker

Bram Stoker died over 100 years ago, just days after the Titanic sank. We know him as the author of Dracula, but long before Dracula, he was just a young Irishman, hoping to be a writer, practicing poetry, and enjoying a good joke.

This Lost Journal (now found) is an amazing opportunity to get into the young mind of the Dracula author - to see who he was (law clerk), where he lived (Dublin, Ireland), and what he thought about (everything from walking on the beach and unrequited love to drunken parties at Dublin Castle and sliding in vomit).

Dr. Miller and Dacre Stoker make interesting comments about Bram's entries, and, as they say, some of the short notes are like twittering.

Imagine decoding somebody's twitter messages 141 years from now in the year 2153. Some of Stoker's notes are just that impossible - even for editors Stoker & Miller, who have studied Bram Stoker for years. The most obscure references will provide a field day for Irish history buffs and English professors who want to challenge their students of Gothic literature.

A few years ago, Bram Stoker's great-grandson found in his attic a journal Stoker had kept during the 1870s while he was young and single, still living in Dublin. All of the entries (over 300) are published in this new book, researched by Elizabeth Miller and Dacre Stoker.

The insights provided into Stoker's life and personality are exciting and unprecedented. We get glimpses into his friendships at Trinity College, his office mates at Dublin Castle, family members, his interest in athletics, as well as his travels around Ireland and on the Continent. We also get to know him better as a writer and see how his skills developed.

The editors say Bram Stoker never thought anybody would care about these notes so he wrote for himself, which is so revealing on many levels.

Dracula: Annotated for the 125th Anniversary

Annotated, edited, and in the author's full, original form, Dracula: Annotated is the very first edition of Bram Stoker's timeless classic horror novel to be written by a member of Bram Stoker's family, Dacre Stoker, his great grandnephew, with the assistance of award-winning vampire expert, Robert Eighteen-Bisang.

This book is available in Hardcover, Paperback, and Kindle formats, and includes the entire version of Dracula—not only Constable's text of 1897 and Dracula's Guest, but outlines of Bram's original first, second, and third chapters.

Within these pages are all of the pre-publication deletions from the original typescript, as well as Bram's hand-written changes and the entire abridged edition of 1901—read for the first time the changes Bram made to create his dramatic adaptation of Dracula in 1897 and note the differences in the Doubleday & McClure and William Rider texts.

This exceptional, incredibly unique slice of literary history represents a rare insight into the remarkable creative process of Bram Stoker, the grand master of horror himself.

The Synagogue Horror

Rabbi Avrum Steinberg is so much more than just a horror movie loving rabbi of a small, run-down synagogue on New York City's Lower East Side - he is also a small time private eye, albeit with cases no more exhilarating than locating debtors and errant, deadbeat husbands.

Following the bizarre murder of a young woman in his synagogue, Steinberg begins to suspect that a vampire may be loose in New York, and before long, his suspicions are proven true. It takes the help of Wilomena - a young, mysterious, African-American minister - to help the rabbi hunt down the infamous Count Dracula himself, who is holed up in an abandoned subway tunnel beneath the City's bustling sidewalks.

In their perilous and terrifying journey, the rabbi and Wilomina are joined by a band of elderly Kabbalists and Steinberg's son, and along the way the vampire hunters encounter zombies, fallen angels, some familiar vampires, and even a ghost or two. This unique urban vampire story pits the powers of faith against an ancient, dark power of evil - proving once again, that dispatching the master vampire is by far no easy task

Printed in Great Britain
by Amazon

17228956R10255